To hell with Famous
Amos!
I have Astrid & Ingrid
the Norwegian cookie
bakers.
Love
Sis

Moccasins in the Snow

by

Sissy Nelsen

authorHOUSE™

1663 LIBERTY DRIVE, SUITE 200
BLOOMINGTON, INDIANA 47403
(800) 839-8640
WWW.AUTHORHOUSE.COM

First published by AuthorHouse 12/01/04

ISBN: 1-4208-0741-2 (sc)

Printed in the United States of America
Bloomington, Indiana

This book is printed on acid-free paper.

Also by Sissy Nelsen
Cloned
Sweet Essence of Murder

*In loving memory of my parents, John
'Beaver' Nelsen and
my saintly mother, Beatrice Theresa.*

Chapter One

Leaning heavily on his cane, Hugh McFadden walked up the narrow dirt path that his footsteps had paved over the years. Little by little, with each step taken, the lonely gravestone on the other side of the slope came into view. As he mounted the crest of the hill, he hesitated and looked at the surrounding countryside. In all his years of living in America, the vastness of the fields, edged by the rolling hills, never ceased to affect him. He studied the tall golden stalks of wheat that fluttered in the breeze which were soon to be sheaved and sold.

Slowly, he continued up the narrow path until he stood at the foot of the grave. His figure cast a giant shadow over the plain flat headstone that read; Jane McFadden beloved wife of Hugh McFadden. "Aye, it won't be long now, Jane," he sighed, wondering how many lives had been overshadowed by his own.

With age, the vibrant copper luster of Hugh McFadden's hair had turned to crisp white but he still maintained a burly look about him. From the day he was born it seemed that Hugh's hardiness was a determining factor in his life. His mother died bearing him and his father failed to look upon the brawny lad without resentment. For this reason, and this reason alone, Hugh became a charge of his benevolent neighbors. His father, Patrick McFadden, gladly paid conscience money for the boy's upkeep and board.

1

Seven years with the Sisters of Mercy completed Hugh's formal education. He had a natural aptitude for doing his sums but he had to be forced to attend Mass on Sundays and other religious holidays. Not that Hugh defied God, nor did he find it in his heart to praise Him, but out of his aloneness grew an overpowering belief in one person only, himself.

Although he was quite unaware of it, people rivaled for his attention and friendship. He possessed a quick Irish wit and an even tempered personality. Life to Hugh was a challenge and he took pride in everything he accomplished. Whether it was to plant a field of crops or to set a wagon wheel, hard work was never beneath his dignity. Neither did he think a man's dreams unattainable once a goal had been set.

At the age of twenty-three, with the dream of owning his own land, he left the poverty of Ireland behind him to find work in England. His goal was to save enough money and sail to America. Here too, Hugh's brawniness was a determining factor in his fate. Since having the look and potential of doing double the work of most men, few employers turned their back on Hugh. He was far from being a fool and never hesitated to quibble over money rightfully due him. He began to save what he considered a tidy sum and knew when the right opportunity presented itself he'd be ready. However, what he never anticipated was being smitten by love.

After living in England for two years, Hugh lost some of his Irish brogue and without realizing it had acquired some characteristics of an Englishman. If brought to his attention, no doubt, he'd sourly deny it. Never could he attain the true pose of an English gentleman, neither did he care to. For Hugh was Hugh, and one could hardly mistake him for other than being Irish with the unruly copper hair, and the mischievous blue eyes set off by dark black lashes, and above all his quick wit and hardy laughter. His very being generated warmth and one found oneself smiling at the man for no apparent reason.

Hugh's physical strength undoubtedly was a blessing. Whereas most men of smaller stature were trying to prove themselves, Hugh was devoid of such competitive feelings. Instead, with an inbred air of integrity he regarded each man as his friend, no matter their size, color, race, or religious convictions. He was to be admired amongst men and by some he was secretly envied. The very nature of the man is what attracted John Whitcomb, a wealthy young Englishman.

One evening, after a day's hard toil on the loading docks, Hugh stood at the bar of the local Pub halfheartedly listening to the mindless babbling of men that was brought on by alcohol. His attention was drawn to the three men sitting at the nearby table playing cards. Noticeably out of place in this part of Liverpool was a young chap in fashionable dress depicting a man of means as well as education.

Hugh detected the sleight of hand of one of the blokes at the table. As the evening wore on, Hugh became certain of his deduction. He watched with interest wondering how long it would take the young chap to see through his predicament. Hugh was about to give up hope when the young chap suddenly shot to his feet and roared, "Gentlemen, I'm on to you. Your little game is over!"

In mild disbelief the two men stared up at John Whitcomb.

"What yer talking about, governor?" The one asked in all innocence.

"I believe I made myself quite clear. Your little game of deception is over."

A heavy silence hung over the table as the two men slowly rose to face their accuser. "Are yer calling us cheats?" The larger of the two asked.

A tight lipped John Whitcomb stood his ground. "Is there another word for it?" he asked, only to feel a hard fist spread his nose.

In the scuffle the table was overturned and coins scattered in all directions on the floor. The groans of the young chap could be heard as his opponents unmercifully struck out at him blow after blow.

Hugh cringed at the sight of the young chap being mauled and within three strides crossed the floor. He reached out, grabbing one of the men by the scuff of his neck, and spun him around. "What say we make it an even match," Hugh said, bringing his clenched fist up into the soft pit of the man's stomach. The blow staggered him and he went stumbling backwards. His body slammed into the wall and he slid to the floor. In dazed wonder he looked up at Hugh and his accomplice meekly backed away.

"He called us cheats." The man said in defense of himself.

"Well ye are," Hugh growled, stealing a glance at the sorrowful looking heap of an Englishman lying on the floor. Hugh leaned over and touched his shoulder. "Are you ailing, man?"

A stunned Whitcomb looked up at the giant of a man leaning over him. "Who might you be?" he breathlessly said, wiping at the blood on his face.

"By the looks of you, your guardian angel," Hugh laughed. "How much money did you have in the game?"

Whitcomb shook his head as if clearing it. He sat up and raised a thin hand to his bleeding lip. "About ten pounds," he said.

Hugh busied himself by picking up the scatter coins on the floor. After counting out ten pounds he stopped. He tucked the money in the young man's vest pocket. He'd never seen such a sorrowful sight in his life. The lace bib of the chap's shirt was covered with blood and by the look of it, his nose was broken. There was a cut on his lower lip and his one eye was beginning to swell. "It's best I'd be seeing to taking you home," Hugh said, lifting the chap to his feet.

"That's damn decent of you old man."

Of no other use than catching the wind, Hugh thought, while plopping the fashionable beaver skin hat on the young chap's fair head. All eyes followed the strange pair; a burly Irishman half carrying a wisp of an Englishman through the Pub door.

Hugh had his first glimpse of real wealth as he stood in John Whitcomb's parlor watching two servants scurrying about while administrating to their Master's needs. The parlor had a high plastered rococo ceiling and the room held elegant carved pieces of furniture. Some of the pieces appeared to be gilded, beyond anything Hugh had ever seen. He stood there feeling ill at ease and totally out of place. "I'll be going now," he said, making a move toward the door.

Whitcomb eased himself up on the edge of the settee holding a cloth to his nose. He waved an impatient hand of dismissal at his servants and looked at Hugh. "Stay a bit," he urged. "My God, I don't even know your name."

"It's Hugh. . . Hugh McFadden."

"Please, won't you sit down, Mr. McFadden."

With misgivings, Hugh looked at the small chair he had been motioned to. He hesitated before deciding on the larger chair by the fireplace. A smile of understanding crossed Whitcomb's cut lips as he watched the large man sink into the chair of his own choosing.

"It seems that I am indebted to you, Mr. McFadden."

Hugh glared at the man in anger. "You owe me nothing. I'd do as much for any man."

"Yes," Whitcomb grinned, "I don't doubt it. I wasn't about to offer you money, if that's what you thought. The hour is late and perhaps we could sup together. My father maintains an ample supply of Irish whiskey in the house. . . that is, if you don't mind drinking alone. I'm afraid I couldn't get it past my cut lips. Not tonight," he grinned, lightly touching his lips.

Hugh smiled at the man's frankness and remembered how only an hour ago; he courageously stood up to two men, who were twice his size. "Aye, a bit of whiskey is known to cure all ills."

"You're right," Whitcomb laughed. "It sure as hell won't kill me, not after what I went through. Will you do the honors, Mr. McFadden?" He pointed to a cabinet across the room on top of which sat a number of cut glass decanters and stemware.

Hugh rose to his feet. "When I drink with a man, he calls me Hugh."

"If you will excuse my not standing," Whitcomb said, stretching his hand out, "The name is John. . . John Whitcomb.

Smiling, Hugh clasped the hand offered and within the week they became friends. Oddly enough, the very nature of their opposing life styles is what seemed to fascinate the men. Whitcomb came from a wealthy family and possessed a devil-may-care attitude that never ceased to astonish Hugh. He had a roving eye when it came to women, an obsession for gambling and the means to indulge himself; whereas Hugh, having lived in poverty had earned a deep respect for money. He sorely looked down upon spending his money for other than essential needs.

***

"I don't know, Hugh," Whitcomb grinned. "Once in a while one must part with his money in order to enjoy life's pleasures."

They'd been riding abreast for a half hour and Hugh was still enthralled by the vastness of Whitcomb's family estate in the country. His face flushed with color well aware of what his friend was referring to. "If you mean paying for the likes of an erring sister the other night, I'll be keeping my money."

"I do believe the redheaded wench took a liking to you."

"If she liked me so much, why did she want me money?" Hugh retorted.

"I dare say, the poor girl has to earn her keep. Surely the girls you've bedded in Ireland weren't free?"

"Nay. I had the good fortune to meet up with a few lassies who weren't interested in me money. It was Hugh McFadden that they were taken with, if you rightly know what I mean."

Whitcomb reined his horse as they rounded the curve in the narrow dirt road. Hugh followed suit, looking at the small church and parsonage in the valley below that was their destination.

"Now mind what I told you, Margarita is a real beauty. You'll be taken with her; Jane, the eldest, is rather handsome and on the quiet side. Jessica, their younger sister, is but ten."

"They'll not be taken with an Irishman at their door," Hugh said, in all honesty, tugging at the stiffness of his new shirt collar.

After having accepted the invitation of accompanying Whitcomb to his family's country estate, Hugh was sensitive to the fact that it would cost him a new suit of clothes. He was beginning to have second thoughts about the money he had spent. Other than being buried in his new clothes, he wondered when he'd make use of the fancy bib shirt and tight britches. About the only thing that pleased him was the fine fit of the waistcoat and the handsome leather boots.

"I assure you, Hugh, they are plain country folk," Whitcomb said. "You'll enjoy their company."

"I don't doubt you, John, but I'm not one to be chatting over a cup of tea. For the life of me, I wouldn't be knowing what to talk about to such fine feathered ladies."

"Have no fear; I will keep a stimulating conversation going. Now and again, just nod your head in agreement to what I might be saying; don't over do it. Smile at the ladies and just sit there looking dashing in your new clothes."

Hugh thought hard for the moment. "Suppose I should disagree with what you'd be saying, John, then what?"

"Heaven's don't," Whitcomb warned. "Remember, we'll be in a minister's house and the man fancies himself the keeper of my soul. I'm expected to visit him each time I come here, lest he should think my soul has gone astray."

"Aye," Hugh frowned. "Traveling with the likes of me the man's bound to think just that."

Within minutes of meeting Margarita Wesley, Hugh had to agree that she was the pretties colleen he'd ever set eyes on. Her hair had the sheen of a raven and through long, dark lashes, violet eyes sparkled.

Her two sisters resembled their father, in that they both had flaxen hair and blue eyes.

True to his word, John Whitcomb kept up a lively conversation with the Wesley family. Hugh marveled at how his friend managed to monopolize the conversation and keep their attention at the same time. He spoke of the latest plays that he had seen while in London, the latest books he had read, and to the delight to the women, he described the latest fashions that the women in the city were wearing.

Jane, the eldest daughter, sat in the window seat, her hands busy with a piece of embroidery. Now and again, she would glance up and smile at something that struck her as amusing.

In contrast to his friend, Hugh was ill at ease. The chair he sat on creaked beneath his weight and he had never mastered the art of balancing a fragile tea cup on his knee. After downing two cups of hot tea he felt the closeness of the warm June day in the room. He tugged at his shirt collar and longingly his gaze carried to the open French doors on the far side of the parlor, through which he glimpsed a garden.

"Would you like to see our garden, Mr. McFadden?"

Hugh blankly glanced around the room to find Jane Wesley smiling at him.

"Aye, I wouldn't mind a short stroll. It appears to be a lovely garden you'd be having, Miss Jane," he said, and instinctively realized something was wrong. All eyes were darting back and forth between him and the girl.

"I'm sure," Reverend Wesley said, "that Mr. McFadden wouldn't object to one of your sisters showing him your garden, Jane."

Before giving her father a second chance to object, Jane Wesley quickly rose to her feet and straightened her skirt. "No father," she insisted, "I can manage nicely. I'm sure that Mr. McFadden won't mind putting up with my slow pace."

She was a slim figured small-bosomed girl, and appeared much taller standing than sitting. As she started across the floor the upper part of her torso was held perfectly erect as if compensating for the irregular gait caused by the lame leg hidden beneath the folds of her skirt.

Immediately, Hugh felt a kinship toward the girl who came limping toward him. There was a proud air in her countenance and an undaunted spirit of determination. He refrained from offering his arm, fearing she would interpret his gesture as a form of pity. Instead, he followed her through the open French doors and watched as she tied the blue ribbons of a large brimmed straw hat under her chin.

They had crossed the lawn in silence and entered the rose garden when suddenly she turned to look up at him. "I would think you'd be more comfortable, Mr. McFadden, if you were to undo your collar button. It might help in giving voice to your thoughts."

Her frankness surprised and delighted Hugh; she had managed to sever convention, and at the same time, put him at ease. "You're a girl after me own heart, Miss Jane," he laughed, undoing his collar button.

"I'm beholden to you. Another hour of this tight collar would have meant the death of Hugh McFadden."

"I though as much," she smiled.

They had strolled through the rose garden and through a small plot of land which Jane Wesley was in the throes of converting into a herb garden. For all his twenty-six years, Hugh had never experienced such a close rapport with a young girl like Jane Wesley. Conversation flowed easily and freely and her knowledge of gardening amazed him.

At the foot of the narrow dirt path that rambled on up into the hillside, Hugh, thinking the climb taxing for the girl, hesitated. In good spirits she trudged on ahead leading the way until they reached the hilltop that encompassed a sweeping view of the fields and valley below. A black wrought iron bench was situated beneath the shade of a giant oak tree.

"Father put this here for me," she said in explanation, before gracing the bench. "Please, won't you join me, Mr. McFadden?"

"Aye, I don't mind if I do. Tis a grand view you'd be having from up here, Miss Jane," he said, seating himself. "The fields look like a lake of rippling purple waters, wouldn't ye say."

"Yes, I would," Jane Wesley smiled. "Tell me, have all Irishmen got a way with words? For what you said, just now, brings to mind a poem by one of your countrymen, Thomas Moore."

"What poem might that be?" Hugh asked, with interest.

A little self-conscious and in soft voice, Jane Wesley began to recite from memory: "When Spring adorns the dewy scene,

How sweet to walk the velvet green,
And hear the west wind's gentle sighs,
As o'er the scented mead it flies!
How sweet to mark the pouting vine,
Ready to burst in tears of wine,

And with. . . " Jane stopped on suddenly recalling the next four lines. Out of embarrassment a high flush of color spread over her cheeks. She was thankful that her face was hidden beneath the brim of her bonnet and was mortified on hearing Mr. McFadden's deep voice continue on.

"And with some maid, who breathes but love,
To walk, at noontide, through the grove,
Or sit in some cool, green recess—
Oh, is not this true happiness?"

A seemingly long silence followed. Each appeared momentarily deep in thought, although keenly aware of having shared a very special moment.

"I take it you like poetry, Mr. McFadden," Jane said finally.

Often linking poetry with effeminacy, Hugh's face flushed with guilt. "I've read a bit," he admitted. "You don't think it odd a big bloke like me reading poetry, do you, Miss Jane?"

"No. Should I?"

"I've never breathed a word of it to another living soul for fear they would laugh at me if they knew."

To Hugh's horror the young girl suddenly burst out in a fit of uncontrollable laughter. "I knew I shouldn't have told you," he said. "Now you're laughing at me."

She raised a delicate hand to her lips trying to restrain the laughter that was caught up in her throat. "It's not your liking of poetry that I'm laughing at, Mr. McFadden, but the idea that anyone would be foolhardy enough to laugh in your face."

He looked surprised, as if making a startling discovery about himself. "Because of me size you mean?'

"Yes," she smiled. "Don't you realize that?"

"Aye, I've never given it much thought," he admitted. "But me size doesn't keep you from laughing in me face."

Her hand, like the flutter of a bird's wing, lightly touched the sleeve of his jacket. The breeze caught the brim of her bonnet, turning it upward and unveiling her face. "I'm not afraid of you, Mr. McFadden. Should I be?"

Hugh solemnly studied the girl's face. What was it about the azure blue eyes that regarded him? They sparked with an unbelievable strength and lust for life, compared to the small face and fragile body they belonged to. She wasn't a beauty like her sister Margarita, but a handsome girl in her own right. She fascinated him more than any woman he'd ever met. Hugh swallowed the lump in his throat. "I'd never give you cause or reason to fear me, Miss Jane."

A warm secretive smile edged Jane Wesley's lips. "I knew that, Mr. McFadden. I knew that the minute we met. Father says I'm rather perceptive when it comes to judging people, and I do believe he is right."

On descending the hilltop, Hugh reached out and took her small hand and protectively brought it to rest in the crook of his arm as if it rightly belonged there. He was deeply conscious of her nearness, as with each limping step taken, her skirt lightly brushed against the side of his leg.

Upon reaching the small stone walk that led to the house, Hugh abruptly stopped in his tracks. "I'm forgetting me collar button," he said, and made several fruitless attempts to button it. Out of desperation he helplessly turned to the girl.

Without hesitation, Jane Wesley leaned forward and reached up to button his collar. The brim of her hat grazed Hugh's chin.

The light touch of her fingers at the base of his throat stirred Hugh's emotion. He strained his neck sideways in the hope of catching a glimpse of her face. Unexpectedly, Jane tilted her head back to inspect her work, her hands momentarily resting on his broad chest. "It's fine," she smiled up at him.

For the life of him, Hugh never knew what possessed him for on sudden impulse his hands slid around her small waist, pulling her close. His lips caught the corner of her mouth and he moved his head until the warm fullness of her mouth was on his. With a sudden urgency, for she was certain to bolt from him arms, Hugh kissed her soundly.

Jane Wesley stood frozen as mixed emotions surged through her body. She was surprised by his behavior, but not outraged. All her senses seemed wondrously confused as she stood in his arms experiencing her first kiss. Warm lips touched her closed eyelids, her cheeks and languidly claimed her lips again. Somewhere in a remote corner of her mind fear struck. Fear what he would think of her unladylike behavior for not rebelling. She breathlessly broke away from him.

"Jane?" Hugh murmured in anguish, collecting himself. "Are you angry with me? I wouldn't blame you. Saint's preserve me; I don't know what to say for my unpardonable behavior except to ask for your forgiveness."

Unable to meet his eyes, Jane stood silent with head bowed. She blinked back the sudden tears that clouded her eyes.

Her silence unnerved Hugh, and out of desperation he reached out and gently cupped her beneath the chin turning her face upward. He was distraught on seeing tears in her eyes.

"Oh God," he groaned. "Wish at will that I could relive these last few moments that have given you cause to cry. I never intended to hurt you or give you pain. I only hope that you can find it in your heart to forgive me by accepting my apology for my ill manners."

She was moved by his declaration, but more so by his deep need for understanding. "Tears are not always brought on by pain, Mr. McFadden; they are also products of joy. At the moment I'm uncertain as to their real cause; other than never having been kissed before."

It was the desolate look on her face that stopped Hugh from laughing out loud with relief. For little did he realize that at one time, Jane Wesley, like any normal girl her age, had envisioned this very moment; the moment of her first kiss. But each night, as she undressed for bed, she faced the cold facts of reality, a lame leg. It was a constant reminder that she was different from other girls and hardly to be sought after by men. With time, she had succumbed to the idea that she would never be kissed, courted or married.

"Then glad I be," Hugh smiled, "that I was the first to have the privilege of kissing you."

John Whitcomb was conscious of his friend's unusual silence as they left the Wesley house and journeyed homeward. As they neared the road that lead to the stable, he asked, "What did you think of Miss Margarita, Hugh?"

"Aye, she's the prettiest colleen I ever laid eyes on."

"So that's what's ailing you," Whitcomb grinned. "I knew you'd be taken with her the minute you saw her."

"You're wrong, John. It's not Miss Margarita I was taken with, but her sister, Miss Jane."

In shocked disbelief Whitcomb pulled at the reins bringing the chestnut mare to an abrupt stop. "You can't be serious, Hugh," he frowned. "Jane has an affliction."

Hugh reined his horse as well as his temper. "It's not Jane that has an affliction, but you, John. More's the pity that you can't see beyond a pretty face and into the true nature of a woman."

Whitcomb shrugged with indifference. "When it comes to women, I truly believe that variety is the true nature of man."

"And that same true nature will take you to an early grave, my friend."

"So be it," Whitcomb laughed. "But first let me give you a word of advice, Hugh, and I will say no more. Bedding a lovely creature is one thing and wedding one is another. The Wesley girls are the most dangerous of their species, for without benefit of savoring; they were raised to be wedded. I, for one, prefer to taste of the wine, making certain as to its sweetness and hardy bouquet before having to purchase the whole bottle. Unless you have honorable intentions, my good man, it's best to stay clear of women like that."

"Aye. My intentions are honorable and I'll be asking Miss Jane to honor me with her hand in marriage."

"I'll be damned! You can't be serious, Hugh. Do you really mean what you are saying?"

"Aye."

The shocked look on Whitcomb's face was enough to make Hugh laugh, but at the moment his thoughts were in earnest. "If it be right with you, John, I thought I'd come by on Saturdays and Sundays and work for you. It appears to me you have a fine store of horses that could do with some exercise and grooming. I've noticed you can do with another hand. And in return,

I'd be obliged if I could borrow a carriage on Sunday afternoons to take Miss Jane for a ride. It's only proper and fitting that I court her before we marry. . . come September."

"Come September! Good God, Hugh, have you taken leave of your senses? You mean to tell me that you actually planned all this in the last hour? Why you hardly know the girl let alone marry her in two month's time. Tell me, so I can fully understand this sudden madness of yours."

Hugh's hand came to rest in the long strains of the horse's mane. He sat there gently stroking the creature as he spoke. "It's a sad day when an Irishman lacks for words, John, but this be one of them. I only know what I feel and how I feel since meeting her," he said, and added with a ray of hope, "maybe some day you will have the good fortune to know how I feel."

"Maybe," Whitcomb said doubtfully. "But right now I'm willing to wager you——that she won't marry you."

Hugh roared with laughter. "Why it would be like stealing your money, John. I couldn't do that to my best friend. Honored though, I would be, if you were to stand up for me on my wedding day."

"Pray tell," Whitcomb said in exasperation. "Is there anything else you'd be asking of me?"

Hugh hesitated. "Aye, one more thing," he said. "Seeings how your family owns a good deal of property in Liverpool, might there be a chance of your finding me a proper flat to rent for me and my bride? Mind you, it can't have too many stairs to climb and I would like it near a park so Jane can go for strolls whenever she has a mind to. Aye, near a park," he said decidedly. "Jane would like that."

In the hope of shattering his friend's irrational dreams, without injury, Whitcomb sought an answer. "I'll do better than that," he said finally. "If you, being Catholic, can succeed in persuading a minister into giving his daughter's hand to you in marriage, I will find a flat and gladly absorb the rent for the first three months. That will be your well deserved wedding present after facing up to Reverend Wesley. For I don't envy the position you have chosen to put yourself in."

"'Tis more than I deserve," Hugh smiled. "I can't believe the good fortune that has befallen me; to find a girl like Miss Jane for a wife and to have you, John, for a friend."

Whitcomb's face flushed with guilt and he said no more.

The house was quiet and in the stillness of her bedroom, Jane Wesley undressed for bed. She slipped into the long sleeved nightdress, the weight of which fell straight to the floor. She blew out the candle in the silver candlestick holder that sat on top of a chest of drawers. Sleep was evasive and in the pale moonlight that streamed through the window she made her way over to the window seat. She curled up, hugging her knees to her chest and peered out the window at the rose garden bathed in moonlight. Their fragrance drifted in the warm evening breeze and carried into the bedroom.

Some of the excitement of the day still lingered on Jane's mind, but at the moment she was in a pensive mood and her thought strayed to her mother. She missed terribly the loving comfort of her mother who, on an evening such as this, would have sat with her and helped to resolve some of life's mysteries that plagued her mind. She always had the privilege of speaking her mind to her mother, more so, than her father. Quite frequently, her mother had intervened on her children's behalf against their father's loving but strict attitude.

With the death of her mother, three years ago, all the responsibilities of the household had fallen upon Jane's shoulders. A loving daughter, she took to her duties without complaint and without regard for herself. It wasn't until the last year that the atmosphere between daughter and father had changed. With discretion Jane had learned to impose her views, but left the decisions to her father's judgment. More recently, he sought out her company, confided in her, and asked her opinion. He took full credit for all decisions even when based upon her opinion. She soon learned to hold her tongue and smile to herself. A man's ego, she learned, was never to be trespassed upon and especially not by a woman.

Jane felt the heat of a blush rise to her cheeks as her thoughts strayed to Hugh McFadden. She found him to be a handsome man and there was no doubt in her mind that other females bore the same feelings. Judging from the bold way he had kissed her, he was well schooled when it came to women. The question that weighed heavily on her mind was his reason for kissing her.

She was well aware of her plainness thereby ruling out attraction. Was he just a brazen young man when it came to women? Or was it just a sudden impulse? At the thought of kindness or pity, Jane shuddered. Suddenly, the reason was of no importance to her. For the first time in all her eighteen years she had been kissed by a man and a handsome one at that. It was something she would remember the rest of her life and she had Hugh McFadden to thank for that.

Jane awoke the next morning feeling warm and loved. She resolved that it would take time to forget Mr. McFadden, but the excitement of the kiss would linger forever. In jubilant spirits she dressed for church and went down to breakfast.

Sunday breakfast was more amiable than most mornings. With the text of his sermon completed and soon to be delivered, Reverent Wesley's disposition was more congenial. Jane was conscious of her father's unusual silence and how his eyes were drawn to a letter that lay beside his plate. The letter had been delivered earlier by one of the servants from the Whitcomb household. It was obvious that something was troubling him and when his announcement came, it was of no surprise to Jane. "When you finish your breakfast, Jane, I would like to see you in my study for a few minutes."

She followed her father into a small room lined from floor to ceiling with books. She had always loved this room and never entered without envisioning her mother sitting in one of the large winged-chairs by the fireplace. Her hands would be busy with a piece of embroidery, or the mending of her family's clothes. Her father would be seated behind the large oak desk in the scholarly task of writing a sermon. Frequently, he would read out loud to his wife and listen to her comments.

Jane graced one of the chairs in front of the fireplace and watched as her father paced about the room, looking grave and anxious.

"What do you make of this, Jane?" he asked, waving the letter in his hand. "Mr. McFadden is asking my permission to call on you this very afternoon and take you out for a carriage ride. It seems John Whitcomb has loaned his friend the use of a carriage."

At the mention of Mr. McFadden's name, Jane felt a strange flutter in her heart. She stared at her father and the note in his hand, completely stunned by its contents.

"What say you?" Her father scowled.

"I don't know what to say," she honestly admitted. "I'm as surprised as you by the invitation."

He gave thought to her answer and nodded. "What do you suppose Mr. McFadden's intentions are by extending such an invitation?"

"It would be presumptuous of me, father, to declare Mr. McFadden's intentions, when I know not what they are. However, I did find him to be a very amiable man."

"I find no fault with him personally, Jane. But you must realize that the man is Catholic and opposes all that we hold dear."

Jane chose her words carefully. "It would seem to me, father, that Mr. McFadden has taken that into consideration and is well aware of my being a minister's daughter."

"Yes, yes, that's true. But it still puzzles me why he has extended such an invitation and to single you out."

"Begging your pardon, father, I think you are making too much of this invitation. On singling me out, I surmise, he is only showing appreciation for the hospitality afforded him yesterday and nothing more. Since I am the oldest lady of the house, so to speak, he might have thought it rude to invite my younger sisters and not me."

''Perhaps you are right, Jane. Nevertheless he has put me in a very awkward position. It would not do for me to offend a guest of John Whitcomb, who is one of the chief benefactors of our church. I'm afraid my dear, that I have to impose upon you to accept this invitation and you're to take Jessica with you. Margarita can see to the evening meal. I do hope you understand."

"I clearly understand your predicament, father. You can put your mind at rest and accept Mr. McFadden's invitation on my behalf."

"Thank you, Jane," he said and hurriedly walked to his desk to answer the letter. "What time do you suppose would be convenient for both parties?"

"Two o'clock, I would think," she smiled. "The heat of the sun will not be directly overhead."

Jane dared not to hope, even to herself, that Mr. McFadden's invitation was extended out of generosity and nothing more. And after sitting in the carriage for over a half hour, with her younger sister seated between them, of this she was certain. Their conversation bordered on the weather and the features of the landscape.

In pleasurable silence, Jane watched as Mr. McFadden took it upon himself to teach her younger sister, Jessica, how to handle the reins. He showed remarkable patience with the child and succeeded in drawing her out of her shyness. In a short while he had the child laughing and her eyes shown with admiration for the man.

"John tells me," Hugh said, "that there is a nice inn not too far from here. If it's to your liking, Miss Jane, we could stop for a spell and have a cup of tea?"

"Oh, could we, Jane? Please, could we? I've never been to an inn for tea," Jessica begged, beside herself with excitement.

"That would be pleasant," Jane smiled, "proving it's not too much trouble for Mr. McFadden."

"Trouble?" Hugh laughed. "Why tis more like a blessing. It's not every day a man has the privilege of taking two lovely ladies to tea."

His compliment started the child giggling and seemed to set the perfect mood for their tea party.

It was a small reputable inn that was built on the edge of a cliff overlooking the ocean. They chose a table outdoors blanketed with the greenery of a grape arbor. They sat at leisure, enjoying the ocean view while eating sweet cakes and drinking tea. A cool refreshing breeze came in over the ocean and carried with it the clean pungent smell of salt in the air. The droning sound of the waves could be heard washing onto the small beach.

Jessica, having finished her tea, longingly watched a number of children down on the beach collecting sea shells. "May I please be excused," she murmured. "I would so like to go down to the beach and collect shells."

"First let me see if I can find you something to store your treasures in," Hugh said, rising to his feet, and seizing the opportunity to be alone with Jane.

He left them for a short span and went into the inn. He returned shortly with a small wicker basket and held it out to the child. "Mind you, Jessica," he teased. "If you find a hidden treasure of gold on the beach, we'd be sharing it."

"Oh, yes. Oh, yes," she squealed with delight, taking the basket from his hand. "I truly promise to share everything with you and Jane."

Hugh roared with laughter as he stared after the child, who with basket in hand, half ran to the footpath that led to the beach. "She truly is a love," he sighed, seating himself.

"Yes," Jane agreed, smiling after her sister. "She gives me endless hours of pleasure. That was very kind of you, Mr. McFadden, to find the basket for her."

Hugh shrugged as his thoughts went racing on ahead. "I suppose," he said, "you'd be missing her terribly when it comes time for you to marry and move away."

Jane thought his statement odd but in all sincerity answered, "Yes, I would miss her very much but there's no fear of that happening. More than likely, Jessica will be leaving me when she is old enough to marry."

"Forgive my impertinence, Miss Jane, but is that your heart's desire, to stay at home? Have you not thought of marrying?"

"Every girl thinks about marrying, Mr. McFadden," Jane sighed. "But I'm not insensitive to the fact that most men are seeking moral as well as physical perfection in a wife. Unfortunately, good morals are invisible to the eye compared to that of having a physical disability."

"Then blind they be to the true beauty of a woman," Hugh frowned. "Before I go making a damn fool of myself, Miss Jane, I would like your permission to ask your father for your hand in marriage."

The acute silence that followed unnerved Hugh and he mistook her silence as rejection. "Ah," he sighed in despair, "you think I would have learned by now to keep my thoughts to myself."

"No, no, Mr. McFadden it's not that," Jane pleaded. "I'm honored by your proposal but I truly believe that my father will object."

Hugh smiled. "Aye, no doubt he will. But I'll tell you this much, he's going to have a real fight on his hands. I'm not about to take no for an answer."

Jane looked at him and smiled. She dared to hope that there was a possibility that Hugh McFadden could stand up to her father.

That evening Hugh took the seat offered, tugged at his collar and, remembering his manners, said, "It's very good of you to see me, sir, on such short notice."

Reverend Wesley politely nodded. "What can I do for you, Mr. McFadden?'

"I'd be honored, sir, if you would favor my request of asking for your daughter Jane's hand in marriage."

"Jane's hand," he said in shocked voice. "Am I to believe you are asking for her hand in marriage?"

"Yes, sir," Hugh smiled. "I'd be honored to have her for my wife."

I bet you would, were the Reverend's black thoughts, while trying to regain his composure. "Your request I'm afraid has taken me by complete surprise, Mr. McFadden."

"Aye," Hugh smiled. "No more than my having fallen in love with your daughter."

"I'm afraid . . . I'm afraid it is out of the question, Mr. McFadden."

"Why would that be?"

"I would think it obvious; you're of a different religion. You can't possibly expect Jane to give up her religion for you."

"No, I'd never ask that of her or anyone. What a person believes comes from the heart and no one has the right to change that. Now that we have that settled, would there be any other problems that you foresee?"

"The fact that I raised my daughter to be a lady, Mr. McFadden, and I do find your brashness very offensive. That you should even entertain the idea of asking for her hand in marriage shows a lack of respect for me and my daughter."

"You're right," Hugh agreed. "Jane is, and always will be far above me, but that still doesn't stop us from loving each other."

"Am I to believe that you already made a declaration of your intentions to my daughter?"

"Yes, I'm afraid I have. The only problem she could foresee was your objecting."

"Apparently, Mr. McFadden, my daughter has more sense than you do. I do object."

For the longest time Hugh stared at the shriveled up old man sitting behind the desk as if keenly aware of his feelings. "Why would any father want to stand in the way of his daughter's happiness is beyond me," Hugh said. "Could it be the thought of losing a daughter who caters to his every whim and out of fear of loneliness he won't let her go? Meaning no disrespect, sir, but Jane has served you well all these years, isn't it time for her happiness?'

"How. . . how dare you," he stammered.

"Oh, I dare, sir. If it means Jane's happiness I will dare anyone in this world."

The truth of Hugh's words infuriated him and at the same time set Reverend Wesley to thinking. He always considered himself a just man and in clear conscience wouldn't stand in the way of his daughter's happiness. Perhaps he had misjudged the man although he couldn't imagine what his daughter saw in him. He would have chosen another man for Jane, instead of the brash Irishman that sat before him. Another thought that consumed him, there never were suitors to choose from, since few men would marry a girl with an affliction. This well may be her only chance. Pulling reins on his emotions, Reverend Wesley finally resolved. "I will tell my daughter of your offer, Mr. McFadden. It will be up to Jane to make the decision, not me."

A triumphant smile crossed Hugh's lips. "Thank you, sir."

When Hugh didn't make a move to leave, a puzzled Reverend Wesley asked, "Is there something else?"

"Yes," Hugh smiled. "What would Jane's dowry be?"

"Her dowry?" he said in shocked voice. "Am I to understand that you want to know what her dowry will be?"

"Yes," Hugh nodded. "I believe it's customary. I assume you have set aside a dowry for each of your daughters, I'd only be claiming what rightful belongs to Jane."

The Reverend had never anticipated anyone asking for his eldest daughter's hand in marriage and now it posed a problem, his never having set aside a dowry for her. At the moment he was at a loss for words. "Let. . . let me think about it."

Hugh smiled. "In three weeks time, after the bans are posted, we'll be wed."

Hugh would never let it be said that he married Jane Wesley for her dowry, so on their wedding night he gave her the money.

"I don't understand, Mr. McFadden," Jane smiled at her husband. "Why did you ask for my dowry if you had no intention of keeping it?"

"It was a matter of principal. Why shouldn't your father give you a dowry if he has full intention of doing so for his other daughters? The money is yours, Jane, to do what you please; I'll never touch a penny of it." Little did Hugh realize that a year later his words would come back to haunt him.

***

Customarily while in Liverpool on business, their mutual friend, John Whitcomb, would call on the couple. He enjoyed their company and the fact that Jane McFadden set a good table was an inducement to his not having to eat alone. It was on such a night, after dinner, the men sat in the parlor enjoying a cigar and whiskey.

"I tell you, Hugh, you did all right for yourself. Jane is a wonderful cook and I must say, marriage certainly agrees with her. She seems to have filled out some."

Hugh was beside himself with laughter. "Marriage had nothing to do with her filling out," he laughed. "Jane was always endowed but her father, set in his ways, thought it improper for ladies to show their true attributes and insisted she wear binding to flatten her body."

"You can't be serous," Whitcomb said in shocked voice.

"If you're surprised," Hugh laughed, "just think what a shock I had on me wedding night, finding this voluptuous woman in my bed."

After their guest had left, Jane McFadden noticed the unusual quietness of her husband and the deep frown of what she perceived to be worry that masked his face. "Is something troubling you, Mr. McFadden?" she asked.

"Aye," he said, shaking his head from side to side. "I was just thinking about what John told me."

"What was that, may I ask?"

"That in the Americas their Congress will be passing a bill called, a Settlement Act. It will allow any man who will start a settlement to become the owner of one hundred and sixty acres of free land. Can you believe that; one hundred and sixty acres of free land to any man? It would be taking me half a life time before I could afford a piece of land like that here in England."

Although he rarely mentioned it, Jane knew that his heart's desire was to own his own land someday. "Is John sure of what he states?" she asked.

"Aye, the man knows what he's talking about. The thing he says is to be there before they pass the Bill and start a settlement."

"Yes, I can see where that makes sense," Jane said, and drew in a sharp breath that pained her heart. "When, will you be leaving, Mr. McFadden?"

A shocked Hugh turned to look at his wife sitting on the settee, her hands busy with a piece of embroidery. "Leaving?" he frowned.

"Since we can't afford passage for both of us, I thought you'd want to leave first and I will join you later."

"Jane, do you hear what you're saying?"

Setting the embroidery aside, Jane looked up at her husband. "If it means owning our own land someday, then sacrifices have to be made. I'm willing to stay here and wait until you can send for me."

"Aye," Hugh sadly smiled. "It's an angel the Lord gave me for a wife. But even if I could afford to go to America, how could I afford to leave you behind?"

"My dowry," she said flatly. "There's enough money to buy you passage and for me to live on for a year. If worst should come to worst, I could always move back with my family."

"Oh no," he fumed. "I won't be touching a penny of your dowry."

Jane smiled. "You won't be touching it, Mr. McFadden, since I will be buying the ticket for your passage."

Chapter Two

Baggage in hand, Beth Carney waited at the gate for someone to fetch her. Her threadbare cape was little comfort against the harsh winds of January that chilled her to the bone. Eerie sounds came out of the darkness and it seemed like an eternity until she caught sight of a speck of light. Although she could not see what manner of person carried it, her green eyes were fixed on the lantern that slowly moved towards her. Within arm's length of her, the lantern was thrust through an opening in the gate, then raised and lowered, bringing her into full view of the bearer.

"Would you be the new girl, Beth Carney?" a woman's voice asked.

"Yes," Beth answered, and detected the sound of the sucking of a tooth in disappointment.

The woman set the lantern down in the snow and pulled a number of jingling keys from her pocket. She proceeded to unlock the heavy wrought iron gate. It was opened but a fraction to let her small frame slip through, and then quickly locked behind her. Beth strained for a glimpse of the woman's face hidden in the shadows of the bonnet brim, but failed.

"It's a bit of a walk." The woman warned, picking up the lantern to lead the way.

Holding fast to her baggage, Beth followed in silence. As they rounded the bend in the road, Beth's mouth dropped open. She stood at a standstill. Chesterton Hall loomed upward into the darkness of the sky, with supporting twin towers on each end. It was far larger than she had ever imagined.

"Move along child, it's cold."

Beth finally found her voice. "How many people reside here at the Hall?" she asked.

"There be but four; his Lordship and Lady and the two young masters."

"Four people, you say? What would they be needing with so many rooms?" Beth asked in puzzlement.

"Never you mind, child. Move along."

The house was dark, the hour late, and the bolting shut of the huge door through which they had entered echoed in the stillness of the marbled floored hall.

Beth's eyes grew enormous in her pale face as she looked about the huge entrance hall. A number of oil paintings climbed the walls along with the oak banister staircase that led to the floor above. Most of the paintings were of men in fanciful dress uniforms; medals and ribbons adorned their chests. Although the flickering light of the lantern played tricks, each face that covered a canvas seemed to hold a common resemblance—sharp featured men with dark black hair.

She was led through a passageway, down a small flight of steps and into a clean scoured kitchen. The sudden brightness of the room hurt her eyes.

A well-fed fire burned in the hearth, the flames of which reflected in a dozen or more assorted copper saucepans that hung down from the overhead beams. The room was bathed in a warm glow of amber, and the nostalgic aroma of a pastry shop filled the air. Beth was enveloped by a sense of warmth and a strange sense of security, as if she belonged there.

"Here, let me give you a hand with that."

The woman leaned over and began to unfasten the ribbons on Beth's bonnet. She looked up at the woman's face but a few inches from hers. It was a pleasant oval face, clean scrubbed, mellowed with age, and suited to the room they were standing in.

"I'm Mrs. Cosgrove," she said. "Before long you'll be calling me Maggie just like young Masters Elwood and Elton do. And you'll be coming into my kitchen to pinch a few of my sweet biscuits. You're a wee-bit of a thing to be a seamstress' helper."

"Yes," Beth smiled. For it was true she was quite small for her age but had intentions of growing. She was struck with a sudden fear that because of her size she'd be sent back to the orphanage. She pulled herself up to her full height and thrust out her chin. "I may be small but my skills are many."

"Aye and a bit of a tongue to match that red hair of yours, I see." The woman laughed. "Go sit by the fire, child, and warm yourself while I fix a sandwich or two and a cup of tea."

At the thought of sitting Beth frowned. Her body was stiff and her buttocks sore after having traveled fifteen hours in the coach. The woman seemed to read her mind.

"Then watch if you will. You can help by fetching the dishes out of the cupboard on the far wall over there."

Beth watched in fascination as Mrs. Cosgrove sliced cold meat, put the kettle on the fire, and within minutes had made dainty sandwiches. She set them down on a small table next to the hearth. In time it would become Beth's private table when visiting the kitchen to see Mrs. Cosgrove.

The woman appeared pleased as the child ate with relish the sandwiches and several fruit tarts along with her tea.

The late hour, the warmth of the fire and a satisfied appetite began to take its toll; the child's head began to droop. "It's time we got you to your bed, Beth Carney," she announced. "Come along child."

Beth had a vague recollection of following the woman through a dark hallway and up a back staircase that led to the second floor.

"This be my room," Mrs. Cosgrove announced. "If there be anything you'd be needing you'll find me here. Your room be at the top of these stairs." She turned and started to climb a narrow spiral staircase opposite that of her bedroom door. "After tonight, you won't catch me climbing these stairs; they're hard on me knees."

When they finally reached the top landing, they entered a small room the likes of which Beth had never seen. It was round, not one corner in the room. Bare windows faced out in all directions through which the blackness of the sky could be seen. It took her a few seconds before realizing she was standing in one of the towers that she had seen earlier.

Off to one side was a small fireplace in front of which sat a small wooden stool. An ample supply of cut logs lay at the hearth as well as a scuttle full of coal. The only other furniture was a bed and rickety old dresser. Next to the bed sat a small night stand with drawers on top of which lay various size candles and holders. Several pegs jutted out from the wall to hang one's clothes on.

A heavy stupor was closing over Beth and she was thankful for the hands that helped her undress and draw the night shirt down over her head. Her body ached and she welcomed the thought of sleep although she found the mattress to be hard and lumpy. An old musty smelling feather quilt was being pulled up over her. She welcomed the warmth of it. Without thought Beth answered all questions put to her by the soft gentle voice.

"How did you get those scars on your back, child?"

"I was whipped for breaking my slate and forgetting to clean the ashes out of the hearth."

"Nobody will whip you here child; Maggie will see to that!"

Something soft and warm gently brushed Beth's forehead and she knew she had to be dreaming about angels, for it felt like a kiss.

When the bright light of daybreak streamed through the windows of the room, Beth sat up with a jolt. It took her a few minutes before realizing where she was. How strange, she thought, to wake up in a silent room without the bustling sound of twenty girls scurrying around and getting dressed. Although small, stranger yet was to have a room of one's own. The thought pleased her.

Fearful that she had overslept, Beth sprang from bed and pushed the wooden stool over to the dresser. She climbed up and poured water from the pitcher into the large matching basin standing atop the dresser. She took a deep breath of the sweet rose fragrant bar of soap that awaited her use. After washing and dressing she set to the task of hanging up her clothes on the pegs—another dress and a pinafore. Her personal belongings—a prayer book and sketchpad—she stored in a dresser drawer along with her undergarments. Out of habit, she automatically saw to the straightening of the bed and took the time to look out each window. The view was beautiful; it was like living in the sky. She had a clear view of all the grounds below and just like a bird, she could see over the tree tops. When she looked straight down the distance to the ground was somewhat frightening. The fairytale of Rapunzel that was told to her by one of the older girls in the orphanage came to mind. She remembered how Rapunzel let her hair down in order for her Prince Charming to climb up and free her from the tower. In awe, Beth stared at the ground below while trying to calculate how long it would take for her hair to grow to such a length. "Cripes," she sighed. "I'd be an old lady of thirty years before my hair would reach the ground. What prince would want an old lady?" Dejectedly, she turned from the window.

Like a path leading to the kitchen, the aroma of fresh baked bread came floating up the staircase from the kitchen below. Upon reaching the second landing, Beth could hear the murmur of voices as she made her way down to the kitchen. "What's she like?" The distinct voice of a young girl asked.

At the threshold Beth caught her breath as all conversation stopped and all eyes turned on her. A group of five adults and a young girl, who she judged to be several years older than herself, were sitting at the table breakfasting.

On seeing Beth, Mrs. Cosgrove rose from her chair to greet the girl. "I didn't expect you up at this early hour, Beth, seeing how tired you were last night. Did you sleep well?"

"Yes, thank you," Beth answered and was surprised to see that with the coming of morning, Mrs. Cosgrove hadn't changed into a stern faced woman. The pleasant smile was still there along with the sincere regard and concern for her welfare. She laid a gentle hand on Beth's shoulder, urging her toward the empty chair at the table next to where she'd been sitting.

After introductions were made, Beth thought them to be a strange lot sitting at the table breakfasting. A Mr. and Mrs. Moore and their young daughter, Lottie, occupied the one side of the table. Mr. Moore, as well as being the gardener, helped manage the stables. He appeared to be more interested in his second helping of gruel than his wife and daughter who openly stared at Beth. From what she gathered, they lived in the village and came to work each day at Chesterton Hall with the exception of Sundays. Prior to this, they had lived in London and their speech and mannerism were characterized by a heavy cockney accent which at times proved quite impossible to understand without the continual begging of their pardon.

At the far end of the table sat Miss Amelia Applegate, a stern-faced spinster of fifty. Miss Applegate was the head housekeeper and without a doubt could be entrusted with the keys of Her Majesty's kingdom. She had already begun to issue the orders for the day to Mrs. Moore and her daughter, Lottie.

On Beth's left sat Madame Dupont looking the epitome of neatness, in a starched white cap and pinafore. She was personal maid to Her Ladyship and appeared to be a rather congenial woman in her mid-thirties whose native French tongue colored her speech. Beth found this most agreeable to her ear.

"Lottie will be showing you about today and she'll be telling you what your chores are to be," Miss Applegate informed Beth.

At the prospect of working with the young girl and possibly finding a new friend, Beth was overjoyed, but within seconds her heart sank when out of earshot of everyone in the room. Lottie grumbled, "I dunno, she must have something agen me to send me up these blooming stairs with the likes of you. Get a move on," she commanded with a supercilious air.

Beth soon learned that Lottie's innermost thoughts, if she manifested any, were kept to herself. She was neither inquisitive nor interested in learning. She tolerated each day as it came. At times Beth found herself envious of the girl's ignorant and complacent manner. Nevertheless, they did share one thing in common; they dreaded the nights that Her Ladyship decided to bathe. Under Madame Dupont's bidding they were obliged to carry bucket after bucket of steaming hot water up the back staircase and down the hall to what Madame Dupont referred to as Her Ladyship's boudoir.

It was on such a night, Lottie climbing the stairs ahead of Beth, both struggling under the weight of the buckets, that Beth chanced to notice the small casement window on the staircase. "Lottie, does that window open?'

"I dunno," she snapped. "Who gives a sixpence whether it do or don't?"

Beth set the vessels down and began to carefully examine the small window. It took some doing but she finally managed to open it. She leaned out and just as she had surmised, the kitchen door was directly beneath her. Quick ideas flashed through her mind only to be shattered by Lottie's grumbling on her getting a move on. Beth closed the window.

In the week that followed, every free moment Beth had was spent at the window diligently working on the scheme that was evolving. Fortunately, in the stables could be found the tools and equipment necessary for the efficient execution of her plan. Her project completed, she anxiously awaited the coming of the evening that Her Ladyship would decide to bathe.

When they finally were summoned, it took some persuasion on Beth's part to get Lottie to climb the stairs empty handed, open the window and wait for her command.

In the yard below Beth stood with three steaming vessels at her feet. She leaned over and tied the handle of one of the buckets to the length of sturdy rope that dangled from the pulley above. "Now pull at your end of the rope, Lottie. Hoist the pail up," Beth commanded.

Timidly at first, Lottie began to pull her end of the rope, lifting the vessel ever so slowly from the ground and into the air. When she finally grasped the idea of Beth's plan, the pail went sailing upward, spilling half of its contents.

"Blimey! Blimey!" Lottie yelled. "You've a'ead on yer shoulders, Beth Carney!"

Bucket followed bucket to the sound of their joyful laughter. Subsequently, Beth gained Lottie's respect and admiration but never found the deep, intimate relationship that she longed for and one seeks in a true friend.

By March Beth had settled into her new life, gaining a great deal of knowledge as to how the nobility of England lived. Chesterton Hall was divided into what she considered two halves. The east wing was for servants, while the west wing was for His Lordship's family and guests. Room after room seemed to depict their pleasures, music room, game room ballroom and library.

Most of Beth's day was spent in the sewing room where piles of bedding needed hemming or the intricate embroidering of monograms and sometimes the family coat of arms. The work was pleasant enough, although she had envisioned the hemming of fashionable gowns of delicate fabric and laces for Her Ladyship. Under the guidance of the village seamstress, after proving her apprenticeship, a year later Beth got her wish.

She was allotted one afternoon a week for herself. On mild and clear days, she would ramble in the woods or venture into the village on an errand for Maggie. Inclement weather would keep her to her room where she spent hours reading her prayer book or took to sketching. When overcome with loneliness on such afternoons, she would run down to the kitchen and seek out Maggie's company. Maggie had the gift to make her laugh. In Maggie's kitchen she willingly lent a helping hand and soon learned the art of cooking and the making of the sweet rose fragrant soap. Some nights she'd sit at the small table doing sums and learning how to read under Maggie's guidance.

Although curious about the library, Beth never set foot in the room since it was under Miss Applegate's domain. The day arrived when she did enter and, in an extraordinary way, it changed her life forever.

That autumn Miss Applegate came down with a bad fever and was bedridden for a week. After much persuasion on Maggie's part, Miss Applegate finally agreed to let Beth take over her duties in the library. After a lengthy speech by Miss Applegate as to what would be involved and the responsibility of the valuable properties in the room, she rather reluctantly handed the key over to Beth. "Now remember, Beth, you're to make certain there's a good fire in the hearth and you're to be out of the room before the clock strikes eight. Masters Elwood and Elton start their lessons at eight sharp. Make certain as to a fresh pitcher of water on Mr. Carver's desk."

With a small curtsy, Beth took the key from her hand and headed directly for the library in the west wing. Mentally she kept going over all that had to be done before eight o'clock but when she unlocked the door the sight of so many books in one room overwhelmed her. It would take a lifetime to read them and more than two hours to dust the shelves. With good intentions she set about her task, of first lighting the fire to take the chill out of the room, then setting a fresh pitcher of water on the desk. She noticed how two desks were situated facing the blackboard and a larger desk. A small spiral staircase led to a loft above where rows and rows of books were shelved. Clean from top to bottom, she mentally said to herself, while climbing the staircase with feather duster in hand.

At one point she had to climb a small ladder to reach the top shelf in order to give it a proper dusting. Beth lost her footing and tumbled to the floor taking several books down with her. She hastily scrambled to her feet and started picking up the books when she noticed the third one lay open. It was a book of poems. Her eyes carried over the open page and she began to read the poem having noticed it was written by a woman.

When I am dead, my dearest,
    Sing no sad songs for me;
Plant thou no roses at my head,
    Nor shady cypress-tree:
Be the green grass above me
    With showers and dewdrops wet;

And if thou wilt, remember,
    And if thou wilt, forget.

I shall not see the shadows,
    I shall not feel the rain;
I shall not hear the nightingale
    Sing on, as if in pain:
And dreaming through the twilight
    That doth not rise nor set,
Haply I may remember,
    And haply may forget.

Again and again, Beth read the poem trying to commit it to memory. She never knew that such beautiful writing existed. How long she stood there, she didn't know; the slamming shut of the library door below brought her back to reality. From where she was standing she could see the man who had entered. He was short and wearing a black flowing gown that trailed over his suit. He quickly headed for the blackboard in the room. A set of spectacles seemed to pinch his nose. With a quick hand be began writing on the board. The door opened and the two young Masters came scrambling in with a "Good morning, Mr. Carver, sir." They spoke in unison while heading for their desks.

For a few seconds Beth stood frozen not knowing what to do. She quickly closed the book in her hand and sank to the floor hiding behind the first row of shelves.

Beth watched as the man set down the chalk and turned to face his students. "Good morning, gentlemen," he smiled. "Let's see which one of you can solve the problem on the board first."

Beth squinted trying to read the writing on the blackboard. With the exception of the word apple she couldn't make out the remainder of the sentence.

"Elton? Elwood? Do you have the answer?" he asked.

"Three." They answered in unison.

"Ah," he laughed. "Read it again carefully. It is a trick question. If there are five apples and you take away two, how many do you have?"

"Three," they repeated.

"Wrong again," he said, shaking his head from side to side.

"But, sir," Elton objected.

A frown crossed Beth's brow as she ran the trick question through her mind. The question posed was, how many you have not how many are left, she told herself. I'd have two apples not three.

"The answer, gentlemen, is two. The trick question was how many you have, not how many were left. If you took away two that would mean you'd have two apples in hand, not three."

On hearing that her answer was correct, Beth smiled, but what tickled her most was the fact that the two Masters, who were much older than her, had failed. She watched in fascination as Mr. Carver went to the board to write out another trick question. He started to write, hesitated, erased and then started all over again, only this time in larger hand. Beth could actually read the problem without having to squint.

The morning class, Mr. Carver announced, was to stimulate their minds and teach them how to us reasoning and logic in a clear and consistent manner.

By midmorning a spellbound Beth had stretched herself out on the loft floor holding her chin in her hand, as she looked down on the classroom below. She hung on to every word spoken by Mr. Carver. The half hour of Latin class she had found confusing since never having studied it outside of the few words she had learned in church. She was mesmerized by the literature class when the two young Masters had to read aloud a play by Shakespeare in which Mr. Carver would comment on the true meaning of a line.

Finally Mr. Carver dismissed his two pupils to partake of their midday meal. Beth saw it as her opportunity to leave the library without anyone knowing she'd been there. She kept waiting for Mr. Carver, who was seated at his desk sifting through papers to leave. Beth waited, waited and waited.

"When do you have the intention of showing yourself, young lady?"

Beth froze on hearing his voice. She summoned all her courage, scrambled to her feet and with shaking knees descended the staircase.

From over the rim of the spectacles that were perched on his nose, Mr. Carver closely regard the young girl standing in front of him. "Well," he grumbled, "when did you intend to leave?"

"Right after you, sir," Beth said.

"I see. Did you enjoy the morning class?"

"Oh, yes. Very much, sir."

"What is your name, child?"

"Beth. . . Beth Carney."

"Well see that this doesn't happen again, Beth."

"Yes, sir." Beth gave a small curtsey before heading for the door.

Peaked by curiosity, Mr. Carver called to her, "Just a minute, Beth. I would like to know what you learned, if anything, this morning."

Beth drew in a sharp breath, not knowing where to begin, when she remembered the trick question about the apples. "What I've learned sir, is to reason and think carefully before making a decision. If one takes two apples from five that leaves them with two in hand and not three that were left."

"Well," he sighed. "I'm glad to hear that my lesson didn't fall on deaf ears."

"No, sir. It didn't."

"Be gone with you child, I have work to do."

Beth gave another curtsey before scurrying toward the door.

That evening as Beth sat in the kitchen wrapping the cakes of soap that Maggie removed from the molds, she could not contain herself any longer. Maggie listened in awe as Beth told her what had transpired in the library that morning. "Do you know how lucky you are? It's a good job that Mr. Carver didn't go a running off and report you to Miss Applegate. Mind you, Beth, she told you that you had to leave the library by eight sharp."

"I know that. It was an accident my being there, honest, Maggie. It will never happen again."

"Someday you're going to be the death of me, child," Maggie said, giving thought to the problem at hand. There was still time. If Mr. Carver went running off to Miss Applegate, there would be hell to pay knowing Beth disobeyed her. Ideas flashed though Maggie Cosgrove's mind. "Beth, see to putting the kettle on and get one of the good plates with matching tea cup out of the cupboard and be quick about it."

Beth did what she was told but not without wonder. She watched as Maggie cut into the large fruit pie she had baked and set a generous wedge down on the plate. "There isn't a man alive who could refuse a taste of my fruit pie and a cup of tea to wash it down."

It was true, as far as Beth was concerned; Maggie's pies left one craving for more.

"Now see to getting your hands and face washed and your hair could do with a combing, while I fix the tea."

"I don't understand," Beth said.

"What's to understand, child. You'll be bringing Mr. Carver a cup of tea and a piece of fruit pie to his room and while you're about it, you can tell him how sorry you are for what you did. Tell him the truth and shame the devil. He'll not open his mouth to anyone after tasting my fruit pie."

Hair combed, face and hands washed, Beth stood outside the door to Mr. Carver's room holding fast the tray containing a slice of fruit pie, teapot with cup and saucer that matched the blue plate. While balancing the tray in one hand she knocked on the door.

"Come in." The words sounded muffled.

51

Apprehensively, Beth turned the doorknob and entered. Mr. Carver was sitting at his desk with a book spread open in front of him. He looked up from the book and stared at Beth. "What have we here?" he asked.

"Begging your pardon, sir. Cook said, I was to apologize for this morning and thought you'd be liking a cup of tea."

Beth quickly set the tray down in front of him and was surprised to see him smile.

"I could do with a cup of tea. Ah. . . and fruit pie to go with it, I see. Seems cook must hold you in high regard, Beth Carney, to go through all this trouble."

"Yes, sir. We're the best of friends. She's always looking after me."

He picked up the teapot and began filling the cup. "Why did you tarry in the library if you knew you should have left by eight o'clock?"

"I wasn't tarrying on purpose, sir. I had a bit of an accident. I was going about my chores when three books fell off the shelf that I was dusting and there, right before my eyes, the one book lay open at my feet. It was a book of poetry written by a woman and when I read the first line, I just couldn't put it down; the words were so beautiful I had to finish reading them. . . and. . .and that's what made me late."

"Do you remember the woman's name who wrote the poem?" he asked with skepticism.

"It was a foreign name, sir. Christina. . . Christina Rossetti, I believe."

"Christina Rossetti," he sighed. "Do you like to read, Beth?

"Yes, but the only book I'd be owning is my prayer book."

"Interesting," he said, more or less to himself while taking another bite of pie.

"What, sir?" Beth frowned.

"Your interest in the poems of Christina Rossetti at your age, and a girl at that."

"Begging your pardon, sir. I don't know what you mean."

"It's a known fact, Beth, that the intelligence of men is far superior to that of women," he said flatly.

"Why would that be, sir?"

"The fact that women have smaller heads than men; therefore their brain is smaller, which makes it impossible for them to comprehend as much."

"Oh, I didn't know that," Beth said aghast, at this shocking discovery. She watched as Mr. Carver finished off the last bit of pie on his plate and drained the tea cup dry.

"Tell cook her pie was delicious; as for you Beth, I think I may have a book around here that you might enjoy reading. Let me see if I can lay hands on it." He rose from the chair and began searching the shelves behind his desk, looking through a number of books. "Ah. . . here it is," he said in surprise. "Take it with you and when you finish reading it, I'd like to have your opinion on the story. It's written by Charles Dickens who I think will become one of England's greatest authors."

A flabbergasted Beth took the book from his hand and held it to her chest as if it were a precious gift. "Thank you, sir. Thank you, sir. I'll take good care of it." She curtseyed several times while backing toward the door.

"Beth," he smiled, "you're forgetting the tray. The next time you pop in, should the cook have an extra piece of pie, I'd be delighted to eat it for her."

It became a regular routine for Beth to pop in on Mr. Carver at least twice a week with the excuse of returning a book she had borrowed along with a slice of Maggie's pie. Sensing her insatiable appetite for learning and her quickness of mind, Mr. Carver began tutoring her, even though she was a girl. Little did he realize that Beth put the first lesson he had taught her to good use—that of reasoning and logic. Often, when passing a looking–glass she'd study the size of her head in comparison to other girls her age. True, her head was smaller than some, but she knew for a fact that other girls with larger heads were far dumber than she. She resolved that the size of a person's brain or sex had nothing to do with their capacity to learn.

It wasn't long before Mr. Carver, a sentimental old bachelor, took a liking to the girl. He found himself looking forward to Beth's evening visits. In a way she brought a ray of sunshine into his lonely life, and before his very eyes the young helpless waif was beginning to blossom into a very refined young girl.

On a warm summer's eve, catching the last light of day to read by, Beth was curled up on the window seat engrossed in her reading. Across the room, Mr.

Carver was seated at his desk working. He glanced up and suddenly found himself openly staring at the girl. A sense of pride stole over him while wondering where the years had gone. Through the French doors that stood ajar could be heard the sound of music and the gaiety of laughter from across the courtyard. On sudden impulse, Mr. Carver set his quill down and stood up. "Beth, close your book; that's enough reading for one evening. I would like you to accompany me onto the courtyard. Quickly girl, before I change my mind."

His strange behavior surprised her, but without question Beth swiftly closed the book and sprang to her feet. She followed him through the French doors and onto the courtyard where he stood waiting for her. He appeared to be deep in thought.

"What is it, Mr. Carver?" Beth asked, as she stood in front of him.

"Do you hear that, Beth?" He raised a hand in the direction of the ballroom. "It's music. A waltz by Strauss, I believe."

"Yes, sir, I hear it. It's beautiful."

"There's more to life besides burying one's head in a book, my dear girl. There's music and dancing."

"Dancing?" she giggled.

"Yes, dancing. I may be old, and some may think me a bit crotchety, but I still remember how to dance. Intelligence is one thing, but a lady has to have beauty of motion, form and manner and know all the social graces. Dancing is one of them."

"Am I to understand, Mr. Carver that you expect me to dance when I don't know the first thing about it?"

"Come, come now, Beth, don't be shy," he said, waving her closer. "It's just a matter of counting and that's what I'm here for, to teach you."

From her bedroom window that overlooked the courtyard, Maggie sat catching a bit of fresh air and listening to the music after having worked in a hot kitchen all day. She frowned in puzzlement on seeing Mr. Carver, who was soon followed by Beth; step out onto the courtyard below. What's he up to now, she thought. Maggie watched with interest as Beth curtsied and presented her hand to Mr. Carver. Before long, after a few stumbling steps, they went gliding around the courtyard in time with the music.

"By-Jove! He's teaching her how to dance," Maggie laughed. "What a sight for me sore eyes. My, how she's grown."

Apparently, Mr. Carver and Maggie weren't the only ones to notice how Beth had grown; the two young Masters also noticed. With lame excuses they would come down to the kitchen to seek out Beth and find a reason to speak with her, a missing button or torn shirt sleeve. More often than not, Maggie would intervene, sending them on their way for interfering with the work that had to be done in her kitchen. Although she couldn't keep an eye on them all the time, she would thank the Lord for making her a light sleeper the night they decided to invade the servant's quarters.

Maggie was awakened by a strange creaking sound and voices in whisper outside in the hall. She groped for a candle and match on top of the night stand. After lighting the candle she made her way across the room and flung open her bedroom door. "Who's there?" she asked.

In the flickering candlelight she could see the two young Masters who appeared to be frozen in motion. They were standing on the small spiral staircase that led to Beth's room.

"Just where did you think you'd be going? Get down here, the pair of you," Maggie ordered.

A nervous giggle passed the lips of Elton, the youngest. "We just wanted to visit with Beth."

"At this hour?" Maggie fumed. "If you think that highly of Beth you can invite her to tea tomorrow."

For a moment they appeared at a loss for words.

"A servant girl to tea? That wouldn't be proper," Elwood said stiffly. "We just wanted to have some fun and teach her a new game we've learned."

"And what game might that be, Master Elwood? Would it be, Dunk Yer Diddle? Would that be the same game the two of you've been playing with Lottie? Now be off with the pair of you this very minute before I wake Her Ladyship and tell her what you've been up to. You're to leave Beth alone."

She watched as they went walking down the corridor and disappeared into the darkness of the night. First thing the next morning, Maggie saw to having the gardener put an inside bolt on Beth's door.

In addition to dance lessons, Mr. Carver began giving Beth lessons in etiquette. Over the years, in comparison with other girls in her walk of life, Beth had received a well rounded education. Rounder still was Mr. Carver's appearance after having eaten eight years of Maggie Cosgrove's pies.

It was a sad day for the household when the two young Masters left to go to a university, but sadder still for Beth. Mr. Carver's services as tutor were no longer required at Chesterton Hall. Before leaving he made a point of visiting with Maggie Cosgrove in her kitchen. The main topic of conversation, over a cup of tea, turned out to be about Beth.

"Sometimes I wonder if I did the right thing by tutoring her," he said solemnly, shaking his head from side to side.

"What's to wonder about, Mr. Carver?" Maggie frowned. "You've done a real fine job of it. She's a real proper lady, my Beth, and I'm beholden to you. I'm sure proud of her and you should be too."

"That I am," he smiled. "My only worry is that she's educated beyond her station in life which can make it very hard on her. She has no social rank or family and will always be looked upon as an outcast in our society."

"Ah. . . that be the truth. I never thought about that," Maggie admitted. "With her having book learning, I though she might open her own dressmaker's shop someday or become a nanny. Beth knows her place in life, so don't you go fretting none about her."

58

"I hope you're right," he sighed. "There's one other thing, Mrs. Cosgrove, which I think you should know."

"What might that be?" she asked.

A high flush of color spread over his face and he appeared ill at ease. "It's a rather delicate subject and I find myself in a very awkward position having to speak about my charge," he said. "If it wasn't for Beth's sake, I'd hold my tongue. I thought you of all people should know. I don't mean to offend you by bringing up such a subject but Master Elwood and Elton, as of late have not conducted themselves in a gentlemanly like manner as I would hope they would and—-"

"Say no more," Maggie interrupted. "I've had me eye on those two scoundrels for a long time. I know what they've been up to."

A sense of relief stole over Mr. Carver. "Where is Beth? I'd like to bid her farewell."

Maggie nodded her head toward the kitchen door. "She'd be out in the rose garden picking petals that I'll be needing when I makes me fragrant soap."

For along time Maggie stared after the man as he went through the kitchen door. She could only imagine his heartache over having to say good-bye to Beth. Like herself, over the years he had grown fond of the girl. Maggie considered Beth blessed for having had the acquaintance of such a fine gentleman.

When Beth came walking in from the garden with a basket full of rose petals over her arm, she was too choked to speak and fought hard not to cry. Roughly she wiped at the uncontrollable tears that clouded her eyes.

"Now don't be pining away over Mr. Carver's leaving us, Beth. Instead you ought to be thankful for all the book learning you had. He made a proper young lady out of you, I dare say."

"Oh, I shall miss him terribly," she sniveled. "I will miss him more than Lottie's leaving us. At least he had the decency to say good-bye. Why do you suppose Lottie went running off like that?"

"Never you mind where Lottie went," Maggie said, and quickly changed the subject. "Here, give us a hand with clearing off this table."

Beth's thoughts often reflected on Mr. Carver and how much she missed him. As for Lottie's leaving, she had little regard since they never were truly friends. It would be by chance that Beth would find out the true reason for Lottie's strange disappearance from Chesterton Hall.

On a rather bleak day in November, Beth set out for the village on an errand for Maggie and to purchase some blue silk thread that was needed to mend one of Her Ladyship's gowns. As she came out of the millinery shop, having purchased the thread, and was crossing the village square, she saw a girl who, although fatter, bore a striking resemblance to Lottie. Beth called out to the girl and when she turned around she knew it was Lottie. She ran up to where Lottie was standing and breathlessly asked, "How are you, Lottie?"

"How'd you think I'd be, carrying all this extra weight around with me?" Lottie snapped.

In all innocence Beth replied, "If you didn't eat so much, Lottie, you wouldn't gain weight."

"You'd be thinking this comes from eating," Lottie snapped, poking her protruding stomach. "I'd be having a babe."

Beth openly stared at Lottie's protruding stomach. "When did you marry, Lottie?"

"Marry?" Lottie laughed. "Whooo'd marry me? You don't think that either one of the Masters would marry the likes of me after having their way with me. Why buy the cow when the milk is free? That's what they said."

A shocked Beth stared at the girl, only to have Lottie suddenly burst forth in a fit of uncontrollable laughter.

"Can it be, Beth Carney," Lottie laughed, "f'all yer fine airs and book learning that you wouldn't be know'en the first thing about what men and women be doing?"

"Of course, I know," she said indignantly. "What I don't understand is how you could be so foolish to let the two Masters take such liberties with you?"

Lottie laughed. "It was a bit of fun for me at times when they weren't in a hurry or worried about getting caught with their britches around their knees."

A bit of fun, Beth thought angrily, and had the overwhelming urge to reach out and give Lottie a sound shaking for never thinking of the consequences. Orphanages were full of abandoned children by women with the same attitude. "What about the babe?" she asked with concern. "What will happen to it?"

Lottie shrugged with indifference. "It will be a bastard, seeings how neither one of them will own up to being the father. But His Lordship will be giving me folks a bit more in their wages for me and the babe."

"Oh," Beth sighed with relief. "You'll be keeping the babe. I'm so glad to hear that."

"What else would I be doing with it?" Lottie frowned.

"Never mind," Beth smiled, and on sudden impulse dug into her purse. She gathered all the coins in her possession. She reached out and grabbed Lottie's hand and placed them in her open palm. "That's for the babe. Promise me you'll take good care of it." Never having had more than one coin in her possession at a time, a dumb struck Lottie stared at them. She quickly closed her fist, fearful that Beth might have a change of heart.

"Promise me," Beth repeated.

"Beth Carney, you'd be as daft as they come. I promise you."

Mind bogged with thought over what Lottie had said, Beth walked back to Chesterton Hall with the last of Lottie's words of warning ringing in her ears. "Make certain ya have a ring on yer finger, Beth, before you let any man have his way with ya'."

Lottie's ignorance was one thing, but being taken advantage of by the Masters, who knew better, infuriated Beth. Suddenly, she realized Maggie's reason for having a bolt put on her bedroom door. "Oh, Maggie," she sighed, "Mr. Carver is gone. Lottie is gone. How blessed I am for still having you."

The weeks just seemed to fly, and before long the young Masters came home for the Christmas holidays. Within two days of their arrival, they began seeking Beth out with their lame excuses of having something that needed mending. A silent Beth obliged. On the fifth day when the two Masters stood before her with buttons that had come undone, Beth lost her temper. "It seems to me that I remember sewing this button on your shirt once before, Master Elwood. As for your button, Master Elton, it's the same one I sewed on your vest the day before yesterday. If you ask me, it's the buttons on your britches that could do with some mending."

"Our britches," Master Elton laughed.

It was Master Elwood who quickly grasped the true meaning of Beth's remark. "I think that's rather impertinent of you, Beth, to suggest such an undertaking when it doesn't concern you."

"Begging your pardon, Master Elwood and Master Elton," Beth said, "I never meant to be impertinent. For in truth, I believed a gentleman having had all the advantages bestowed upon him through circumstances of birth would not take advantage of one beneath him in station. Nor would he take liberties or improprieties with a lowly soul under his domain, who loyally serves him. In my eyes, an honorable gentleman would take full responsibilities for the consequences of all his actions, and for the rest of his life make restitution for his unpardonable behavior."

"How. . . how dare you? How dare you speak to us in such manner? How dare you take the liberty to impose upon us your views, without invitation?" Master Elwood sputtered.

"You should be horsewhipped," Master Elton added.

Beth rose to her feet, picked up the two buttons on the table along with the shirt and vest, and handed them back to their owners. "No," she sighed, looking them straight in the eye. "It's the pair of you that should be horsewhipped."

Without further ado the Masters turned on their heels and left the kitchen.

Maggie, who was within earshot of all that had transpired, came running over to Beth's side. "What got into you, Beth? You know better than to speak to your superiors in such a manner. That sharp tongue of yours is going to get you into a lot of trouble someday."

"Oh, Maggie," she sighed. "All I could think about was the poor babe who won't have a father and Lottie for its mother. What will become of it?"

Maggie placed a comforting arm around her shoulder. "There's a lot of ills in this world, Beth. It's best you learn now, you can't cure them all."

That March Maggie was stricken ill, her head burning with fever and every bone in her body was aching. Over and over again, she prayed for God to give her strength for the heart-rending task that faced her.

"Beth," Maggie said, forcing a smile on her pale lips.

Tossing the coverlet aside, Beth sprang from the chair she'd been sleeping in. "Yes, Maggie, I'm here," she said, laying her cool hand on Maggie's feverish brow.

"Beth, my sweet child you have to listen to what I'd be telling you. It's important."

"Yes, Maggie," she answered, leaning over the bed and tucking the covers up higher.

"I think the Lord has seen fit to take me," Maggie whispered.

"Don't say that, Maggie," Beth cried. "Don't even think it."

"Aye, Beth. It be the truth."

"No, Maggie. No, Maggie. I won't have you talking like this."

"It's not my way, Beth, it be the Lord's way and that we can't change. What I want you to do is, go into the closet and take out the purse that's hidden inside one of me old shoes. Do what I tell'ya, Beth."

Reluctantly Beth turned from the bed and walked across the room and opened the closet door. She looked at the old scuffed up pair of shoes on the floor and slipped her hand inside the one shoe. She felt something that had been stuffed into the toe of the shoe. She pulled out a small, soft leather purse that jingled with the sound of coins inside and carried it over to the bed, setting it within reach of Maggie's hand.

"No, Beth. I want you to have it. It's me life savings."

"I. . .I can't—-

"Listen to what I'd be telling ya and listen with a good ear. There be just enough money saved to get you to America. I fear for you living here. You'd be a free

65

woman in America, Beth. If you work hard, you could have your own shop some day and be beholden to no one. That be the dream I have for you, Beth."

"No, Maggie. No, Maggie. I won't leave you. If that is your dream, we'll do it together."

"Aye child, that be my dream and I'll be counting on you to see that my dream comes true. Now take the money and leave, the sooner the better. There be no sense of you staying here another night. Come morning, I'll be gone."

"No, Maggie," Beth cried. "I'll not leave you. It's your fever that's talking."

"No, Beth. It be me, Maggie talking. Now give us a hug and be on your way."

"Please, Maggie, don't do this to me," Beth begged, as she leaned over and rested her head against the softness of Maggie's bosom. "Please, Maggie, let me stay. Together we can go to America."

Lovingly, Maggie's hand swept the girl's copper tresses of hair. "Ah, Beth," she sighed. "You've given me more joy than I ever dreamed of having. And you've grown to be such a lady. You've done me heart proud. I'll always be with you, Beth; love never dies. Now it's best you be on your way."

Through a blur of blinding tears, with baggage in hand and drudging footsteps, Beth walked to the village. Once again fate had dealt her a terrible blow; she was all alone in the world. The only thing she heard in the stillness of the night was the melodious song of a lonely nightingale calling to its mate. To mind came the words of Christine Rossetti that she had memorized so long ago; I shall not see the shadows, I shall not feel the rain; I shall not hear the nightingale sing on, as if in pain.

Chapter Three

The H.M.S. Bristol left Liverpool in the early morning mist, only to become caught up in the late afternoon storm that had followed her out to sea. Swelling waves came crashing down across her bow, tossing and heaving her about like a mustard seed being carried in the wind.

For three hours the crew of the H.M.S. Bristol was successful in defying the whiplash of an Atlantic gale, while the passengers were confined to their cabins.

On desk, under the steady eyes of Captain Stanton, the young helmsman stood fast. His biceps wrenched with pain from the strenuous task of trying to keep the ship on course. He licked his lips only to have the taste of salt on his palate. He smiled to himself knowing that within a short time he would be relieved of his duty. His dry throat ached for his daily allotted ration of rum. As his thoughts strayed to the passengers below in steerage class, he sadly shook his head. The three words he mumbled were carried in the wind; "The poor bastards!"

Beth's green eyes appeared enormous in her pale, drawn face. It seemed like an eternity since she first sat on the hard covered bunk that was to be her new bed for the next few weeks. Over and over again, she found herself groping for the post of the bed to support herself against the ship's rocking motion.

Oddly enough, the raging storm was of little concern to her compared with the sights she beheld in the room

69

that she had been destined to share with strangers. In the far corner of the room a group of boisterous men were playing a game of chance. Beth watched as they greedily grabbed at the few coins atop their makeshift table. A communal jug of rum was being passed amongst them and from all appearances some of the men were drunk already. Children aimlessly ran about while their parents' warnings went unheeded. The smallest of the lot clung to their mothers' skirts shrieking in fear. A filthy blanket tacked to an overhead beam would be rolled down at night to separate the men's quarters from that of the women passengers.

The young woman, whom Beth had befriended, unbuttoned her bodice, reached in and lifted a breast out. She guided it to the mouth of the wailing child in her arms. Beth's cheeks flushed at the woman's shocking behavior in mixed company. But within the last few hours she had already learned that modesty was a luxury not afforded to one in steerage class.

She tried to erase the negative thoughts that came creeping to mind. Maybe it would have been wiser to stay in England and obtain a position as a governess or ladies' maid. Surely, she was above her own class in education and manners, but lacking the necessary essentials such as money and family. She wasn't foolish enough to believe a gentleman of good breeding would consider her a proper maiden to marry. What one needed, she resolved, was money and family. Her only hope lay in a new life in another country.

Suddenly overcome by the reek of vomit, cheeses and soiled clothes, Beth stood up, wrapped her cape round her, drew the hood up over her head and stumbled toward the ladder. She needed air, fresh, clean air or she was likely to become ill.

The young woman, who was nursing her child, called out after her. "Mind you Beth, be careful; we're not supposed to go up on deck!"

Ignoring her warning, Beth climbed the ladder that led to the deck and to the promise of fresh, clean air.

Beth stood on deck hungrily breathing in the fresh air. A welcome spray of salt water dotted her face as the thunderous waves splashed against the sides of the ship. Unmindful of the wind ripping at her cape, she found herself wishing she could remain on deck for the rest of the voyage. The thought of returning to steerage class below actually nauseated her.

At dusk, Beth caught a glimpse of another woman. She came down the staircase from the upper deck and stood at the railing about fifteen yards away from where Beth was standing. There was something about the desolate figure of the woman that caused Beth to stare. Suddenly, the woman grabbed the railing, hoisted herself up and willfully jumped into the turbulent sea. Screaming, Beth ran across the deck to where the woman had been standing. She grabbed the rail, leaned over, and frantically searched the dark, swelling waves. It was hopeless.

How long she stood there she did not know. Her hands were numb and her clothes had become drenched with water. The distressing sight had shocked her.

Beth was startled when a firm rough hand grabbed her arm tearing her away from the railing. She found herself looking up into the weather beaten face of an old seaman. Through purple tinged lips, he yelled. "You know you're not to be up here now, Miss. The Captain will have my hide if he finds out!"

Forcefully, he dragged her along the deck to the staircase that led to the upper landing. Beth's attempts to free herself were futile as well as her attempts to explain what she had seen. She was being dragged up the staircase and down a long narrow passageway.

The seaman stopped short and with his free hand flung a door to a private cabin open. Firmly but gently he pushed Beth inside before closing the door behind him.

Dripping wet and speechless, Beth watched as the man struck a match to light the oil lamp hanging from the ceiling. His giant shadow was cast on the wall.

"You know you might have been washed overboard!" he roared and turned to look at her. Was it the sorrowful eyes, set in the pale face or the bedraggled appearance of the young lassie drenched to the skin that made him take pity on her? "Captain Stanton is expecting you to be seated at his table and I don't think he'd like it one bit if anything happened to you," he said softly. "Now stay put in your cabin, Miss and I'll come fetch you shortly when dinner is being served."

Just before closing the door behind him, the man stuck his head back in. "Don't you go fretting none about this storm, Miss. It will all blow over in another hour. You mark my words," he smiled, a toothless grin.

Totally perplexed and exhausted, Beth stared at the closed door. Then her eyes quickly surveyed the small cabin taking in the two open trunks of the floor that, from all appearances, contained women's clothing. Although it was open, all the contents appeared to be intact. There was a woman's comb and brush set on the dress with the initials A.W., embossed in silver. Several long strands of dark hair were entangled in the brush. A gold chain with a pendant that consisted of a star sapphire surrounded by small diamonds lay there. Beth suddenly realized it was a case of mistaken identity on the part of the old seaman; he had mistaken her for another passenger. She was about to leave the cabin for fear of being caught by the rightful owner, but the solitude of the cabin and the lovely, faint, fragrance of lavender made her linger. It was while she was eyeing the comfort of the bed that Beth spied the letter lying on the pillow. Out of curiosity, Beth leaned over and peeked at the letter. The two opening words drew her full attention, "Forgive me."

Crystal tears spilled from Beth's eyes and splattered onto the pages as she reread the letter. Beth now knew that Abigail Whitcomb was the name of the desolate figure of the woman who jumped overboard.

It was a letter beseeching her uncle, a John Whitcomb of Devonshire to forgive her for taking her life. But unbeknown to her uncle, she was in love with a Lieutenant who three months prior had died in India while in the Queen's service.

In professing her love for the Lieutenant, it grieved her that in good faith she could not marry her uncle's choice for her; a man named Albert McFadden who was the eldest son of Hugh McFadden. Not wanting to inflict pain on a friendship of long standing between Hugh McFadden and her uncle, whom she loved dearly, Abigail Whitcomb had chosen death.

The letter was written with tenderness and regard for all concerned. In closing, Abigail Whitcomb again professed a love so strong for her Lieutenant, never once doubting it would be carried into eternity with her death.

Beth carefully folded the letter as if it were a precious gift. Never having known or witnessed such an intense regard of one person for another, she deemed it a privilege to have touched upon such devotion, although in tragic form. She found herself wondering if life would ever unfold such a devoted love on her behalf.

A cold chill ran through Beth's body. She looked down at her drenched cape and decided to bring the letter to the attention of the Captain and then return to steerage class to change her clothes before catching a death of a cold. As she reached for the door latch the fragrance of lavender and the solitude of the cabin engulfed her once more. Suddenly a devious thought crossed her mind. That such a thought had even entered it, Beth found frightening.

Ever so slowly her hand began to withdraw from the latch. She raised her hand to her lips in shock. She turned once more and looked at the luxury and comfort the small cabin afforded while her will to survive grew strong.

Her wet cape dropped to the floor as she sat down on the edge of the bed to stop her legs from trembling. Quick thoughts kept running through the corridors of her mind. Who would she harm? She could reimburse the uncle for the use of the cabin when she acquired a position in America. If she failed, she'd be put back in steerage class, but if she succeeded, she would have her own private cabin until the ship docked in America. Why not? Of what harm would it be?

Beth ran to the trunks and quickly started to rummage through their contents. A sigh of relief escaped her lips on seeing the luxurious dresses were her size. Abigail Whitcomb without doubt was a lady of fashion. Tossing the dresses to one side she hastily sat on the floor and removed her old, worn shoes. She rummaged through the trunk again only this time looking for shoes.

At the bottom of the trunk she found several fashionable pair of shoes and sat on the floor struggling to put them on. Pair after pair was a size too small. Her feet felt tight and cramped in the shoes, but their discomfort would be a small price to pay for the luxury of having a private cabin of her own.

***

Standing bare-chested in the center of his cabin, Jason Rockwell snapped shut the pouched compartments of his money belt. He picked up a pair of dainty, diamond earrings that were lying on the dresser and wrapped them in a piece of paper. He tucked them in the last cavity of the belt for safe keeping. He smiled to himself on visualizing the adoring face of the recipient of his gift. No doubt, he thought, there'd be a reproachful tongue because of his extravagance.

After tying the belt securely around his waist he picked up the clean, white shirt that he had taken out of his trunk. Slipping the shirt over his head and pushing his muscular arms through the sleeves, he became conscious of the tightness of the garment on his frame. He cursed under his breath while fumbling with the tiny buttons on the bib of the shirt. Lifting the collar to a standing position he encircled it with a thin, black band that he tied in bow fashion. As he folded the collar back down, automatically he tugged at it to loosen it from around his neck.

In the dimness he looked at his reflection in the dull mirror hanging over the dresser while running a partly toothless comb through his thick, black hair trying to smooth it to the contour of his head. He laughed at his own fruitless attempts which displayed an even set of gleaming white teeth from beneath the black mustache that his upper lip supported.

That English fashion should demand a man to dress in such constricting clothes in order to be considered a gentleman was ridiculous in his eyes. He longed for the comfort of his old clothes and most of all, his home in Kansas where he was born and raised.

If it weren't for Hugh McFadden and the promise I made him, I never would have left Kansas in the first place, he thought. The lines around Jason's mouth softened while thinking of the elderly man. A man whom he respected, and only to himself admitted, he loved like a father.

For some inexplicable reason, as long as Jason could remember, a request by Hugh McFadden was one he could never deny. It hadn't taken much persuading on the older man's part to get him to make the trip to England for him. Jason was fully aware of the problems that weighed heavily on the older man's mind.

While adjusting the money belt beneath his shirt, Jason felt an air of self-satisfaction. With what he considered to be shrewd bargaining on his part, he sold the furs in England for a substantial amount of money. One of the joys of returning home would be to see the older man's face when he gave him his share of the profit.

The mirror reflected a frown across Jason's brow as he thought of the second promise he had made. If it hadn't been for the second promise, he pondered, he could rid himself of the ridiculous clothes and be traveling in steerage class among the people he enjoyed and free from the constraints of formality.

Although Jason had been tutored by the patience of Jane McFadden, he was more at ease with common folks. Like them, he had a natural born love of working the land and a reverence for nature. He wasn't one to engage in polite, idle conversation, and dreaded the thought of having to be seated at the Captain's table for dinner, especially with ladies present. The art of keeping the conversation light and amusing for their delicate ears he found to be a troublesome bore. While in England he tried to acquire this social grave, for benefit of the fair sex, but without much success.

Most of the women he had met in the last four months seemed to have difficulty in raising their eyes above the bib of his shirt while conversing with him and concealed their true emotions behind a fluttering fan. This coquettish behavior on their part annoyed the hell out of him.

He thought of the spunky, vivacious women he had known in America. He laughed while visualizing them hiding behind a fluttering fan or playing a coy game by demurely dropping their eyelids. Thank God, they weren't like that, he mused.

Jason slipped into the black vest, buttoned it and picked up the gold watch and chain that Hugh McFadden had given him for his twenty-ninth birthday. Before placing the watch into his vest pocket he checked the time. It was six-thirty; time enough to enjoy a drink of brandy and a few puffs on a cigar.

With brandy bottle in one hand and cigar in the other, Jason sat on his bunk waiting for time to pass. He was beginning to feel like himself again. The trapped, caged feeling he had while living in London was beginning to pass, as his thought strayed to his home in Kansas.

Tilting the bottle up to his lips he took another generous gulp before recapping it. He placed the bottle back in his baggage and glanced at his watch. It was time to join the other passengers for dinner.

As he put on the last piece of garment befitting a gentleman, his waistcoat, an amusing thought struck him. Perhaps the afternoon's storm had confined some of the delicate creatures to their beds. If so, dinner should be a pleasant affair without the company of females. With this thought in mind Jason left his cabin.

At the dinner table, after the usual formalities of introductions were made, Jason sat down on the right hand side of Captain Stanton. It was apparent that the storm had taken a toll on some of the guests; three chairs remained empty. While engaged in conversation with a Mr. Hilliard and his wife, Jason glanced up to see a young lady standing in the doorway. He watched with interest as she squarely set her shoulders back, lifted her head high and proceeded across the room. Her left hand was buried in the folds of the blue dress she wore, lifting it ever so slightly so as not to touch the floor.

"Captain Stanton?" she smiled, directly at the fat man seated at the head of the table with highly, polished, brass buttons on his uniform.

The Captain turned and abruptly stood up while Jason and Mr. Hilliard slowly followed suit. "Why you must be Miss Whitcomb," the Captain beamed.

She uttered a soft sigh of relief. "I'm sorry to be late." Her soft voice held a note of apology in it as she graced the chair that the Captain held for her.

"I'm so glad you're up to joining us, Miss Whitcomb," Stanton said, resuming his chair. "Your uncle, John Whitcomb, was good enough to come to see me this morning before we set sail. I must apologize for not being able to meet with you sooner——the storm you know." His eyes twinkled. "Your uncle has solicited me to watch over his precious cargo for him. But I must say," he chuckled, "I wasn't aware of its beauty until this very moment."

"You're very kind Captain, but I'm afraid my uncle is inclined to be overly concerned about my welfare," she smiled.

Jason found himself staring at the long, copper curls that came to rest on the girl's milky white shoulders. Although her green eyes had met each guest with direct contact while being introduced, he thought it odd that her hands trembled. His faint show of interest didn't go unnoticed by the Captain.

"Miss Whitcomb is betrothed to Hugh McFadden's eldest son, Albert, and is on her way to Kansas. I promised her uncle that I would see to her safety while aboard my ship."

"I envy you for your good fortune, Captain," Jason smiled, "but it appears that I also will have the honor of being in Miss Whitcomb's company as a traveling companion since we will be journeying in the same direction. Hugh McFadden happens to be my neighbor."

"Your neighbor?" Beth gasped.

"Yes," Jason smiled. "It appears we are going to be neighbors. Hugh McFadden owns acres of property that are adjacent to mine on the west border."

"Jason, I'm sure Miss Whitcomb isn't interested in knowing about McFadden's property. I believe she'd be more interested in your mentioning something about his eldest son, Albert," Captain Stanton smiled.

"I take it you've never met your betrothed, Albert McFadden," Jason said, curious as to what possessed a woman to travel halfway around the world to marry a man she didn't even know.

"No," she murmured. "I've never had the pleasure."

If meeting Albert McFadden was a pleasure, Jason was totally unaware of it. He considered the young man spoiled and arrogant but found himself saying, "What would you wish to know about the man?"

It was obvious to Beth that the man was laughing at her and suddenly she became infuriated by his bad manners. Her fiery, green eyes bored into his. "I'm afraid Captain Stanton is misinformed as to my wanting to know more about Mr. McFadden," she paused, taking in a deep breath. "You see, Mr. Rockwell whatever you might say about the gentleman would be of your opinion and judgment—-which in your eyes, no doubt would be correct. However, never having met the man, I can neither agree nor disagree with your opinion or judgment. I would rather you withheld talking about Mr. McFadden until I've had the privilege of meeting him myself. I'm quite sure that, he being a gentleman would extend the same courtesy to me, should the occasion arise."

Everyone at the table was staring at her and Beth realized her mistake. A lady of Abigail Whitcomb's up bringing would never have lost her temper or raised her voice.

The sharpness of her tongue brought a smile to Jason's face. "I find that very commendable, Miss

Whitcomb. However, you are quite mistaken in thinking for one moment that I would have given you my opinion or judgment of the man. My intentions were to tell you what most young ladies seem to deem necessary to know about the man they're about to marry. And this is——Mr. McFadden is of handsome stature with fair hair and blue eyes," Jason grinned.

"You are highly mistaken, Mr. Rockwell," Beth snapped, "if you think that I, for one, consider these attributes as constituting a man. I personally wouldn't care if Mr. McFadden were of olive complexion, dark hair and eyes. There are more important…" she stopped out of the shocking realization that she had described Mr. Rockwell's coloring.

The other guests were amused as well as Mr. Rockwell. Beth felt the color rising to her cheeks.

"What you mean, Miss Whitcomb, is that I have a chance of marrying?" Jason laughed.

Beth lowered her eyes as well as her voice. "Your marital status is of no concern of mine, Mr. Rockwell," she said, resolving she had said quite enough for the evening. Rather than create a discourse at the table, she would refrain from encouraging further conversation with such a man.

Throughout the rest of the meal, Beth's replies were curt and concise; although she couldn't help but hear Mr. Rockwell's interesting stories about America while conversing with the other guests, Mr. and Mrs. Hilliard.

Whether or not it was for her benefit, she had no way of knowing, but Mr. Rockwell repeatedly made mention of the McFadden family, his neighbors. By the end of the evening Beth had gained considerable information about the family. Besides Albert McFadden, her supposedly betrothed, there were two younger children, Jenny, a young girl of fourteen and Timothy, a boy of ten.

Although he never mentioned the eldest son again, one became conscious of his strong, warm, affection when speaking of the younger children, Beth noted—- a characteristic which she had earlier assumed him devoid of.

Beth was standing next to the Captain conveying her compliments on the lovely dinner that had been served when the door to the room loudly banged open. A young sailor made his way across the room at a fast pace. The strain on his face suggested that something was wrong. When he approached the Captain's side he whispered something in his ear before quickly taking his leave. A solemn faced Captain Stanton stood staring at his guest.

"What's wrong?" Jason asked. "Can I help in anyway?"

The Captain shook his graying head from side to side. "It's very distressing news. It appears we have a young lady from steerage class missing since earlier this evening. The crew has searched the ship in vain. I'm afraid she may have been washed overboard." He took a deep breath and went on, "She was last seen by a woman passenger going up on deck at the height of the storm."

"Have they told her family?" Mr. Hilliard asked.

The Captain's eyes were fixed in a hard stare. "No. The woman who made her acquaintance said the girl was orphaned at birth. Her name was Beth Carney. It appears she was traveling alone."

Beth's face drained of color and suddenly the room seemed to whirl. At that instant from behind her came two powerful hands impersonally holding her about the shoulders.

"Are you all right, Miss Whitcomb?" Jason asked, supporting her weight with his own body.

Beth found herself looking up into the dark brown eyes of Mr. Rockwell. She shook herself free of his touch while recovering herself. "Thank you, I'm fine," she said, in strained voice.

"I'm sorry, Miss Whitcomb," Captain Stanton apologized. "I should have had the good sense not to mention such distressing news with ladies present. I was overcome by the negligence of my own responsibility. In all my years of duty in the service to the Queen, I prided myself on never having lost a passenger."

Suddenly, Mrs. Hilliard took it upon herself to reassure the Captain that he was not at fault for the tragedy. To enlighten the Captain she decided to state what she though would compensate for the tragedy. "You might say, Captain Stanton, that the young lady's misfortune, without doubt, was a blessing in disguise. After all, she was an orphan."

"Mrs. Hilliard," Beth gasped. "How you can consider a person's death being a blessing because of their unfortunate circumstances at birth, is beyond my comprehension."

"Here, here," murmured the Captain.

Mrs. Hilliard's mouth dropped open and then closed. By the look in her eyes it was clear that she and the young lady would never become compatible travelers.

Jason saw the uncontrollable tears that welled-up in the young girl's eyes as she blinked several times over to keep them from showing.

"If you will kindly excuse me," Captain Stanton said gravely. "I would like to personally make some inquiries about the tragedy. Jason, would you be so kind as to escort Miss Whitcomb back to her cabin."

"My pleasure," Jason answered.

Through the narrow passageway they walked in silence. Sensing the girl wanted time to wipe the tears from her eyes, so as not to be noticed by him, Jason walked a few steps ahead of her. Had it been the death of the girl that affected her, he wondered. Or was it the ignorant statement uttered by Mrs. Hilliard?

He had suppressed the urge to console her. At the moment, she appeared weak and stripped of her haughty spirit. Fearing any kindness on his part would be misinterpreted, he chose to remain silent.

Unlocking the door to the cabin, Jason turned and placed the key in her outstretched palm. Without delay he bid her good night and headed down the passageway to his own cabin.

Once inside the locked cabin, Beth ran to the bed and flung herself down. She buried her face in the pillow and began to cry. The strain of masquerading as Abigail Whitcomb had physically as well as emotionally drained her. She could not erase the haunting picture of the young woman jumping overboard into the turbulent sea.

Totally spent, Beth lay on the bed, when suddenly a light tap on the door startled her. She jolted upright in bed and hastily brushed at the wetness on her cheeks. The tapping grew louder and she envisioned an enraged Captain Stanton standing outside the door ready to drag her out of the cabin and below to steerage class. "Who. . .who is it?" she stammered.

"Miss Whitcomb?"

She breathed a sigh of relief on recognizing the voice to be that of Mr. Rockwell. She rose from the bed and crossed the floor. "What do you want?" she asked.

"Open the door!" His voice sounded urgent.

Beth momentarily hesitated before turning the key in the lock. When she opened the door Mr. Rockwell stood with one hand leaning against the doorjamb and in his other hand he held a bottle of liquor. He was without jacket or vest. The bib of his shirt was partly undone and the band that was once neatly tied in a bow trailed down the front of his shirt.

"What do you want?" she asked, appalled by his appearance.

He thrust the bottle of liquor in front of her face. "Here, drink some of this." His voice was gruff.

"I most certainly will not!"

"Damn it! Do what I tell you, woman," he roared.

He roughly grabbed her hands and firmly wrapped them around the neck of the bottle, pushing it up to her mouth. Under his cold, hard stare, Beth tilted the bottle up to her lips, squinted and took a mouthful. The wetness on the mouth of the bottle only confirmed what she had surmised; he'd been drinking from the same bottle. As she swallowed, the burning sensation in her throat made her cough and gasp for air. She finally caught her breath when he ordered. "Once more!"

The first sip had already begun to warm Beth's small frame. A slight flush crept into her pale cheeks and without warning she sent the bottle slapping down hard against his open palm. Her fiery spirit had returned. That he had ordered her like a child infuriated her, but that she had succumbed to his authority was more upsetting. She was about to retaliate for his rude behavior when suddenly he commanded. "Now lock your door and go to bed!" With that he turned on his heels and left her standing there with her mouth agape.

Midway down the passageway, Jason heard the sound of an indignant foot stomping the floor. It was soon followed by the slamming shut of a door and clanking sound of a key being turned. The corners of his mouth curled with a grin.

Chapter Four

Hugh McFadden was only allowed to indulge himself in a few moments of reminiscing before his daughter Jenny's voice erased all thoughts of the past from his mind.

"Father! Father!"

He looked up from his wife's grave to see his daughter running up the path and waving what appeared to be letters in her outstretched hand. Behind her, trying to keep up with her long stride was Timothy, his youngest son. Hugh smiled at the sight of his children and proceeded down the path to meet them.

"We picked up two letters in town," Jenny said breathlessly. "And one is written in Jason's hand."

Hugh studied the two envelopes and smiled on recognizing the familiar hand- writing of one; the other letter puzzled him. Out of far-sightedness he brought the letters up close to his face and examined the postmarks and stamps. Both were posted from England and within a week of each other.

"Aren't you going to open them?" Timothy asked anxiously.

Hugh patted his son on the head. "In due time, son. First, we'll get out of reach of the noonday sun. Let's go into the house."

His children sat crossed-legged on the parlor floor close to his chair patiently waiting as Hugh rummaged in a table drawer looking for his glasses. He carefully broke the seal of the envelope written in the familiar hand and scanned its contents before deciding to read it out loud. "Dear Hugh, Jenny and Timothy, "

"This will be the last letter you will receive from me as I have booked passage on the H.M.S. Bristol which sets sail next Thursday from Liverpool. Hopefully, in a month from now I will be on your doorstep.

"Hugh, I can only say that it has been an interesting and somewhat adventurous journey. I'm glad you persuaded me to make this trip to England, but more so I'm glad to be returning home.

"I consider myself a fortunate man for having had the advantage of living in two different worlds. Now, without a doubt, I am able to choose the one more suited to me, or perhaps I should say, more suited to the life I choose to live. I miss seeing the golden fields of wheat at sunset, and the fragrance of new moan hay. Above all I miss Jenny and Timothy.

"Jenny must have grown a good foot since last I saw her and Timothy must be the best shot in the entire county since having entrusted my rifle to him. Give my love to both of them.

"Hugh, you can rest easy. I discretely checked to find that the merchandise you're expecting will be on board when I sail. As promised, I will do my best to see that no harm or danger befalls my charge.

God's speed, respectfully,

Jason"

"Oh," Jenny sighed, "I'm so glad Jason is coming home."

"Well, I'm not!"

The three of them turned to see Albert McFadden, Hugh's oldest son, standing in the doorway. Obviously, he had been standing there while his father read the letter.

"Albert," Hugh McFadden said, coolly acknowledging his presence while carefully refolding the letter. Out of the corner of his eye, he watched as his son went over to the sideboard and picked up the decanter of whiskey and poured himself a drink. Hugh shook his head in disgust.

"So you sent him to England to keep an eye on your precious cargo," Albert said, taking several gulps before turning to face his father.

"Suppose I did," Hugh said. "Isn't it a bit early in the day to be drinking, Albert?"

"Is it? Wasn't it you who said, a good Irishman could drink any time of the day?"

"True, I've said that," Hugh nodded. "But aren't you forgetting something Albert?"

"What might that be?" he frowned.

"You're only part Irish," Hugh said, and glanced down at his youngest children sitting on the floor. "Jenny, will you see to getting some firewood in? I noticed the bin was empty this morning. And Timothy, you can start the milking; I'll be out to help you shortly."

The children scrambled to their feet and as they headed for the door, a concerned Jenny glanced back over her shoulder at her father.

"What's troubling you, Albert?" Hugh asked.

"Do you really want to know?"

"If I didn't," Hugh sighed, "I wouldn't have asked."

The glass in Albert's hand came down hard on the sideboard. "You sit there and without my consent, choose a wife for me; a niece of a friend of yours, who you haven't seen in over thirty years or more. In all probability a homely old maid that nobody in England, who was in their right mind, would marry. And if that isn't enough, you have the nerve to send a half-breed over to England to see to her safe journey here. Why didn't you send me?"

"You know as well as I do, Albert, it wouldn't be proper for a betrothed couple to travel together. As for Jason, I can rely on him. He will discreetly see to Abigail Whitcomb's safety without her knowledge. I thought Jason better suited for the job."

"Better suited," Albert sneered. "It seems to me, Father, that he's always been better suited than your own son!"

"That's not true, Albert!"

"Isn't it?"

"Why do you have this animosity towards Jason?" Hugh frowned. "What has he ever done to you?"

"As long as I can remember, my life has been spent in his shadow and you have the nerve to ask, what has he done to me?"

Hugh sighed. "If you've been in his shadow, Albert, it's because you placed yourself there. I've given you more than enough chances to prove yourself."

"Prove myself!" Albert yelled. "Why, you haven't even given me the benefit of choosing my own wife. Just because the girl happens to be the niece of your friend, John Whitcomb, why must I marry her?"

"Abigail Whitcomb happens to be an educated lady," Hugh said, "and that's what I want for the mother of my grandchildren—-a lady. Not some dance hall girl from Abilene."

"What makes you think she'll be a lady when Jason gets done with her?"

With cane in hand, Hugh sprang to his feet. He lashed out at his son, only to knock the glass of whiskey to the floor. The sound of the shattering glass was followed by a heavy silence.

"Don't you ever judge Jason by your own morals," Hugh hissed.

"Since when is he a virgin when it comes to women?"

Hugh's face turned purple with rage. "His morals aren't in question, yours are. He's worked the land I've leased to him. He's made something of himself. That's more than I can say for you."

"Yes, and in doing so you made us the laughing stock of Abilene. Since when does a white man lease his land to an Indian squaw and her son?"

Hugh pulled himself up to his full height; the knuckles gripping the cane turned white. "I'm under no obligation to explain my actions to you, Albert. Don't let me hear you call Gay Feather a squaw. How easily you forget how she helped to raise you and your sister and brother long after your mother died."

"And what of your comfort, father, did she see to that?'

Albert staggered under the blow of the cane that came down hard across his left shoulder. He regained his composure and stood there with a pasted grin on his face. "Am I to be your whipping boy?"

Dejectedly, Hugh leaned on the fireplace mantel; his voice was coarse with anger. "Get out."

"Oh, I'm leaving all right," Albert smiled. "I'm going to Mexico and then I'm going to join a cattle train in Texas. By the time I get back my fiancée will have arrived. And I'm going to look her over real good before I put my brand on her and give you the grandchildren you so justly deserve."

"Perhaps, Albert, she will see beyond that charming veneer of yours and not want to marry you. Did you ever think of that?"

He blinked at his father's words. A forced laugh caught in his throat. "If that be the case," he smiled, "then it would give me all the more reason to charm her. Good day, father."

Hugh crossed the floor and sat down in the armchair. For a long time he sat there wondering what mistakes he had made in raising Albert. The fact the he looked so much like his mother had stopped him many a time from coming down hard on the boy. But he wasn't a boy anymore and would have to face up to the responsibilities of being a man and raising a family.

It was then that Hugh remembered the second letter that arrived. He picked it up from the table, put his glasses on again and opened the letter.

The letter was from a barrister in England. It stated that John Whitcomb had a heart attack and died the night his niece Abigail had set sail for America. One of his last wishes was that his best friend, Hugh McFadden, should be the girl's guardian. There wasn't much of an inheritance to speak of, since John Whitcomb had gambled most of the estate away.

Chapter Five

In the days that followed Beth stayed within the quarters of her cabin, only venturing out for her meals. Fearful of being recognized by a passenger from steerage class, she waited until dark before walking on the upper deck for her much needed exercise.

On several occasions while strolling on deck she unexpectedly met with Mr. Rockwell. She made it a point to inform him of her liking to stroll at a certain hour hoping this would prevent their meeting again. And yet, on several evenings she met him but not by chance; he appeared to be waiting for her. Without asking her consent he joined her but never chose to speak a great deal. Nor did she encourage engaging conversation with the man.

It wasn't until the last evening before the ship reached port that Mr. Rockwell met with her again, but this time, he talked excessively. It was more of a sermon than a civil conversation, she thought. He seemed to be warning her of the hard and lonely life that was in store for her in the wilds of Kansas for which she supposedly was heading. He compared it with the social life she had been living in England. Several times, Beth covered her mouth to keep from laughing at his ignorance of her circumstances. If he only knew, she thought, of the hard and lonely life that had brought her this far.

On the day that the ship docked in Philadelphia, Beth was happy to give up masquerading as Abigail

Whitcomb. It had finally come to an end, although the guilt of her actions weighed on her mind. Her spirits began to soar on being in a new country and most of all, on being able to resume her identity, but she was mistaken.

Captain Stanton had made it his personal responsibility to escort her to the train that left for Topeka. From there he assumed she would venture forth to Fort Riley by stagecoach and on to Abilene, Kansas.

For hours, Beth sat sulking looking out the train window. She was utterly annoyed at having to make a needless journey and annoyed by Captain Stanton's good, but interfering intentions that now forced her to resume the identity of Abigail Whitcomb. She refrained from telling him the truth about herself for fear he might make her return to the ship and go back to England. She finally resolved that she would leave the train at the first opportunity in a large city. When she had saved enough money to repay John Whitcomb she would relocate to the part of the country that suited her fancy, instead of the wilderness. Her anger began to subside as she finally felt free of Captain Stanton and anyone else who might interfere with her life again.

"Abigail? It is Abigail, isn't that what Captain Stanton said?"

She looked over at the young woman sitting opposite her and the two small boys. "Yes. It's Abigail Whitcomb."

"Would you like to join me and my children for lunch? You're welcome to share what we have."

Amy Cooper was on her way to Topeka to join her husband who worked for the Union Pacific Railroad company. She was a frail, plain looking woman who didn't look old enough to have two children or the means to afford passage on the train. From beneath her seat she pulled out a wicker basket lifted the covering and peered inside. She took out a loaf of bread and began slicing it. On top of four slices she set a small wedge of cheese and began handing the bread and cheese to her children. As if to lift their spirits she said, "We have some nice apples for dessert."

Having noticed the meager amount of food in the basket and that of the disappointed looks on the children's faces, Abigail felt guilty while eating the slice of bread and wedge of cheese offered but she was hungry. She was trying to think of a way she could reciprocate for the woman's generosity when to her horror she looked up to see Mr. Rockwell coming through the car door. She had no idea that he was on the train.

"Good gracious," she gasped.

"Is something wrong?" Amy Cooper asked.

"No," she said, trying to recover her shock and watched as Mr. Rockwell came walking directly toward them. "I. . .I've just seen an acquaintance that I met aboard ship."

"Oh, how grand," Amy Cooper smiled, while turning to look at the man who was coming down the aisle.

"Miss Whitcomb," Jason smiled, "how nice to meet up with you again."

Abigail bit into her lower lip. "Mr. Rockwell," she said, forcing a smile to her lips. "May I introduce you to Mrs. Cooper; we've just been having our lunch."

"Mrs. Cooper," he smiled, tipping his hat, "nice to meet you, ma'am."

"Would you care to join us, Mr. Rockwell," Amy Cooper smiled. "I'm afraid all I can offer you is a wedge of cheese on bread."

"That's very kind of you, ma'am, but I've already eaten. However, I wouldn't mind joining you for some company. I can't tell you what a relief it is to get out of that cigar smoke filled car and stretch my legs a bit."

"Henry," Amy Cooper said, "Come over here and sit next to your brother so Mr. Rockwell can have your seat."

As demurely as possible, Abigail finished off the last bite of cheese and bread that she held in her hand as Jason Rockwell sat down next to her. When, she thought, will I ever rid myself of this man?

The conversation between Amy Cooper and Mr. Rockwell seemed to flow incessantly. They talked about her husband's work, the future of the country once the railroad reached California. At one point, to the delight of the children, Mr. Rockwell took a deck of cards out of his vest pocket and entertained them with card tricks. Abigail had to admit to herself that his company for two hours had taken her mind off the grinding sound of the train wheels and the discomfort of the hard seat she sat in.

"He's a very nice man," Amy Cooper smiled, "such impeccable manners. How fortunate you were to have him as a traveling companion abroad ship."

"Yes," Abigail agreed, while her mind went racing on ahead wondering how she'd ever escape Mr. Rockwell's company when she left the train in Topeka. He had the uncanny ability to know her every move.

With the coming of evening and the shifting of the wind they had to close the car windows to the black soot that came pouring in from the engine. The stuffiness of the car and the gnawing of an empty stomach put Abigail in an ill frame of mind. When she saw Amy Cooper reach for the wicker basket well knowing its meager contents and two hungry children, she politely refused joining them.

"At least have an apple," Amy Cooper insisted. "There are four apples here."

"No real. . ly," Abigail stopped, on seeing Mr. Rockwell entering their car again. He came walking down the aisle directly toward them carrying a large wicker basket.

"Miss Whitcomb, Mrs. Cooper," he said, tipping his hat. "I was wondering if you could do me a big favor."

The unmistakable aroma of fried chicken caught at Abigail's nostrils as she stared up at him. "Yes, Mr. Rockwell," she said hesitantly.

"As you must know, in the last car most of the men get together to play poker. I won this here basket. It seems my opponent was short on cash and insisted I take it. Now I'm stuck with this basket of food that will only go to waste if someone doesn't eat it."

"You won it gambling?" Amy Cooper asked, in shocked voice.

"Yes, ma'am," he said guiltily. "I know you probably look on gambling as a sin and I don't blame you, Mrs. Cooper. The way I see it, it would be a bigger sin for all this fine food to go to waste." He lifted the cover of the basket and looked in. "There's fried chicken, corn bread, a jug of milk and what looks to be some ginger cookies. Do your boys like ginger cookies?"

"Yes. . . yes they love ginger cookies, but I really don't know, Mr. Rockwell," Amy Cooper sighed.

"I think," Abigail interjected, with mouth salivating, "Mr. Rockwell is right. It would be a bigger sin to have to throw the food away." She reached up for the basket in his hand.

"Thank you, Miss Whitcomb, that's very understanding of you," Jason said, and with a lopsided grin he turned to leave the car.

A flabbergasted Amy Cooper and her two children stared as Abigail opened the basket. "I never would have thought it of him," Amy Cooper said. "I would never have taken him for a gambling man."

As Abigail gnawed on the chicken leg in her hand her thoughts strayed to Mr. Rockwell. She wondered if he truly won the basket of food playing cards or did he buy it from someone? Was he, like herself, sensitive to the impoverishment of the Cooper family? She wondered.

The Topeka train platform was situated a few blocks away from the business district of the town. After saying good-bye to the Cooper family, Beth trudged along the hard, dirt road with baggage in one hand and purse in the other having left her trunk at the station. She became conscious of people gaping at her clothes as she passed them in the roadway. Although she considered the full green skirt and lace eggshell blouse proper attire for daytime wear, it was quite apparent the clothes she wore were of high fashion compared with the simple cotton dresses and bonnets worn by most of the women she had seen. To her surprise, the simplicity of the men's attire was also startling. Their open shirt collars, wide brim hats, high boots and faded pants did not go unnoticed. But the most startling of all was the heavy, leather belts that hung low on their hips and supported a gun on each side.

Stepping onto the wooden planking she slowly walked along the store fronts. A couple of hand printed notices in windows advertising for help caught her eye. Her hopes soared on seeing two positions she deemed herself qualified to fill without difficulty. One was an advertisement for a clerk, another for a waitress.

Beth stopped a minute, raised her hand over her eyes and squinted against the glaring sun. The growling sound in the pit of her stomach seemed to subside on seeing a sign in bold lettering that read: EATS. She put her thoughts into priority. Breakfast first, a reasonable place to lodge and the comfort of her old shoes. Tomorrow would be time enough to acquire one of the positions she had seen advertised. And tomorrow the painstaking job of writing to John Whitcomb and informing him about his niece's death.

A little apprehensive as to spending the money she had found in the purse, Beth ordered a cup of tea and toast hoping it would sustain her until her evening meal. Since the money rightfully belonged to John Whitcomb, she kept an accurate tally of what she spent in order to justly reimburse the man.

The young waitress who served her was more than hospitable and willingly complied to her many questions. She voluntarily told her of a reasonable and safe place for a young woman to find lodging.

Despite her sore feet, Beth quickened her step and anxiously followed the directions that the waitress had given her. As she turned the corner and headed down one of the side streets, automatically her back arched on hearing an unforgettable sound that haunted her from childhood; the swishing sound of a whip cutting the air.

A few feet in front of her the whip came down unmercifully across the back of a horse tied to a wagon. Beth dropped her baggage and ran towards the man holding the whip. She grabbed the man's arm that held the whip causing the second blow to fall short of its mark. "Stop it!" she cried out. "Stop whipping the poor defenseless creature!"

"What in tar nation do you think you're doing lady?" The burly looking man glanced down at her while pulling his arm free of her grasp.

"There's no need of whipping a defenseless animal like that," Beth hotly retorted.

"It's none of you're damn business, lady, this happens to be my horse!"

The end of the whip started to leave the round as the man raised his arm. Beth jumped up and clawed at his arm. "You have no right, I tell you!"

The muscles in the man's arm tightened and he was about to give her a push that would have sent her sailing to the ground when a loud clear voice cut the air. "You heard the lady!"

Beth's head spun round to the sound of the familiar voice. It took her a few seconds before recognizing Mr. Rockwell standing there in different attire. His eyes went directly past her and were fixed in a hard stare, watching her opponent.

With interest, Beth watched as the man seemed to resign himself. She wondered whether it was Mr. Rockwell's hard stare or the fact that on each of his thighs rested a gun.

"I didn't mean anything by it." The man floundered.

"Good," Mr. Rockwell smiled, stood straight and slowly walked toward them. With one scoop he picked up Beth's baggage that lay in his path. His eyes never wavered from the stranger's face. With his free hand he seized her by the elbow. "Shall we go, Abigail?" he said politely, although his touch was compelling her to move.

Confused and bewildered by the moment, Beth found herself being dragged along the road in the opposite direction in which she had been headed. She was well aware that Mr. Rockwell had called her by her

Christian name as if implying they were good friends in front of the stranger.

She struggled to keep up with his long stride and finally caught her breath. "Where are you taking me, Mr. Rockwell?"

He stopped short and blankly stared down at her. "Across the road," he said and continued dragging her by the elbow.

Beth gazed at the other side of the road to see a stagecoach standing in the roadway. The two men sitting on top were watching them with interest. She also spotted her trunk, the one she had left at the station tied on the roof of the coach. "Okay, Hank, we can leave now," Mr. Rockwell yelled while effortlessly tossing her baggage up to the driver's companion. In the next instant Beth found herself being pushed up the steps and into the coach. Mr. Rockwell leaped in behind her and closed the door. The slamming of the door, like that of a signal, seemed to set the stagecoach in motion. It took off with a jolt that had Beth holding on for dear life. She was speechless.

"It's a good thing I found you when I did," Jason grinned. "You were headed in the wrong direction and if you missed this coach there'd be another day's wait until the next one left for Fort Riley."

Beth's plans shattered before her eyes. She had a sudden impulse to tell Mr. Rockwell the truth about herself for the sheer joy of wiping the smug, interfering grin from his face. But fearful of what he might be capable of doing, Beth refrained.

"Yes," she said from between gritted teeth. "It was a bit of good luck your finding me."

"I didn't know you were a lover of horses, Miss Whitcomb."

"I'm not."

"Well back there. . . " he stopped.

"It was the fact that the man was whipping the poor creature. No one has the right to whip another living creature." She glared at him and was somewhat annoyed that she had to explain her actions to him. Yet, she thought, he did intervene on her behalf. Or was it on behalf of the horse, she wondered. It was at this point that she looked at the other passenger sitting in the far corner. He was an elderly man, rather portly, dressed in black. In his hands he held what resembled a Bible. At the moment he was openly staring at her and Mr. Rockwell with interest. She could only imagine what the man must have been thinking.

"Hum," he said, clearing his throat. "I couldn't help but overhear the gentleman call you, Miss Whitcomb. By chance, you wouldn't be Abigail Whitcomb?"

"Y...yes," Beth said hesitantly, not knowing what might lay in store for her.

He smiled with delight. "God works in mysterious ways. Let me introduce myself, Chaplain Charles Fillmore, at your service. It was only a week ago that I received a letter from my old friend, Hugh McFadden asking me to make certain of your comfort and lodging over night while you're at Fort Riley. I must say, Mrs. Fillmore is looking forward to having you as our guest. Having a visitor all the way from England is a rare

107

honor. As for you, sir, Hugh also made mention of your being a neighbor of his, a. . .Mr. Rockwell, am I correct?"

"Yes, that's right," Jason smiled.

"I'm sorry our small home only allows us to have one guest, Mr. Rockwell."

"You can put your mind at ease, sir. I'm quite sure that I will find lodgings in one of the barracks."

He clasped his hands together and smiled. "I'm so glad that's settled. If anything, I wouldn't want to disappoint an old friend."

"How long have you known Hugh McFadden?" Jason asked with interest.

He frowned. "Let me think now. We go back a long way together; even before they built Fort Riley. I remember his coming here without his wife and talked about having his own settlement and by George the man did it."

With half an ear Beth listened to the conversation that transpired between the two men while wondering what she had gotten herself into. Once more she was forced into assuming the roll of Abigail Whitcomb. If Hugh McFadden had written a letter to the Chaplain over his concern for Abigail Whitcomb, he certainly held her in high regard. Beth could only imagine what he would do to her when he found out the truth. Hopefully, she would be able to escape Mr. Rockwell and his well meaning intentions and never have to face Mr. McFadden. If it wasn't for his interfering ways she would have found lodgings and possible a job in

Topeka by now and be wearing her own comfortable shoes.

She could hear snatches of their conversation and the fact they were now traveling over what once was Indian Territory. Aboard ship she remembered some of the gruesome stories that Mr. Hilliard told about Indian raids and now traveling in their territory was far from enlightening news to her ears. "Excuse me, Chaplain Fillmore," she said. "If this is Indian Territory, as you claim, why are we traveling through it when it belongs to them?"

"You don't understand, my dear lady, our government purchased this land from them and now they want it back."

"That is very confusing, sir. If they sold it, why do they want it back?"

"It seems they're not satisfied with the land that our government allowed them."

"Why?" she asked in all innocence. "What's wrong with it?"

Her question appeared to make him ill at ease. "Nothing, that I can think of," he finally answered.

"It would appear to me," she said, "that if it were an even exchange of land, they wouldn't want to come back here."

Jason broadly smiled. "I do believe Miss Whitcomb has made a very good point, Chaplain. Had our government given the Indians land that they could cultivate and hunt for wild game, they would be happy on the land."

"Yes, yes," he mumbled. "Well, my dear, there is nothing for you to worry about; Fort Riley is well equipped to handle such matters. On the lighter side, I think you should be thinking about going to the dance this evening. It's going to be a gala affair from what I've heard. Good food, dancing and even an orchestra. The only problem I can foresee is getting you a chaperone. Mrs. Fillmore and I rarely attend such functions. Poor Elizabeth, she's not up to it; her arthritis is acting up again."

As if making certain as to what she heard, Beth asked, "There's going to be a dance?"

"Yes," he nodded. "They have one every year on May Day."

"Oh," she said, forgetting herself, "I've never been to a dance."

"You haven't," he said in surprise. "I find that hard to believe."

"I mean on May Day," Beth quickly corrected herself.

"Then you must go. I'll try to find you a chaperone, although on such short notice it may prove difficult."

Beth's heart sank on her hearing his words. When to her surprise Mr. Rockwell leaned forward in his seat and said, "I'll be only too glad to avail my services to Miss Whitcomb. Would eight o'clock be time enough to pick her up?"

Again the Chaplain clasped his hands in delight. "Eight o'clock is fine. I can't thank you enough for putting my mind at rest."

"Is that agreeable with you, Miss Whitcomb?" Jason grinned.

Hardly, she thought, but if it meant going to the dance with the devil himself, she would. She had never attended a dance and a May Day dance at that. Forcing a soft demure note to her voice she replied, "Thank you, Mr. Rockwell, that's very considerate of you."

For the rest of the journey she sat there mulling things over in her mind. What gown should she wear? Should she wear her hair up? Would she remember all the steps of dancing that Mr. Carver had taught her that seemed so long ago while teaching her the social graces? And most important of all, she must think of herself as Abigail Whitcomb.

While descending the small staircase that opened onto the parlor below, Abigail caught the flicker of admiration in the dark eyes that boldly swept over her. The all too meaningful look quickly faded from Mr. Rockwell's eyes, but not before confirming the uncertainty as to her having chosen the proper gown for the dance.

The white gown gave the allusion of being light and airy, a perfect selection, she thought, for a summer's eve. The neckline she had considered a bit daring, but the deep blue velvet piping that edged it was striking against her fair skin. The same edging trimmed the large puff sleeves that hugged her bare shoulders. Accentuating her small waist was a matching blue sash that tied in a large bow in back with streamers freely flowing down the length of the white skirt. From beneath the scalloped festooned skirt of the gown, as if held in place by delicately embroidered forget-me-nots, peeked ruffles of blue satin petticoats.

"Oh my, Abigail," Elizabeth Fillmore sighed as she looked at the young girl. "That has to be by far the prettiest gown I've ever seen in my life. Are you sure you have your key, dear?"

"Yes, Mrs. Fillmore. It's in my evening purse."

"And you make certain, Mr. Rockwell that she's in by a reasonable hour."

"That I will, ma'am," he smiled.

Although conscious of the silence of the man who walked beside her, Abigail was determined not to let him spoil her evening. "It was very kind of you, Mr. Rockwell, to take the time to escort me to this dance."

"My pleasure, Miss Whitcomb," he grinned. "I had nothing better to do."

He had nothing better to do, Abigail thought. Oh, the man is insufferable; he doesn't even try to make polite conversation. Why do I bother?

Abigail felt her heart pounding against her ribs as they entered the hall. Unconsciously her hand tightened on Mr. Rockwell's arm causing him to glance down at her. Her green eyes, enormous with wonder, darted about the room. Never having seen so many uniformed men, Abigail was taken aback by the sight.

The officers appeared handsome in their meticulous dark navy uniforms. Their black boots were polished to perfection as well as the gleaming sabers that swung at their side. A sea of clean shaven faces, some with neatly trimmed mustaches turned in her direction. The scarcity of women was quite evident.

"Good gracious, why are they staring?" she whispered, as they crossed the floor.

"I know why the men are staring," Jason grinned, his eyes carrying over the neckline of her gown.

Abigail flushed with anger as well as embarrassment. "No doubt, Mr. Rockwell, they're not accustomed to seeing a man in civilian dress," she hotly retorted.

He laughed good-naturedly and escorted her across the room to where their host and hostess stood waiting, a Captain Blanchard and his wife Margaret.

Like a flickering candle that allures insects to their death, Abigail was faced with a small group of officers rivaling for her undivided attention. While soldiers clamored to be introduced, some of the women bombarded her with questions. Was her gown from Paris? Was her hair style, the wearing of curls on the crown of the head the latest rage? Was it true that some women were bobbing their hair? What color was fashionable for fall? Did she know the Weatherbees of Lancashire? Abigail was thankful for the sudden roll of a drum that brought everyone to attention. There was a hushed silence and as the music started, everyone stood at attention and raised their voices in song. Abigail supposed it to be their national anthem. She stood silent while listening to the vibrant voices of the men drowning out the few female sopranos. She noticed that Mr. Rockwell, like her, stood silent.

The song ended with an enthusiastic round of applause and the orchestra started to play a waltz.

"The Captain and his wife asked that we join them in the first waltz. I take it; it's considered an honor of some sort."

Abigail stood frozen for the minute, never anticipating having to dance with Mr. Rockwell and by the look of him; he wasn't considering it an honor, but a duty. She wanted to flatly refuse but she saw the Captain and his wife smiling their way. Suddenly she didn't care who her partner was. If it meant dancing with the devil himself, she was going to enjoy her first dance. On sudden impulse, she turned to Mr. Rockwell and in ladylike fashion, swept him a low curtsy making certain he had the full advantage of seeing her low neckline while her eyes defiantly met with his.

Contrary to the grin that edged his lips in amusement, the hand he extended to help her rise gripped into the flesh of her wrist. "It's one thing to play teasing games with some of these young boys who are your age, Miss Whitcomb, but another with men." His whispered warning rang in her ear.

Somewhat mortified by her own unladylike behavior, Abigail could not meet his gaze. She kept her eyes lowered while dancing, but her mind wondered into a thousand avenues trying to think of a civil conversation she could start. She resolved that she'd be more appreciative of her next partner, but at the moment she had to admit to herself that Mr. Rockwell was an amiable dance partner. As he swung her around, her skirts gracefully bellowed and the dark blue ribbons of her sash aimlessly flowed in the air. "It's a lovely waltz. What is the name of it?" she finally said.

Jason glanced down at her as if suddenly aware of her presence while reciting the words to the song. "Drink to me only with thine eyes and I will pledge with mine. Or leave a kiss within the cup and I'll not ask for wine."

Face flushed, Abigail stared up at him.

"By no means a declaration, Miss Whitcomb."

"I should hope not!"

She heard the deep rumble of laughter that escaped his lips and felt a bit foolish and angry at herself. Why did he have the power to make her feel beside herself? He truly was a hateful man.

Having observed earlier the scarcity of unattached females in the room, Abigail didn't prize herself on her beauty for the competitive attentiveness of the soldiers. However, she became attuned to their loneliness for female companionship and allotted one dance to each gentleman who asked.

While dancing she managed to keep the conversation as light and amusing as possible. When a question that fringed on being personal was directed at her, she tactfully and cleverly answered with another question, thereby, turning the conversation back to her partner without his realizing it.

Although clever, in certain aspects, she was naïve to the fact that she could obtain a man's devoted attention, had she chosen to do so. If she had bestowed her attention on one particular bachelor in the room, without a doubt, a proposal of marriage would have occurred by the end of the evening.

The youngest of the officers, sandy-haired, freckle-faced Lieutenant Wilbur Harrison pushed his way through the small group of men that surrounded Abigail. On approaching her side, he stammered, "I. . .l believe this our dance, Miss Whitcomb."

Abigail's eyes quickly flashed around the circle of men that surrounded her and smiled, "Will you kindly excuse me gentlemen, I promised this dance to the Lieutenant."

Unexpectedly, a strong hand tightly clamped down around Abigail's small wrist and she found herself being dragged in the opposite direction. "I'm afraid you are mistaken, Lieutenant." The voice of Jason Rockwell boomed as he skillfully maneuvered Abigail through the small group and onto the dance floor before the Lieutenant had a chance to object.

When Abigail finally caught her breath she fumed, "I did promise this dance to the Lieutenant!"

"Did you now?"

"You had not right——"she stopped on seeing the brown eyes that glared down at her in contempt.

"I have all the right in the world. You see, Miss Whitcomb, I'm trying to keep you from making a damn fool of yourself."

"How dare you! How dare you speak to me in such an uncivil manner?"

About to bolt from his arms, the hard pressure of his hand on her back gave her warning. "Smile, Miss Whitcomb!" he commanded. "Smile before everyone in the room surmises we are having a spat."

On the next full turn, Abigail glanced over his shoulder to see a number of people were openly staring at them. She tilted her head back and clinched her teeth into a smile.

"That's better," Jason said, returning a forced grin. "As I was saying, Miss Whitcomb, you are making a damn fool of yourself. In this part of the country an engaged girl doesn't flaunt herself at ever available male in the room," Jason paused, concentrating on the next full turn. "Personally, I don't give a damn what you do, but there are others to be considered besides yourself, such as the McFadden family."

Abigail glared up at him. "I assure you, Mr. Rockwell, I'm not, as you so callously put it, flaunting myself at these gentlemen. What possible harm can there be in dancing? Am I not in full sight of everyone in the room? I believe I used very good judgment by dancing with several of the officers, rather than dancing with one gentleman all evening. Indeed, people would have something to gossip about!"

Jason didn't answer, instead he thought hard about what she had said; it made sense.

The corners of Abigail's lips suddenly curled up in a sneer. She titled her head back and her green eyes bored into his. "Tell me, Mr. Rockwell, since you are concerned as to what people might prattle about, may I ask; why are you dancing with me for the second time?"

The effect was immediate. Jason didn't answer, but a deep shade of anger spread over the finely chiseled features of his face.

The remainder of the waltz he was silent and when the music stopped he dutifully escorted her back to where her next partner anxiously stood waiting. To Abigail's surprise she overheard him openly apologize to the young Lieutenant. He stiffly nodded to her before turning on his heels.

Jason's anger was directed at himself. Perhaps he was a bit harsh on the girl but he could think only in terms of the gossip hurting the McFadden family. He made his way over to the punch bowl, hoping by now that someone had courageously strengthened its content with something more delectable to his palate than the sweet fruit juice it usually contained.

Delightfully enjoying the evening, Abigail gave little thought to Mr. Rockwell and what he had said. She caught several glimpses of him dancing with a pretty brunette and was surprised to see the woman was actually laughing at something he had said.

"My, you're a proficient dancer," Abigail smiled up at her robust host, Captain Blanchard.

"Well, at my age one would be," he chuckled. "Mrs. Blanchard insisted upon my learning the grace ever since we first were married.'

"Bully for her!" Abigail laughed.

Captain Blanchard looked into the pretty face of his partner. "I must say, I couldn't help but notice what striking couple you and Jason made while dancing. I'm afraid quite a few of us were staring."

"Mr. Rockwell?"

"Yes," he nodded.

Abigail reflected for a moment only to realize that although they had been quarreling, not once did she have to concentrate on Mr. Rockwell's maneuvering of her. Somehow the thought of finding him a suitable dance partner annoyed her. "I find him to be an extremely disagreeable man," she said.

"Really? From all appearances one wouldn't think that of him. At times, he's been known to be a bit headstrong, I grant you, but other than that." The Captain thought for a moment. "To be honest I wish some of my men had half his knowledge about this wild country and its horses."

"Why, horses?" Abigail asked.

"Out here, Miss Whitcomb, a man's life can depend on a good horse. It's been said, if a man has to choose between his horse and his wife, he'll take a good horse any day. And when it comes to breaking the wild horses, Jason has a way with them."

"Yes, I don't doubt it," Abigail nodded. "One can easily visualize the man beating the poor creatures within an inch of their lives until they submit to his headstrong will as you so rightly put it."

Surprise touched the Captain's face. "On the contrary, Miss Whitcomb, it's my men who whip horses, not Jason. In fact, there's a wager as to his breaking a fiery, black stallion tomorrow."

"A wager?"

"Yes. Some of my men goaded Jason into it since they haven't had much luck with the creature. The horse cost me two good men already. One man has a broken arm and the other injured his leg."

"Tell me, has Mr. Rockwell accepted the challenge?" Abigail asked with interest.

"Yes, but the majority are betting he won't succeed. Are you a gambling lady, Miss Whitcomb? Perhaps you would like to place a small wager on Jason's success."

"You are mistaken, Captain. I prefer to wager five shilling as to his failure."

"Five Shillings?" he laughed.

Abigail's laughter joined his. "I'm still having difficulty as to your currency; what I probably meant to say is five dollars. Yes, five dollars." A feeling of guilt stole over her knowing the money in her purse wasn't rightfully hers to gamble.

"When will this venture take place, Captain?"

"Tomorrow morning about sunup; before the stagecoach leaves for Abilene, I should think. I'll gladly take your wager. Will you be there to watch, Miss Whitcomb?"

"I wouldn't miss it for the world, Captain," she said while wondering what would please her more, the thought of easily winning five dollars, or the thought of Mr. Rockwell breaking his neck.

The last strains of the fiddle were heard and the small group of soldiers who participated in the orchestra were beginning to pack their instruments. A few of the older women had embarked on the task of clearing the buffet of the remaining food, while Captain and Mrs. Blanchard stood at the door bidding their guests good night.

Attentively standing alongside of Abigail stood young Lieutenant Wilbur Harrison. Having preferred his light and amusing conversation to that of his fellow officers, Abigail had graciously accepted his offer to escort her back to her quarters. To heck with Mr. Rockwell, she thought.

Outside, a large cloud drifted over the evening moon shrouding Fort Riley in darkness. In the distance, a mere speck of light could be seen coming from one of the officer's quarters. Abigail and Lieutenant Harrison strolled past several barrack buildings that ran parallel to the vast parade ground. Out of fear of stumbling in the dark, Abigail held fast the arm that the Lieutenant had gallantly offered.

"Is it usually this dark?" she asked.

The Lieutenant laughed. "We don't consider this dark, Miss Abigail. When you can't see your hand in front of your face, then it's dark."

Abigail found his words far from comforting as she strained to see his face in the dark. They had rounded the bend passing St. Mary's Chapel on their right and headed toward the Chaplain's quarters that lay beyond.

"Tell me, Lieutenant, the wager between Mr. Rockwell and your company of men; where will that take place in the morning?"

"Down by the corral, I would imagine. Why do you ask?"

"I would like to be there," she honestly admitted, and felt his arm stiffen beneath the sleeve of his uniform.

"I really don't think it fitting or proper for a young lady to be there, Miss Abigail."

"Pish-posh! I have every intention of being there since I have already placed a wager with the Captain."

"I see."

They were approaching the small footpath that led to Chaplain Fillmore's quarters. The two-story, box-shaped house loomed out of the shadows and Abigail rummaged through her purse feeling for the key that Mrs. Fillmore had given her. She was conscious of the Lieutenant's sudden silence and thought little of it, other than his being perturbed by her placing a wager. On reaching the top porch step she held out the key to him. "Would you be so kind, Lieutenant?"

The slight touch of her hand, the fragrance of her lavender cologne and her nearness awakened the young man into an impulsive frenzy of passion. He clumsily groped for her in the dark and his lips eagerly covered her face with kisses while making a declaration of his undying love for her.

"Lieutenant!" Abigail protested in shocked horror while attempting to break free. It was useless. The more she struggled the more he ardently pursued.

The sudden flare of a match striking within five feet of the young couple startled them. The Lieutenant quickly released his hold on Abigail.

The sharply chiseled features of Jason Rockwell's profile appeared in the flickering light as he raised the match which was cupped in his hands to light the cigar wedged between his teeth. He was half hidden in the shadows of the porch pillar that he nonchalantly stood leaning against. The aroma of the cigar filled the air after what appeared to be several pleasurable puffs. He blew out the match, pulled himself up to his full height and came strolling toward them. "The lady's key," he said coolly.

Without protest, a dumbfounded Lieutenant Harrison handed Jason the key. He stammered a few unintelligible words while making a hasty retreat. He stumbled over the porch steps and disappeared into the blackness of the night.

The small comfortable parlor became bathed in light as Jason adjusted the wick on the lamp and blew out the match. He glanced over at the girl. Her face appeared drained of color and from all appearances she seemed visibly shaken. She was gripping the back of a rocking chair to help support herself.

"Come, come now, Miss Whitcomb, it wasn't as bad as all that."

Abigail finally found her voice. "I'm indebted to you, Mr. Rockwell. If you hadn't been here I hate to think——"

"I assure you the young Lieutenant's actions were those of any red blooded young boy his age and nothing more."

"Nothing more!" she gasped. "How can you say that after witnessing his inexcusable behavior?"

"What did you expect? Surely, a few harmless kisses——"Jason stopped. His lips edged into a grin as his gaze slowly swept her. "Could it be, Miss Whitcomb, that you've never been thoroughly kissed by a man and not knowing the difference——"

"Mr. Rockwell," she gasped. "You are far from a gentleman to pursue such an avenue of conversation"

She glared at him wondering how it was possible to be thankful for his presence one minute and hating him the next. She watched in silence as he gruffly tossed his cigar into the empty fireplace and started for the door. Within a few feet of her he stopped in his tracks. He pushed at the brim of his hat in an exasperated manner, unveiling the half shadows that cover his face. It was evident that he was angered by her remarks but the brown eyes that boldly studied her held a spark of amusement in them. "Gentleman or rogue, Miss Whitcomb it's about time you learned!"

Before Abigail realized his intentions, Jason's large, strong hands shot out and tightly gripped the sides of her head like a vise.

"Close your eyes," he commanded. His face was but a few inches from hers.

Contrary to the roughness of his hands the lips that sought hers were warm, moist and gentle. Playfully they nibbled at her lips until they succeeded in parting them. She could feel the strength of his hands as they somehow managed to slip from her head and encircle her small waist, lifting her from the floor. She was being crushed to his chest while his mouth tenderly and languidly moved over hers.

A wave of uncontrollable emotions surged through Abigail's body while experiencing the most profound kiss in her life. She was plunging into unknown depths one minute, and then, soaring into exhilarating heights.

Finally, his lips breathlessly parted from hers only to take refuge in the soft whiteness of her throat. A shattering wave of tingling impulses surged through her body. As if hanging on the edge of a precipice, she clung to him.

It was inconceivable to Abigail how her body turned traitor to her mind as she willfully turned her head to meet the lips that urgently and passionately sought hers again. Then quite unexpectedly Jason abruptly released his hold on her. Abigail's feet hit the floor with a forceful jolt that jarred her back to reality.

Breathless with uncertainty they stared at each other; until Jason's deep voice broke the silence. "May I commend you on being an apt student, Miss Whitcomb," he grinned, and executed a curt bow.

Caught in an ambivalence of her emotions, Abigail's cheeks turned crimson while out of rage her hand went flying into the air hoping to slap the infuriating grin from his face. She winced with pain as Jason roughly seized her wrist before meeting its mark.

In mild disbelief he shook his head from side to side. "Temper, temper, Miss Whitcomb, it's far from ladylike behavior to slap someone." He released his hold from about her wrist and headed for the door.

"Mr. Rockwell," Abigail gasped, trying to clarify her thoughts while seething rage shook her body.

In the doorway he turned to face her. "Yes, Miss Whitcomb?" he grinned.

Abigail clutched her hands together to keep them from shaking and she forced what she hoped to be a dazzling smile to her lips, but her voice was strained. "I would like to wish you Godspeed on your venture tomorrow morning," she said demurely and paused. "And the speedier you break your neck the better!"

In a gallant gesture, Jason tipped his hat. "Anything to oblige a lady."

Although he closed the door behind him, she still could hear the sound of his laughter and footsteps fading into the night.

With the dawn of the new day came the shrill notes of a bugle sounding reveille; Fort Riley burst forth into life again. The wind carried the sound of driven hammers, carpenters fast at work building a new barracks. The tramping of horse's hooves and the shouts of command echoed across the parade ground.

Since sleep proved to be evasive, Abigail was already dressed and packing her trunk. All night long she had tossed and turned as bits and pieces of the evening flashed through her mind. Her gown was by far the loveliest at the dance and without doubt she had been the center of attention. Secretly to herself she admitted enjoying ever minute of it. But for the most part, her mind tarried on the close of the evening and Mr. Rockwell's shocking behavior. Men without scruples often preyed on women who travel alone and Mr. Rockwell was one of them. She would discourage any further conversation with the man and hopefully there would be other passengers on the coach she could converse with. She'd have to see that her trunk was on the stagecoach and then find her way to what they called the corral to witness what she hoped would be Mr. Rockwell's defeat. Any injury that would befall him was of little concern to her, other than his being detained at the Fort and leaving her to travel alone. The thought pleased her as she grabbed her bonnet and headed for the door.

After having a rather congenial breakfast with her host and hostess, Abigail left their home and headed directly for the corral. She was surprised to see that a number of people had already gathered. Aimlessly, they stood leaning against the railing waiting. She searched the crowd but there was no sign of Mr. Rockwell. It would be just like him not to show, she thought, while noticing that most of the spectators were men.

Within a few minutes she was soon joined by Captain Blanchard and his wife. "Ah," he smiled, "you haven't forgotten about our wager, have you, Miss Whitcomb?"

"No, Captain Blanchard, I haven't," she smiled, looking at the large black stallion that three men were desperately trying to lasso in the corral. The odds were in her favor, she thought, the animal was powerful. There was a good chance that Mr. Rockwell would break his neck.

"Did you enjoy our dance, Miss Whitcomb?" Mrs. Blanchard asked. "I guess it must have seemed pretty dull compared with those you're accustomed to attending in England."

"Gracious, no," Abigail said, on hearing the note of apology in the woman's voce. "I can truly say it was one of the loveliest dances that I ever attended."

"Really," Mrs. Blanchard smiled, "how kind of you to say so."

Suddenly all heads turned in the direction of the gate and all eyes were on a man who walked in the midst of other men. Someone broke from the crowd and ran ahead to open the gate for him. Abigail recognized Mr. Rockwell who was dressed in riding clothes and carrying what appeared to be a blanket beneath his arm.

He walked directly over to where the black stallion was lassoed and held down by three men. "Huh—Huh," he loudly uttered as if announcing his approaching presence to the horse. From beneath his arm he quickly unfolded the blanket that he was carrying and sent if flying into the air and across the face of the stallion with a loud guttural sound of "Shuh! Shuh!"

Back and forth he sent the blanket flaring across the stallion's face until suddenly it stood perfectly still. All eyes were on him as he reached into his pants pocket and removed what appeared to be a long narrow string of rawhide. He made several attempts to touch the stallion's nose but its head kept nodding from side to side, warding off his touch. To everyone's amazement, as if picking up the scent of Mr. Rockwell's hand, the stallion stopped nodding and allowed Mr. Rockwell to rub its nose. A murmur of surprise ran through the crowd.

With deft hands, Mr. Rockwell tied the long narrow string of rawhide around the horse's nose and brought it up over his head. He continued to stroke the animal while making hissing sounds and finally flung the blanket over the animal's back. He began to lead the stallion around the outer perimeter of the corral.

It wasn't until after his third round-a-bout that he stopped and very cautiously mounted the stallion. The horse weaved back and forth under the weight of the rider for a few moments and appeared that it would buck. Mr. Rockwell pulled on the strip of rawhide and the animal began to jog along at a slow pace until Mr. Rockwell spurred him on. A hush fell over the crowd as Mr. Rockwell rounded the corral for the second time in perfect coordination with the stallion that he had broken.

Throughout the event Abigail could hear the Captain muttering a number of expletive words under his breath for which his wife kept apologizing.

"By George," he finally said, "the man is good, there's no denying it."

A high flush of color rose to Abigail's cheeks as Mr. Rockwell, spotting her in the crowd, made a gallant show of tipping his hat to her. It was the smug smile on his face that infuriated her. And it was at the precise moment that Abigail was handing the Captain her five dollar wager.

Chapter Six

Benito Hernandez had a streak of good luck, inside his shabby pants pockets, weighing him down, jingled twenty pesos. More money than he made in months as a dirt farmer.

His steps quickened on the dry crusted, dirt road as he headed in the direction of the local cantina. The dryness in his throat seemed to subside at the mere thought of being able to afford a whole bottle of tequila.

The guilt of breaking his promise made him sweat, more than that of the hot noonday sun beating down on his sombrero. With gnarled hands he pulled at the red bandanna around his neck and used it to wipe his brow.

She has a lot to learn about life, my little one, Benito thought. What does she know about a man's needs, my sweet angel of God? A man must have a drink once in a while if only to replace the sweat of his brow. Juanita understands. Yes, she understands a man's needs. Madre de Dios, how she understands.

Benito shuttered at the thought of how his oldest daughter, Juanita, earned her living. He thanked God that his wife never lived to see the disgrace. He quickened his pace trying to erase the degrading pictures of his oldest daughter that sprang to mind.

On turning the corner of the adobe walled cantina, Benito was taken aback by the sight of the two horses tied to the hitching post out front. A rare sight, for no one who patronized the rundown, Mexican cantina was rich enough to own such animals, let alone the handsome saddles that were strapped to the creatures' backs. Some lost gringos, Benito thought. With a shrug he entered the cantina.

As his soft brown eyes became accustomed to the dimness, Benito could see that the cantina was empty, with the exception of two gringos who were standing at the middle of the bar. His good friend, Miguel Lopez, the proprietor, was serving them.

Wary of the two Americans, Benito made his way over to the far side of the bar and waited to be served.

"Buenos dias, Benito," Miguel smiled. Automatically, from a bottle of tequila he poured a drink and set it down in front of Benito. He was about to replace the bottle on the back of the bar when Benito's voice stopped him.

"La botella," Benito announced.

"La botella?" Miguel frowned.

Smiling, Benito reached deep inside his one pocket and placed the cost of a bottle of tequila down on the bar. He made certain his friend could hear the remaining money that jingled in his pocket. The astonished look on Miguel's face was reward in itself.

"Did you find a gold mine, my friend?" Miguel asked, while making change.

"No. . .a game of chance," Benito laughed. He looked up to see the fair-haired Americano watching and listening to the small transaction that had taken place. There was a smile on the young man's face and from all appearances his manner seemed friendly.

To Benito's astonishment the young man raised his glass in midair and gestured to him in a form of salute. "Here's to Lady Luck, may she always smile on you, Senor."

"Gracias, Senor." The deep creases in Benito's weather-beaten face folded into a warm smile. He drained his glass and poured himself another drink. The second shot of tequila seemed to take hold and give courage to his tongue as Benito looked at the young Americano. "Are you a man of chance, Senor?"

The stranger's blue eyes sparked with amusement. "One might say that."

"What the hell are you up to now?" Slim Anderson muttered under his breath.

"Just being neighborly," McFadden grinned.

Slim Anderson knew better. They'd been traveling together for over a month now and he had seen the dark side to his traveling companion. Well hidden beneath his display of charm was a mean streak more deadly than the venom of a rattler. "For Chris' sake, Al, he's nothing but a poor dirt farmer."

Ignoring his friend, McFadden turned his attention back to the lonely soul sitting at the far end of the bar. "What does one do around here for amusement?"

"Amusement?" Benito repeated the word unfamiliar to him. He blankly stared at the young man.

"What I mean is; what does one do for fun? Pasatiempo."

"Si, pasatiempo," Benito nodded. He thought hard for a moment before shrugging. "I'm afraid there is nothing of interest here, Senor. This is a very poor village."

"But surely there must be some way to pass the time of day. I could not help but hear you mention a game of chance."

Benito nodded his head in agreement and smiled. "Si. But that was last night and I am sure that a few pesos would not be of interest to you." He already appraised the fine leather boots and holsters the two men were wearing.

McFadden carefully chose his words. "That's where you are wrong, my friend. It is not the money that counts, but the skill one uses to play the game. And since you appear to be the winner, Senor, I must commend you for being a man of great skill. Is this not so?"

On openly hearing the compliment that he secretly admired in himself, Benito's chest swelled with pride.

"Oh, forgive my poor manners," the young man continued. "May I introduce myself? My name is Albert McFadden but my friends call me Al." Reaching out, he roughly threw his arm around the shoulder of his companion. "And this, Senor, is my friend Slim Anderson."

The two men nodded to each other.

"And might I ask you name, Senor?"

"Benito . . . Benito Hernandez."

"Well then, Senor Hernandez——"

"Please, call me Benito."

"Benito," Al McFadden nodded. "Would you do us the honor of playing a game of chance with us just to help pass the time of day? We'll gladly leave the stakes to your choosing."

Benito needed time to think. While deciding he quickly poured himself another drink of tequila. To be asked to play cards with two rich Americanos, he considered an honor. It would give the people of his small village something to talk about for years to come. He could hear the echo of their voices in his head. "Remember the day Benito Hernandez played cards with the rich Americanos and won!"

Benito quickly erased the negative thought of losing that popped to mind. One does not lose when Lady Luck was with them. Didn't he have a pocket full of pesos to prove it?

Benito pulled himself up to his full height and stood straight and proud; as proud as the great patriot Benito Juarez whom he was named after. He tightly gripped the neck of the bottle of tequila using his thumb to cap the open top. With his free hand he gestured toward the two empty tables in back of the room and disregarded the look of warning in Miguel's eyes when he asked for a deck of cards.

As the cards were shuffled and dealt amongst them, McFadden kept a friendly line of chatter going while his friend Slim Anderson only spoke to bet his hand.

Benito was having second thoughts about playing with the quiet one, but for his companion's friendly manner which help put his mind at ease. Without a doubt, the young fair-haired man, who called himself Albert McFadden, was an honorable man. He spoke of their plans to join a cattle train and that they, like

Benito himself, were farmers. He also spoke about the wheat fields he owned in a place called Kansas. The only topic of conversation Benito could find to talk about was his sweet daughter Rosa, with which he had been blessed.

Till late afternoon the cards had come Benito's way and he had more money neatly stacked in front of him than he had seen in a lifetime. His heavy winnings only led him to believe that he was unbeatable. With winning came the grasping desire of greed and Benito began to double his bets.

Slowly, Benito's luck began to change and little by little the money began to move to the opposite side of the table. With each hand he lost Benito found reason to pour himself another drink. Within the next hour Benito lost ever peso in his pocket. His heavy lidded eyes closed and his head made a dull sound as it hit the table. He lay in a stupor, one hand clutching the empty tequila bottle.

McFadden burst out laughing at the sight of the man. "God, he was funny. I thought his eyes would fall out of his head when all the money was on his side of the table. Did you see the way he kept looking at the money he was winning?"

Slim Anderson didn't answer; instead he slipped some coins off the table, leaned over and put them in the old man's shirt pocket.

"Why'd you do that?" McFadden frowned. "We won it fair and square."

"It's one thing to win a man's money and another to leave him without money for a meal."

They looked up to see a young barefooted girl quietly approaching their table. They watched in silence as she timidly reached out and gave Benito's shoulder several gentle nudges. "Papa?" her voice was a whisper. "Papa? It's me."

McFadden studied the slim figured girl. From beneath the cheap blouse she wore, he could see the hardness of the nipples of her young undeveloped breasts. The skirt round her slim hips hung straight to her ankles. Her shiny, black hair trailed down her back, touching her waist. The whole of her held the promise of being a beautiful woman one day.

"You must be Rosa," McFadden smiled.

The mention of her name on a stranger's lips brought the color rising to her cheeks. Her gray innocent eyes flickered over the two men before quickly being lowered. "Si, Senor."

"I'm afraid your papa has had too much tequila, Rosa," McFadden grinned.

The girl nervously looked about the room for help. There wasn't any. "Papa, papa," she said, soundly shaking her father's shoulder. She watched in dismay as the salt-and-pepper head of her father lifted and turned to find comfort on the table.

"If I were you, Rosa, I'd let him sleep it off," McFadden suggested, while his eyes hastily searched the room, as if seeing it for the first time.

From where he sat, he could see Miguel, the proprietor, taking a siesta in a chair behind the bar. On spying a curtained doorway, to his extreme right, a sudden excitement within him began to mount. His glance quickly came back to the young slim figured girl.

"Let's go," Slim Anderson said.

"No. . . not yet," McFadden grinned, "it seems I'm needed here."

Anderson stared at his companion and on seeing the way he looked at the young girl his own face clouded in disgust. "Jesus Christ, Al, she's only a kid."

"That's what you think," McFadden grinned. "They learn real young down here."

Deeply concerned and humiliated by her father's condition, Rosa wasn't aware of the two Americans talking about her. She was preoccupied with another troubling thought. Her father had made a promise to her as well as to God never to get drunk again. She would forgive him, that much she knew, but what weighed heavy on her mind was the fact that maybe God would not forgive him.

"Rosa?" McFadden smiled at the girl and began to gesticulate as he spoke. "There are some packages that belong to your father in that room over there." He pointed to the curtained doorway.

The girl frowned at him in puzzlement. Finally, after repeated tries she began to understand the young man. He was going to help to carry her father out of the cantina, but first, she had to get something that was in the other room. With hope soaring, Rosa half ran to the curtained doorway. She glanced over her shoulder to see the blond-haired man putting her father's sombrero on his head.

In the excitement of searching the small room, Rosa, never heard the footsteps behind her until it was too late. Al McFadden's right hand came down hard across her mouth, splitting her lip open against her teeth and stunning her. With one forceful yank the thin cotton blouse she was wearing shredded in his hand.

Instinctively, Rosa backed away from the man only to find herself trapped in the corner of the room. She pulled at her blouse trying to cover her nakedness, while her panic-stricken eyes darted back and forth searching for a way to escape. She had never witnessed such rage and in all her innocence wondered what she had done to offend the man.

Suddenly, she was mortified on seeing the stranger opening his belt buckle. Never once, in all her twelve years, had she given her father reason to whip her, let alone a stranger.

Rosa tightly closed her eyes in the anticipation of the first lash of the belt. Instead, she was startled by the roughness of the man's hands on her body as he pushed her to the ground and fell on top of her.

McFadden stood brushing the dust from his pants and tucking the tails of his shirt in. He leaned over, picked up his holster and buckled it securely around his hips. His glance carried over the listless half-naked body of the young girl sprawled out on the dirt floor. Her eyes were wide open and fixed in a hard stare on the ceiling. Her body was a mass of tremors and a thin streak of blood trickled down the corner of her mouth.

"Come on, get up," he urged. "It always hurts the first time. You'll get over it." He jabbed the tip of his boot into the bare skin of her buttocks without a reaction. The girl lay motionless, staring up at the ceiling. He shrugged with indifference, dug deep inside of his pants pockets and grabbed a hand full of coins and threw them at her. "That should make you feel better," he said, turned and disappeared from sight through the curtained doorway.

Four large, smooth stones, placed in a circle on the dirt floor made up the hearth in the two room adobe built house. Squatting close to the fire with a black, battered frying pan in her hand was Juanita Maria Hernandez. Her usual pleasant, oval face was set in a grim frown. Suddenly, she sent the frying pan slamming down onto the ground almost emptying it of its contents. It was the third time she had reheated the pan of frigjoles in the expectation that her father and sister would be coming home for dinner.

Juanita sprang to her feet and, with determination in each step, headed for the door. One glance from her large, saucy, brown eyes at the setting sun only added fuel to the smoldering anger within her. As Juanita crossed the barren fields her eyes were fixed in a hard stare on the cantina in the small village ahead.

I should have gone looking for him in the first place instead of sending a child, she thought. Why wasn't he in the fields working today like the other men? He never has money for firewood or food but always time and money for cards and tequila; that lazy good-for-nothing father of mine. If it weren't for me, both of them would starve. I should have gone for him myself but I think it's time Rosa learns what he really is. . . a lazy, good-for-nothing. Dios mio! That child has so much to learn about life. Why doesn't she see the poverty and cruelties of this world? No, not Rosa, she does not see the barren fields only the pretty wild flowers. She doesn't see the small portion on her plate but is so happy and content with so little. Dios mio, that child is a saint, always finding the good of this world and not the cruelties. She'll be a daughter of God someday. I know that is her dream and she'll have her dream, even if I have to break her father's head to get it for her. Dios mio, will she still love me when she knows what I've become?

The cantina was alive with a group of field hands who, after finishing a hard day's work, stopped in to quench their thirst before going home to their evening meal.

Surprise touched the faces of some of the men standing at the bar as Juanita Hernandez came storming through the open door. Those that knew her well and availed themselves upon her services were about to pass some flippant remark, but one glance from her blazing eyes gave them fair warning.

Juanita spied her father slumped over the table in the back of the room and headed directly toward him. Out of anger, she raised her hand and brought it down hard across his shoulder, knocking his sombrero to the floor.

Benito's eyes blinked open, more to the noise of the slap than the sting of it. Through a blurred haze he looked up into the raging face of his oldest daughter.

He was about to make some limp excuse but the shrill of her voiced stopped him. "Where's Rosa?"

"Rosa?"

"I sent her here over two hours ago."

There was a moment of silence as father and daughter glared at each other. Both were aware that the young girl would never disobey.

"Miguel, was Rosa here?" Benito called out to his friend.

Miguel silently shook his head.

It was but a whisper that called Juanita by name but enough to make her turn in the direction of the curtained doorway. She screamed; "Ay! Dios Mio!"

A hush fell over the room as all eyes turned in the direction of the disheveled figure of the young girl standing in the doorway. Rosa limped toward her sister with one hand clutched to her small breasts holding the remnants of her blouse together. Silent tears streamed down her cheeks. On the one side of her face the innocent tears fused with the blood that ran down the corner of her mouth and splattered onto her white blouse. She made an effort to reach the outstretched arms that waited to comfort her, but failed. She sank to the floor.

Juanita sprang forward and dropped to the floor beside her sister and cradled her in her arms. She rocked back and forth on her knees holding the limp body of Rosa in her arms.

The men at the bar came running. They formed a circle round the Hernandez family and each in turn gazed at the childlike figure in Juanita's arms. It was clearly evident what had taken place. Anger masked their faces.

Through Rosa's incoherent mumbling, Juanita slowly pieced together some of the vile details of what had happened.

"Quien es el rubi?" She asked her father.

"Impossible," he gasped.

"Look at her!" Juanita screamed, tears spilling from her eyes. "Look at her and tell me it was impossible. You foolish old man."

Benito forced himself to look at his youngest daughter. He didn't want to believe that the young fair-haired man, who was so friendly, had raped his young daughter. At the sight of the helpless childlike figure in Juanita's arms, Benito began to cry. He broke down and through uncontrollable sobs told as much as he could remember.

Juanita listened intently. Already her mind began to register the important fact. Albert McFadden. . .fair-haired. . . farmer. . . Kansas.

A defeated Benito sat sobbing. It was his entire fault. He had broken his promise to God. Now God was punishing him.

Juanita's eyes scanned the faces of the men who silently looked on and came to rest on the richest man in the group, Miguel Lopez. "Miguel, I have a favor to ask of you," she said. "May I have the use of your horse and wagon?"

"Si, Juanita."

"What are you going to do?" Benito asked.

"I'm going to take Rosa to the mission," she sighed, "where she truly belongs."

"No. . . no," Benito protested.

"For once in your life think of her." Juanita's words cut through him like a knife.

"We can go after them," Benito said, only to realize how foolish his words were. By now, the two men had crossed the border. He was engulfed by a feeling of total helplessness.

For the first time in her life, Juanita truly felt sorry for her father. Maybe he was a lazy good-for-nothing, but one thing she knew for certain; he truly loved his youngest daughter. He would have given his life for his sweet young daughter. Juanita reached out and gently patted his hand. "This man, Albert McFadden," she said, "he will not get away with what he had done. I swear to you father, I swear to you on my mother's grave, he will pay."

A soft chorus of agreement echoed from the small group of men looking on. Those that knew Juanita knew it was no idle threat; the Americano would pay for his black deed.

Chapter Seven

Beth was dispirited as she stepped onto the stagecoach; another day of walking in someone else's skin. She was surprised on finding Mr. Rockwell already sitting in the coach and the fact that they were the only two passengers.

"Morning, Miss Whitcomb," he smiled. "You're up bright and early. Did you enjoy the recreation this morning?"

"It was interesting," she said coolly, while seating herself.

"How much money did you lose on you wager with the Captain?" he grinned.

"Enough," she said stiffly, and busied herself with the straightening of her skirt.

Jason sensed her mood and bit into his lower lip to keep from laughing out loud. He slouched down in the corner of his seat and stretched his legs across the aisle resting them on the empty space across from him. He pulled the well-worn hat he was wearing down over his face screening the flickering sunlight that came through the open window. He tucked his thumbs under the leather holster that hung low on his hips. He was and looked the picture of comfort. Within a short time the rocking motion of the coach lulled him to sleep.

On hearing the short raspy sounds coming out of her fellow traveler's mouth, Abigail leaned over, lifted her skirt, and unbuttoned the top half of her shoes. Last night's dancing in tight shoes hadn't helped any. She sighed with relief and longingly thought of her own comfortable old shoes lying in the baggage somewhere overhead.

As the grinding wheels of the coach rolled rapidly along the narrow, dirt road, Abigail sat looking out the window. She became enthralled by the desolate vastness of the land. Every now and then her thoughts strayed to the man who was now loudly snoring under the hat.

For want of something to do, she untied the strings of her purse and removed the small book of poetry that she had found in one of the trunks. She set about reading.

Engrossed, she never heard Mr. Rockwell stir and his sudden actions startled her. He had jumped up onto the seat of the coach and in one fluid movement his body was halfway out the window while holding fast to the frame. Abigail could hear him yelling something to the driver. When he lowered himself back down into the safety of the coach the troubled frown on his face was quite evident. He jumped off the seat and with outstretched arms braced himself against the rocking motion of the coach and leaned over her. "Abigail, I want you to listen carefully to what I have to say." The note of urgency in his voice stopped her from asking questions. "In a few minutes we'll be coming to a bend in the road, and when we reach it, the driver is going to slow the pace of the stagecoach. At that precise moment I'm going to lower you to the ground outside. When you hit the ground, roll down the embankment and for God's sake stay put! Don't move; it's imperative!"

Her frightened eyes searched his.

"There's a small band of Comanche Indians who have been following us now for the last half hour."

"Good heavens," she gasped.

"Believe me, they mean business. Our chances of outrunning them in this stagecoach are nil. We'll have a better chance if they're led to believe the coach was empty. I'm going to jump out after you. Stay put until I find you. Do you understand?"

She nodded her head in answer. "What about the driver and the other man?" she asked with concern.

He avoided looking directly at her. "They'll have to take their chances." He swung open the door of the coach and turned to her. "Okay, are you ready? We haven't much time; we're coming to the bend in the road."

Jason's eyes held hers just before spinning her around. He grabbed her beneath the armpits and waited. He felt the pace of the stagecoach begin to slacken and through the open door saw that they were rounding the bend in the road. "Here'ya go," he warned, and with one heave lifted her off her feet and out the open door. He leaned out as far as possible before releasing his hold on her. There was a thud sound as her body hit the ground. Jason watched as the bundle of petticoats went rolling down the embankment and disappeared from view. The seriousness of the moment kept him from laughing out loud. He held fast to his hat and leaped out just as the pace of the coach started up again.

Stunned by her fall, a few minutes passed before Abigail regained her senses. She found herself sprawled in a dry gully, flat on her stomach. She lifted her head and stifled a sneeze as the dry dust tickled her nose. A number of galloping horses were heard on the road above.

Beads of perspiration began running down her forehead and into her eyes. She lifted a sore hand and wiped at her dirt-covered face. She could hear more horses passing on the road above and as the sound of their hoof beats faded, it was replaced by the sound of her thumping heart. She raised her head again only to have a thicket of tall grass block her view. Her ears became attune to the stillness of the surrounding countryside. On hearing a twig snap in the nearby brush she tightly closed her eyes.

Unexpectedly, a rough hand came clamping down hard across her mouth causing the imprint of her teeth to be felt on her lips. She was being turned on her side. Instinctively, Abigail clawed at the hand that covered her mouth.

"It's all right, Abigail!" It was only a whisper but enough to make her whole body go limp. Mr. Rockwell was lying in the grass beside her. He slowly lifted his hand from her lips and brought it to rest on her far shoulder. Abigail clung to the arm across her chest suddenly finding comfort in its strength.

"There's one more Comanche up there. We'll have to wait," he whispered against her ear.

It seemed like an eternity to Abigail as they lay there waiting until the Comanche's horse passed overhead.

Conscious of her grip on his arm, Abigail slowly removed her hand. As she felt Mr. Rockwell stir beside her she scrambled to her feet. She busied herself with the straightening of her petticoats and skirt and brushed at the wisps of hair that clung to her damp forehead. She spied her purse a few feet away and picked it up along with the book of poetry that lay beneath it. When she finally felt satisfied with her appearance, she pulled herself up to her full height and stood straight and as dignified as circumstance allowed. Her face was streaked with dirt from the gully and her green skirt was torn in several places. She was unaware that the lonely ostrich feather on her bonnet, no longer pointed skyward, but limply fluttered in the breeze.

For fear of laughing at the unsightly look of the girl, Jason turned his head and preoccupied himself with the surveying of the surrounding countryside. His sudden turn startled her. "Do you see that group of trees over there in the distance?" He raised his hand and pointed. "Well I want you to cut across the field and make your way over to them. Keep low, on your hands and knees, and move slowly. As soon as you get within the grove of trees stay there," he ordered.

In disbelief she stared at him. "I have no intention of soiling my clothes."

"Your clothes be damned, woman," he roared. "If the Comanche's catch you they'll strip you naked!"

The impatient set of his jaw stopped her from asking questions. Instead she crouched over and slowly began inching her way through the tall, stalks of grass. Several times she pulled at her skirt and petticoats as they became entangled in the underbrush. She could feel the heat of the sun baking down on her back causing her blouse to become drenched with perspiration. Halfway across the field she stopped to catch her breath and rest. She turned around in search of Mr. Rockwell. There were no signs of prevailing movement in the brush so she slowly continued on.

Tired and exhausted she came out onto the clearing and crawled to the shade of the nearest tree and sat with her back leaning against it. She wearily inspected the small, painful, bleeding grass cuts on her hands, but at the moment they seemed insignificant compared to the unbearable pain of her cramped toes.

Questionable thoughts began running through Abigail's mind as time passed without sight of Mr. Rockwell. Why did he insist she cross the field first and alone? If he had any intention of following her, where was he? What could be detaining him for so long? She sat up with a jolt as the thought of him being captured by the Comanche Indians crossed her mind.

Abigail raised her legs to her chest and encircled them with her arms as if trying to console herself in her aloneness. Her eyes frantically searched the grassland for movement. As if willing him to come out of the field, she softly began repeating his name over and over again like a prayer. "Mr. Rockwell. . . Mr. Rockwell. . . Mr. Rockwell——

"Don't you think that under these circumstances, you can drop all the formality and start calling me Jason?"

At the sound of his voice her head snapped round to see him nonchalantly leaning against the same tree.

God knows how long he was standing there watching her. "Where were you?" she demanded.

He crouched down next to her in the grass holding out his clenched fist. As he opened it little bits of white and green pieces of cloth became visible.

"What are they?" Abigail frowned.

"Those damn petticoats and skirt you're wearing left a trail a mile wide that any Comanche could follow with his eyes closed!"

She was speechless. The painstaking job of covering her tracks had detained him and could have cost him his life.

He sat down beside her and exchanged the tiny bits of cloth for a half chewed cigar and a match from his shirt pocket. He scratched at the tip of the wooden match with his thumb nail until it flared. After lighting the cigar he blew out the match and put it back in his pocket. His eyes never wavered from the grassland.

"There's only one thing we can do," he declared after giving it much thought.

"What do you suggest?"

He hesitated. "About ten miles from here there is a small Cheyenne village. Once we get there we may be able to buy a horse and make our way to Abilene."

She stared at him in disbelief. "You mean to tell me," she shrilled, "that you tossed me out of a moving coach and made me practically crawl here on my hands and knees to escape from savages and now you expect me to walk another ten miles into a village of savages!"

The anger in his face was evident as he turned to look at her. "Don't believe everything you've heard about Indians; not all Indians are savages. Now go behind one of those trees over there and take off that damn, heavy skirt and at least two to three of your petticoats and whatever. It's going to be a long, hot day and the less you have to drag along with you the better!"

"I most——"

"Move Abigail!" It was an order.

The rustling noise from behind the tree was accompanied by low, indignant mumbling that brought a smile to Jason's lips.

Head high, shoulders back, Abigail slowly came out from behind the tree. The strings of her purse rested in the fold of her arm, causing it to swing loosely at her side. In front of her she carried the neatly folded bundle of clothes like a shield of armor. Perched on top of the bundle sat her green bonnet. Her hair flowed freely about her shoulders and with each step taken she was conscious of the movement of her breasts and buttocks as she walked. Well hidden within the bundle of skirt and petticoats lay her stockings and corset.

Jason sprang to his feet and met her halfway. He picked up the bonnet and with one tug stripped it of the broken feather before firmly plopping it on her head. "You're going to need it," he said, removing the clothes from her hands. The silhouette of her body beneath the flimsiness of her one petticoat caused him to avert his eyes, only to find himself staring at her highly flustered face.

Abigail watched in silence as he buried the clothes under a small mound of rocks. Then she quietly followed as he turned to lead the way.

Scared of losing sight of him, Abigail clawed at the rocks of the slope and scrambled toward the top. She had been following him for what seemed like hours and each step was torment to her cramped feet. She found Mr. Rockwell standing on the crest of the slope occupied in watching a flock of long winged birds circling about in the far distance. "What kind of birds are they?" she asked with interest.

"Vultures."

She thought for a moment. "Some poor creature must be lying out there dead for them to be circling like that."

"It's not an animal they're circling over."

She frowned at his words while looking deeper into the horizon. This time she noticed the curving dirt road that headed in the direction to where the birds were flying. "Oh my God!" she grabbed at his arm. "It's the driver and the other man. There lying out there dead, aren't they?" Her eyes searched his for the truth.

He didn't answer.

"Let's go. We have a long way to go." he said. Then, to encourage her he added, "There's a small creek at the bottom of this slope. At this time of year there should be some nice, cool water in it."

At the thought of water a smile crossed her dried, parched lips. She closed her eyes for a second trying to erase the picture of the birds circling in the sky but failed.

A half hour later, on reaching the bottom of the slope and seeing the water, Abigail lost all her ladylike dignity and went running on ahead of Mr. Rockwell. She flung herself to the ground, leaned over the embankment, and with cupped hands drank several handfuls of water while managing to splash some on her face. Then, on sudden impulse, she sat up, lifted her petticoat above her ankles and plunged her feet, shoes and all, into the coolness of the water. She uttered a sigh of relief as the cold water touched her burning feet. She watched the tiny air bubbles rise to the surface and slowly begin to disappear as her shoes became submerged in the water. For the first time in all the hours they had traveled, she began to feel almost human again.

"Aren't you thirs. . ." she stopped, on seeing the gun in Mr. Rockwell's hand that was pointed at her. "Merciful God!" she screamed. Her eyes closed as the sound of the shot crackled in the air. She felt something hit her back but there was no pain. When she opened her eyes she could see him coming closer with gun in hand. There was no doubt in her mind that he had intentions of killing her. She hurled herself head first into the stream. Scrambling to her feet and waist deep in water, she hurriedly waded toward the opposite embankment. Midway she heard him yell to her. "Damn it woman, this is no time to go wading!"

She spun round in the water to see him standing in the spot where she had been sitting. The gun now rested in the holster. She raised her hand to her brow and watched with interest as he crouched down and picked up something in the grass. He stood up holding a large dead snake in his hand. After carefully examining it he flung it into the nearby brush.

Mortified by her own behavior, Abigail pulled at the weight of her wet petticoat around her legs and headed back. Mr. Rockwell reached out an impatient hand to help her up the embankment. "You look like a drowned squirrel," he laughed.

Abigail was furious with indignation. She was well aware of her disheveled appearance and his mentioning it only angered her more. "I don't need you to tell me what I look like," she snapped. "Do you realize that you could have missed killing that snake and shot me?"

"Don't think I didn't think about it," he honestly admitted a flicker of amusement hidden in the hard set line of his jaw. "But I had no choice. If the snake bit you, it would have meant a slow and unbearable death. On the other hand, had I missed and shot you by mistake, I would have seen your death as being quick and merciful. And I'd have seen to giving you a true Christian burial."

A cold shiver ran through Abigail's body. There was no doubt in her mind that he would have no qualms about killing her, should the occasion arise.

"See to whatever you have to. I'll be waiting on the far side of those trees over there." Jason turned and left her fully aware that the shot he fired to save her life was heard for miles around. They'd have to move fast now, he thought.

Abigail took personal advantage of the privacy of the moment. Before leaving she thirstily drank several more handfuls of water hoping it would fill the emptiness in the pit of her stomach.

The only sound in the wilderness as she trudged behind Mr. Rockwell was the sloshing of her wet shoes with each step taken. It was a constant reminder of her sore feet.

They came out of the forest only to face a bare rock-covered ravine that stretched along for several miles. In the distance could be seen another slope covered with trees and the promise of shade.

Jason carefully studied the ravine for signs of movement. Without uttering a word he reached out and roughly pulled at the brim of the girl's bonnet bringing it down onto her forehead, shading her fair skin from the glaring noonday sun.

As they crossed the ravine, Abigail could feel the stiffness of her shoes as the sun baked them dry against the flesh of her feet. She stumbled repeatedly over the rocks but kept her eyes fixed in a hard stare on Mr. Rockwell's back.

The sure-footedness of his walk and the way he carried himself as if out for a mere stroll only irritated her more. He seemed to know every rock, tree and blade of grass in the area. He had the ability to sense a jack rabbit in the brush even before it crossed his path.

Ever more, intense waves of heat rose from the ground, making the air heavy and harder to breathe. Abigail's drenched blouse stuck to her body. The skin of her hands began to feel stiff and dry from the scorching sun's rays.

By the time they reached the end of the ravine the heat was beginning to diminish. Jason sat down cross-legged under the shade of a tree, patiently waiting for the girl to catch up with him.

Her disheveled figure finally came stumbling onto the grassy knoll a few feet away from him. He watched as her legs buckled under her and she wearily leaned against a tree trunk. He couldn't see her face under the brim of the hat but he heard the sigh that escaped her lips. He felt a pang of pity for her and said, "You can rest awhile."

Abigail's parched lips and dry throat made it impossible for her to answer. Through half-slit eyes she peeked out from under the brim of her bonnet and looked around at the tall trees, the cool green grass and closed her eyes again. She took consolation in knowing it was a lovely, peaceful spot for one to die in. She doubted her feet could carry her another inch. Either Mr. Rockwell would have to shoot her or let the Comanche's capture her, she didn't care. She vaguely heard him talking to her. Something about it being safe now and they didn't have far to go.

Jason watched as the girl's breathing became even and her head began to droop to one side. Soon he heard the soft wheezing of one in sleep. He decided to let the girl sleep while he enjoyed a few puffs on a cigar. He sat there trying to get his fill of the countryside that he had missed for the last four months while in England.

Early dusk had fallen when Abigail's eyes blinked open. Immediately, she glanced over to the spot where Mr. Rockwell had been sitting. It was empty.

As she moved her body, she was conscious of the sore stiffness of her muscles. The burning sensation of her feet had subsided, only to be replaced with unbearable throbbing pain. Involved in her own misery, it was a few moments before she fully awoke to the horrible, low, groaning sound that seemed to be coming from the nearby brush.

Stumbling to her feet she headed in the direction of the noise. With her heart in her throat, Abigail cautiously made her way up the slight incline. Her first thoughts were of Mr. Rockwell. Somehow the Comanche Indians had found him and he was out there dying. God give me strength, she prayed, as she slowly made her way up the slope wondering how she would survive without him. A wave of relief that almost sent her to her knees, swept over Abigail as she spied Mr. Rockwell alive and whole. He was standing a short distance from her. All his attention was on watching something in the clearing ahead. She could see the broad smile on his face.

Abigail inched her way close to the edge of the clearing to see what he was looking at. The first thing that caught her eyes was the large pole sunk in the ground with a rope tied around it. The rope suddenly lifted from the ground and a loud, bloodcurdling, whooping cry pierced her ears. It was then that she saw the young Indian man stripped to the waist and tied to the end of the rope. The blood was running down his chest from two vertical cuts that penetrated his pictorial muscles. The flesh between the cuts had been lifted from the bone and the rope was threaded though his skin and knotted in front. The perspiration ran down his slim body as he whooped and yelled, trying to rip his flesh free of the rope without the use of his hands.

"Merciful God!" Abigail screamed, gathered her petticoat and went running into the clearing to help the man. Within arms length of him a strong arm circled her around the waist stopping her flight in mid air by lifting her off her feet.

"Don't touch him!" Jason yelled.

The young man's soft, brown eyes grew enormous in his face as he stared at Abigail. She watched as he gave a violent jerk to his body ripping the flesh of his chest open. The blood ridden rope fell to the ground. He stood frozen for a second, not realizing he had succeeded in freeing himself and that his anguish had ended. Without warning another thunderous whoop fell on their ears as the young man joyously jumped into the air and swiftly ran in the opposite direction and disappeared from sight.

"Merciful God," Abigail gasped, her body went limp. She could feel Mr. Rockwell's hold on her tighten and, with what little strength she had left, she turned and began beating her fists against his chest when remembering him smiling at the young man's torment. She succeeded in wrenching herself free and crumpled to the ground. For a moment she thought she was going to become ill and just sat there supporting herself with her arms. "What kind of man are you?" she hissed. "How for the love of God could you stand there and watch his suffering and not help?" She blinked back the tears in her eyes, raised her head to look up at him in shocked disbelief. "Did you do that to him? Did you hurt him?"

"No," he said gruffly. "You just don't understand."

Her face clouded with scorn. "I don't understand? What is there to understand—that you enjoy seeing people suffer?" Her green eyes bored into his.

The lines around Jason's mouth hardened. Bridling his temper he knelt down beside her in the grass. "What you have just witnessed is an old Indian custom" he said, "that is a spiritual undertaking. No one is allowed to help set him free." Unexpectedly, Jason chuckled. "He can thank you for coming out of the brush and scaring him half to death. You shortened his agony by your surprise visit. He probably never saw a redheaded woman in his life and was scared out of his wits."

"How can you laugh at his pain?"

"I'm not laughing at his pain. If you think his pain was so unbearable, just think for a moment about the person who had to inflict those cuts into his chest. The cuts you've seen were probably made by his father, who happens to love him very much. I believe that the father's pain was far greater than that of his son."

She stared at him. "And to you, this display of savagery is love of a parent for a child? I believe you can condone such savagery because brutality is to your liking," she said bitterly.

Jason's temper soared and he clenched his hands tight to keep from striking her. "Don't condemn something you don't understand. Speaking of love for their children, Miss Abigail, it may interest you to know that there are no orphans in an Indian village. As

long as there is one Indian man or woman alive that
child will be cared for and loved for the rest of his life.
They're not ostracized from the society in which they
grew up in because they are orphans. They're not put
into buildings to be raised by strangers and worked to
death. That's more then I can say for your so-called
civilized English society," he paused, and then added,
"There's a lot you can learn from savages." He stood
up abruptly, brushed at the dust on his pants. "The
village I mentioned earlier is a short distance from
here. We should be there before nightfall." He turned
on his heels and headed in the same direction that the
man had taken.

Abigail scrambled to her feet and followed. She
never knew when she had despised another human
being more in her life than she did Mr. Rockwell.

Darkness had fallen as they approached the
Cheyenne village. The outline of several small teepees
and a lodge could be seen in the distance. It was
strange coming out of the wilderness to hear the sound
of child's laughter and dogs barking and running free.
Ahead of her Abigail could see Mr. Rockwell patiently
waiting for her to catch up with him. When she reached
his side he announced, "I'm going to tell them that
you're my wife."

Even in the dimness he could see the shocked look
on her face. "I don't like it anymore than you do, but I
think it will be for the best. Now just do as I tell you.
Don't speak unless spoken to. And, if at all possible,
try to be a little humble and gracious."

His words were like a slap in the face. Humble, she thought in anger, just her appearance in itself was humiliating. Her disheveled appearance, her dirty petticoats, add to this was the hunger that now gnawed in the pit of her stomach.

As they entered the lodge Mr. Rockwell removed his hat and stood for a minute fixed in the doorway. Abigail, who stood beside him quickly, estimated that there were about thirty people in the room. She was conscious of the hushed silence that fell over the room and surprise touched their faces as all eyes turned to look at them. An old man who seemed to be sitting in a place of honor let out a joyous whoop and with surprising agility jumped to his feet.

Abigail trembled at the sight of the man. The deep scars that ran across the hollow of his cheeks and the wild, long head of hair that was adorned with feathers alarmed her. For a moment the only sound that fell on their ears as he walked toward them was the clicking together of the bleached bones that he wore down the front of his chest as a breast plate. The old man suddenly grinned and reached out and roughly grabbed Jason around the back of his neck and embraced him.

To Abigail's astonishment, Mr. Rockwell was laughing and answering the man in his own language. Then, without warning, he suddenly turned to her and ordered, "Go sit over there."

Again, she found herself infuriated by his rude behavior. A command that one would give to a dog, she thought, crossing to the vacant spot that he had pointed to. Apparently, segregation was in order, for she found herself sitting with the other women in the room.

Abigail folded her legs up under her but her eyes stayed glued on Mr. Rockwell and the man he was talking to. In the flickering fire light, his scarred face even appeared more grotesque. Just looking at him made her shudder.

Loud laughter came from the circle where the men were sitting. Abigail could see the old man's keen eyes carefully studying her. A faint flush rose to her cheeks as his laughter grew a bit louder. It became obvious to her, that for some reason, their topic of conversation was Abigail.

For want of something to do she removed her bonnet letting her hair fall freely down her back. A mumbling sound ran rampant among the women who sat behind her. One by one, they reached out and began touching her long, red hair. It was too late. To replace the bonnet would only offend them. She arched her back and tried to ignore the light tugs to her head. She caught Mr. Rockwell watching with an unmistakable glint of amusement in his eyes. Damn him, she thought.

She diverted her attention to a group of women who appeared to be bustling around someone lying on a blanket in the far corner of the lodge. She found her eyes locked on those of the man she had seen earlier in the clearing. The women were doctoring him. As he looked at Abigail, a proud and triumphant smile crossed his young face.

Several younger boys sat with feathers in their hair and their chests and faces were streaked with paint. They appeared to be listening to his eager tale of woe.

Through the open doorway situated a few feet behind the boys stood a tripod with a large pot hanging down over a small fire. Abigail's mouth began to salivate while watching the women dipping a ladle into the pot and filling bowls with warm food. They carried the bowls over to where the men were sitting and began serving each one in turn. Without so much as a thank you, she noted, the men began gulping at their food while continuing to talk.

An older woman, short and plump, with streaks of gray running through her dark hair, pushed a bowl of food in front of Abigail's face, while with her free hand she tossed some berries into the lap of her petticoat.

Somehow, Abigail managed to smile as she thanked the woman. Without napkin or benefit of silverware she set about to eat the ground mush in the bowl with her fingers. The strong taste of what she thought to be fish greeted her palate. She was thankful for the warmth of it in her stomach if nothing more. After she emptied the bowl, one by one, she ate the sweet berries that helped to cleanse her mouth of the lingering fish taste.

Later the same woman returned holding a hot cup of dark green liquid out to her. She hadn't the vaguest idea what she was drinking but found it to be delicious and slowly sipped, trying to make it last as long as possible.

Abigail soon found herself fighting to keep her eyes open and her head from drooping. She was just about to give up hope when she saw Mr. Rockwell rise to his feet. A quick nod of his head sent her scrambling to her feet. She quietly followed him out of the lodge and into the blackness of the night. When they reached the third tent from the lodge, Abigail watched as Mr. Rockwell leaned over and held back the flap of the doorway and motioned to her to go inside.

The only light was a small candle that had been sunk in the ground, glowing for all its worth. Across from where she was standing Abigail spied the rolled up blankets lying on the ground.

"I'm going to have to leave you for a short while," Jason announced, while reaching up for a length of rope that hung over the entrance.

Speechless and tired, Abigail headed for the blankets at the thought of a night's sleep ensued. As she leaned over to pick one up he warned, "Wait a minute. I'm sorry to have to do this to you, but it's for your own good."

Swift hands tied the rope around her waist and quickly brought the length of it down the front of her petticoat. She felt the roughness of the rope as he tied it around her ankles. "What in God's name are you doing?" she gasped.

"It's for your own good," he offered.

"For my own good!" she shrilled.

With one scoop, Mr. Rockwell lifted her into his arms, leaned over and dumped her down on one of the blankets. He unrolled another blanket and tossed it over her. Everything seemed to be happening so fast.

Abigail managed to prop herself up on her elbows and shouted, "You're mad! You're a madman!"

"Abigail," he said in exasperation, lifting his hat and scratching his head. "It happens to be another old Indian custom. When a man leaves his wife alone at night she usually ties herself up to prove her loyalty. No man will violate her if she is tied. It would mean his death."

"Loyalty? Violate?" she repeated, not having the slightest idea what he was talking about.

"It's what you might call a chastity belt," he said.

"A what?" she frowned.

"You heard me," he grinned.

"You expect me to believe that? Why you'd go to the ends of the earth just to torment me," she hissed.

In the dimness she watched as he walked toward the opening in the teepee. He turned, shrugged his shoulders with indifference as he looked at her. "Think what you will. Make sure you blow out the candle; they're a luxury in these parts. Good night, Abigail." He stooped over and went through the slit opening in the teepee and disappeared from sight.

Whether it was the smell of whiskey or someone touching her hair, Abigail wasn't certain but she had awakened with a jolt. She felt the weight of someone straddling her across her thighs and instinctively she struck out. Blindly she struck her attacker only to have each blow retaliated across her face. She pulled at the braid that touched her neck only to feel the grease covered face of her attacker rub against hers. She tried to roll over on her side but the weight of her opponent pinned her to the ground. Her tied ankles kept her from kicking. She succeeded in pushing herself up onto her elbows only to have a hard blow knock her back down. She heard her blouse tear as she pushed at the hands that roughly touched her body. Suddenly, the hands moved down to her waist and touched the rope around her waist; all movement stopped. The man snorted something under his breath and clumsily rolled off of her. Abigail watched in dazed wonder as he staggered toward the door mumbling to himself. In the moonlit doorway she caught a glimpse of his silhouette. He was bare-chested with a long braid that had feathers sticking out of it.

Hot tears of anguish stung Abigail's eyes. She snatched at the blanket to cover her body, a mass of tremors. She reached up and gingerly felt the bruises on her cheeks and began to cry. Over come by sheer exhaustion she fell into a deep sleep with one thought running through the corridors of her mind. As long as she lived, she would never forget the incident and she would never give Mr. Rockwell the satisfaction of knowing that the rope he called a chastity belt had saved her from being raped.

The hour was late, and Jason quietly entered the teepee to spread the blanket he had carried with him on the ground. He wearily sat down and removed his shirt, laying it on the ground next to his hat. While removing his holster and boots he remembered the rope he had tied around the girl and decided she'd be more comfortable without the harness.

On his hands and knees he crawled over to where she lay sleeping. He reached inside his pants pocket and removed a double blade knife and a match. He struck at the match with his fingernail until it flared and lit the candle. The girl was sleeping with one arm covering her eyes. He lifted the blanket gently to cut the rope from around her waist and that's when he noticed her torn blouse sleeve. He quickly reached for the candle bringing the light closer to her face. The read and white paint smears only confirmed what he had suspected. He cursed under his breath at the young buck who had entered the teepee while he was gone. He stuck the candle back down in the ground and gently slipped his hand beneath the rope and cut it apart. He crawled to her feet and cut the rope freeing her ankles. Dejectedly, with a feeling helplessness on her behalf, he went back to his own blanket, cursing himself for having left her alone for a single minute.

Daybreak streaked the ground through the opening of the roof of the teepee. Jason was already awake but lay there mentally planning their day's journey. He was pleased with the stallion he had bought from Great Bear, but anxious to know whether the girl would like the spotted pony.

He was slipping into his shirt when he glanced over at the girl and the pitiful sight of her in daylight shocked him. It wasn't long before he realized that the heavy breathing coming from her throat wasn't normal. He crawled over to where she lay and reached out and touched her forehead. She was burning with fever.

"Abigail?"

Flying arms came into the air warding him off. He grabbed her small wrists pinning her arms to her side. "Abigail, its Jason, tell me what's wrong?" he asked with concern.

Through half-slit eyes she looked up at him and weakly mumbled, "My feet."

Puzzled, he leaned over and lifted the end of the blanket. The fact that she was still wearing her shoes only led him to believe she was too tired to take them off. Clumsily, he began to unbutton one of her shoes when the redness around her ankles became prevalent. As he pulled at the tongue of the shoe he heard her groan. The flesh of her foot stuck to the leather leaving it bleeding and raw. She moaned with pain.

"Damn it, woman! Why didn't you tell me?" He couldn't control the anger in his voice.

She groggily lifted her head to look at him. "I. . . I was afraid you'd shoot me."

"Shoot you? My God, whatever gave you that idea?" He was totally baffled.

She never answered him; instead she succumbed to the blackness that ensued.

Wrapping her in a blanket, Jason carried her down to the river edge. A number of women were already there beating their families' wash on the smooth stones of the river bed. They watched him closely as he laid the girl down in the shade of a tree while cutting the ruffles from the bottom of her petticoat. He washed both ruffles in the river and set one out in the sun to dry; to be used later for bandaging her feet. With the remaining ruffle he gently washed away the red and white paint from her face. A deep-seated anger rose in his throat on seeing the number of bruises on her face. "If I ever get my hands on the bastard," he mumbled under his breath.

He draped the blanket over her head bringing it down to her knees before lifting her in his arms. He carried her down to the embankment and, like a child, held her in his lap while letting her feet dangle over the edge into the cool water below. He was hoping the coolness of the water would comfort her and, at the same time, bring the swelling down. Her feverish brow rest against his chest and he sat there listening to her incoherent mumbling.

Doctoring, he knew, was considered to be woman's work in an Indian village. Although he received a number of skeptical looks, not one woman came forward to offer him help. He was well aware of their fears and couldn't blame them. That's when he decided to bring the girl back to the teepee for the dreaded task of removing the blood ridden shoes that stuck to her feet. By now, he hoped that the water had softened the leather, making his job a lot easier and less painful for her.

With a grimace, Jason lifted the girl's leg with his one hand while his other grabbed onto the heel of her shoe. Slowly he began to ease the shoe off her foot only to hear groans escape her lips. He breathed a sigh of relief on removing her one shoe and started on the other. Unbelieving he stared at her raw, blister-covered feet before tearing the dry ruffle in half and bandaging them. He felt a sense of guilt for having driven her so hard and not taking the time to see to her needs.

Suddenly, the light of day that streaked the ground was blocked; a giant shadow appeared on the ground. Jason didn't have to look up to know it was Great Bear stooping over and entering the teepee while two of his bravest warriors waited outside. He had been anticipating the visit well knowing that news traveled fast in a small camp.

"What's wrong with your woman?" Great Bear asked, standing fixed in the doorway.

Jason finished placing the cool wet ruffle on the girl's feverish brow before answering. "She has a fever. We walked many miles to get here and her feet became inflamed." He rolled back the blanket so the Indian chief could see what he was talking about.

"I would like to see her body."

It wasn't a request; it was an order and Jason knew he'd be a fool to refuse. He leaned over and clumsily unbuttoned Abigail's blouse, draping it back over her shoulders.

A disgruntled grunt told him that the old man wasn't satisfied. He had already taken out a long blade knife from his waistband and was holding it out to Jason.

Jason reluctantly took the knife offered and at the same time glanced at the girl's face. She appeared to be in a deep sleep. His only hope was that she would remain that way. Willfully stripping a lady of her clothes was not his idea of pleasure. He preferred it to be a voluntary act, but under the circumstances he had no choice.

He sucked in his breath and swiftly slashed at the lace straps of her petticoat and flung them back down to the ground. The faster the better, he thought. With the tip of the knife, he moved the opal pendant that hung from her neck and was nestled in the cleavage of her breasts to one side. He slid the tip of the knife beneath the small gape in the center of her petticoat and brought the blade up. Swiftly, he cut three slashes into the petticoat down to her waist. Then he made two more cuts running parallel with her small waistline. With the tip of the knife he flapped each side of the petticoat back and watched as Great Bear's eyes gave her smooth, white skin a thorough examination.

The old man nodded his head in approval and the scars on his face softened into a smile. A chuckle caught in his throat. "Her skin is like snow. We will call her White Snow."

Although Jason's eyes agreed, he thought it best to warn the old Chief in case the girl suddenly woke up. "Her skin is like white snow but her tongue is like red, hot fire." Quickly, he covered her nakedness with the blanket.

"I'm sorry, Jason," Great Bear apologized. "But too many of my people have died from the white man's spotted fever and I had to be sure. You and your woman may stay here."

An understanding smile passed between the two men.

Free from the dreaded fear of the white man's disease, Great Bear relaxed and moved forward into the teepee. Surprise touched his face on seeing the bruises on the girl's face. "She does not please you?" he asked, in puzzlement.

Jason bit into his lip to keep from laughing out loud. It was obvious that the Chief thought the bruises were inflicted by him for rebuffing his ardent advances. "No, she is not pleasing to me," he lied, trying to make his voice sound convincing.

Great Bear was an old man, but far from a fool. His eyes were fixed on Jason in a hard stare. "I find that strange," he said. "Why do you worry over a woman who you say does not please you?"

The guilt of his lie sent the color rising to Jason's face. He didn't answer but made a show of handing the old man back his knife. "Who is the young warrior, who like a woman, hangs beads around his neck? He is not Cheyenne."

"You have a very keen eye." The old man smiled. "He's an Arapaho. His name is Lazy Boy. He came here to buy a horse."

Jason nodded his head in understanding.

A prevalent twinkle sparked the old man's eyes. "I will send Songbird to take care of the woman although she does not please you." He turned to leave, shaking his head from side too side. "Strange," he mumbled to himself. "Strange, that she should wear shoes that are too small."

A dumfounded Jason stared after him. He found himself wondering if vanity played a part in women's fashions to the point of them crippling their feet.

As promised, Songbird, Chief Great Bear's wife, entered the teepee her arms laden with articles. The most important of all was the medicine pouches that hung from her belt; herbal salves and cure-alls. With fluttering hands, she chased Jason out of the teepee assuring him that doctoring was woman's work.

Knowing that the girl would be in good hands, Jason went to the lodge and joined a number of men in a hunting expedition. The scarcity of meat at the evening meal had been noted by him.

A small flicker of light shone in the doorway of the teepee as Jason headed toward it. He stooped over and on entering he could smell the heavy odor of the burning candle. He walked over to where the girl lay and looked down at her. It was apparent that she had been given excellent care. She was wearing a blue calico trade cloth dress that had been hand beaded around the neckline. Her hair had been combed and fashioned into braids. The long red braids came down to rest on her shoulders. The familiar odor of healing herb salve greeted his nostrils as he bent down and lifted the end of the blanket that covered her feet. They had been neatly bandaged with the ruffle he had cut from the bottom of her petticoat.

He was about to blow out the candle and get undressed when he heard a strange clicking sound. He moved closer to the girl to find her shivering under the blanket. The strange noise came from her mouth; her teeth were chattering. Through heavy eyelids she starred up at him.

"It's all right, Abigail," he whispered. "It's your fever breaking."

Her words came muttered through uncontrollable chattering teeth. "I'm.. . .I'm. . .free . . . zing. . . to death." With trembling hands she made several fruitless attempts trying to draw the blanket up close to her neck.

Jason removed his hat and boots and sprawled out beside the girl under the blanket. He put his arms around her and gently began rubbing his hands up and down her back trying to warm her. She clutched at his shirt and snuggled close to the warmth of his body. Within a half hour he felt her breathing become regular and he lifted his head to see her face. She was sound asleep in his arms.

On sudden impulse he bent his head and lightly kissed her on the lips. Mortified by his own irrational behavior he forcefully dropped his head back down only to bang it hard on the ground. Serves you right, he thought, maybe it will knock some sense into you. He swore under his breath, blew out the candle and went to sleep.

Daybreak brought Songbird back to the teepee. The chant she softly sang to herself caught in her throat and was replaced by a large toothless grin. The sight of the young couple huddled together under the blanket reminded her of her youth when she was the only squaw in Great Bear's life.

Through half an eye, Jason squinted up at the dumpy, shrunken old woman who stood blocking the light of day. Her all too meaningful grin at the moment annoyed him. He cast a quick glance at the girl and was relived to see that she was still sleeping. Slowly he eased his one arm free from beneath her and scrambled to his feet. With a grunt he grabbed his hat, boots and holster and lit out of the teepee door under Songbird's twinkling brown eyes.

Outside, he struggled with his boots and squarely set his hat only to find himself standing there at a total loss with nothing to do. Usually, at this early hour, a group of men could be found forming a hunting party. Jason quickened his steps and headed for the lodge. He needed something to occupy his mind and at the same time he could repay Great Bear for his kindness. The unmerciful killing of the buffalo by the white man for their pelts had only added in the starvation of the small village. Maybe he'd have some luck in killing a few rabbits or wild turkey, if only to repay for Great Bear's hospitality.

Early afternoon brought a successful Jason back to the campsite. He left three rabbits at the lodge before returning to check on the girl.

Surprise touched his face as he stooped over to enter the teepee. The girl was sitting up and sipping water out of a tin cup. Their eyes locked and a short uncomfortable silence seemed to hang in the air.

"I thought you left."

"Left?" he frowned.

"I thought you went on to Abilene without me."

"Why would I do that?" he asked, tossing his hat down on the blanket and wearily sitting down next to it.

"Why wouldn't you?"

"Well, I can hear that you're much better by the sharpness of your tongue," Jason grinned.

The color rose to Abigail's cheeks. "You didn't answer my question."

Jason thought hard for a moment with two objects in view. First, he had to cool her tongue and secondly, relinquish her fear of his wanting to shoot her. "It may interest you to know," he drawled, "that I anticipate asking for a handsome reward from Hugh McFadden for the troublesome task of delivering you safe and sound. Furthermore, I'd be a fool to shoot the goose that laid the golden egg, wouldn't I?"

By the shocked look on her face, he knew he had succeeded. At the moment she appeared to be groping for words. The tin cup in her hand came down with bang. "Let me not detain you a moment longer, Mr. Rockwell, with a troublesome task. If you will kindly leave, I'll get ready and we can be on our way."

"You're not fit——"

She cut him short. "Will you kindly leave?"

Jason angrily rose to his feet, leaned over and picked up his hat before stalking out of the teepee. Behind him he heard the soft whimper of pain as she struggled to her feet. "Damn her and her pride," he swore as he set about to fetch the horse and pony.

He could see her leaning in the doorway as he approached with the horse and pony in tow. She was wearing a buckskin dress that was fringed about the ankles and sleeves. Her purse, in Indian fashion, hung from the beaded belt that tied around her small waist. On her bandaged feet were the booted moccasins that

177

Great Bear had thoughtfully left for her along with the dress. Her pigtails hung loosely down her back. With the exception of hair and skin coloring, she could be taken for a young Indian maiden. Jason had trouble keeping his eyes off her.

"Have you ever ridden a horse?" he asked, on approaching her side.

Abigail shook her head, trying to hide the fear in her eyes.

"I didn't think so. That's why I got the pony for you; they're easier to handle."

Without warning, he reached out grabbing her around the waist and lifted her off the ground. "Swing you leg over his back," he ordered.

At first Abigail hesitated, and then she awkwardly followed his instructions. She found herself straddling the creature, well aware that women of good breeding rode sidesaddle. She sat there mortified and embarrassed with her bare legs hanging out from beneath the buckskin dress.

"Are you comfortable?" Jason asked.

"Yes," she lied.

He stood there for a few seconds studying her. "If I were you," he said finally. "I'd relax my spine a little. There's a possibility of it breaking under such rigid pressure." He grabbed the reins of both animals and led the way back to the lodge. Abigail held on for dear life, grabbing the pony's mane to keep from falling.

Outside the lodge, Mr. Rockwell tied the reins to a nearby post and left her sitting there without so much as an explanation. Within a short time he returned carrying a rolled up blanket under his arm and in the company of the Indian with the badly scarred face who frightened her. Behind them walked the elderly woman who had taken care of her. A pang of loneliness engulfed Abigail as she watched the three of them laughing and talking together. On a whim, she reached up and unclasped the pendant from her neck and held it clutched in her hand.

As Mr. Rockwell began tying the rolled up blanket to the back of the saddle Abigail interrupted his conversation by calling to him. "Will you kindly give this to the woman and thank her for her kindness."

With a visible scowl on his face he reached out to take the object from her hand. He gazed down at the precious necklace in the palm of his hand then at the girl. The generosity of her gift baffled him.

Abigail watched with interest as he presented the gift to the woman along with her message. The old woman's face beamed with delight, but it took a good deal of persuasion on Mr. Rockwell's behalf before she finally accepted the gift.

Suddenly the old man stepped forward as Mr. Rockwell mounted the horse. To Abigail's surprise he spoke in English. "Jason,' he said, a serious note edged his voice. "In winter when a man is thirsty he fills his cup with white snow. The eager man puts his cup into the fire only to have it melt and become too hot to drink," he stopped. "Then he must wait for it to cool before he can drink of it. But a patient man slowly melts the white snow within his cup and, with each precious sip, his thirst will be quenched."

Abigail was at a loss trying to understand the fable. When she looked at Mr. Rockwell he was smiling from ear to ear. Obviously he knew what the Chief was talking about.

Then quite unexpectedly the old man reached out and gently touched the moccasin on her foot. "May your moccasins make tracks in many snows yet to come, my daughter."

Abigail was deeply touched by his gesture. From the beginning she had a sense of sadness among the three of them. There appeared to be a finality in the way they said good-bye, as if they would never meet again.

Again Abigail found herself staring at Mr. Rockwell's back as the pony bounced and jarred along with him holding the reins. It was remarkable, she thought, how he and the stallion seemed fused. She was shocked by the realization that she knew very little about the man. She began bringing to mind their first meeting aboard ship to the present day, only to find it was of little help. The only reason for her being in his company was the fact that he was Hugh McFadden's neighbor. Other than that, she knew nothing about him. If he owned land west of the McFadden's he must have a home there, she mused. If he has a home that could possibly mean a wife and children. But didn't he once say he wasn't married. Why couldn't she remember? Mercy, why didn't she think to ask? What difference would it make? But she should know more about him; it wasn't proper to travel with a perfect stranger.

Could it possibly be only four days ago that their paths had crossed in Topeka and they were thrown together? It seemed so long ago. And yet, in a way he wasn't a stranger. Wasn't she accustomed to his despicable moods? Like the one he's in right now; never making an attempt at civil conversation. And that annoying way he has of grinning and not knowing what he was truly thinking. Well, if he's married, the poor dear has my sympathy. I wonder what his wife looks like.

They stopped to water the animals and Mr. Rockwell left her sitting in the grass while he made his way down the slight incline to the river's edge.

Abigail stretched out on the cool grass and rolled over on her stomach, giving her hind quarters a much needed rest. With renewed interest, she watched Mr. Rockwell standing with the animals. There was a gentleness in his manner as he stood there, petting the horse and pony. She believed she could actually see him talking to the animals. But the remarkable thing about it, they seemed to know what he was saying as their tails swayed to and fro.

When he climbed back up the hill, he sprawled out beside her in the grass. He pulled at a long blade of blue stem grass and sat there toying with it. "That was very generous of you to give Songbird your necklace," he said. "I know how much it must have meant to you."

Abigail's complexion deepened with guilt. The necklace wasn't hers to give in the first place and was of no sentimental value, as he believed. She had felt the immense need to repay the woman for her kindness and had no other possession to give. "I only wish I could have given her more. The dear woman held me in her arms the whole of the night and comforted my chilled body as though I were her own sick child."

"Did she now?" he nodded, with the unreadable grin on his face.

It soon faded when Abigail asked the next question. "What did the old man mean when he was talking about a man's thirst and a cup of white snow?"

Jason was caught off guard by her question and for the first time found himself floundering. "If. . . if the time should ever come, I'll tell you."

The abruptness in his voice told her their conversation had come to an end as far as he was concerned. He stood up and gave her a helping hand. It was time to leave.

They had traveled a long way since noon, only stopping to eat and water the animals. Abigail's buttocks was numb as well as her legs. Her bladder felt as if it was about to burst, but modesty kept her from complaining.

Several times her hopes falsely soared on thinking they would stop for a spell, when Jason slowed their pace. He'd linger for a moment to check the brush as if in search of a lost article and then continued on.

At present he was engrossed in searching the ground anew. He brought his horse to a halt and dismounted. With an air of satisfaction he came walking toward her. "We'll camp here for the night," he said, reaching up to help her down from the pony's back.

Abigail's legs buckled beneath her, like a toddler she had to be held until the circulation returned. After a short duration, Jason asked, "Can you manage?"

She nodded in answer and out of necessity hobbled across the small clearing toward the only upheaval of rocks in the area.

Jason stared after her, a quiet smile on his lips when seeing the buckskin skirt of the dress she was wearing being lifted in readiness. She disappeared behind the mound of rocks.

The horse and pony had been hobbled with a thin strip of hide tied around their ankles. The meager supplies Great Bear had given them were unpacked and lying about on the ground. Jason was busy spreading one of the blankets on the ground as Abigail came from behind the rocks walking rather stately. She stood in the center of the clearing eyeing the vast sea of grass being rippled by the wind. The tall grass stretched to the horizon. The sky was streaked with brilliant shades of yellow and orange, embedded in a breath taking purple.

"Beautiful, isn't it?"

She was startled by the sound of his voice close to her ear. "Mr. Rockwell, you have the unpardonable habit of sneaking up on a person and scaring them half to death."

"Sorry, about that," he laughed and removed a gun from his holster. "I don't think you'll need this, but just in case. I'm going to gather some brush to make a fire."

Abigail drew back from the gun in his outstretched hand. "I detest guns. Furthermore, I don't know how to use one."

"It doesn't matter," he said. "No man in his right mind would come within twenty feet of a woman holding a gun in her hand. You may need it to ward off an animal. If so, just fire a shot in the air that should do it." He grabbed her about the wrist and firmly placed the gun in her hand.

"But. . .I. . ." she stammered.

Before she had a chance to protest, he disappeared into the nearby brush. She looked down at the cold, blue, steel barrel of the gun in her hand with disdain. She gingerly held it off to one side, as if it were infected with a communicable disease. She walked over to where Jason had spread the blanket and sat down, carefully laying the gun to one side.

Magnified in double measure by the stillness of dusk came eerie sounds out of the wilderness. Oddly enough, the strange sounds were of little concern to Abigail compared with her having to spend another night in the company of Mr. Rockwell. The man definitely was the most disagreeable man she had ever met. More often than not, she was conscious of the uncomfortable silence that hung between them.

Long before she caught sight of him coming through the brush she heard him whistling. He entered the clearing like a stiff back English soldier with the refrain of "God Save the Queen."

For a split second Abigail thought he'd gone mad, until she realized he was play acting. His grand entrance was in answer to her earlier accusation of his startling her. It was the sight of a dead hen dangling from his left hand that made her burst out laughing. His gallant stand and whistled tune was inappropriate to the dead hen in hand.

Jason's own deep laughter accompanied hers as he closed the distance between them. He set the bundle of dry brush down on the ground along with the dead prairie hen. "Meaning no disrespect to the Queen," he laughed. "It was the only tune I could think of."

"I'm quite sure the Queen would be pleased," she choked with laughter. "It's not every day that Her Majesty is saluted with a dead bird in hand."

"Is that a fact?"

Tears of laughter spilled from Abigail's eyes while envisioning the throngs outside of Buckingham Palace saluting the Queen Mother with a dead bird in hand.

Jason watched as she lightly brushed at the shimmering tears in her eyes. Under his direct gaze a high color rose to her fair cheeks. There was an awkward moment upon realizing it was the first time they had laughed together.

Abigail watched in silence as Mr. Rockwell skillfully removed the gizzards of the hen and started the fire. It wasn't until he sat down next to her, clumsily dry plucking the prairie hen that she could contain herself no longer. "Here, let me have a go at it," she said, a note of impatience edged her voice.

A bit reluctant, Jason handed her the hen, feet first. He sat back and was amazed at the deftness of her hands pulling at the feathers and sending them flying into the air. It was obvious to him that the chore was far from being unfamiliar to her; the thought perplexed him.

In fact, there were quite a number of things about the girl that puzzled him. Until today she had the manners and gentility of a lady. Yet, here she sat, dry plucking a hen, like an experienced scullery maid. He found her squeamish about holding a gun in her hand, but thought nothing of holding a bloody, dead hen. And her feet, that was something else again. Most women would have cried if they had sustained such blistering, but not her. Still, her remarkable green eyes that could chill a man to the marrow of his bones had grown warm and soft with tears of laughter. Women, Jason mused, who could understand them?

He watched a she gave the hen a gentle slap on the rump in an air of self-satisfaction for a job well done, before handing it back to him.

There was a sharp cool nip in the night air and Abigail huddled close to the fire, finishing the generous portion on the tin plate that Mr. Rockwell had given her. They had eaten their meal in silence for which she was thankful. Hunger had gnawed at her and she wholeheartedly preferred concentrating on the food rather then having to make polite conversation. She never anticipated the long tedious chore of cooking over an open fire. Or the necessary trips that had to be made by Mr. Rockwell in order to accumulate enough wood to keep the fire going. Dead tree branches were sparse and at one point they had tried burning dry grass, only to be choked by the smoke of the fire.

"Abigail!"

To the sharpness of his voice she automatically came to attention.

"We're going to have a guest for dinner. Don't be frightened. Just make sure you serve him as a dutiful wife would."

Confused and baffled, but keenly aware of the serious tone of his voice, openmouthed, she peered into the surrounding darkness. A gasp caught in her throat; her heart pounded wildly in her chest on seeing the silhouette of an Indian not more than ten feet from where she was sitting. Her head spun round to look at Mr. Rockwell. He nonchalantly sat there chewing on a hen's leg.

Slowly, ever so slowly the figure of a half-naked Indian loomed out of the darkness and into the flickering light of the fire. Wide-eyed, Abigail watched as Mr. Rockwell unhurriedly rose to his feet. With hands resting on his hips he stood there squarely facing the approaching intruder.

The Indian presented himself in a noticeable bold and arrogant manner as he came within arms length of Mr. Rockwell. He wore leggings of greased buffalo hide and his long, black hair was parted in the middle and braided. Strands of beads hung from his neck adorning his bare chest. A grave moment of uncertainty prevailed as the two men eyed each other like contenders in a boxing ring.

Mr. Rockwell made a sweeping welcomed gesture with his right hand, while his other hand rested a few inches from the gun in his holster.

The Indian hesitated, distrustfully glanced about before deciding to seat himself on the ground; Mr. Rockwell joined him. From over the flickering flames of the fire Abigail watched in awe at the alternating gestures they made with their hands in sign language. Frequent, deep, guttural sounds escaped the stranger's lips. For some unexplainable reason she sat rigid, in sudden fear for her life.

A second call from Mr. Rockwell sent Abigail scrambling to her feet. She hastily scraped the bones from her plate onto the fire and replaced them with the remaining carcass of the hen. She hobbled on her sore feet and with legs that felt like straw slowly circled half way round the campfire to where their guest sat. Hands trembling, she leaned over and held the plate of food out to him. He acknowledged it with a grunt but chose not to look up at her.

Abigail stepped back and was about to return to her place when Mr. Rockwell grabbed her about the wrist and roughly pulled at her arm forcing her to sit beside him. Puzzled as to his reasoning she silently sat down. She remembered how like servants the women in the village had seated themselves off to one side while the men ate and talked. She tried hard to avoid looking at their guest as he noisily wolfed down his food. Occasionally, he'd glance up from the plate only to smile at Mr. Rockwell, who in turn smiled back. She was thankful his eyes never wandered in her direction. At close range, she was surprised how she had misjudged the man's age. There was firmness and hardness to his lean body that was the unmistakable mark of youth. He was younger than she had surmised but the darkness played tricks. She lowered her eyes in embarrassment when she caught herself scrutinizing his half-naked body.

The clank of the tin plate tossed to the ground announced that their guest had finished his meal. He seemed pleased and cordially expelled sever loud belches.

On seeing Mr. Rockwell reach into his shirt pocket, she thought, cigars after dinner? He held out a small object between his thumb and index finger and placed it on the ground in full view of their guest. Curiously, the man leaned forward and studied the small object. His face registered shock as if making a startling discovery. For a split second his dark eyes flashed to her face just before he sprang to his feet. Mr. Rockwell quickly jumped to his feet and flung his hat to the ground. Abigail saw as well as heard the hard drive of Mr. Rockwell's fist hit the man's jaw; stunning him for a moment. The man quickly recovered and with one sweeping movement pulled a knife out of his waistband.

Slightly crouched, knife in hand, he lunged at Jason. He grunted and leaped about while thrusting his knife. With remarkable agility Jason succeeded in fending off each drive. But on the fourth attack the knife made contact and cut deep into the flesh of his upper right arm. Abigail heard him swear, and out of rage he leaped forward and with both hands grabbed the arm holding the knife. The weight of his powerful body plowed into his opponent, knocking the breath out of him and casting the knife to the ground. With a swift kick Jason sent the knife sliding to the edge of the firelight past a wide-eyed Abigail who was too stunned to move.

A hard blow on the back of his neck momentarily stunned Jason. With full strength he firmly clasped his hands together, spun around, and with driving impact brought them up under his opponent's chin. The man fell backwards to the ground heavily. His listless body was sprawled out beside the campfire, he lay motionless. Instinctively Abigail groped for the knife and quickly hid it from sight under the blanket. She forced a glance over her shoulder and an involuntary short scream, a release, to counter the brutal sight she was witnessing escaped her lips.

Breathing heavily, Jason towered over the body and viciously stomped his foot down on what appeared to be the man's face. The girl's scream momentarily baffled him. He darted a glance in her direction while continuing his vicious attack.

Abigail fought hard against a sweeping nausea in the pit of her stomach. Finally a hush of silence fell on her ears; the stomping noise had stopped. She slowly opened her eyes and immediately focused them on the only part of the Indian's body that was visible to her, his legs. To her amazement the man was rising to his feet. He staggered and cautiously backed way from where Mr. Rockwell was standing. Abigail held her breath. Once clear of Mr. Rockwell, the man turned and ran for all his diminishing worth into the brush and disappeared into the darkness. But not before Abigail spotted the smoking, stump like pigtail that jutted out from his scalp. Ordinarily, she would have considered it a laughable sight but she was utterly drained by fear and her own false assumption as to the attack on the Indian. To the fading sound of hoof beats, denoting their guest's hurried departure, she breathed a sigh of relief and utterly drained, sank to the ground. She sat there trying to control her emotions when she remembered Mr. Rockwell's arm having been injured. She saw him sitting on the blanket. He was hunched over, making several fruitless attempts at bandaging his arm with the neckerchief from around his neck.

She hobbled to her feet and walked over to the blanket. "Here, let me do that," she said, sinking to her knees beside him.

"It's not a pretty sight," he warned.

Ignoring his warning she tore the rest of the shirt sleeve open. A large chunk of flesh flapped down exposing pink tissue of muscle beneath; his arm was drenched in blood. The color drained from her face.

"I warned you," he said, gruffly pulling his arm free of her touch.

Quick thoughts flashed through Abigail's mind as she scrambled to her feet in search of her purse. Once found, she hastily spilled its contents on the ground. She sifted through the articles until she found what she was looking for, a small wooden spool of thread with needle entwined. At the gleam of the steel needle in her hand Mr. Rockwell flinched. "What the hell do you think you're going to do with that?"

191

She blinked at his words. "Your arm has to be stitched."

Dumfounded, he stared at her calm, sure, manner while having to admit to himself that she was right. He thought of the pain involved, but thought more of having a fainting woman to contend with. It was then that he noticed the small spark of amusement that shone in her eyes; it seemed to be challenging his masculinity. He knew damn well he could take the pain but he wondered if she had the guts to stitch his arm. With that, he folded his arms across his chest holding tight the elbow of his injured arm. Teeth gritted, statue-like in form, he stared straight ahead, anticipating the first painful prick of the needle.

To keep from fainting, Abigail mentally fortified herself by envisioning the flesh of his wound to be that of a torn, delicate piece of lace that needed mending. Her years of experience as a seamstress showed in the deftness of her hands. With remarkable speed and gentleness she began stitching the wound close. She disregarded the sticky wetness of the blood that seeped out of the wound and over her fingers. Beads of perspiration broke out on her forehead and at one point she felt light headed. There was no struggle for words as the pent up fears within her released themselves in verbal form. "You knew that man and you've been tracking him down all day. Haven't you?" She didn't wait for his answer. "You knew he would see our campfire and join us. In fact, you invited him with the full intention of picking a fight with him. Will you kindly tell me what all this was about?" She then realized she had blurted out her innermost thoughts and waited for his reply.

"It wouldn't be of interest to you," he said, from between clenched teeth.

"It wouldn't be of interest to me!" she exploded. "A savage joins us, almost takes your life, had he succeeded, would have taken mine and you have the unmitigated gall to tell me it wouldn't be of interest to me." The needle in her hand dug deeper into the flesh of his arm.

"Watch what your doing!"

"Sorry," she half whispered feeling his pain. She concentrated on the last stitch that had to be made. Pulling the needle through a loop of the thread, she made a knot.

"If I thought for one minute that your life was in danger, I would have shot him," he said, matter-of-factly.

Leaning back on her haunches, Abigail stared at the hard set line of his jaw. Until that very moment it never occurred to her that at any given time he could have used his gun had he chosen to do so.

The warmth of her breath on his arm made his head snap round and for the first time he looked to see what she was doing. Using her teeth, she gnawed at the remaining length of blood ridden thread. It broke off.

"There that should do it," she weakly smiled, brushing the wetness of his blood from her lips.

He was astonished by the neat, skillful job she had done and sat there almost admiring it. From one of the pouched buffalo hides that they carried with them, she got some water and washed the blood from his arm as well as her hands. She covered the wound with a fine, white handkerchief that was in her purse. Using his faded blue neckerchief she tied it around the arm securely holding the bandage in place. She sat back and was drained by the appalling thought of what she had just accomplished. Now that the crisis was over she was visibly shaken.

"Thank you Abigail, you've done a real fine job of it," he smiled over at her.

Too weak to reply, and out of fear of becoming ill, Abigail turned her back on him and sprawled out on the blanket.

"Are you all right?" he asked with concern.

"Yes," she lied. "Just a bit tired."

With his good arm Jason grabbed the rolled up blanket and covered her. He removed his holster and laid it to one side before sprawling out next to her. With the remaining half of the blanket he covered himself. Before bringing the brim of his hat down, in readiness against the early morning sun, he glanced at the star filled sky above. Sleep would come easy.

"Jason?"

He smiled to himself on hearing her use his first name. "Yes, Abigail?"

"You were tracking that man, weren't you?

"Yes, I was after him."

She weighed his answer before asking, "Why?"

"Well, if you really must know," he said, with a note of impatience in his voice. "He's an Arapaho by the name of Lazy Boy; his name describes him well. It just happens that he was the man who tried to rape you the night before last."

She sat up with a jolt. She was shocked by what he had said and more so by the unexpected nearness of him lying beside her. "How. . . how did. . ., "she stammered.

"By the bruises on your face."

How nitwitted of her, of course they showed, why hadn't she realized that? She raised her hand to her face and touched the still tender spots. "How did you know he was the man?"

"I found one of his beads next to your blanket."

She was stunned by his candor but more so by the fact of his seeking retribution on her behalf. An overpowering feeling of femininity swept over her knowing he had fought for her honor. "Oh, Jason," she sighed. "I don't know. . .I really don't know how to thank you."

On hearing the unusual quality of softness in her voice it became obvious to him that she had misinterpreted his actions entirely. The idea that she might bask in the glory of him fighting to save her virginity irked him. He summoned a deep sigh of disgust from deep within his throat. "This may come as a surprise to you, Abigail, but don't go getting the notion that I was about to die for your honor alone. Lazy Boy was a guest in that village and contrary to what most white people think, the Cheyenne, above all, have strong moral laws and virginity in their women is one of them. There were a number of young maidens sleeping in that village besides you. I meant to teach him a lesson and that's all there was to it," he said, adding as an after thought, "I was protecting my own interest as well. After all, my reward might have diminished by delivering slightly used merchandise to the McFadden's."

Anger brought the color back to Abigail's cheeks. "You are without a doubt the most despicable. . ." she gave up. In a huff, she turned her back on him. As she lay there huddled beneath the blanket she vowed it would be a frosty day in hell before she spoke to him again.

Self-satisfied and grinning, Jason closed his eyes only to reflect on seeing the girl bending down to pick up the knife. "While I think of it, what did you do with Lazy Boy's knife?" he asked out of curiosity.

In all the excitement, Abigail had completely forgotten about it. She reached down and felt the small mound under the blanket near the curve of her waist. "I'm keeping it!" she hotly retorted. "I just might cut my bloody throat with it! I hope you'll be amply rewarded for the deliverance of my corpse!"

About to laugh he thought better of it. The somber bitter note in her voice baffled him as to whether she would take her life he wasn't certain. There was no question, she had the most fiery temper he'd ever seen; added to this was the fact that she was totally unpredictable. Her remark suddenly erased all thoughts of sleep from his mind.

A short time passed before Jason heard her even breathing. He sat up and leaned over her small frame searching diligently for the knife. He was about to give up hope when he felt the small bump beneath the blanket near the curve of her waist. He stretched out his left hand and slowly pushed at the knife trying to inch it out from under her and toward the outer edge of the blanket. Without warning the girl turned in her sleep, pinning his arm.

Jason sucked in his breath as she cushioned her head on his shoulder, nestled close, and brought her arm to rest across his chest. At first, he didn't move for fear of waking her. Then he shifted his weight and made himself comfortable. He was thankful that it wasn't the shoulder of his sore arm that she had opted to lean on.

Chapter Eight

In late afternoon, they stopped to water the animals and sat beneath the shade of a cottonwood tree. Abigail was keenly aware of Jason's ill tempered mood. He hadn't spoken a word since morning. Mustering up her courage she decided to ask him a question. "How much further is it to Abilene?"

"About another hour's ride from here."

She was shocked. "Then why are we sitting here? Why don't we leave now?" she demanded.

He took the long blade of grass that he'd been chewing on out of his mouth, his glance slowly sweeping her. "I thought it best that we wait until dark before we enter the city. I didn't think you'd want anyone to see you dressed like that."

She was overwhelmed by his consideration, since she had never given thought to her appearance. "Thank you. It's very considerate of you, Jason, to think of my feelings."

"I wasn't thinking of you," he grinned. "It just happens that I have a number of friends in Abilene and I wouldn't want it to be spread all over town that I rode in with a redheaded squaw."

If he was hoping to give her a taste of her own sharp tongue, he knew he had succeeded. For the remainder of the afternoon she sat sullen.

Dusk had given way to evening as they rode through the back streets of Abilene. A few scattered stars were visible in the cloudy, dark sky. A heavy ring around a quarter moon was evident and the streets were deserted. The only light visible shone from windows of the wooden framed houses that were repetitiously trimmed with white, picket fencing. Peering into the windows one could see families sitting down to their evening meal.

Behind one of the two story buildings in the area Jason reined his horse and dismounted. He tied the reins of both animals to a nearby post. Without explanation he disappeared around the corner of the building leaving Abigail sitting in the deserted alley way.

A short time later, Abigail looked up to see him making his way down the open back staircase of the building. As he reached the middle of the landing he announced, "I got you a room for the night."

On approaching the last step he came towards her and reached up to help her down from the pony's back. When her feet touched the ground a whimper escaped her lips. He thoughtfully looked at her and then at the flight of stairs they had to climb. "I think I better carry you."

"No, no," she protested. "I'll manage."

It was too late. He had grabbed her left wrist and was swinging her arm over his head. He leaned over bringing his shoulder up into the pit of her stomach, knocking the breath out of her while effortlessly tossing her over his shoulder like a sack of meal. He began climbing the steps as his right arm tightly closed around her dangling legs.

The undignified manner in which Abigail found herself being carried brought the color rising to her cheeks more so than her inverted head.

Through the open banisters of the upper corridor, Abigail caught a glimpse of the hotel lobby below. It was empty with the exception of the desk clerk who, at the moment, was straining his neck to catch a glimpse of her. Probably never seen a redheaded squaw, Abigail thought, angrily.

At the end of the corridor they entered a room. The only thing visible to Abigail was the blue carpeting on the floor and the back of Jason's pants. The slats in the bed creaked as he dumped her onto it. She sat up with a jolt, her eyes darting around the room. She quickly took in its cleanliness and simplicity. She looked up to see Jason watching her.

"I'm going down to the kitchen and see if I can get you something to eat," he announced. "I'll be back shortly."

Before she could answer him, he was out the door. She fluffed up the pillows behind her back and studied the room. Hardly luxurious, but it was clean and comfortable and would be heaven compared to sleeping another night on the hard, cold ground. She suddenly realized how long it had been since she had slept in a full size bed.

Without the courtesy of a knock, Abigail noted, Jason had reentered the room carrying a large wooden tray. He crossed the floor and set it down in her lap. "It's the best I could do at this hour," he said, pushing his hat back onto the crown of his head.

Sitting on a heavy white platter was a juicy browned steak accompanied by home fried potatoes and sweet peas. On the corner of the tray sat a small dented silver teapot. Next to it was a rather fragile looking blue and white tea cup and saucer. The best he could do, she thought as the aroma of the food tantalized her nostrils. "It's wonderful," she smiled. Her smile went unnoticed.

"Go ahead and eat before it gets cold," he ordered.

It was the first order that he had given her, barring a verbal rebuttal. She resourcefully started cutting into the steak and hesitated. "What about you?" she asked. "Aren't you going to eat?"

"I'll eat later." He was standing at the dresser pouring water from the large white pitcher into the basin. He rolled up the sleeves of his shirt, and stood there washing his hands. With the large white bath towel in hand he came across the room and sat down at the foot of the bed. Spreading the towel over his lap he warned, "I'm going to have a look at your feet."

Dumbfounded, Abigail watched as he lifted each foot in turn onto his lap. How in God's name does he expect me to eat with him touching my feet, she thought.

Painstakingly he removed the bandages with the same gentleness Abigail had witnessed with the stallion and pony. She looked over at him to see him taking something out of his shirt pocket. The familiar odor of the herbal salve permeated the air. She could feel the soothing coolness of the salve as he spread it over her feet. She was touched by his thoughtfulness.

"That should do it," he said. "But leave the bandages off for the night."

His sudden reply startled her and she choked on the last morsel of food in her mouth. Out of desperation she reached out for the cup of tea.

Lifting her feet, he inched his way out from under them and carefully lowered them back down on the towel he had spread out on the bed. He stood up and glanced at her empty plate with what appeared to be approval. "I'll take this back down to the kitchen," he said, removing the tray from her lap.

"It was delicious." Again, Abigail's smile went unnoticed.

In the doorway he hesitated. "The facilities, or should I say the water-closet, is down the end of the hallway to your left. I'll see you in the morning."

"Good night, Jason, and thank you," she called out after him but it was too late; the door closed. Or was it? She heard the key being turned in the lock and then it was followed by a strange scraping sound on the floor. She glanced down to see the key being pushed under the door from the other side.

Abigail found his strange quiet attitude perplexing and downright irritating. When he yelled at her she could retaliate but silence was irreproachable. Reaching out she turned down the oil lamp on the night stand and stretched out on the bed. No doubt, she thought, tomorrow he'll be yelling at me. Tomorrow, but where was he sleeping tonight? Why didn't he tell me where he was lodging?

Sleep helped to erase all questions from Abigail's mind.

A good night's sleep, a proper meal, and a proper bed had rejuvenated Abigail. She had awakened at an early hour only to find herself a prisoner in her room. Where could she go without the proper attire? Again they'd have to wait until night fall to travel, she thought. For want of something to do, she sat by the window and studied the people walking in the street below. At the sound of a knock on the door and the idea of company she eagerly hobbled across the floor, leaned over and picked up the key. She opened the door to find a young girl standing there. In one hand she expertly carried a tray while the other hand dragged a large wooden tub on wheels into the room. "Your breakfast and bath, ma'am," she announced.

Outside in the hallway, Abigail could see a row of buckets filled with steaming water. Two at a time the young girl, who Abigail judged to be a year or two younger than herself, carried in the buckets and filled the tub. The girl was a frail creature and struggled under the weight of the buckets; it was a chore all too familiar to Abigail. How many times, she thought, have I filled tubs for the pleasure of others?

She uncovered the tray of food only to be shocked and disappointed by its contents. A browned steak, home fried potatoes and peas, the same meal she had for dinner. She once heard that Americans were in the habit of eating a hearty breakfast. She picked at the potatoes and drank some tea.

Among Abigail's many virtues, cleanliness was foremost. She slid down into the tub of warm water and extravagantly used the soap, filling the water with a sudsy lather. She was enjoying the luxury of the bath when a knock on the door was heard. In the expectation of the young girl bringing warm water to be added to her bath, without hesitation, Abigail called out permission to enter.

The door opened, and a strange woman came walking into the room. Their eyes locked and a heavy rouged smile crossed the woman's face. It was then that Abigail noticed Jason standing behind the woman.

"Abigail, I would like you to meet Lucy. . . Lucy Stone." He was smiling from ear to ear as his eyes darted back and forth looking at the both of them.

Abigail was speechless. Was he oblivious to the fact that she was bathing? How dare he enter and with a stranger?

By appearance alone, Lucy Stone was what Abigail was raised to know as a woman of the streets. Her face was heavily made up and the low cut neckline of her dress was quite improper for daytime attire. A bright red feather boa hung loosely around her neck and down to her waist; Abigail thought it deplorable.

"Hi, Abby." Lucy's husky voice filled the room as she strutted like a proud peacock looking the room over.

"My name is Abigail," she corrected.

The woman shrugged with indifference, but it was Jason's eyes that gave her fair warning. "Lucy happens to be a very good friend of mine."

Abigail sunk deeper into the tub till the water covered her bare shoulders. She was thankful for the heavy layer of bubbles that floated on the surface covering her nakedness.

The woman stopped in her tracks and brought her hands to rest on her hips as she stood there staring down at Abigail in the tub. "Well, I can't tell a damn thing this way," she said in exasperation.

Jason laughed, turned his back and cleared his throat. "Abigail stand up for a minute."

"I most . . ."

"Stand up, Abigail!" It was an order.

Mortified and embarrassed, she tightly gripped the sides of the wooden tub and slowly raised herself until she stood knee deep in the water.

The woman circled round the tub impersonally glancing at Abigail. When she finished she waved her back down into the water. "Okay, Jason, you can turn around now," she said.

"Well," he said eagerly, "do you think you can manage?"

"It's a cinch," she laughed. "Anything that I wouldn't be caught dead in will do the trick."

Jason's hardy laughter accompanied his friends as they stood there whispering amongst themselves. Aggravated by their rude behavior, Abigail's face flushed in anger. She watched as the woman looped her arm through Jason's and steered him toward the door. "Ya'know, Jason," she laughed. "She's an honest ta'goodness redhead. No dye job there."

Having all to do to restrain his laughter, Jason turned to close the door but a loud thud stopped him. He glanced down to see the cake of soap at his feet that had been hurled across the room. He stood there shaking his head in a disapproving manner. "Temper, temper, Abigail," he grinned.

Abigail sat sulking in the tub while listening to the sound of their laughter and footsteps as they went down the corridor.

In late afternoon when another tap was heard on the door, Abigail found herself a little reluctant to answering. She hobbled across the floor minus one moccasin. Where the other had disappeared to, she didn't know. She had searched the room in vain. She unlocked the door and in quick stride, Jason pushed past her. His arms were laden with packages which he dumped onto the bed.

"I think this should do it," he said, "everything you'll be needing should be here."

Speechless, Abigail stood there looking at all the packages on the bed.

"Oh, there's one more thing," he murmured. He unbuttoned the front of his shirt and reached into one of the cavities of his money belt. He removed the small piece of paper containing the diamond earrings and held them out to her. "I thought you might want to borrow these for this evening. I know how some ladies feel lost without wearing jewelry. I'll meet you downstairs in the dining room for dinner." He lifted his pocket watch out of his vest pocket, opened it and glanced at the time. "Shall we say for seven that will give you an hour to dress?"

"Seven," she repeated, somewhat bewildered by the mound of packages on the bed and Jason's jubilant mood. She had never seen him like this and she reflected on the idea that perhaps his friend Lucy Stone had something to do with it. She didn't know why, but the thought disturbed her. She stood there with her mouth agape and watched as Jason left the room as hurriedly as he had entered.

Abigail unfolded the small packet of paper in her hand and founded herself staring at a beautiful pair of dainty diamond earrings. Then her glance carried over to the pile of boxes on the bed. The excitement within her began to mount, wondering about their contents. After a short deliberation she decided to open the smallest of the lot first. Ever so carefully she untied the strings on the box to find herself the owner of two new purses; one was black, quite plain and ordinary compared with the other, which was of white silk and beaded with pearls. Suddenly her hands seemed to gain momentum and she found herself tearing the packages open. A comb and brush set, two pairs of shoes plus the missing moccasin she had spent the morning looking for. She quickly grabbed at the larger boxes and found herself the owner of two new shirtwaist dresses, one of pale lavender and the other sky blue. Another large box held an assortment of lace undergarments that sent the color rising to her cheeks at the thought of Jason having purchased them. It wasn't until she opened the last box that a squeal of delight escaped her lips. She unfolded an emerald green dress of the finest cotton that was delicately trimmed about the collar and cuffs with satin. Unmindful of her sore feet she danced about the room holding it to her body and watching the generous folds of the skirt bellow in the air. She stopped suddenly as the thought of dressing in an hour crossed her mind. She flung the dress down on the bed in exchange for the hair brush. Hastily she pulled apart the pigtails in her hair and vigorously sent the brush running through it.

Jason sat in the hotel dining room with eyes fixed on the doorway and one hand curled around a glass of bourbon. The last time he looked at his watch it was going on seven o'clock. A warm grin spread over his lips and his eyes gleamed with admiration. The girl, like a painting, stood framed in the open doorway to the dining room. Just like he had envisioned, her red hair was striking against the emerald green dress she was wearing. That she had chosen that particular dress to wear pleased him. It was the one he had selected.

When she caught sight of him, she descended the steps. He detected a slight limp in her walk as she came across the floor. He sprang to his feet and pulled out the chair opposite him. "You look lovely," he said, as she graced the chair.

Somewhat shocked on hearing his compliment, but please, Abigail smiled, "Thank you."

Jason suddenly realized as he sat down opposite her that he had unconsciously chosen the green dress because it matched her remarkable eyes. He picked up the bottle of wine he had ordered and began filling the empty glass in front of her. "I think you'll like this . . . it's not too strong and most ladies seem to enjoy a glass of wine with their dinner."

Abigail sipped at the wine, having already observed that Jason had also changed his clothes. He was wearing a dark jacket and vest with a white ruffled shirt. "I see that I'm not the only one wearing new attire," she smiled.

"No," he laughed. "I had to buy a new suit." He found himself wondering when he'd ever wear it again other than being laid out in it.

Setting the wine glass down, a serious note edged Abigail's voice, "Jason, I'm afraid you were rather extravagant in your buying. I don't know how I'll ever be able to repay Mr. McFadden for all the articles you've purchased for me."

"I wouldn't worry about it, if I were you."

The tone of his voice told her the subject was closed.

"How do the shoes fit? Are they comfortable?" he asked.

"Fine. Just fine," she said. "It was very clever of you to take the moccasin along for sizing."

Whether it was the wine that had loosened her tongue or the atmosphere of the hotel dining room, but it was the first time they began conversing in a very civil manner. Perhaps it was false courage from the wine, but Abigail no longer feared the man. She was at ease in his company and even found herself laughing at some of the things he was saying. By the end of the evening however, Abigail's curiosity had gotten the best of her as to the rightful owner of the diamond earrings. She nonchalantly touched her ear lobe and said, "These are lovely earrings and I'm quite sure your wife will be pleased by your selection."

He blanked stared at her. "I'm not married," he smiled.

"Oh?" Although surprised touched her face, she couldn't help but wonder why his admission pleased her for the moment. "I was assuming you bought them for your wife."

"I'm afraid there isn't a jewel in the world worthy of the lady those earrings are intended for."

A vague picture of them being worn by Lucy Stone flashed through Abigail's mind. But if they were intended for her, why hadn't he given them to her this morning, she mused.

"You see," he offered, "the lady they're intended for is a rare species of womanhood." Jason watched with amusement as the girl's eyebrows arched in unison with her backbone.

"Pray tell," Abigail snapped, "what is so rare about the lady, may I ask?"

Jason leaned back in his chair and thoughtfully gazed into space while picturing the woman he spoke of. "I find it difficult to put into words, but one can say that she softly walks through life and her cloak is woven of the finest threads; one being kindness and the other gentleness. I myself consider her most prized virtue to be that of patience and warmth," his deep voice trailed off.

The sincerity in his voice was perceptible and Abigail was sorry she had ever asked. He was waiting for her reply. "You're very fortunate to have found such a lady," she murmured.

"Yes, I know I am," he grinned. He began making a mental comparison of the girl sitting opposite him to that of the woman he had spoken of. How different they were, he mused. The girl opposite him was sharp tongued, hot tempered with damnable pride. Why am I concerned about her welfare, he wondered. She's going to marry Albert McFadden and good luck to them. Oddly enough, the thought of her marrying Albert McFadden made his blood boil. He now found her nearness disturbing and began mumbling an excuse in order to leave her company. He stubbed out the cigar he was smoking and abruptly stood up. "I'm sorry I have to leave," he said, forcing a smile. "I have to see about renting a rig and buying some supplies. I'll meet you in the lobby at noon tomorrow. Good night, Abigail."

His abruptness surprised Abigail, and she stared after him as he hastily left the dining room and disappeared from view. She sat there wondering if it was something she had said. She shrugged to herself, picked up the wine glass and drained it of the last few drops that sparkled in the bottom of the glass. Tomorrow, Abigail Whitcomb will arrive at her destination, she mused. What then?

Jason groggily sat up on the edge of the bed holding what he imagined to be shattered pieces of his head in his hands. Through eyelids heavy from sleep he looked around the familiar room. He was thankful that nothing had changed but at the same time wished that it had. The décor of the room was deplorable to him. The brightness hurt his eyes and the clutter made him feel caged in.

"Here, try some of this." Lucy's clicking heels seemed to echo in his head as she crossed the room to where he was sitting. She was scantily clad; a sheer robe draped over her corset. In her outstretched hand she held a cup of steaming hot coffee. Dangling out of the corner of her mouth was along, thin cigar. She was smoking.

Jason reached out for the cup. "Will you please do me a favor and tiptoe out and take that damn cigar out of your mouth."

She gave him a cold, hard stare and ignored his comments as she slipped back into the next room. She plopped herself down in the nearest chair at the table and picked up her cup of coffee. The heavy make-up caked in the lines of her face as she frowned in thought. Setting the cup aside in exchange for a deck of cards that were on the table, she began to play a game of solitaire.

Minus a boot, Jason came hobbling into the room. "Did you see my other boot around here?"

Languidly, Lucy raised her and pointed to the red satin settee where his boot lay on the floor.

"Thanks," he said, sitting down on the edge of the settee. He picked up his boot and sat there, struggling with it. "Okay, Lucy, let's have it, what's bothering you?" he asked.

"Nothing."

"Hell's bells, Lucy, I know you long enough to know that the only time you smoke them damn cigars is when you're mad."

She didn't answer but drew harder on the cigar sending smoke rings floating into the air.

Jason rose from the couch and leaned on the table squarely facing her. "Let's have it. What's wrong?"

Her move startled him as she sprang from the chair. Her hands went flying into the air as she started pacing back and forth across the room. "You, me, the whole thing is wrong," she shrilled.

A puzzled frown crossed Jason's face as he looked at her with concern. They had been friends for years and it was the first time he could remember her yelling at him. He had often seen her temper, but never directed at him. An odd feeling stole over him as he looked at her. Perhaps she had met someone else while he was gone and this was her way of breaking up their friendship. "Have you met someone?" he asked.

She glared at him. "No! It's not that. You know I'd have told you."

He smiled with a sense of relief. Yes, she would have told him straight out. One thing about their relationship, they had always been honest with each other. More so than some married folks, he thought. "Damn it. What is it?" he roared.

"It's you, Jason."

"Me?" He blankly stared at her.

Lucy sucked in her breath. "Damn it, Jason, you were so tender and so. . . as if I were a virgin!" she exploded.

He burst out in a roar of laughter. "And you're made at me for that!"

"Damn you, Jason. Don't you understand," she shrilled. "It wasn't me you were making love to, but another woman and I hate you for it!"

He shook his head as if clearing it. "What the hell are you talking about, Lucy? As far as I remember, I went to bed with you."

She stared at him in disbelief. "Oh, Jason, is it possible you don't know?"

"Know what? I thought I had a lot to drink last night but something tells me you're still tipsy. I don't even know what the hell you're talking about."

"Jason," she sighed, "you're in love with that Abigail girl. Can't you see that?"

He raised his hand and pointed a finger in her face. "Now. . . now I know you're crazy."

"Am I?"

"Don't even joke like that, Lucy," he warned.

"I'm not joking, Jason," she said evenly. "Maybe it takes another woman to know these things, but last night it wasn't me you were sleeping with but her. I only wish it had been me."

He clenched his hands several times over. "Abigail Whitcomb is going to marry Albert McFadden. My job was to see that she arrived here safely and that's all that there was to it."

"That well may be, but it so happens you've fallen in love with the girl."

Anger got the best of him; he crossed the floor to where she was standing, reached up and pulled the cigar out of her mouth. He roughly drew her to him and kissed her full on the mouth. "Why, she's nothing but a scrawny kid to me," he grinned.

"Nice try," Lucy said, pushing herself free. "But it won't work. I know when someone is trying to bamboozle me. You better look again, she's no scrawny kid."

Jason's hands fell helplessly to his sides and he swore under his breath.

Lucy turned her back on him and walked over to the window. She had a clear view of the main street in town. "We'll see," she murmured. "You'd better get a move on, she's probably sitting in the lobby of the hotel waiting for you right this minute."

"Damn it," he roared. "Let her wait!"

Silently he finished buttoning his shirt and then picked up his jacket. His glance slowly swept Lucy's back as she stood at the window. "Thanks, Lucy," he said forcing a smile. "I'll be seeing you the next time I come to town."

"Yeah, be seeing you," she said flatly, staring out the window but seeing nothing

As the door softly closed behind him, Lucy reached up and brushed at the silent tears that ran down her cheeks. "Good-bye, Jason," she whispered against the pane of glass as she watched his lean figure cross the street. Suddenly his pace seemed to quicken as he headed in the direction of the hotel.

"Men," Lucy said in disgust. "None of them are any damn good." She turned from the window, picked up the cigar and wedged it between her teeth. She plopped down in the chair and shuffled the deck of cards.

On entering the hotel lobby Jason spotted the girl sitting in the far corner of the room. Her head was buried in her book of poetry. A pang of guilt ran through him on seeing her in the blue calico dress that Lucy Stone had picked out. But more disturbing was hearing Lucy's words still ringing in his ears; "You're in love with that Abigail girl." As he watched the girl a surge of warmth ran through his body and he cursed under his breath when realizing that Lucy had seen in him something he hadn't realized until that very moment. He had fallen in love with what he considered a red headed spitfire of a girl. Mixed emotions surged through him as he looked at her. One was knowing he loved her, and the other was knowing he could never have her.

As if sensing his presence the girl glanced up at him and hastily closed the book. A warm smile spread over her lips. "Good morning, Jason."

He avoided the green eyes that looked up at him and asked, "Did you eat?"

"Yes, I've eaten."

"Good. I'll see to the tally, and then we can be on our way."

Outside, as they walked the three blocks to the livery stable, out of the corner of his eye Jason could see the girl struggling to keep up with his stride. He slowed his pace.

After tying the stallion and pony to the back of the rig, Jason climbed up and took his place beside the girl. He untied the reins, clucked at the horse and started them into motion. The rig rocked and jounced on the deeply rutted dirt road leaving a trail of cloudy dust as it moved westward to the outskirts of town.

Beth was conscious of the stillness in the air as well as the stillness in the man sitting next to her. "How long of a journey is it?" she asked.

He shot her a sideward glance. "About an hour's ride on the main road and then another half hour's ride after we reach the cutoff," he offered. "We should be there way before sun down."

At the thought of having to face Mr. McFadden, the nervous tension within her began to mount. What would he do to her when she told him the truth? Mentally, she began rehearsing what she would say. The thought of Jason hearing the truth panicked her. Wasn't he anticipating to be handsomely rewarded by Mr. McFadden for the safety of Abigail Whitcomb? Not one penny would be paid for Beth Carney, she thought. She stole a look at the finely chiseled features of the face of the man sitting next to her. The hard-set line of his jawbone brought one thought to mind; I'll be dead by nightfall.

Unexpectedly, as if seized with a compulsion to talk, Jason's voice interrupted her thoughts. Oddly enough, he repetitiously warned her of the hard and lonely life that was in store for her. Added to this were numerous chores that would be expected of her. With the exception of riding a horse and driving a wagon and using a rifle as well as any man, her hands had tackled some of the chores he had named.

That he had spoken in earnest was obvious, and for one inexplicable moment she had the feeling he was sorry to see her come to America.

Again he sank into his own silence and Beth found herself studying the countryside. There was a loneliness to the vastness of flat land that seemed to surround them. She only remembered passing one home since they had left Abilene, a log cabin.

"Abigail, move closer to the outside edge of your seat."

The command in his voice was enough to make her move without question. She watched as he fingered his holster and brought his hand to rest on his knee. His eyes were fixed in a hard stare on the roadway ahead.

In the distance she could see what appeared to be two men on horseback approaching. As they drew closer, Jason slowed the pace of the team. In the bend of the road the men had reined their horses sideways, blocking the cut off. The rig stopped short but a few feet in front of them.

"Well, will you look what we have here now?" The taller of the two drawled as a sardonic smile tightened across his lips. His companion's beady eyes were already studying Abigail.

"Funny, I was just saying to Frank the other day, wonder where good old Jason's been keeping hisself. Didn't I, Frank?"

"Yeah, yeah, just the other day." Frank O'Conner parroted.

Although Jason nodded his head in understanding, he could not contain the venom in his voice. "I went to

219

Europe. I wasn't aware of your missing me or I would have hurried back sooner."

Slim the taller of the two, forced a laugh that was immediately taken up by his brother. "Mind your manners, Jason, and introduce us to the lady."

Jason forced a smile while managing to keep his temper in check. "Abigail Whitcomb, I'd like you to meet Slim and Frank O'Conner."

Slim O'Conner removed his hat and stood up in his stirrups. With hat in hand he made a sweeping gesture like that of a bow.

Abigail silently nodded her head. Her instincts warned her that the two men meant trouble. By the look of them alone she was appalled. The breeze carried the stench of them in the air and the restlessness about them was quite notable.

Slim O'Conner's smile quickly faded into anger. "Does she know? Does the young lady know she's traveling with a half-breed, Jason?"

"Know what, Mr. O'Conner?" Abigail demanded. For the second time she was provoked by the rude manners of Americans who always seemed to talk around her but not directly to her.

"Why ma'am, Jason here is a half-breed, ya'know. One part of him is white while the other part of him is—Injun."

It was the first time Jason looked over at the girl and he was sorry he did. He would never forget the look in her eyes as long as he lived.

Quickly recovering from the impact of the shock, Abigail turned to face the man. "I'm well aware of Mr.

Rockwell's origin," she lied. "And if you and your brother would kindly move your horses, Mr. O'Conner, we would like to be on our way."

The clear note of authority in her voice baffled the O'Conner brothers.

"She sure talks funny," Frank frowned.

"That's the way ladies talk, stupid."

Frank O'Conner glared at his brother. "Who you calling stupid?"

"You, little brother," Slim laughed, and unmercifully dug his spurs into the animal's side. The horse reared and Slim uttered a loud hoot and set the horse into a fast gallop down the road. An angered Frank O'Conner followed, biting the dust in pursuit of his brother.

Jason picked up the reins and turned the rig onto the cutoff, conscious of an acute silence that hung between them.

"Why didn't you tell me?"

Her voice was barely audible yet each word cut into him like a knife. "I had my reasons."

"What possible reason . . . "she stopped.

He had pulled at the reins bringing the rig to an abrupt stop. He turned and squarely faced her. His brown eyes bored into hers. "I had enough trouble getting you this far without your knowledge that I was part Indian. Can you imagine what it would have been like had you known?" he sneered.

She didn't answer, although a lot of things began to make sense to her. His skin coloring, for one thing, and the way he was accepted into the small village of Cheyenne people and the fact that he spoke their language.

"I'll tell you what it would have been like," he scowled. "Every minute of the day you'd have been scared out of your wits wondering when I would slit that pretty throat of yours. Or perhaps, scalp your copper locks, rape you or inflict some treacherous torture that us so called Injuns are known for."

His voice dripping with sarcasm sent the color rising to her face. He turned in his seat, pulled at the reins and clucked at the horses, sending the rig into motion.

It was sometime later before he chose to speak to her again. "My mother is Cheyenne and my father was a white man. Now don't misunderstand, I'm not apologizing for them," he said curtly.

Whatever led him to believe an apology should be had, she thought. Suddenly she was conscious of the deep scars within the man himself. Scars obviously inflicted by being born a child of a mixed marriage. How strange, she mused, when her own suffering was caused by being born an orphan and never having known her parents. Now, fully aware of fate having dealt both of them a difficult hand, she began to reevaluate her judgment of the man sitting beside her. A feeling of compassion was aroused in her for a man who, only a few days ago, she thought she despised. Perhaps her acquaintance with him under such extraordinary and perilous circumstances may have clouded her judgment. But wait, she thought, wait until he finds out my true identity.

Chapter Nine

The sunset on the horizon set the wheat fields ablaze. Jason thoughtfully studied the fields while Beth's interest was drawn to the house that suddenly loomed in the distance. A faint line of smoke could be seen coming out the chimney and spiraling upward in the sky. She could see the large, open front porch that ran the length of the house. The only greenery around the house was a cluster of trees for shade. Aside from that, the rest of the land was flat and rather desolate to the eye. Beyond the house was a barn with a corral where two horses freely roamed.

Suddenly, from around the back of the house, a young girl appeared holding a bucket in her hand. She headed directly for the water pump on the side of the house and set the bucket beneath it and began priming the pump vigorously. On hearing the wagon approach, she stopped, raised her hand to her forehead and peered in their direction. She stood there watching the wagon.

Beth's stomach suddenly felt squeamish. Although she had thought of this moment many times, now that it was at hand she was frightened. Once the truth was known she could only wonder what would happen to her.

As Jason turned the wagon onto the dirt road leading to the house Beth spied the sign hanging on a post. It stated: Welcome to Safe Haven. There was something comforting about the name of the farm but it could hardly apply to the circumstances of her being there.

They were halfway down the road when the young girl picked up her skirt and as if the devil were biting at her heels, came running towards them. "Jason! Jason!" she squealed with delight.

He pulled at the reins stopping the wagon and tied them to the whip stock before jumping down to meet her halfway. Within a few feet of him she stopped in her tracks as if overcome by shyness. Then, laughing, she lunged forward into the arms there were held wide to greet her. Their laughter echoed across the open fields as he lifted the girl off the ground and swung her around in the air before setting her back down on her feet and planting a kiss on her forehead.

The front door of the house opened and a young boy came running down the porch steps two at a time. The young boy also got the same treatment but, instead of a kiss, a hug and a handshake followed.

From where she sat Beth watched their joyful reunion and found herself smiling as they came walking toward the wagon. After Jason helped her down and introduced her, Beth found herself being steered toward the porch steps where an older man stood watching them. He was a robust looking man with gray hair that still held traces of red. In his right hand he held a cane. It was the hugeness of the man that made Beth's legs suddenly feel weak. If anything, by appearance alone, she wouldn't want him for her enemy.

"Before you ask, Jason," he smiled, "your mother is fine."

"Thank you," Jason said, climbing the steps to shake hands. An understanding smile passed between the two men.

Hugh McFadden's gaze carried past Jason and to the young redheaded girl who forlornly looked up at him. "Abigail?"

Beth hesitated for a second, then anxiously nodded her head and stumbled up the steps and into the arms that were held open to receive her. "Welcome to our home, Abigail," Hugh McFadden smiled down at her and planted a fatherly kiss on her forehead while warmly embracing her.

The friendliness of the old man seemed to regenerate her very being and she found herself smiling up into the warmest blue eyes she had ever seen. Later, she thought, there'd be time enough to tell him the truth but at the moment she was experiencing something new in her life. Meeting Hugh McFadden was one thing, but to be welcomed with such sincere love from all was a new experience and she desperately wanted to savor the moment.

She found herself being caught up in a whirlwind. Everything seemed to be happening at once. She had a vague recollection of Jenny showing her their comfortable home and what was to be her own private room. Anxiously running back and forth to the wagon to bring in her belongings was the boy Timothy. Ceaseless questions about her trip were being asked with genuine concern. But, most of all, there was an unmistakable joy of their wanting her with them. Laughter seemed to ripple forth like a waterfall.

The excitement of the day finally subsided as they sat down to their evening meal that the young girl Jenny had prepared. A substantial meal, Beth noted, but lacking that of culinary skill. She sat there half heartily listening to the conversation at the table that of a number of questions put forth by Timothy as to their having stayed at an Indian village. A feeling of remorse suddenly stole over Beth knowing it would all end soon; the truth had to be spoken. It was while she was helping Jenny clear off the table and wash the dishes that Timothy came into the kitchen to fetch her. She was summoned to join Hugh McFadden and Jason in the parlor.

The minute Beth entered the parlor, by the grave look on their faces, she knew something was amiss. With trembling legs she quickly graced the chair that Jason had offered her. Surprisingly, he knelt down beside her chair and before she realized what was happening, he took hold of her trembling hand in his as if to comfort her. "I'm sorry, Abigail," he said, a sincere note of warmth in his voice. "I'm sorry to have to be the one to tell you this, but your uncle, John Whitcomb, has passed away. It seems he had a heart attack on the very day your ship set sail."

"John Whitcomb's dead," she gasped.

"Yes, my dear," Hugh McFadden said sorrowfully. "I received a letter last week telling me of the unfortunate circumstances. I'm truly sorry, Abigail, but I want you to know that although there is no inheritance to speak of, he did authorize me to be your guardian. I deem it a privilege and our home will be your home."

The last thing Beth remembered was tightly gripping the hand that held hers as the room began to spin and blackness ensued. When she regained consciousness she found herself lying on the settee and a concerned Jason, with a glass in hand, was sitting beside her.

"Here," he said, holding the glass to her lips, "take a couple of sips. It's brandy. You'll feel better."

She followed his orders with a thousand thoughts flashing to mind. John Whitcomb was dead, Abigail Whitcomb was dead; how could she tell them the truth after such distressing news? Why couldn't it have been me that died instead of Abigail? God, what am I to do?

"It's been a very trying day for you, my dear," Hugh McFadden said sympathetically. "I'll get Jenny to take you to your room and, after a food night's sleep, you'll feel better."

The words of Sir Walter Scott came floating to Beth's mind; Oh, what a tangled web we weave when first we practice to deceive. There was so much she had to think about. "Yes," Beth murmured. "Yes, I think I'll go to my room if you don't mind."

Jason helped her to her feet and with a comforting arm around her waist Jenny led her across the floor. Halfway across the room, as if remembering her manners, she turned and looked at Jason. "Thank you, Jason," she murmured, "thank you for all your kindness."

He silently nodded his head in answer as he stared after her.

For the longest time, Beth lay in bed staring up at the ceiling, her mind muddled in thought. The death of John Whitcomb had shocked her and left her without the recourse of writing him a letter and telling him the truth about his niece. Now Hugh McFadden deemed it a privilege to be chosen her guardian. She had no family, or friends, or money, where would she go? What was to become of her? It was clear that all doors opened to a girl named Abigail Whitcomb while the name, Beth Carney, was of little value but to herself. Wasn't it Shakespeare who wrote, "What's in a name? That which we call a rose by any other name would smell as sweet." With this thought in mind Beth sprang from bed and walked over to the small mirror that hung over the dresser. She stood there peering into the mirror at her reflection. What would change? Certainly not her personality or her heart; she'd still be the same person only answering to another name. With the name of Abigail Whitcomb came a guardian, Hugh McFadden, and most of all, a family. For the longest time she just stood there staring at her reflection until she could summon up the courage and finally say, "Good-bye, Beth Carney, Good-bye." She blew out the candle and went to bed.

Within one week of living with the McFadden family, Beth knew she had made the right decision. For the first time in her life, she felt like she truly belonged and was part of a family.

Life on a farm was hard work, but not without compensations. There was always plenty of food to eat and the joy of watching your endeavors take hold.

On the south side of the house Abigail started a flower garden. In the cool of some evenings she would plant all the wildflowers she had gathered during the day while working out in the fields planting with the rest of the family. Other evenings she'd sit on the porch with Hugh McFadden and listen to his expectations of what the farm would be like in a couple of years. It would yield enough crops to be sold at market and make a profit to comfortably support the family. His dreams became hers.

It was on such an evening that Abigail truly saw the fair-mindedness in the man himself. "I know you are betrothed to my oldest son, Albert, and that was the full intentions for your coming here. Now with the death of your Uncle John, no doubt you will want the proper time to mourn and a wedding at this time would be out of the question. I will respect your wishes whatever they may be, Abigail, but this much I want you to know; whether you marry my son Albert or decide otherwise, there will always be a home for you here with us. You're free to do what pleases you, my dear." From this, Abigail gathered that he truly loved her like a daughter and put her happiness first.

One night she learned, quite by accident, that Jason Rockwell had voluntarily seen to the safety of her journey without compensation as he had led her to believe. Nor did he submit a bill for all the purchases he had made on her behalf. The strangeness of the man often perplexed Abigail whenever she thought about him. Oddly enough, something would occur that would remind her of him like at the moment, as she walked home after help planting the corn field, her back hurt from bending over, her hands rough and grimy. But all her cares seemed to fade as she looked at the rows of tall stalks of corn growing on each side of the path. She had left the fields earlier than usual to prepare supper before the rest of the family came home.

Her first thoughts on approaching the house were to go inside and wash up, but as she passed her flower garden, on seeing some unsightly weeds, automatically she leaned over and began pulling them out. Before long, she was down on her hands and knees tidying up the flower bed and totally absorbed in her work.

"Do my eyes behold a living and breathing hybrid rose amongst the wildness of these flowers, or is it a fragment of my imagination. Speak so I know my eyes are not tormenting me."

Abigail's head snapped round to see a man standing in the kitchen doorway. He was fair headed, slim of stature and noticeably handsome. A soft smile covered his lips. How long had he been standing there watching her, she wondered, while slowly rising to her feet. "May I help you?" she frowned.

"Ah," he smiled. "She is a real rose amongst the wildflowers; my eyes do not deceive me. By chance would her name be, Abigail?"

"Y. . . yes," she stammered. "But you have the advantage of me, sir. What is your name?"

He smiled, "Albert. . . Albert McFadden."

A high flush of color rose to her cheeks. She had envisioned meeting him many times, but not under such conditions. Her hair was unsightly, her hands grimy and her clothes untidy. Self-consciously she brushed at the wisps of hair that clung to the sides of her face. "Welcome home, Albert," she managed to say evenly while brushing the dirt from her hands.

His bold blue eyes slowly swept her. "And happy I am to be home."

In the months that followed life at Safe Haven farm, with Albert's intervention, suddenly changed for Abigail. It was beyond any joy that she had imagined. His devoted attention to her comfort and pleasure overwhelmed her, as well as his generosity. Whenever he went to town he'd bring back a small present for her, pearl combs for her hair, a book of poetry, a pair of garnet earrings. Socially, her life also changed. On Saturday nights, he'd take Jenny, Timothy and her to a church function where there'd be dancing or a play. On several occasions, with the excuse of having to meet someone in town on business, he'd leave them and pick them up later and take them home.

Under his guidance Abigail learned to drive a team of horses and her fear of guns soon diminished. Albert taught her how to use a rifle and took pride in her becoming such a good marksman.

Although he never gave voice to his love for her, oddly enough, she would find love letters written in his bold hand lying on her bed pillow at night when she entered her room. Several times he wrote her lengthy letters declaring his admiration and love for her, and a proposal of marriage. She supposed this was his way of addressing the subject without giving offense to her state of mourning.

Slowly, Abigail began to admire and respect Albert, but was in no haste to be married.

Chapter Ten

The night's heavy rainfall had left the streets of Abilene ankle deep in mud. From his office window, Sheriff Blake Saunders watched the six o'clock stagecoach as it pulled up in front of the hotel. Out of habit, he made it his business to know who came and who left Abilene of their own accord. From where he was standing he had a bird's eye view of each passenger without their knowledge. His three years of experience as sheriff taught him to judge the cut of a man, or woman for that matter, in one easy glance. From the heavy mug that he held in his hand Blake took a sip of black coffee and watched with interest as the first passenger stepped down, out of the coach.

A man stepped down who Blake judged to be about his own age, middle thirties. He was short and stocky, wearing a store-bought suit. A tinhorn salesman from the East, who never did a hard day's lick of work in his life, except run off his mouth, Blake mused. The man turned and stretched out his hand to help a woman down. She looked like an overdressed, stuffed peacock as she stood smiling and laughing up into the man's face. She held tight the arm he offered as they entered the hotel, like a dance hall girl selling her wares. Definitely not the man's wife, probably his traveling companion, Blake concluded.

Blake relaxed knowing that the two strangers were far from a threat to his sleepy, peaceful town. He was about to turn from the window when he saw a third party slowly stepping down out of the coach. It was a woman, the likes of which Blake had rarely seen in this part of the country, a young Mexican woman. She stood gazing up and down the street as if deciding which way to go. She was poorly clothed against the harsh autumn winds. There was a pathetic look about her, but she stood straight and proud as if above all pity, barricading herself from her fellow man.

Blake felt a prickle as the hairs on the back of his neck began to rise, a familiar omen that the girl meant trouble.

"Sure enough, she's gone and done it!" Blake snorted as he put down the mug in his hand and hastily headed for the door.

Outside Blake looked up and down the street for help, but at this early hour the streets of Abilene were empty. His boots sucked deep in the mud as he ran over to the woman; she was sprawled on her side in the muddy road. Her eyes were closed and there was a chalky pallor to her skin. Blake leaned over and effortlessly scooped her up in his arms along with a small worn carpetbag that she had been carrying. She was weightless. He mumbled, "When was the last time you've eaten, girl?"

Inside the jailhouse, Blake laid her down on his cot rather than on one in the back cells and was quite taken with seeing her up close. She was younger than he had suspected twenty-three or thereabouts; a fine looking woman whom he found pleasing in face as well as figure. He helplessly looked about, deciding what to do next when he remembered her baggage. He had second thoughts about opening it, but then reminded himself that he was the law. He sifted through the contents of the baggage, only to find another change of clothes. He was about to give up hope when he spied the small piece of paper tucked in an old shoe. A deep frown spread over his face as he unfolded the paper and tried to decipher the four words written in childish, misspelled scrawl. He finally made out the words to read Albert McFadden, farmer, Kansas. With renewed interest he glanced from the paper in his hand to the girl lying on the cot. How the likes of a poor Mexican girl knew McFadden other than being hired help baffled Blake. With this thought in mind he went back to the cot and turned to the task of washing the caked mud from the girl's face.

To the cold wetness of the cloth, the girl's eyes blinked open. Intent on what he was doing, a few moments passed before Blake realized she was watching him. Under her large, brown questioning eyes he felt a bit foolish and awkwardly stood up.

"You fainted smack in the middle of the road," he told her.

She didn't answer. Her glance slowly swept over him and came to rest on the silver badge pinned to his shirt.

"I'm Sheriff Saunders," he offered, wishing she would say something instead of staring at him. Suddenly he realized that perhaps she didn't understand a word he was saying. The few words of Spanish he knew flashed to mind only to be rejected for being profanity. He helplessly glanced about, uneasy under her intensive stare. He wondered how a small creature like her had the ability to make a man of his size feel self conscious. He caught her eyeing the coffee pot that was sitting on the black potbellied stove and was angry at himself for not thinking of it sooner. He went over and poured a cup of coffee and brought it back to where she lay. Slowly, she sat up on the edge of the cot accepting his hospitality. Her face shriveled up like a prune to the first sip of black coffee and Blake, laughing, ran for the sugar bowl. She weakly smiled up at him as he held the sugar bowl out to her. It was a warm smile displaying a beautiful set of even white teeth, but it lacked something. Blake realized the warmth of her smile never reached her eyes. Cold, penetrating, they watched his every move.

One thing for certain, she wasn't afraid of him or any living creature on God's earth. Like a mirror, her eyes reflected her true feelings and Blake was disturbed by what he saw. The sugar bowl became lost in his large, strong hands as he fumbled with it. "No one around here speaks Spanish; don't ask me what I'm going to do with you lady."

She was leaning over studying her mud covered skirt. "There's no need that you find someone who speaks Espanola," she said.

Blake spun around to the soft murmur of her words. A broad grin covered his face. He was pleased by the fact that she spoke English, but more so, by the soft quality of her voice.

She stood up facing him with eyes searching the room. "Is there a place where I change the clothes?" she asked.

"Yeah. . . yeah sure," he stammered. "You can use one of the empty cells in back."

She made a move toward her baggage but Blake beat her to it. He picked it up and led the way to the small spare room, next to one of the cells that he used for himself. "I wasn't expecting company," he laughed, quickly picking up his clothes that were strewn around the room. There was a full pitcher of water and a basin standing on top of the dresser. Pushing his shaving mug and razor aside, he made room for her baggage.

The girl never said a word but somehow he knew she wasn't offended by the unsightly room. He backed out the door, closed it, and took a deep breath before making a beeline for the hotel across the street.

A half hour later, when Blake returned, he found the girl standing next to the stove drying the sleeve of her jacket that had been covered with mud. Her shiny black hair was neatly combed and pulled back, accentuating her high cheek bones. She had changed into a clean blouse and skirt. There was a look of distinction about her compared with the women he had left.

Blake set the tray that he was carrying down on his desk and carefully weighed his words, hoping they'd sound convincing. "I took the liberty of getting us some breakfast. It's not everyday that I have company. I hate eating alone and a sheriff's job is mighty lonely at times."

Distrustfully, her glance carried from him to the tray; a spark of anger shown in the brown eyes. She arched her back and stood straight as if her feathers had suddenly been ruffled. "No. . ."

"What's so bad about eating breakfast with a sheriff?" Blake said indignantly.

She thought for a moment. "Nada, I believe."

"Well good! Let's eat!" Blake knew if he waited long enough the aroma of the food would win her over even if he couldn't. He busied himself with arranging the two plates, each containing fried eggs, hash brown potatoes and sliced ham. He set the tray aside and refilled their coffee cups.

A little apprehensive, the girl slowly walked over and hung her jacket over the back of the chair before sitting down. Blake took his usual seat behind his desk and began to eat. Halfway through the meal he asked, "What's your name?"

"Juanita, Juanita Hernandez," she murmured.

"Well, Juanita, are you planning to stay long in Abilene?" he asked, only to realize he was sounding like a sheriff.

"I no sure."

Remembering the piece of paper he had found in her baggage he asked, "Do you have any friends here in Abilene?"

She was toying with the last piece of ham on her plate. She looked up with eyes squarely meeting his. "No, I know nobody." Then, she smiled and added, "Except you."

The humor in her reply brought a smile to Blake's face. Unconsciously he found himself studying her hands. Although tan, they appeared soft and smooth. Each nail was long and tapered, hardly the hands of a woman whose daily work was toilsome.

With a sigh, she set down the cup in her hand. "Gracias, Sheriff that was muy delicioso."

"You're quite welcome." Blake was pleased by the sight of the empty dish and the color returning to her cheeks.

"What are you planning to do now?" he asked.

Juanita slowly rose to her feet and picked up her jacket and slipped into it. "I look for work," she said, buttoning the jacket.

Blake frowned. "There isn't much work to be had around here at this time of year."

She leaned over, picked up her baggage and headed for the door. Just before opening it she hesitated, turned and looked at the big strapping man sitting behind the desk. A sad, sardonic smile touched the corners of her mouth. "That's where you are wrong, Senor. Always there is work for a woman like me. In every pueblo in all the seasons of the year." she softly closed the door behind her, leaving Blake Saunders, who had just finished eating a second breakfast on her behalf, with an empty feeling in the pit of his stomach.

Chapter Eleven

Abigail raised an arm to brush at the small beads of perspiration that dotted her forehead and continued to divide the large mound of dough she'd been kneading into four equal parts. At moments like this, her thoughts reflected on Maggie Cosgrove bustling about in the large kitchen of Chesterton Hall. On remembering, tears welled up. Maggie would be proud of me, she thought, as her glance carried over the small kitchen. She had made the kitchen clean and functional; it held a certain charm, what with the curtains and tablecloths that she had made. Many times over she had blessed Maggie for teaching her how to cook. Here in the wilderness, fresh fruits and scores of items were considered a luxury and one had to make do with what the earth would yield. With the basic knowledge of what Maggie had taught her, and her own improvisation, she managed to set halfway decent meals on the table and surprised the McFadden family as well as herself.

In the months of living with the McFadden family, everyone else seemed to remain the same, except for her. True, she helped Timothy and Jenny with their lessons, but in a sense she had come to have a broader education. She could husk corn as well as any man and fire a rifle and hit what she aimed at. She learned to drive a team of horses as if the devil were after them and milk a cow without wasting a precious drop. The one thorn in her side was the fact that she had not mastered the art of riding a horse, a necessity in these parts. She had tried under Albert's supervision, but within a short time he'd lose patience with her. With an air of self-satisfaction Abigail covered the four loaves of bread and had contrived to putting the hour before the bread would rise to good use. She would go riding.

A determined Abigail headed for the barn to saddle the only horse in the stable, a large stallion named Charger. It took some doing, but she managed to saddle the horse and mount it and in a slow trot leave the barn.

On approaching the main fork in the road, Abigail pulled at the reins, deciding which way to go. To avoid meeting with Timothy and his father, who were working the south field, she chose to go west. She smiled to herself on the new adventure of exploring a new territory.

After a half hour of trotting along on the main road, she began to feel confident. The wide open grassland that ran parallel with the dusty road began to look inviting. She pulled at the reins, diverting Charger into the grassland and at a full gallop started across the field. The excitement within Abigail began to mount as she and horse became one. The wind played havoc with her long hair and the crispness of the autumn air bit her cheeks. The exhilarating sound of the horse's hooves drove her on. The countryside became a blur to her vision as she egged the horse on and her thoughts aimlessly drifted.

It was the sudden loud shout of her name that brought Abigail back to reality. She glanced over her shoulder to see the familiar figure of a horse and rider relentlessly following her. There appeared to be a promise of a race at hand. Throwing caution to the wind, Abigail spurred the horse on as her pursuer appeared to be gaining ground. It was too late when she realized his shouts were meant in warning. Out of the brush a stone wall loomed up in front of her. The last thing she spotted was the small log cabin in the clearing beyond the wall. The ground came up to meet her as Charger scaled the wall with one smooth arch of his back that sent Abigail flying through the air.

A stunned and dazed Abigail lay sprawled out on her side. When she raised her head, a sharp pain tore through her right side taking her breath away. She inched over on her back and propped herself up on her elbows as the hoof beats of her pursuer's horse came to a halt but a few feet away from her.

"What the hell were you trying to do, kill yourself?" he said, jumping down off his horse. Within three strides he towered over her.

Through blurred vision Abigail looked up into his drained but angry face. "It seems," she gasped, "I'm to be indebted to you once more, Mr. Roc..k..." She succumbed to the ensuing blackness that finally engulfed her.

Jason's arm shot out circling her shoulders before her head could hit the ground. "Abigail?"

She didn't answer.

"Damn you woman," he snorted, pushing his free hand beneath the folds of her skirt. Gently his hands ran the length of her legs checking each in turn for broken bones. Satisfied, he began to lift her into his arms and to the pressure of his hand on her side an involuntary groan escaped her lips. He shook his head in dismay as he carefully lifted her from the ground.

Through the heavy brush he carried her along the length of the wall until he came to an opening. His steps quickened as he headed directly for the cabin not more than twenty paces away. Using his shoulder he pushed the front door open, crossed the parlor floor and entered one of the bedrooms situated in the back part of the cabin. Her small frame appeared lost in the massive bed as Jason carefully laid her down.

Tilting her chin to one side, he carefully examined the small cut on the side of her forehead. It was beginning to swell. In exasperation he glanced down at her clothed body wondering where to beginning while facing the task of having to undress her.

Just as he suspected, when he got down to removing her petticoat the rib cage on the right side of her body was badly bruised. At the foot of the bed he began ripping the bottom of the sheet into long strips and with painstaking effort, he bandaged her rib cage. He stood up and couldn't help but admire his work. On seeing the small beating pulse in the hollow of her throat he sucked in his breath as his eyes traveled to the inviting softness of her full rounded breasts. He leaned over and slowly drew the blanket up, covering her nakedness. "Believe me woman," he said in warning. "The next time I have to undress you, it will be for my pleasure."

It was while he was seeing to the deep cut on her hand that he sensed someone standing in the doorway watching. He turned around to see his mother standing there with a meaningful smile on her face.

"It's not what you're thinking," he said.

"And what am I thinking?

"That I brought home a wife."

"Can you blame me? I would like to have grandchildren someday." She crossed the floor and stood on the other side of the bed looking down at the young girl lying there. "Who is she?'

"It's Abigail. She's had a pretty bad spill from a horse."

"Mmm. . . so this is Abigail," she smiled, leaned over and examined the bruise on the young girl's head. "You never told me she was a beauty."

He didn't answer. "I had to tape up her ribs. It's possible she fractured them. She's badly bruised on her right side."

"When did this happen?"

"About a half hour ago."

"You better ride over and tell Hugh; he's probably worried sick about her."

"What I can't understand is, what the deuce was she doing riding Charger? He's too strong of a horse for her. Why wasn't somebody with her?" he frowned.

"I met Jenny and Albert. They were going into town for supplies and I saw Hugh and Timothy working in the south field."

"That explains it,"" Jason said, shaking his head from side to side. "She took it upon herself to ride Charger. She's as pigheaded as a mule. Had Hugh or

Albert been there, they never would have allowed it. She's lucky she didn't break her damn fool neck."

"I'll see to her. It's best you go and tell Hugh what's happened."

Midway across the floor Jason stopped and turned around to look at his mother.

"What's wrong?" she asked.

"When she wakes up she's liable to ask about her ribs being taped."

With a fluttering hand, a smiling Gay Feather shooed her son toward the door. "To save her the embarrassment I'll tell her I did it, all right?"

"If I didn't know better, I'd swear you're happy over what's happened."

A soft chuckled escaped her lips. "I guess in a way I am. It will be nice having another female in the house to talk to instead of a grouchy son."

Abigail's eyes blinked open and in mild confusion searched the strange room in wonder. She raised a hand to her head and winced with pain. Slowly she began to recall her spill from the horse and Jason Rockwell's appearance. She became conscious of the tightness of the bandaging around the rib cage of her body with each breath taken, and at the same time the strangeness of the white night dress she was wearing. She lifted the collar of the gown to have a better look at it.

"I'm afraid it's a bit large for you."

To the sound of the voice Abigail turned her head to see an older woman come walking into the room carrying a tray in her hands. Her hair was severely pulled back, accentuating her high cheek bones. A crown of black braids, with strains of silver running through, encircled her head. It was the dainty diamond earrings she wore that gave her cause to wonder. She remembered only too well Jason's description of the woman who would rightfully own them. She softly walks through life and her cloak is woven of the finest threads, one being kindness, the other gentleness.

"How are you feeling, Abigail? May I call you Abigail?'

To both questions a dumbfounded Abigail nodded her head. She was enthralled by the gracious way in which the woman carried herself and her stunning beauty. She watched as she set the tray down on the night stand. There was something hauntingly familiar about the woman's face. The high cheekbones, the whiteness of her teeth as she smiled and the dark brown eyes that held a glint of amusement in them, all so familiar to her. Out of a startling realization she asked, "Are. . . are you Jason's mother?"

"Yes," she softly chuckled. "My name is Gay Feather."

"Your resemblance to your son is striking," Abigail blurted out.

"You seem surprised at my being here. Didn't Jason tell you that I lived with him?"

"No," Abigail honestly admitted only to notice the injured look on the woman's face. Immediately, she clarified her statement. "He did tell me that his mother's people were Cheyenne, but aside from that, Jason and I rarely held what one would consider a civil conversation."

"Then let me apologize for my son's ill-manners," Gay Feather smiled.

"Oh no, you shouldn't apologize. I'm afraid that I was partly to blame. I'd be beholden to you if you could lend me a wagon so I could return home."

Her request surprised Gay Feather. "You're in no condition to travel, child."

"I can't stay here."

"Why not?"

Abigail searched her mind for the right answer without giving offense. "It's very kind of you but I don't think Jason would like having to put up with me."

Gay Feather regarded the young girl for a moment. "Abigail, are you afraid of my son?"

She was momentarily taken off guard by the woman's frankness. "No," she said. "It's not that I'm afraid of him exactly, but I am rather uncomfortable in his presence."

The honesty of her reply set Gay Feather to laughing. "I would think it would be the other way round. I doubt Jason has ever met a young girl like you. Your ladylike candidness possibly confuses him. You must remember that most women in these parts have rather placid personalities. It's the men who have the opinions and not us women. Why, only a half hour ago he considered your riding Charger a pigheaded notion."

Abigail looked down at her neatly bandaged hand. "I have to admit he was right about that."

Gay Feather pulled up a chair next to the bed and sat down. "Now let's see to getting some hot tea into you," she smiled holding the cup to Abigail's lips.

The next time Abigail opened her eyes, the only light in the room came from the candle burning on the night stand. She could hear the familiar voices in the next room and knew them to be those of Albert and Hugh McFadden, in what sounded like a heated discussion. She had the sinking feeling that whatever was going on, she was to blame. Suddenly, she saw Albert come walking into the room and smiled at the sight of him.

"Abigail," he said, with an edge of sharpness in his voice. "Do you feel fit enough to travel now?"

Surprised by the directness of his question, she hesitated. "Why?" she asked, keenly aware that he never inquired about the injuries she had sustained.

"Why?" he frowned. "I should think it would be obvious to you that you can't stay here for the night. These people. . . they're not like us, Abigail. They're vulgar and uncivilized. You must know that."

"I know nothing of the kind, Albert. Gay Feather has been very gracious and kind."

"Fine. But for all concerned, I think it best you come home tonight. I have a wagon outside."

"What does you father think?" she asked.

"To hell with what my father thinks. You're engaged to me, not my father. I think you should come home right this very minute."

Hugh McFadden's having entered the room saved Abigail from answering. "Heard you had a pretty bad spill from a horse," he smiled down at her. "Judging from that cut on your head, we're lucky to still have you. How are you feeling, Abigail?"

"A little bit out of sorts. I'm sorry for all the trouble I've caused you."

He took hold of her hand and patted it. "Never you mind. The important thing is for you to get better. A good night's rest will do you a world of good. I've talked it over with Gay Feather and we agree its best not to move you. Albert can come back and fetch you in the morning."

Albert was about to protest, but Hugh's hand on his son's shoulder stopped him. "She needs her rest, Albert. It's best we leave now. Gay Feather will see to her needs."

She heard them leave the cabin and listened to the sound of their horses' hooves as they faded into the stillness of the night. Gay Feather came walking into the room carrying a tray. She set it down on the night stand and smiled over at her guest. "I thought you could do with a bowl of soup and another cup of tea."

Abigail suddenly realized she was hungry. "Thank you, I could do with a bite to eat."

The woman sat bedside while Abigail began eating the food on the tray that was set before her. "I hope you don't think me impertinent for asking, but how did you learn to speak English so well?"

Gay Feather chuckled. "I was fortunate to have Jane, Hugh's wife, as my neighbor. Over the years she taught Jason and I how to speak English."

Abigail listened intently as the woman, in a reminiscing mood, went on to tell her what life was like when Hugh McFadden first came to settle in the wilderness and how she helped him get started. "It wasn't until Hugh had the house built that he sent for Jane. Jane was a rather delicate creature physically, and working the fields was too hard on her. In time, after her first born, she took to staying in the house and I would leave Jason in her care while Hugh and I worked the fields together. She taught Jason how to read and write and he in turn began to teach me."

"I would imagine that the McFadden family must be beholden to you in a lot of ways," Abigail said, while wondering what the foundation for Albert's disparaging remarks was earlier.

"I wouldn't know about that," Gay Feather said and rose to her feet. She reached out for the tray in Abigail's lap. "You better get some sleep. Before you know it, Albert will be here to take you home."

Sleep was evasive and Abigail lay there studying the bareness of the room. A small woven rug lay beside the bed and in the far corner sat a dresser. Three hooks on the wall held men's clothes and from this she gathered it was Jason's room. She turned to the sound of movement coming from the other room and through the open doorway she caught glimpses of Jason moving about in the next room. He was rolling out a bedroll in front of the fireplace on the floor. It disturbed her to think that she was the cause of his having to sleep on the floor. Another thought that surfaced to mind was the fact that he had never entered the room since he carried her into it, or made an inquiry about her well being.

Sometime during the night Abigail was awakened by the sensation of a full bladder and to her dismay, realized she didn't know where the facilities were. Restlessly she kept turning from side to side, trying to alleviate the pressure on her bladder.

It was the continuous sound of the squeaking bed that brought a concerned Jason hurrying into the room. He was busy slipping into his shirt as he approached the bed. He stood there looking down at her. "Abigail, what's wrong?" he asked.

"I. . . I. . . " she stopped thoroughly embarrassed.

A faint smiled edged his lips on realizing her predicament. "I guess my mother overdid it with the soup and tea."

He reached out and pulled back the bed covers and leaned over to lift her. "I'll show you where the shed is."

"No, no," she protested. "I can walk. There nothing wrong with my legs."

"Suit yourself," he said, backing away from her and watched as she slipped into her shoes.

She followed him to the back of the cabin and through what appeared to be a kitchen. He held the backdoor open for her before leading the way down the path to what Abigail could see in the moonlight was a small shed. Halfway down the path he stopped and stood there lighting a candle which he held out to her. "I'll wait here for you."

With candle in hand Abigail continued on the well worn path heading for the outdoor toilet. She was beginning to learn that some ladylike proprieties became lost when living in the wilderness. When she came out of the shed she blew out the candle. No sense in wasting it, she thought while looking up at the bright moonlit sky. She could see Jason with one hand leaning against a tree waiting for her. His back was to her and she marveled how he and the tree appeared in silhouette form, both tall and strong, as if they could withstand anything that the surrounding fields and forces of nature could level upon them.

He heard her approach and turned to face her. In silence he led the way back to the cabin. He saw her to her room and thoughtfully pulled the covers up over her. "I was wondering," he finally said. "If it's not an imposition for you, Abigail, would you come visit my mother when Jenny and Timothy come. She never gets company out here and I know how lonely it is for her."

"You needn't have asked," Abigail said. "I've already had it in my mind to call if only to thank her for her generous hospitality."

"Thank you," he smiled, "I should have known better than to ask."

"And while you're here, Jason," she said, "I'd like you to know I'm truly sorry for any inconvenience I've caused by making you give up your bed."

"It seems to me," he grinned jauntily, "if you're truly sorry, Abigail, you'd move over a little so I could fit. It is a large bed. It's not as if we haven't shared a blanket before if you think about it."

"Oh," she said indignantly. "You're impossible!'

His deep laughter echoed in the room as he headed for the door.

For the longest time a smiling Abigail stared after him when realizing he had been teasing her. Stranger still was the fact that she found his nearness disturbing. Just the thought of him sleeping in the same bed brought the color rising to her cheeks.

Even before the dawn of the new day broke on the horizon, Albert arrived at the cabin with a team of horses and wagon to take Abigail home.

Chapter Twelve

Blake Saunders paced the floor of his drab office. Something was sticking in his craw and this night of all nights, Christmas Eve, he couldn't shake the feeling. He stopped in his tracks, leaned over, and opened the bottom desk drawer. He rummaged through a stack of old Wanted posters, until his hand came in contact with the bottle of whiskey hidden beneath them. He opened the bottle and took a generous swig. While replacing the bottle he accidentally slammed the drawer closed on his thumb. The abusive language he directed at himself did little to relieve his pain but helped to release the tension he was feeling.

From one of the cells in back, Jeremiah Dunn, the town drunk, was making loud off-key overtures in an effort to sing a Christmas carol. Blake smiled to himself and shook his head in understanding. Jeremiah was at home in the only home he knew, the Abilene jailhouse. At the thought of having to spend Christmas Eve with Jeremiah for company, Blake felt a twinge of loneliness. He walked over to the window and looked out at the large snowflakes that were beginning to blanket the sleepy town. Most folks were at home with their loved ones; even the shops had closed early.

The sight of the deserted streets only added to Blake's loneliness. Resigning himself to the inevitable, he sat down, stretched his legs up bringing his boots to rest on the corner of his desk. He sat there for some time mulling things over in his mind while eyeing his hat and jacket hanging on one of the wall pegs beside the door. On sudden impulse Blake leaped to his feet and made a grab for his hat and jacket. "What the blazes have I got to lose?" He told himself.

Outside, he held tight the brim of his hat against the wind while locking the jailhouse door. His long stride quickened as he headed west, in the direction of Lucy Stone's house of ill fame.

Blake had to hand it to Lucy; she owned one of the nicest houses in town. It was a large wood frame house with a porch that swung clear around to the side of the house. Fancy wood trim hung from the eaves which Lucy saw to having painted every three years along with the white picket fence that surrounded her property. On the small plot of land next to the house Lucy planted a vegetable garden in summer. Many's the time, he'd seen her working in the garden and figured a woman who loved the land couldn't be as bad as people claimed. Still, till all hours of the night, one could see the red lamp that shone from the parlor window.

On the porch Blake stomped the snow from his boots, shook his hat and jacket free of snowflakes and drew in a deep breath before turning the doorknob.

Blake found himself standing in a large hallway facing a red carpeted staircase that circled clear round to the second floor. Shiny, gold wallpaper with small Cupids in flight, the likes of which Blake had never seen, covered the walls. At the far end of the hallway a door stood open and he caught a glimpse of the kitchen. The large parlor doors on his right were open and

Blake could hear a conglomeration of voices coming from the room. He walked over and stood fixed in the doorway.

A woman was sitting at a piano pecking at it with two fingers while two of Lucy's other girls looked on. A couple was sitting on one of the settees looking mighty friendly towards each other. Blake saw Lucy standing behind a bar that ran the width of the room. She was talking with two men whom Blake knew to be drifters. When she caught sight of him, she raised her hand and waved. "Hi, Sheriff," she yelled, "Merry Christmas."

All movement in the room stopped and every head turned in Blake's direction. He pulled himself up to his full height and smiled, "Merry Christmas, Lucy."

Blake removed his hat and with a nod acknowledged the others in the room. In quick stride he closed the distance between him and the bar. He looked around for a place to hang his hat and decided to put it back on his head.

From the far end of the bar Lucy came strolling toward him. She was all decked out in a bright red dress that glittered. "What do I owe this honor to?" she smiled. "Are any of my girls giving you trouble?"

Her question took him by surprise. "No. . . no trouble," he stammered.

"Don't tell me you're here for pleasure?" Lucy was about to laugh but the sober look on his face stopped her. "How about having a drink, Blake? Would you like a drink?"

She saw him hesitate and smiled. "Don't worry, drinks are on the house being it's Christmas. That's about the only time of the year you'll catch me giving something away for nothing. So, you might as well take advantage of my generosity."

Her honest admission brought a smile to his face. "Since you put it that way, I guess I'll have a whiskey."

Lucy's dark eyebrows knitted together as she opened a fresh bottle of whiskey and set two shot glasses down on the bar. All the while she studied the big, strapping man opposite her. In comparison with other sheriffs she had met, he never found reason to give her trouble. Neither did he use the weight of his badge for free drinks or the pleasure of one of her girls. In fact, in all the years she knew him, she couldn't recall his ever visiting her establishment before. Whatever was troubling him had to be serious so she came right out and asked, "What's wrong Blake?"

He fingered the shot glass in his hand and cleared his throat. "It's about the Mexican girl who drifted into town several months ago."

"Juanita?"

"Yes that's her name."

"Is she in some kind a trouble?" Lucy frowned.

"No. . . nothing like that," he said. "Let's just say it's a personal matter."

A glint of amusement sparked Lucy's eyes on seeing the deep flush of color that covered his face almost matching the auburn hair on his head and neatly trimmed mustache. "Well," she shrugged, "there's not much I can tell you about her. She's a loner, if you know what I mean; a loner if ever I saw one. Take right now for instance. Here it is Christmas Eve. Okay, the joint is dead, but you'd think she'd be a little sociable and come down and join us. Mind you, I like her. She minds her own business, but I wish ta'God she'd talk to customers. After all, I am running a business based on sociability among other things."

To keep from laughing out loud, Blake chewed into his lower lips. "Do. . .do you think I could take her out for supper tonight?"

At first, Lucy thought he was joking, but a second glance told her he was dead earnest. "Sorry, Blake, house rules; none of my girls are allowed to leave the premises. It's not good for business."

Although he nodded his head in understanding it was the disappointed look on his face that succeeded in making Lucy have a change of heart. "Oh, what the hell!" she said in exasperation. "It's Christmas and there's never any business in a cat house during the holidays. It seems to me it's the only time of year that men get conscious stricken and remember they're married." Her dark head nodded toward the door. "She's upstairs in her room. It's the second door on your left. Go on now, git, before I change my mind!"

"Thank you, Miss Lucy," he beamed, and was halfway across the room before she could change her mind.

Lucy smiled after the man.

For a few seconds Blake stood outside the door to Juanita's room. Mentally he was rehearsing what he would say to her. On hearing the soft murmur of her voice in answer to his knock, he quickly opened the door. He stepped inside and leaned against the closed door, taking comfort in its support.

The girl was sitting in a chair by the window brushing her hair. The brush in her hand froze in midair at the sight of him. The large brown eyes narrowed as she stared at him.

Blake's mind went blank and his tongue suddenly felt paralyzed. He'd forgotten how pretty she was. She made a lovely picture sitting there brushing her dark hair. Her dark waist length hair made a striking contrast against that of the light blue satin robe she wore.

Slowly, as if each move was mechanical, Juanita rose to her feet. She sighed in despair, "You just like all the rest."

Reaching out she turned down the lamp and the blue robe slipped from her shoulders and fell to the floor. She turned her back on him and headed toward the bed.

Blake stood frozen; his glance having swept her naked body. The smooth softness of her skin, her full inviting breasts, the small waist accentuating the round, firmness of her hips; just like he had imagined. "For the love of God, Juanita," he exploded. "Put that damn thing back on before you drive me out of my mind!"

Totally confused, Juanita turned to see him make a beeline for the small closet and open the door.

"I didn't come here to sleep with you, if that's what you're thinking," he said, over his shoulder. With a critical eye, Blake inspected each article hanging in the closet. He finally seemed satisfied with his find, a plain, dark blue shirtwaist dress that buttoned to the neck. Compared to the other gaudy dresses, it was out of place. He tossed the dress down on the bed. "This will do," he said, "put it on."

He turned to look at her and somehow, she had managed to slip back into her robe while his back was turned.

"Why I should wear that dress?" Her voice was barely audible.

"Because," he grinned, "I'm taking you out for supper. The hotel usually fixes something special for Christmas Eve."

"You are taking me to supper?"

"That's right. Now get dressed. . .I'll wait for you on the front porch." He turned and headed for the door.

"Bl-ake?"

It was the first time she had called him by name and he liked the way it kind of got caught up in her throat.

"Blake, no puedo. I cannot allow you."

He frowned. "Allow what, Juanita?"

"No is good that someone sees you with a woman like me. The people will laugh."

Within three strides he stood in front of her. He raised his hand and lightly touched her warm cheek. A thin smile crossed his lips while hoping to sound convincing. "No one in this town laughs at Blake Saunders. Remember that, Juanita. Now hurry up and get dressed."

Juanita stared at the door as it softly closed behind him.

The snow had stopped and the quiet stillness in the air seemed to match the hushed silence that hung between them as they walked, side by side, toward the heart of town. A number of times they had passed each other on the same street with nothing more than a slight nod of their head in acknowledgment.

They had climbed the steps of the hotel porch and Blake reached out to open the door. "You'll like the supper, Juanita," he said. "I promise you, you won't be sorry you came."

Juanita drew in a deep breath as if fortifying herself. Her eyes searched his. "Oh, I no sorry, pero. I hope that you no be sorry."

Chin high, Juanita held fast the arm offered as they entered the hotel and in perfect step they crossed the lobby to the candlelit dining room.

Juanita was not insensitive to the feelings of others. Although he was a large strapping man and could probably hold his own in any barroom brawl, it took another kind of courage for him to be seen in her company. Such news traveled fast in a small town and by tomorrow everyone would know that he had taken a prostitute out to dinner. Not Juanita Hernandez but the dark haired foreign woman who worked at Lucy Stone's place. One thing was certain; being in her company would be damaging to his career as Sheriff. For all she knew, maybe the man was a bit loco.

Juanita was relieved to see that the majority of faces turned in their direction were those of strangers. They were travelers who were stranded in Abilene over the holidays or just passing through on business.

Suddenly Juanita's heart sank as Myrtle Thompson, the proprietor's wife, came walking toward them. There was no mistake in the hard set line of the woman's jaw and the long beaked nose that seemed to twitch with each step taken. Ordinarily, Juanita would have found the sight of the woman amusing if it hadn't been for her companion.

"Good evening, Blake," Myrtle Thompson said, forcing a smile while completely shunning Juanita. "Where would you like to sit?"

Immediately, Blake took the situation in hand. "I really don't know, Myrtle," he smiled. "I suggest you ask the lady."

Myrtle Thompson made an attempt to say something but failed.

"I think the table in the back by the window is good," Juanita interjected.

"Are you sure?" Blake frowned.

"Si," Juanita smiled. "The table by the window, please."

"Okay, Myrtle, you heard the lady, we'll take the table by the window."

Within minutes of Myrtle taking their order and leaving, a stern faced man came walking toward their table. With each step his clean shaven face deepened in color. By the time he got to their table his pouchy cheeks were apple red. Even without benefit of collar, Juanita knew the man to be the new preacher in town, Reverend John Finch.

"Blake, what is the meaning of this?" he demanded. "I should think you'd have better sense——"

Blake had shot to his feet towering over the man. He grasped the man's limp hand that was at his side and firmly shook it. "Merry Christmas, Reverend," he said with exhilarating joy. "Sorry, were you about to say something?"

"Must I remind you that there are ladies here and children?"

Blake's eyes carried over the room and came to rest on Juanita. "I'm well aware of there being ladies present, Reverend. Did I say or do something wrong?"

"You know perfectly well what I'm referring to." His small beady eyes swept Juanita.

Blake shifted his weight blocking the man's view. "No, Reverend," he said. "I'm afraid I don't know what you're driving at."

"Well," he said in indignation. "I suggest you think about the election for Sheriff that is coming up soon. And remember you'll be judged by the company you keep."

"And I suggest, Reverend," Blake retorted, "you should spend more time reading the good book. Judge not, and ye shall not be judged."

The two men glared at each other. With great indignation the Reverend turned on his heels and stormed back to his table.

Juanita sat shaking her head from side to side. "I knew. . . I knew this would happen."

As Blake eased himself into his chair he reached over and patted her small hand that was resting on the table. "Now you're not going to let that righteous ass ruin your dinner, are you? The man's the biggest hypocrite in town. He sells religion; he doesn't practice it. It's a known fact that he brutally whips his horses. Just take a look at his wife and children sitting over there. Why it wouldn't surprise me none if he whips them."

Juanita had to agree that they were far from a jovial looking family. "He'll hurt your election."

"That's real funny, Juanita," Blake laughed, "seeing how I'm not about to run again."

She stared at him in disbelief while waiting for an explanation.

"The way I figure it, within another year the railroad will be coming to these parts. That can only mean trouble. When they start bringing the cattle drive here to Abilene it won't be a fit place to live. They'll probably need a Marshall to keep law and order. I've bought myself a piece of land outside of town and last year I built a small cabin on it. Come spring, I'm going to plant my first crop of corn. Most folks say the soil in these parts is real good for farming and one can make a fairly decent living at it. I know it's hard work and it may take me a couple of years before it begins to pay off, but being a sheriff can only mean sure death. I'd rather die from hard work than a stray bullet because some whiskey drinking cowpoke wants to shoot up the town."

Juanita sat listening to Blake's dreams of becoming a farmer. His strong conviction and enthusiasm led her to believe that without a doubt the man would succeed where others had failed. She was surprised to learn that he always wanted to be a farmer but, with the death of his young wife, three years ago, he had taken the job as sheriff.

Throughout the evening, Blake made several attempts trying to draw Juanita into the conversation but there was very little she cared to tell about herself. With the exception of several humorous anecdotes on how she was taught to speak English by a missionary, she never volunteered any information about herself.

In spite of the outward show of hostility by Myrtle Thompson while serving the meal, the food compensated for the woman's rudeness. The dining room was beginning to empty of guests and Juanita lingered over the cup of coffee in front of her, hating the thought of going back to Lucy's house. Outside in the desolate street they silently walked toward the outskirts of town and Lucy Stone's house. On the front porch Juanita turned to look at Blake once more before entering the house. He was standing at the foot of the porch steps watching her and made no attempt to follow.

"Gracias, Blake, I had good time and the food was delicious," she smiled. Trying to hold onto the evening she added, "Maybe someday I see your cabin."

Suddenly struck by an overpowering impulse, Blake two at time climbed the steps and grabbed her hand. "It's early yet," he said breathlessly. "I could rent a rig and we can ride out there now, if you like."

Misinterpreting her silence, he let her small hand slip from his. "I guess it wasn't such a good idea."

"Oh no! Oh no, Blake! I love to go." She looked at the front door and shrugged helplessly.

"Then what are we waiting for? Come on, let's go, ta'hell with Lucy." He roughly snatched at her hand and they flew down the porch steps and out into the middle of the road. Hand in hand, like two children whose wicked stepmother was in hot pursuit, they ran to McGregor's livery stable to rent a rig.

The unpredictable weather had changed during the last hour of their journey. A light, blinding snow carried by the harsh winds across the open plains slowed their pace. Juanita huddled beneath the blanket that Blake had thoughtfully taken from the jailhouse while leaving Jeremiah Dunn's cell door open. She strained to see the outline of the small cabin on the side of the slope which Blake had eagerly pointed out to her.

Once inside the cabin, and refuged from the wind, Blake held the kerosene lamp up and objectively glanced around the cabin. He took in the warped floors and the partly partitioned bedroom that he had been meaning to finish. The bed was unmade and his work clothes were strewn about the room. A heavy musty smell of dampness hung in the air. He began to have second thoughts about bringing the girl to the cabin.

Juanita, busy studying the sturdy structure of the logged walls and fireplace, gave little thought to the bareness of the cabin. She could see the potential of it being a fine home someday. "You done good. Good building, Blake." Her sincere smile, although hampered by chattering teeth, erased all his doubts.

Blake picked up a chair and carried it over to the fireplace. "Sit here, Juanita, and keep that blanket wrapped around you until I get a fire going."

Within a half hour the black potbellied stove was laden with burning wood and a blazing fire in the fireplace. The musty smell of dampness was soon replaced by the savory aroma of coffee perking. Blake melted down a scrub bucket of snow and when the temperature met his satisfaction, he made the girl remove her shoes and stockings and soak her chilled feet in the hot water. Between the hot cup of coffee and the soothing warm water, Juanita soon shed the blanket as well as her cape.

After attentively seeing to her comfort, Blake went out into the cold again to take care of the horses. He unhitched the rig and tied the horses to one of the posts of the lean-to that he had built on the south side of the cabin. The cold nipped at his ears and several times he blew on his hands trying to warm them. Again, he was having second thoughts about bringing the girl to the cabin. With face frowned in worry, he reentered the cabin.

"What is wrong, Blake? Your face she is troubled."

"The temperature is dropping like crazy," he said, hanging up his hat and jacket on a rusty nail. "It's going to be hell for you going back tonight. It really was a dumb idea bringing you out here in this kind of weather."

Juanita silently studied the man as he stood basking his hands in the warmth of the fire. She would never consider him a handsome man, but if one took the time as she was doing, there was a warmth and gentleness in his looks and manner, especially when he laughed. His hugeness was almost intimidating, and yet, for a man his size, he carried himself well and moved with an astonishing agility.

He caught her staring at him and asked, "Are you hungry? I could rustle up some beans and biscuits and there's a rind of bacon. . . "

"No," she laughed, "all I need was a coffee. Why you no sit down and enjoy the fire?"

He poured himself a cup of coffee and appeared to be at a loss with nothing to do as he sat opposite her staring into the fire.

"Blake? If you are worried for going back to town tonight, why we no stay here until morning? Maybe the weather will be changed in the morning?"

A deep flush covered his face. "I was thinking about it," he honestly admitted, "but I didn't want to be the one to suggest it."

"Bueno. We stay till morning."

Having settled the question, they sat silent for sometime enjoying the crackling sounds of the fire and out of reach of the wind that howled in the chimney.

"Are you sleepy?"

"Un poquito," Juanita yawned.

"Why don't you stretch out on the bed for a spell? I won't mind."

Through the open studs that had the promise of becoming a bedroom wall, Juanita eyed the comfort of the bed. She set the empty coffee cup down on the floor and began to dry her feet. "And you?" she asked, picking up her shoes and stockings.

"I'll stretch out here beside the fire on the floor," Blake smiled.

Barefooted, Juanita crossed the room and slipped between two of the open studs. She could feel the cold penetrating right through the floor boards as she undressed.

The bed sounded with a creak as she jumped into it and hastily pulled the quilt up over her. As she puffed up one of the pillows her glance carried into the next room to see Blake busy feeding the fire. The thought of him sleeping on the cold floor worried her. "Blake? The floor she is like ice, you catch a cold of death. There is no reason of the world why you do not sleep in your bed."

She heard him suck in his breath.

"You're asking a helluva lot of me, Juanita," he said.

Her eyes swept the huge, massive man who at the moment appeared to be having trouble looking at her. "Si," she sighed. "Come to the bed."

He turned his head and even in the dimness she could see his eyes and she managed to out stare him. She watched as he slowly came walking into the room and quietly undressed. The bed creaked as he sat down on the edge of it and Juanita noticed his hands gripping the edge of the mattress.

On sudden impulse Juanita rose to her knees and curled up behind him. She slipped her arms around his waist and brought her cheek to rest on his bare shoulder. "Blake . . .," she whispered.

The warmth and softness of her body nestled close to his suddenly became a hot branding iron burning his flesh. A dozen or more sordid pictures of her making love with other men flashed through his mind. Pure rage surged through his body. "Don't do that, Juanita!" he exploded. Stunned, she drew back on her haunches and looked at him.

"You don't have to force yourself on me. It's not as if I were going to pay you!"

Her face crumbled and uncontrollable tears spilled from her eyes.

On seeing her cry, Blake felt about as hollowed as a sucked egg and wished he had bitten his tongue. He slid into bed and leaned over her, gently removing her hands from her face. "I'm sorry, Juanita, it's just. . . Juanita, please don't cry," he begged. "I'm sorry for what I said. It's just. . .," he struggled for words. "Well, damn it all, with you shining up to me like that I felt like one of Lucy's paying customers. God knows, I'm not a handsome man, Juanita, but I still have some pride."

Through thick wet lashes, Juanita looked up at him. "I reached to you," she sobbed, "for the first time in my life I reach to a man." A new onslaught of tears flowed from her eyes.

Her words struck him like a taut harpoon that was ready to snap and he found himself holding tight the end of the line. He wanted her; he ached for her, but knew he had deeply hurt her. He restrained from touching her knowing whatever happened between them had to be of her own free will and initiative.

Blake bent his head and lightly kissed her closed eyelids and then her trembling lips. "Juanita reach for me," he whispered.

She lay motionless.

"Juanita, please reach for me," he begged, voice deep with passion.

Ever so slowly her eyelids blinked open, a faint smile of hope crossed Blake's lips. "Por favor," he whispered.

She giggled at his attempt to speak Spanish and timidly her arms reached up and encircled him about the neck. As their lips met, Blake felt the warm softness of her body as it conveniently slid beneath his.

The light of dawn streaked through the windows and Blake's eyes lazily blinked open. He was conscious of every fiber of his huge, muscular body and a warm smile of contentment spread over his lips as he stretched his arms up in the air. He sighed, relaxed and glanced over at the pillow next to his. He was jarred awake on finding the other half of the bed empty. The familiar sound of a frying pan being shuffled on top of the kitchen stove caught his ear and he smiled. He turned on his side to gain a better view of the adjoining room and peered through the open studs. He lay there anxious for his first glimpse of the girl.

A well fed fire was burning in the fireplace and the aroma of fried bacon and coffee perking taunted his nostrils. Suddenly, the girl came into view. She was struggling to push the large wooden washtub in front of the fireplace clad in nothing more than his blue plaid shirt the length of which covered her to the knees. The sleeves had been rolled up several times over till they reached her elbows. Blake watched with interest as she made several trips back and forth to the kitchen while filling the tub with kettles of hot water. The blue plaid shirt slipped to the floor and she gingerly stepped into the tub of water.

"Aye! Que caliente," she squealed, while hopping about from one foot to the other in the water. On her third try, she finally succeeded in submerging her rump in the hot tub of water.

Blake buried his face in the pillow muffling the sound of his laughter. He delighted in watching her bathe and listening to the sound of her humming. Several times, while scrubbing her back, she glanced over her shoulder in his direction. He'd quickly close his eyes pretending to be asleep.

He watched as she toweled herself dry and slipped back into his shirt again.

With closed eyes he listened to her footsteps as she entered the bedroom in search of her clothes.

Suddenly, he felt the warmth of her presence as she leaned over him. "Blake? I fix breakfast," she whispered, gently shaking his shoulder.

The warmth of her small hand on his bare shoulder sent a wave of emotions sweeping over him. He couldn't move. He couldn't speak. He tried to push the pleasurable memories of their love making out of his mind but failed. He lay in misery. He was torn between wanting her and the fact that she would interpret it as his only reasons for bringing her to his cabin.

"Get up you lazy," she said, playfully pulling back the quilt that covered him.

Blake turned on his side trying to hide his manliness, but it was too late. He heard the soft "Oh," sound that escaped Juanita's lips. In fear of seeing her face masked in disgust, he tightly closed his eyes in anguish. "Please, Juanita. Please go in the kitchen and get dressed," he groaned.

Juanita climbed up on the bed and curled up beside him. She felt the involuntary quiver that swept his body as her hands gently caressed his back. "Three years a long time with no woman," she said against his ear. "I reach to you last night, now you reach to me."

Chapter Thirteen

"But I promised," Timothy whined. "Don't you understand, it's going to be my foal and I promised I'd be there to help?"

Abigail reached out and touched his feverish brow. "I know how disappointed you must be, Timothy, but you can't go. . .not with a fever. I'm sure Jason will be able to manage."

"No," he said obstinately, "he told me I should be there when Grasshopper is born and I promised I'd help; that was our agreement. And a man is only as good as his word and I gave my word."

Abigail smiled to herself as she leaned over and pulled the covers up to his neck. "Well, it seems to me you got yourself in quite a pickle giving your word like that and not being able to go. Do you suppose we could send someone else in your place?"

He stared at her in wonder. "Who?" he frowned.

"Jenny can't go; she's got too much homework. Albert went into town and I expect he won't be home till the wee hours in the morning. As for your pa, he's dead to the world sleeping in the parlor so I guess that leaves me," Abigail said.

"Do you mean it, Abigail, would you go? Do you honestly mean it?" he said excitedly.

"If you promise me that you will stay in bed, I'll go help Jason. Lord knows what I get myself into sometimes."

"Oh, Abigail, I love you dearly," he sighed.

She leaned over and planted a kiss on his feverish brow. "I guess this means I'll be Grasshopper's godmother," she laughed.

He smiled after her and said, "Just knowing you're there, I'll rest easy."

It had been a long cold winter and with the coming of spring it seemed to rejuvenate Abigail's spirit. She was looking forward to planting her flower garden and working in the fields. Only a month ago she had paid a visit to Gay Feather and the fields were covered in snow; and now as she rode west, one could see a jade world on the horizon.

The cabin was swallowed up in darkness as Abigail tied the rig to the hitching post. She pulled her shawl up tighter around her shoulders and headed for the faint stream of light that was coming from the open barn door. As she crossed the threshold she could see Jason sitting stretched out on the ground reading a book by the light of an oil lamp sitting on top of a milking stool. She suddenly realized that, although she had visited his mother on several occasions, she hadn't seen him in months. In all honesty, she had to admit that she missed him. As if sensing her presence, he glanced up from the book in his hand. Surprise touched his face as his eyes carried past her. "Where's Timothy?" he asked.

"He's home in bed with a fever. Since he gave his word he'd be here I promised to take his place in order to keep him in bed," Abigail smiled, while self-consciously gathering her skirt and sitting down on the vacant milking stool opposite him. Although she found his nearness disturbing, she had to admit she was pleased to see him.

"That's just like Timothy," he smiled. "He'd never break his word, but I'm sorry you had to make the trip. The reason I wanted Timothy to come was the fact that he's never seen a foal born. If a boy is given the chance to see the miracle of life he's not apt to needlessly kill animals."

Although ignorant as to what transpired during the birth of a foal, Abigail shook her head in understanding. She was conscious of suddenly becoming tongue-tied under Jason's direct gaze. The restless movement coming from the stall in back seemed to mirror her own behavior. "Shouldn't we be helping the mare?" she asked.

"It's her first foal and she's a little skittish. It's best to stay out of her sight until. . .

A loud thud sound coming from the stall sent Jason springing to his feet. He ran to the back of the barn and Abigail followed with oil lamp in hand. The mare was laying on her side laboring. "Quick, Abigail, hand me a wet cloth from the basin over there," he said, and pointed.

Abigail watched in silence as Jason gently washed down the mare's hindquarters and legs with the damp cloth she had given him. The strong order of disinfectant permeated the air.

As the mare groaned and strained Abigail spied the protruding membrane beneath its tail. She watched in awe as the membrane grew larger and the small hoof of the foal became visible. Then slowly, the long slender legs came into view with the tiny muzzle nestled in between. All movement stopped and the pitiful sound of the mare's groans continued as it labored in vain.

"For the love of God, do something!" Abigail cried.

Her cry was in vain, for Jason was already kneeling on the ground and pulling at the legs of the foal in an attempt to free its shoulders. He sat back on his haunches and patiently waited for the mare's next spasm. With that he began pulling again and the second attempt freed the foal. It lay on the ground with membrane and umbilical broken.

Curious as to what was happening, the mare lifted her head and looked at her newborn foal as it made several unsuccessful attempts to rise on its scrawny legs.

"Come on girl," Jason urged. "You can do it."

To the sound of his voice the filly mustered its courage, let out a soft wheeze and awkwardly stood up wobbling on all fours. A triumphant smile crossed Jason's lips as he gently ran his hand over the shiny black, curly coat of the newborn foal.

The mare staggered to her feet and nuzzled her nose against her newborn as though thoroughly inspecting it.

Abigail couldn't contain her laughter while watching an exasperated Jason trying to teach the small filly to take nourishment from the mare. It persisted in sucking his fingers that had become covered in milk. It took some doing on Jason's part until the filly got the hang of it.

"She's beautiful," Abigail sighed. "Timothy will be so happy when I tell him."

As if suddenly aware of her presence, Jason turned to look at her. The excitement of the last hour had brought a high color to her cheeks and from where he was standing washing his hands he caught the gleam of shimmering tears in her eyes. He dried his hands on his shirttail and joined her leaning on the railing watching the new born filly. He reached out and touched Abigail's chin, turning her face towards him. "It's nothing to cry over," he smiled down at her.

"I know," she laughed. "But I never realized that life and birth could be so meaningful and beautiful." Her voice shook with emotion and she reached up and touched the hand beneath her chin. Suddenly conscious of their closeness, she quickly dropped her hand and the color rose to her cheeks. The innocent and befuddled look of her brought a smile to Jason's lips. On sudden impulse he leaned over and kissed her. He meant it to be a light gentle kiss but somehow it became fused with the excitement of the last hour. They became swept up in their emotions and each in turn seemed to be demanding, and yielding to each other's passionate kisses.

The torment of wanting her racked through Jason as his lips took refuge in the smoother whiteness of her throat. Unexpectedly, Abigail wrenched herself free of his arms. "No, Jason, please." she gasped.

He stood stunned for a moment with a thousand impulses flashing through his mind. He reached out and firmly gripped her about the throat with his one hand where only a moment ago his lips had been. "You were enjoying the moment as much as I and you know damn well its right between us. Whether you realize it or not, Abigail, and I think you do, it's our time to love. I want you as a man wants a woman." His hand tightened around her throat. "I could force you or bend you to my will but in conquering your physical being, lost to me forever would be the spirit of the woman within you." Ever so slowly, Jason released his hold from about her neck. His hand dropped to his side.

The truth of his words stung like a wasp, Abigail couldn't answer. With bowed head and legs that felt like straw she turned and stumbled toward the door.

Out of fear of doing something drastic, only to regret late, Jason stood frozen. His voice carried a warning note as he called out to her. "Abigail!"

Jason sucked in his breath as he watched her nearing the threshold of the doorway. It took him a few seconds before he realized what had taken place. Momentarily she stood within the framework of the doorway just before making a sharp turn. Instead, she disappeared into the dimness of the empty stall next to the door.

Jason's eyes were glued on the blue shawl that had slipped from her shoulders and had fallen to the ground. He slowly walked toward it, stooped over and picked it up. He fingered the softness of the shawl in his hand and brought it up to his face breathing deep the fragrance of lavender. He entered the stall.

In the dimness he could see Abigail standing there in her bare feet. Her back was to him and at the moment she appeared hesitant on removing the last article of clothing that covered her; her pantalets.

"Everything," he murmured.

Slowly she followed his command and sank to her knees on the hay covered ground. She reached up and removed the pins from her hair causing it to fall loosely down her back as if trying to cover her nakedness.

Jason's eyes never wavered from the lovely picture of beauty and innocence before him. He knelt down behind her in the hay and ran his hand down the length of her silky, red hair to the small, warm hollow of her back. He felt the slight involuntary quiver of her body beneath his hand reminding him of the new born lissome, skittish, filly. He lifted his hand from her back and bent his head burying his lips in the hollow, mouthing the soft flesh of her body until he succeeded in reaching her lips. Hungrily his lips moved over hers while his hands gently caressed her body evoking strange sensations within her that frightened and excited her beyond anything she ever imagined. For the first time in her life, Abigail threw caution to the wind by letting her mind go blank as Jason took command of her body. There was no yesterday, no tomorrow, only the moment as she clung to him.

The silence was so acute that the only thing that could be heard was their breathing. Abigail lay with one arm covering her eyes, her cheeks turning crimson while reliving the last moments that had transpired. The rapture of the moments helped to alleviate the feeling of guilt over her unladylike behavior.

Beside her she heard Jason stir. She raised her arm to find herself staring up into his face. He was leaning over her. "Did I hurt you?" he asked with concern.

Unable to find her voice, Abigail silently shook her head. The smug grin that spread over his lips sent the color rising to her cheeks again. He knew he hadn't hurt her. He was well schooled in the art of making love. As if committing to memory his lips and hands had traveled over every inch of her body.

"When I please you," he grinned, "tell me. Don't bite."

In the overpowering excitement of the moment, Abigail remembered losing all reasoning. She found herself possessed with a primitive urge to scream or strike back at him. Instead she used her teeth. She could see the red imprint of the bite mark on his shoulder. "Whatever possessed me to do such a thing?" she said in shocked dismay.

Jason's head rolled back in laughter.

"What are you laughing about," she said indignantly. "I could have drawn blood."

"The fact that I'm supposed to be the savage," he said, reaching out and drawing her into his arms. "I can tell you one thing," he said, voice filled with passion. "Great Bear was wrong when he said if I slowly sipped of White Snow my quench would be filled. My thirst for you will never be quenched."

"White Snow?" she frowned, clearly remembering the fable.

"Yes, that's what he named you," Jason smiled. "White Snow."

282

Again his hands caressed her evoking strange sensations as he took mastery of her body and mind.

Abigail buried her head against his chest. She took comfort in the arms that held her and comfort in knowing that she had achieved the ultimate joy in a woman's life——the joy of being wanted and loved. But in the back of her mind a negative thought sprang to mind that troubled her. Although he had murmured a number of endearments, never once did she hear the words, I love you. Abigail decided to give voice to her thoughts. "Jason?"

"Hmm."

She raised her head so she could see his face. "Jason, do you love me?" she asked, and heard the deep rumple of laughter that was caught up in his chest.

"Boy," he laughed. "Ain't that just like a woman to ask such a silly question at a time like this?"

"Jason, I'm serious."

"I know you are," he said, "that's what poses a problem."

"Problem?" she frowned, somewhat at a loss, anticipating his declaration of love. "What problem?"

He raised his hand and fingered the long curl resting on the bare whiteness of her shoulder while succeeding in holding back the grin that taunted his lips. "It's not of any importance whether I love you or not, I know, I have to pay the consequences for my actions. It's the gentlemanly thing to do to save a lady's reputation. I'd be a cad if I didn't marry you."

He felt her body go rigid in his arms and unexpectedly she pushed herself free of his hold and sprang to her feet. Stark naked, she went running out of the stall snatching up her clothes on the way.

Jason stared after. "Now what the hell did I do!" he swore, making a grab for his clothes.

When he caught up to her she was fully dressed, busy buttoning the top of her dress. He stood silent, guarding the anger that was caught in his throat. "What's wrong?" he asked, finally.

She avoided looking at him. "Nothing."

"Nothing?" he repeated. "Damn it, Abigail you're madder than a wet hen!"

She pushed past him out into the light of dawn breaking on a new day. She headed for her rig on the far side of the road. Jason followed in silence and waited until she climbed up and seated herself. When she picked up the reins his hand shot out grabbing the hand holding the reins. "Just like that," he said. "No good-bye."

"Let go of the reins," she fumed.

"Not until you tell me what's bothering you."

"Let go of the reins," she shrilled, and made several unsuccessful attempts to free her hand. "Damn you, Jason! Damn you!" she exploded as tears gushed from her eyes. "I can't marry you!"

Although stunned by her words, he began to clearly reason. "Oh," he murmured. "I understand. I'm a half-breed."

"No! God no! That has nothing to do with it. Now will you let go of the reins," she begged only to feel his grip tighten.

Anger crossed the fine chiseled features of his face. "Maybe I should have taken you like the savage that I am."

The sting of his words hit her like a blow. With her free hand, Abigail grabbed the whip from the whip stock and lashed out at him. The tip of the whip cut into the flesh of his cheek.

Jason flinched with pain and his hand tightened on hers like a vice. "I could kill you for that," he said fiercely.

Horrified by what she had done, the whip slipped from her fingers as if burning them. She gasped at the sight of the long thin cut on his cheek. She could see the blood rising to the surface of his skin. She crumbled over as deep compelling sobs racked her body. "For the love of God, Jason, please let me go," she begged.

He was confused by seeing her stripped of her pride and begging, but more so by the fact that she was crying. She wasn't one to use tears as a weapon. He reached up and spun her halfway around in the seat forcing her to face him. His voice was calm and low as he spoke. "Since you set such a store in the words; I love you. Just say, Jason, I don't love you."

Beseechingly, her green eyes held his as uncontrollable tears spilled down her cheeks. She bit into her lower lip which trembled. A soft sob escaped her lips. Mutely she shook her head from side to side, unable to give voice to the words which would be a lie.

Jason slowly released his grip from her arm and stepped back. "That's all I wanted to know," he murmured. "You can go, Abigail."

The hard flap of the reins over the horse's backs sent the rig into fast motion. Jason stood in the dust of the road and watched until it disappeared from sight.

Silent tears streamed down Abigail's face that even the strong winds of the speeding rig could not dry. She felt a deep sinking hollowness inside of her heart where only a short while ago had been overflowing with love. That she loved Jason was undeniable, she had loved him for months. But what he wouldn't understand was the reason she could not marry him. All her life she had been looking for somewhere to belong, a place to call home and a family who loved her. Now she had it all. Hugh McFadden looked on her as a daughter and she in turn looked on him as the father she never had. Since the first day she met Jenny she had become her sister and with each passing day the bond between them grew strong. Just to know Timothy was to love him and here too she looked on him as her younger brother.

A girl could not ask for more than to have Albert for a husband. He was handsome and his manners were impeccable. Since the first day she had met him he catered to her every whim. He was generous to a fault and any girl in the world would consider it an honor to give her hand in marriage to a man like Albert. And that's exactly what she did two weeks ago. To the delight of the whole family, they were to be married this coming Sunday by Reverend Finch. What she lacked was the courage to tell Jason.

It rained the whole of Sunday and in the parlor of the McFadden house, with only the Reverend Finch and his wife Martha as guests, Abigail gave her hand in marriage to Albert. It was far from a wedding that young girls dream about; it was simplicity unto itself.

After a month of married life, Abigail's dreams shattered before her eyes. Marriage didn't change Albert, as she had hoped, or unite the family. Instead she found herself caught in a web. She was torn between her love for the McFadden family and what she considered to be a wife's loyalty to her husband. Time after time, she found herself making excuses for her husband. This she could endure, but it was the marriage bed itself that she had come to loathe and despise. Had she not experienced tenderness and regard in the most intimate of moments between a man and a woman, she would have been led to believe that the marriage bed was meant for man's pleasure alone.

Her husband, she learned, had the ability of showing distinct incompatible patterns of behavior. He could be charming and gracious in the presence of others, but in the seclusion of their bedroom he chose to humiliate and degrade her. It was on such a night, after Albert reminded her of her wifely duties, and had taken his manly fill of her that Abigail lay crying.

"Will you stop that sniveling. How is a man supposed to get any sleep around here with you sniveling?"

Abigail quickly buried her face in her pillow trying to muffle the sounds of her crying. She blamed herself for the failure of their marriage: the failure to see that Albert, in a lot of ways, was a small boy. At the same time the quilt of loving and wanting another man weighed heavily on her mind. "Albert, can we talk?' she asked, raising her head from the pillow.

"Talk? What's there to talk about? And how many times must I ask you to call me Al? Albert, shouldn't you be helping your father? Albert, shouldn't you be working the fields? Albert, shouldn't you do this, shouldn't you do that?" His voice mimicked hers in deep ridicule.

"There was a time when you liked me calling you, Albert."

"That, my dear wife, was before I realized you weren't the prize package I thought you to be."

Abigail's complexion deepened in anger. "I never claimed to be anything more than what I am."

"And that my dear wife adds up to a cipher." With disgust, he rose from the bed and turned to look at her. "Why did you marry me, Abigail?" his voice held a curious note to it.

Taken aback by the question, Abigail found herself stammering. "I . . .I love your family and I. . . "

"You love my family," he sneered. "I guess that's about as good an answer as any."

"Why did you marry me?" she hotly retorted.

He ignored her while hurriedly putting on his clothes.

"That's right, Albert, get dressed and run to Abilene. Run Albert, run, like you always do to avoid facing a problem. Shall I tell you why you married me?" she jolted up in bed with green eyes glaring at him.

"Shut up, Abigail! I've had about as much of you as I can take for one night," he warned.

"You're so right, Albert," she said bitterly. "You had about as much of me as you can take and that's what it amounts to. You don't make love to a woman, you take her. As for your marrying me, it was to gain favor in you father's eyes. Don't you think I didn't know that? You want all the benefits of marriage but not the responsibility. Well, I'm tired of making excuses for you. It's about time you lost some of that boyish charm of yours and become a man!"

Unexpectedly, he brought his one knee down hard on the bed and leaned over and slapped her across the mouth.

Abigail blinked, the blow stinging her lips.

Momentarily stunned by his own behavior, Albert backed off the bed. "See what you made me do," he said. "I told you to shut up."

An acute silence hung in the room.

He resumed buttoning his shirt, struggled to put his boots on and head for the door. When he reached out to open the door Abigail said, "Al. . .bert I'm with child."

She saw his shoulders slump and his hand slipped from the door latch. He turned and faced her. In the dimness she strained to see his face. Was he smiling? Was he happy? Would he beg for her forgiveness? She had envisioned this as being the most joyous of all moments in a marriage.

For some reason she trembled as Albert quietly made his way across the room and silently stood at the side of the bed looking down at her. He reached out and gently fingered a lock of her hair. "Are you sure?" he asked.

"Yes, I'm sure," she weakly smiled as he sat down facing her. This was the husband she always wanted, gently touching her and deeply concerned about her welfare. "But just to make certain, your father is taking me to see Dr. Tillman in the morning."

"My father knows?"

Abigail laughed. "Your father diagnosed my symptoms before I even surmised what was troubling me. I might say he's quite pleased at the thought of becoming a grandfather." Then she quickly added, "I haven't told Jenny or Timothy; I thought you'd like to have the honor of telling them."

She felt the warmth of his hand through the sheerness of her night dress. Slowly and rhythmically it caressed the small mound of her stomach that promised life.

"I can't believe you're with child. God, I'm the most fortunate of men for having you for a wife."

"Albert?"

"Please dear, let me finish," he insisted. "Did I ever tell you how beautiful you are?" His raised hand gently swept through her hair. "This fiery red hair of yours, and your green eyes, are beauty in itself. What I love about you the most is your soft, smooth, flawless skin. It covers a body that any sculptor would give his soul to fashion out of stone."

The color rose to her cheeks on feeling his hand slip from her throat and invaded the bodice of her gown cupping her breast. "So smooth, so flawless," he sighed. "I doubt a sculptor could do you justice."

Quite suddenly he pulled his hand back, almost ripping the gown. "Unless he used white marble. Do you know anything about white marble, dearest Abigail?"

She shook her head.

"Well, for one thing, it's like you. Smooth, cold and to my way of thinking, quite impossible to impregnate!" he sneered, springing to his feet and towering over her. "I doubt very much you're with child. The woman that carries my seed will be alive! And you, my dear wife, are nothing more than a flawless, cold piece of marble!"

"I am with child," Abigail gasped. "I am with child."

Her words filled the silence of the room as Albert closed the door behind him.

The next morning Dr. Tillman confirmed the fact that Abigail was pregnant. The news of her pregnancy delighted the McFadden family, with the exception of Albert. His attitude towards her never changed and he became detached from the rest of the family. It came as no surprise to Abigail, when three days later at the supper table; Albert announced his plans of going to Texas to join another cattle train. His decision appalled the McFadden family and left Abigail with an over laden burden of guilt, the guilt of not caring about the father of her child.

291

Chapter Fourteen

Abigail would remember that summer as being one of the happiest in her life. She shared the same dreams along with her father-in-law that someday the land would yield more than its bounty. Early morning would find her working in the fields with the rest of the family. Before the heat of the noonday sun she'd be sent back to the house to rest. Her arms were never laden with firewood, milking pails or bundles of wash without Timothy or Jenny finding some excuse as to their helping her. Her father-in-law had sent all the way to Virginia and surprised her with three rose bushes and three lavender plants for her flower garden. Pampered she was by her in-laws.

Under her guidance, Jenny applied herself to learning how to sew a pretty hand, and together they became obsessed with making clothes for Abigail's expected child. While their hands were set to toil they delighted in thinking up different names for her expected child.

On cool evenings the sound of hammer and saw could be heard coming from the barn. Hugh McFadden was teaching his son, Timothy, how to fashion a cradle out of wood.

Each day became more joyous than the previous to Abigail as she slowly blossomed forth with child. The most unbearable time of day was the long summer night. At night, in the privacy of her bedroom, she was struck with the aloneness of having a child. She lay in the large bed aching for strong arms to hold and comfort her. She longed for the tenderness that rightfully belonged to a woman in her condition by a loving husband—someone to confide in and help banish her fears of childbirth. Time and time again, she found herself checking the looking glass and studying the visible changes that were taking place in her body. She was happy with the life within her that held the promise of someone to love, but most important of all, she'd be loved in return. When she found the loneliness frightening and unbearable she took refuge in daydreaming. More often than not, Jason appeared in her dreams. She visualized him laughing at something she had said or reprimanding her for some foolhardy thing she had done. Good humored or ill tempered, no matter how she visualized him, his honest air of love and concern for her illuminated each dream. When her dreams faded into clear, cold reality she would lay there crying until the darkness of sleep erased all thoughts from her mind.

It was a dreary day for late August and the overcast sky promised gloom and sadness in itself. It could have been an ill omen, had Abigail chosen to believe so. She stood in the yard busily hanging the day's wash that Jenny had carried out in a basket. When she leaned over to pick up one of Timothy's shirts giving it a final wring before pinning it to the clothesline, she thought she detected movement in the brush beyond the barn. Out of the corner of her eye she saw two half-naked Indians; their faces were streaked with paint. They were watching her. She stood frozen for a minute with her heart pounding against her ribs. With trembling hands she snatched up her skirt and went running back to the house.

Inside the house she screamed for Jenny as she frantically pushed the kitchen table to one side and began pulling up the corner of the rug, unveiling the trap door to the root cellar below.

A startled Jenny came running into the kitchen. "Abigail what's wrong? You gave me such a fright. What are you doing?"

"Help me lift the door," she breathlessly said.

"Why?"

"Don't ask questions, Jenny, just do as I tell you," she snapped.

Somewhat surprised by Abigail's sharpness, Jenny leaned over and together they struggled with the weight of the door.

"Now go down there and stay put, don't make a sound. There are two Indians outside in the yard and they may get a notion to come into the house."

Jenny stared at her wide-eyed.

"Be quick about it, Jenny. Do what I tell you!" Forcefully she pushed the girl toward the ladder that led to the small root cellar below.

"What. . .what about you?" Jenny's voice cracked with emotion.

"Never mind, just do as I say."

"I won't leave you."

"They saw me, Jenny. Now, for heaven's sake, do as I tell you!"

Jenny's face was masked in fright as she watched Abigail lower the door overhead leaving her in total darkness.

Abigail breathed a sigh of relief as she pulled the rug back over the door and pushed at the kitchen table, setting it back into place. It was a relief just to know that Jenny would be safe but as she leaned over the table she was suddenly struck with the startling realization that not only was her life at stake, but that of the child she carried in her womb. The horrifying stories she had heard so often about Indians and their brutality to white women flashed through her mind. Her will to live grew strong as she felt the child in her womb leap.

Abigail didn't have to look up to know that someone was standing in the kitchen doorway watching her. Their bodies blocked the light of the day. She held tight the knife in her hand to keep from trembling as she sliced one of the fresh loaves of bread that she and Jenny had baked that morning. For a timeless moment she stood there slowly slicing the bread; as if magnified, she could hear the sound of her own heartbeat. With an air of nonchalance, Abigail looked up at the two men standing in the doorway while she continued to slice the bread. They distrustfully glanced about the room before deciding to open the screen door and enter. In the closeness of the kitchen she could smell their presence. With the tip of the knife Abigail forked several slices of bread across the table in their direction. Her glance quickly sweeping them to see, that although tall in stature, they were both young.

The taller of the two picked up a slice of bread and sniffed at it and thoroughly examined it before taking a bite. After the first mouthful appeared to meet with his satisfaction, he wolfed down the rest of the slice while tossing another piece in the air to his companion who stood fixed in the doorway.

It was quite obvious to Abigail that they were hungry and she turned to the simmering pot of soup on the stove. Her sudden move startled them and without warning, they pounced on her both tightly gripping the hand that was holding the knife. The knife fell to the floor. In an attempt to free herself, the sleeve of her dress was torn. Suddenly they appeared fascinated by the color of her eyes and began poking her about the cheeks with grubby hands while trying to get a better look at her green eyes. They made a game out of pulling at her cheeks in turn. Their hold on her slackened as they became absorbed in the little game they were playing. With each tug to her cheek Abigail backed away from them, inching her way toward the corner of the room and the only available weapon in sight, a broom. The minute she was within reach of the broom, with one forceful yank she wrenched her arms free and grabbed the broom aimlessly sending it swinging in all directions before she angrily began beating them about their heads with it. They whooped and hollered as a furious Abigail came swarming down on them with broom in hand chasing them around the table. She was in hot pursuit of them when howling laughter suddenly filled the room. She turned to see another young man standing in the doorway who appeared strangely familiar to her. She was about to give him a taste of the broom but her eyes were glued on her two opponents who stood on the opposite side of the table. The one boy seemed to be taking the dusting in good humor as he stood there rubbing his head. It was the older one that Abigail feared. He was making his way around the table slightly crouched, his eyes filled with hate. All hope abandoned her as she caught the gleam of the steel knife in his hand.

Unexpectedly the young man standing in the doorway sprang forward, throwing himself in the path of Abigail's opponent while loudly yelling on the top of his lungs. All movement stopped as his words fell on their ears and to Abigail's surprise, the two of them went scrambling for the door, almost knocking each other down.

An exhausted Abigail leaned on the broom as she looked at the young man still standing in front of her. Under the streaks of paint that covered his face she finally recognized him. Her eyes dropped to his chest where the pinkness of two fresh scars was still evident. Without thinking she reached out and lightly touched the scars remembering clearly the day of his agony. He shook his head in an understanding manner and warmly smiled down at her. He turned to leave, and as if having second thoughts, walked over to the table and picked up the two remaining slices of bread before running out the door to catch up with his friends.

For the longest time, Abigail stood in the doorway and watched as they crossed the field heading toward the barn and their horses. There was only one feasible explanation she could think of for the man having saved her life; he thought her to be Jason's wife. She watched as they mounted their horses and headed out in a southerly direction. How long she stood there, she did not know, when suddenly her thoughts flew to Jenny in the root cellar.

When Abigail finally opened the door to the root cellar she was greeted by a hysterical Jenny. "Oh, Abigail," she sobbed, "I thought you were dead. I thought you were dead. I could hear them shouting and for sure thought that they had killed you."

Abigail steered her toward the parlor and sat there comforting her. She told her about giving the Indians a dusting with the broom stick. The two of them, holding fast to each other and realizing that eminent danger no longer presented itself began to laugh and cry at the same time.

"Let me in on the joke, I sure could use a good laugh."

Simultaneously they turned to see Albert entering the parlor. It was Jenny who sprang to her feet and ran across the room to greet her older brother with kisses and hugs. A shocked Abigail sat perfectly still trying to evaluate her own feelings at the sight of him. She was happy that no harm had befallen him, but other than that, she was devoid of all emotion as she looked at him. Strange she thought, I never missed him and now that he is back I wish he wasn't. If he was anticipating a warm welcome from her, he was sadly mistaken.

"Well, Abigail," he said, approaching her side, "you're looking well."

Abigail looked up into the cold blue eyes that regarded her. "Thank you, Albert," she murmured.

Jenny, perceiving the coolness between the couple, was puzzled. She could only reason that Abigail's lack of enthusiasm on greeting her husband was that the afternoon's events had drained her and began to blurt out the details to her brother. "And then . . . and then," she stammered, "Abigail gave them a good dusting with the broom. You certainly married a courageous woman, Albert. Imagine fighting off three Indians."

"How long ago did they leave?" he asked, with interest.

Jenny shrugged, "About a half hour ago, I'd say. Wouldn't you agree, Abigail?"

"Yes, about a half hour ago," she sighed. "Why? What does it matter?"

He didn't answer; instead he walked over to the fireplace and reached up to take down the rifle hanging over the mantle. "It matters, Abigail," he finally said, while loading the rifle. "Where does a filthy savage get the gall to come walking into our home and scaring women folk? There's still time; I can track them down and teach them some manners."

"With a rifle," Abigail shrilled, springing to her feet. "No, Albert, leave them be. They were young hungry boys looking for food. No harm was——" she stopped on seeing the hard set line of his jaw and the spark of excitement that illuminated the cold blue eyes.

"Which way did they head?" The question was posed to the two of them.

"I. . .I wouldn't know, I was in the cellar," Jenny stammered.

"Which way did they head, Abigail?" he demanded.

Abigail hesitated, knowing that the fate of the three young Indians was in her hands. "The last I saw of them, they were mounting their horses and heading south," she murmured.

He nodded his head as if taking her at her word. "I don't expect you to understand, this is man's work."

In fast stride, with rifle in hand, he headed for the back door.

Abigail ran after him. "Don't do this, Albert," she cried out. "Killing isn't man's work; it's the work of the devil!"

A defeated Abigail stood in the doorway and watched as her husband untied his horse from the hitching post and slipped the rifle into the saddle before mounting. He spurred the horse into a fast gallop cutting across the yard toward the barn before pulling the reins and heading north. Her eyes followed him until he was a speck on the horizon and with sinking heart realized the truth of her own convictions; a loveless marriage was one thing, but without trust it would never endure the test of time.

"This is my entire fault," Jenny cried. "I shouldn't have told him."

Abigail turned to the distraught girl and put a comforting arm around her shoulder. "Nothing's going to happen, Jenny. Albert is chasing the wind."

She blankly stared at her. "What. . .what are you talking about, Abigail? He's going to kill them. You know how much he hates Indians."

Abigail drew in a ragged breath while wondering whether she should tell Jenny the truth, after all, Albert was her brother. But then, she wanted Jenny, who she loved dearly to learn from her experience. "Albert took off to the north," she heard herself say.

"North?" Jenny frowned. "But you told him they went south."

"Yes," she nodded, "but he didn't choose to believe me."

For the longest time a confused Jenny stood there mulling things over in her mind. "I don't understand," she said finally. "Why wouldn't he believe you?"

"Perhaps his lack of integrity makes him judge others like himself. He thought I was lying to him and that's why he headed north. Now we best be getting a meal on the table before your father and Timothy come home."

The unusual silence between them as they prepared the evening meal gave Abigail cause to wonder if she had done the right thing. Jenny had always held her older brother in high regard. If anything, she didn't want to destroy the love that Jenny had for him, but at the same time she wanted her to know the truth of the matter; that her marriage wasn't the romantic school girl notion that Jenny had pictured in her head.

"Abigail?" Jenny said, placing the last plate on the table.

"Yes."

"When you told Albert that they had headed south, were you telling him the truth?"

"Yes, I told him the truth."

"But did you intentionally tell him the truth knowing he wouldn't believe you?"

Abigail wiped her hands on her apron as she turned to look at Jenny standing by the table. "I would have lied to Albert if it meant saving their lives. As it was, I didn't have to; I told him the truth well knowing he wouldn't believe me."

"Oh, Abigail," she sobbed. "I had no idea that you and Albert. . ."

"Not all marriages are made in heaven, Jenny, but you can be certain if I have anything to say about it, yours will."

Jenny ran to the arms that opened wide to receive her. "Oh, Abigail, I truly love you like a sister."

Missing was the jovial spirit that usually presided at the dinner table. Each seemed preoccupied in thought and aware of the empty chair at the table. An enraged Hugh McFadden had already voiced his opinion on his oldest son's actions but it wasn't till later that evening when they were sitting in the parlor that Albert returned home.

"What's this I hear about you tracking down three Indians," Hugh McFadden said, as his son entered the room.

"That's right, I did. But knowing how much you like Indians, father, you'll be happy to know I failed."

"What's got into you, Albert, are you trying to start an uprising? We have no quarrel with them. Let the government handle making the treaties."

"No quarrel," he angrily retorted. "They come into our home, scare our women half to death and you expect me to sit still for this."

"Since no harm was done, what was the sense of tracking them down to begin with?"

"To teach them a lesson," Albert said flatly.

The hypocrisy in his son's statement only angered him more. "A lesson? By God, I should think they taught you one. If you're so concerned about Abigail and Jenny, as you claim, you wouldn't go running off every chance you can get. You'd stay here and work the land and make someth . .ing. . ." Hugh McFadden voice trailed off as he slumped forward in his chair clutching his chest. His body fell to the floor.

Abigail sat bedside staring at the man lying on the bed. He seemed to be resting easy now. At his request, Timothy was sent to fetch Jason and Gay Feather while Albert, taking it upon himself, rode to Abilene to see if he could bring back Dr. Tillman. It took some persuasion on Abigail's part to get a hysterical Jenny to lie down for a spell.

"Abigail?"

It was but a whisper that brought her to her feet and over to the bed. She perched herself on the edge of the bed and took hold of the listless hand lying there and pressed it to her cheek. "How are you feeling?" she asked. "Can I get you anything?"

"No, child," he said, a weak smile edging his wan lips. "But there is something you can promise me."

"Anything," she sighed.

"See that Timothy gets a good education."

"You needn't have asked. I've already had it in mind for him."

A speck of warmth shown in Hugh McFadden's eyes as he looked at her. "We've been blessed for having you as part of our family, but I've always been curious as to how a young colleen, who has the map of Ireland written all over her face, came about impersonating an English woman, whose hair was said to be as black as a raven? You need not tell me, but I would like to know your real name."

It seemed so long ago and as if searching her memory while tears spilled from her eyes, Abigail murmured, "My name be Beth. . .Beth Carney."

"Ah, Beth Carney," he sighed. "Your secret is safe with me."

He closed his eyes and Abigail sat there holding his hand as he lapsed back into sleep. She couldn't believe that from the very onset he had known her to be an impostor and never exposed her. That he truly accepted her as his daughter-in-law and above all, loved her. There were few men in her eyes that could hold a candle to Hugh McFadden.

Long before they even entered the house, in the stillness of the night Abigail could hear the sound of the galloping horses approaching. She was hoping it was Albert bringing the doctor, but she opened the door to Gay Feather, Jason and Timothy as they came running up the porch steps.

"How is he," Gay Feather solemnly asked.

"The pain subsided, he seems to be resting comfortably now. I only wish Albert would get here with the doctor."

Albert arrived an hour later without success and at two o'clock that morning Hugh McFadden's soul passed into the hands of his creator, but not before confessing the guilt that had weighed heavy on his mind for the last thirty years. As he looked up at the concerned faces of his family standing beside the bed, his hand reached out to hold that of Gay Feather's knowing that the very touch of her hand in his would give him strength.

He looked at his three children and said, "You often heard the story of my having to leave your mother behind in England for three years when I first came here. I didn't send for her until I was financially able. What you didn't know my first year of living here I came down with a fever and was at death's door when Gay Feather, defying her father's wishes, came to live with me and nursed me back to health. She's been at my side ever since. . . just like she is now. She helped me work the land and build this house knowing the truth that she would never be the mistress of this house and she bore me a son.

"I often think of the apostle Peter who denied our Lord three times in the course of a day and our Lord forgave him. Jason, I denied you twenty-nine years for not having the courage to tell you. . . you're my son.

306

I couldn't be more proud of having you for a son and only hope that, in time, you will find it in your heart to forgive me for being such a coward. As for the rest of my children, don't ever think that I deceived your mother. She was well aware of the matter and found it in her heart to forgive me. Just remember what she taught you; judge not lest ye be judged." He closed his eyes as his voice trailed off. "Now would you be so kind as to leave this room, I would like to talk to Gay Feather alone."

Jenny ran to his bedside and flung her arms around her father's neck and cried, "I love you, father. I truly love you."

"Jenny, Jenny, my sweet Jenny," he whispered. "You're so like your mother Jane, that sometimes to look at you would take my breath away. Timothy, you're to take good care of your sister and as for you, Albert, see that Abigail wants for nothing."

There was such stillness in the parlor that one could hear the sound of the wind rustling through the tall fields of corn. Abigail sat on the settee comforting Jenny who sat beside her. Timothy stood looking out the window into the blackness of the night trying to hide the fact that he had been crying. Preoccupied in thought, Jason seated himself in the far corner of the room. The jingling sound of Albert's spurs finally ceased as he stood at the sideboard and poured a drink. He quickly downed a shot of whiskey and poured himself another.

Appalled by her husband's ill-manners, Abigail asked, "Would you care for a drink, Jason?"

He looked at her and then at her husband standing at the sideboard. "No . . no thank you."

A curt laugh escaped Albert's lips. "Please excuse my wife's ignorance," he said, "I'm afraid she is ignorant of the fact that it's against the law to serve whiskey to Indians."

"Albert," Abigail gasped in shock. "Jason is a guest in our home."

"All the more reason not to break the law," he retorted.

"Your husband is right," Jason said. "A long time ago we found out from white men that very few men can hold their liquor. It numbs the brain and makes some men cantankerous."

About to retaliate, the mournful chanting coming from the bedroom stopped Albert. "What the hell is that noise?"

A stricken Jason rose to his feet. "I'm afraid Hugh is dead. My mother is praying for his departed soul."

"Get her out of here," Albert yelled. "Get her and her heathen ways the hell out of here!"

Jason blocked his path. "Leave her be, Albert," he said fiercely. "Let her pray in the only way she knows how."

Bewildered Timothy turned from the window and looked at the two men angrily facing each other and suddenly realized that they were brothers. "Father wouldn't like you fighting like this." It was the only thing he could think to say.

A sobbing Jenny, having made a startling discovery, shot to her feet and went running to Jason. With arms clutching him around the waist she cried, "Oh, Jason, if you truly are my half brother that means we can never marry."

Touched by her declaration of love he leaned over and hugged her to him while running a hand down the length of her flaxen hair. "I'll remember this moment for years to come, Jenny, and on your wedding day I'll remind you of this and we'll both look back on it and laugh," he softly murmured.

The chanting suddenly stopped and a somber Gay Feather came walking into the room with a white envelope in her hand. "This is your father's will. It is written in his own hand. He asked me to give it to you, Albert."

With a bang Albert set the glass in his hand down on the sideboard and tore open the envelope giving her a skeptical look. At a quick glance he sifted through the three sheets of paper and said, "Do you know what's in here?"

"I have a vague idea," she admitted.

He glanced over at his wife sitting on the settee and then at his younger brother and sister. "It seems our dear father has left a deed leaving all the land west of here that he owned, to Jason. The rest of the acreage is to be equally divided among the three of us when Timothy becomes twenty-one. Now that you and your half-breed son got what you came for, Gay Feather, will you kindly leave my house?"

An angry Jason stepped forward only to have Timothy block his path. "No, Jason, brothers shouldn't fight amongst themselves."

"I have no quarrel with you, Timothy, nor will I ever have. But it seems to me Albert should mind his manners."

"The day you want to teach me some, Jason, I'd be only too happy to oblige," Albert sneered.

"This is neither the time nor place, Albert," Jason said, fighting to control his temper. "There are more important things to discuss, such as Hugh's funeral."

"Oh, no," Albert shouted. "You'll have no say in the matter. We'll take care of it. Now if you don't mind, I'd like you and your mother to leave."

Jason took his mother by the arm and steered her toward the front door. He opened it only to have Albert shout out after him, "Don't ever set foot on my property again, is that clear?"

In the doorway, Jason turned around and, ignoring the man standing in the middle of the parlor floor, said, "Good night, Abigail. Good night, Jenny. Good night, Timothy. I'm sorry for your loss. As for you, Albert, hell would have to freeze over before I set foot on your property."

The slamming of the front door echoed through the house.

Chapter Fifteen

For months Jason was bothered by an unexplainable feeling of loneliness, to the extent that a part of him was missing. There had always been a hard day's work in the fields, a book to occupy his mind and an occasional visit with Lucy Stone to uplift his spirits. Even his own thoughts had a way of keeping him company, but now they were constantly invaded by Abigail. Somehow she had managed to become part of him. He understood her completely and in a sense, came to understand himself as well. In a lot of ways they were alike. They possessed the same stubborn pride and the same sense of justice. It unnerved him to think that a woman could get such a hold on his emotions and reduce him to his present state of mind.

The whirling winds drew the smoke of the flames up into the chimney while the logs in the fireplace crackled with red glowing embers. From where she sat at her loom weaving, Gay Feather studied her son's face. He appeared to be hypnotized by the flames of the fire. The book he had been reading lay idle in his lap. Too often now, she had seen that faraway look in his eyes and knew something was troubling him. She was engulfed by a feeling of helplessness on his behalf, but knew better than to ask him questions.

"I don't think the storm will last till morning," she said, her deft hands sending the clattering shuttle across the loom.

Absent-mindedly, Jason turned to the sound of her voice. "What did you say?"

"I don't think this snowstorm will last till morning."

He didn't answer.

"Jason, I've been thinking," she said, hoping to get his attention. "There's enough wood to last the winter and we have more than enough food stored till spring, there really isn't that much work around here for two people. I thought perhaps you and Timothy might like to make a trip to the North Country and set some traps; maybe on spring vacation when he has no school. I don't mind being left alone."

"Now what made you think of that?" he smiled.

"It's been a long time since you've set traps. It would be a pity to forget the skills that my people have taught you," she smiled.

Jason leaned forward and picked up a long dry twig and held one end in the flames of the fire until it flared. He brought the twig up to his face and lit the cigar that was wedged between his teeth. "I just might do that," he said, exhaling the smoke of the cigar into the air.

Gay Feather quickly bent her head to hide the smile that covered her lips.

Their attention was drawn to the sound of horses hoof beats approaching the house. It was soon followed by the stumping of boots on the porch. Jason rose to open the door but before he could get there, Timothy came barging into the room. His clothes were covered by a light film of snow and his blue eyes nervously darted back and forth between Jason and his mother.

"It's Abigail;" he said breathlessly, "her time has come."

"Oh," Gay Feather smiled. "Was it a boy or a girl?"

"No, no, you don't understand. Jenny and I need help; we don't know what to do."

"Where's Albert?" Jason demanded.

"He went to Abilene yesterday and he hasn't come home yet."

"Then why didn't you go after him and get Doc Tillman?" Jason roared.

"There isn't time; Jason she needs help now."

Gay Feather studied the hard set line of her son's jaw and silently rose to her feet. She knew all too well that his sworn promise never to set foot on McFadden land was troubling him.

"Please come, Gay Feather," he said through quivering lips. "She's in an awful lot of pain, and Jenny and I don't know what to do."

In true Indian fashion, Gay Feather stood silent, waiting for her son to make the decision.

"You can't let her die," Timothy pleaded on the verge of tears.

Gay Feather ran to the young boy's side and placed a comforting arm around his shoulder. "She's not going to die, Timothy, she's a strong young girl," she assured him, know that the repercussion of his own birth weighed heavy on his mind.

"Damn him anyway," Jason fumed. "Why did he go to Abilene now of all times?"

"The baby wasn't due for another couple of weeks," Timothy said, in defense of his brother.

Jason smiled at his loyalty. "Go hitch up the rig."

"That won't be necessary, I'll ride Thunderbolt, it will save time."

"But you haven't ridden a horse in years," Jason protested.

Gay Feather smiled, "I've ridden horses long before you were born."

A spark of admiration shown in her son's eyes. "Okay, Timothy; you've heard her, saddle two horses and we'll be on our way."

Timothy scrambled for the door and never looked back.

A heavy blinding snow had slowed their pace as they rode in single file on the lonely road that led to the McFadden farmhouse. Each in turn was preoccupied with his own thoughts. Timothy's were frightening, for he was well aware that his mother had died giving birth to him. Gay Feather was disheartened by the fact that Hugh McFadden hadn't lived to see his first grandchild.

Oddly enough, Jason found himself praying: praying that Abigail would live and that he'd have the strength to see the evening through. Wasn't it enough that she married Albert and now he was expected to help with the birth of their first born? Damn it to hell, he thought, how much can a man take?

No sooner had they ridden up to the house when the door was flung open. Light streamed onto the porch and the silhouette of Jenny framed the doorway. She anxiously ran down the steps to meet them. "Thank God you came," she cried. "I don't know what to do."

Once inside the house, Gay Feather removed her brightly colored serape and began issuing orders. "Jenny, see to it that there is plenty of hot water on the stove. Before you take off your jacket, Timothy, I want you to go outside and gather some large stones. Put them in the fireplace and get them warm. Oh, and Jenny bring the sewing basket; I'll need twine and scissors."

The relief of having someone older who knew what to do showed on their faces as they eagerly set about the chores given them.

In the shadows of the dimly lit bedroom, Gay Feather could see the restless figure thrashing about on the bed. Low distressful groans were heard as she approached the side of the bed. She leaned over and drew the blanket back and with deft hands examined Abigail's stomach. "Your child is ready to be brought into this world, Abigail, but you're not helping it."

Through terrified eyes, Abigail looked up at the older woman in dismay. "Leave me be," she gasped, "just leave me be."

With the corner of the sheet Gay Feather gently dabbed at the beads of perspiration that dotted the young girl's forehead. "Don't be frightened; everything is going to be fine," she softly murmured.

To Gay Feather's surprise she turned from her touch as if refusing her help. She solemnly studied the girl on the bed and turned around and headed for the door where a silent Jason stood watching.

"I don't understand," she whispered. "It's as if she doesn't want my help. She's terrified and in tremendous pain. One would think she's part Indian the way she's laying there without screaming."

Jason's face clouded with concern. "To her way of thinking, a thoroughbred doesn't cry or scream; it wouldn't be proper." He weakly smiled at his mother. "I guess it's just as bad as being part Indian."

The evening dragged on and the clock on the parlor mantel chimed twelve times. Jason rose from the sofa and tossed his cigar into the fireplace in passing. He went over to where Timothy had fallen asleep in the parlor chair and shook his arm. "Timothy, go upstairs and go to bed," he said, "I'll wake you up when the baby comes." He turned and looked at Jenny who was fighting to keep her eyes open in a chair by the window. "You too, Jenny, there's no sense in all of us staying up."

"No, no. . . I couldn't sleep knowing she's in such pain."

"You know she's in good hands, Jenny, and there's nothing either one of you can do. Isn't it better you get your rest because she'll be depending upon you to take care of the baby tomorrow and help her? You won't be much help to her if you don't get some sleep." He put an arm around her shoulders coaxing her to her feet and steering her toward the staircase that led to her bedroom.

"You'll promise to wake me if she needs me."

"I promise," he smiled, planning a kiss on her forehead.

Groggy from lack of sleep, Timothy came staggering across the parlor floor. When he reached the staircase he stopped and looked at Jason standing there.

"Jason, I know what it meant to you having to cross the threshold of this house and I want to thank you for coming. Maybe someday Albert will come to his senses and realize how much he's missing by not having an older brother." With that he hugged Jason around the waist. "I love you, Jason."

Jason's arms went around him hugging him tight. "I'm so damn proud of you Timothy. Now git. . .git upstairs and get some sleep before the rooster crows."

He stood there for a while listening to their footsteps over head in their bedrooms. Soon the house fell silent. He walked into the dining room and headed directly for the sideboard and was glad to see that nothing had changed. Sitting on top of the sideboard were three decanters of liquor and finely etched crystal glasses. He picked up the decanter that was labeled whiskey and poured himself a drink. With shaking hands he brought the glass up to his mouth wondering just how much longer Abigail could endure the pain. He found himself wishing that there was a way that he could absorb some of the pain she was feeling. The thought of her blistered feet came to him. "Hell," he murmured, "she's got more guts and spirit than any woman I've ever known."

"Jason?"

He turned to see his mother in the doorway watching him. "What's wrong?"

"I need your help. The foot board of the bed is too high, I can't help her. I think it best we put her on the kitchen table. I'll go get things ready, but I'll need you to carry her into the kitchen."

Jason stood staring down at the figure of Abigail lying in bed. At the moment her eyes were closed and little wisps of hair clung to her damp forehead. Her hands were raised over her head tightly gripping the spindles of the brass headboard. As the pain racked her body the whiteness of her knuckles showed as her hold tightened around the spindles. Tiny beads of perspiration broke out on her forehead as she squelched the scream that welled up inside her throat. Then suddenly her whole body seemed to go limp with fatigue and she lay there gasping for air.

Jason leaned over and forcefully unclasped her small hands from around the spindles. "I'm going to carry you into the kitchen," he warned.

To the sound of his voice her eyes blinked open and she stared up at him. "Go away," she murmured. "Leave me be."

As he pushed his left arm beneath her shoulders he was appalled by the dampness of the bedding as well as her night dress. He could only imagine her pain. With one sweeping movement he lifted her cumbersome body into his arms and carefully maneuvered his way through the bedroom room door down the hallway and into the kitchen.

A clean white sheet covered the kitchen table and oil lamps illuminated the room. In the brightness as Jason lowered her to the table he was shocked by the pale drawn color of her skin and the deep dark circles beneath her eyes. He carefully laid her down on the table and turned to leave.

"Where are you going? I'll need your help."

In an exasperated manner he ran a hand through his hair. "I'll go get Jenny—she can help you."

"I don't think Jenny is strong enough to hold her down."

Gay Feather's eyebrows knitted together as she watched her son. "It's not like you've never seen a foal being born."

"It's not that."

Their eyes locked and Gay Feather made a starling discovery. His uneasiness was caused by seeing the girl's suffering. It's never easy to watch someone suffer, especially those you love. She watched as he reluctantly walked over to the table and lightly placed his hands on the girl's shoulders, pinning her to the table.

From the opposite end of the table Gay Feather's voice cut through his thoughts. "When the next spasm of pain comes, get her to bear down on it."

"I'll try, but I doubt she'll listen to me," he said helplessly.

"Make her."

Abigail's hands groped in vain for something to grasp as a sharp pain racked through her body. Once again she managed to squelch the scream that caught in her throat and a soft moan of anguish passed her lips.

Jason felt her body go limp beneath his touch and he watched the heavy rising and falling of her breasts as she lay there gasping. Without warning, her clenched fists hit the table as another pain racked her body.

Out of desperation, Jason's right hand went flying into the air. "Scream, damn you, scream," he roared, bringing his hand down hard across her cheek.

To the sting of his hand a loud piercing scream escaped her lips and she bore down on the violent pain that racked her body. Her hands flew up in the air, grabbing Jason about the wrists.

"That's it," he urged, "bear down on the pain."

A few seconds later her hands relaxed. Then all too quickly her nails dug into the flesh of his wrists only this time cutting deep as a loud cry of anguish passed her distorted lips. Her cheeks became flushed with color as she strained to support the piercing pain.

There was an acute stillness in the room and from the other end of the kitchen table the soft wails of a newborn's cries were heard.

Jason breathed a deep sigh of relief. "It's all over," he softly murmured.

A faint smile crossed Abigail's lips on hearing the child's first wails. The color drained from her face, with the exception of the deep red welt across her cheek where Jason had slapped her. Her head limply rolled to one side. She passed out with both hands still gripping Jason's wrists.

"It's a girl!" Gay Feather announced and out of the corner of her eye saw her son pick up a kitchen towel and gently wiped the perspiration from Abigail's face and throat.

"She'll be all right," Gay Feather said. "I'll go make up a fresh bed but right now it's the baby I'm concerned about."

"What's wrong?" he asked, in alarm.

"It's her color. Come see for yourself."

Between the fresh linen on the bed and the fresh night dress Abigail was wearing the fragrances of roses seem to permeate the bedroom. For a long time, Jason stood there holding a sleeping Abigail in his arms. He buried his head in the softness of her breasts as if breathing deep her very essence. Lightly his lips brushed the raw lips that had been bitten raw by pain. With a heavy heart he finally laid her down on the bed and pulled the blankets up over her making certain her feet touched upon the warm mound of covered stones at the foot of the bed. With the back of his hand he roughly brushed at the tears that clouded his eyes.

During the early morning hours the snowstorm had subsided and the first light of dawn brought a clear sky with the sun shinning bright on the horizon. Under the sun's reflection the snow on the ground glistened like crystal. From where he stood gazing out the bedroom window Jason watched two black crows soaring in the sky over the barn. That's how life should be, he thought. Smooth and as free as birds winging in the sky. Deep in thought, he watched until the birds were nothing more than mere black specks on the horizon.

"Jason?"

To the soft murmur of his name he spun around to look at Abigail. He walked over to the foot of the bed and checked to see if the rocks he put there earlier still contained heat.

"You shouldn't be here," Abigail said.

"Maybe not," he said. "But I'm here."

He watched as she propped herself up on her elbows with eyes eagerly searching the room. They came to rest on the small cradle in the far corner of the room. A faint smile crossed her lips. "Is it a boy or a girl?"

Jason swallowed hard. "It was a girl. We did everything we could to try to save her, but she didn't have the strength to survive."

"God no," she sobbed. "God no, I wanted that child more than anything in this world."

Suppressing a deep urge to take her in his arms and console her, Jason's hand tightened on the brass foot board. "You're young, there will be others."

"No, no," she cried, "you don't understand. I needed that child."

As much as he loved her, he wondered if he would ever come to understand her. "I guess I don't understand," he said bitterly. "You say you needed that child as if for your own selfish needs. I always thought one wanted a child out of love and to love. Did you need the McFadden name—is that why you married Albert? Now you have his name and one of the best farms in all of Kansas. As if that isn't enough, you expect me to believe you needed this child more than anything in this world. No, Abigail, I'm afraid I don't understand. And I damn you every day for marrying him."

"Oh, God, Jason," she cried. "Is that what you truly think of me?"

"What am I to think, Abigail? Tell me, so I can understand."

She brushed at the silent tears that ran down her cheeks. How could she explain—he'd never understand. There was no love in her heart for Albert, nor would there ever be. He was the only man she loved and to help relinquish that love she planned to bestow all the love she felt for him on her child. No, he wouldn't understand. Nor would he believe her.

"Is that why you stayed?" she asked. "Just to have the satisfaction of telling me what you think of me?"

"No. . . that wasn't my reason for staying," he said solemnly. "If we have another storm the ground will freeze. Rather than give the job to Timothy, I dug the grave and buried your child. That's why I stayed."

Chapter Sixteen

Abilene's public bathhouse had been filled to capacity with men sprucing up for their Saturday night spree. Tomorrow would be time enough to pay for their sins while having to listen to Reverend Finch's lambasting sermon on hell and damnation. At present the majority of men were bent on raising hell.

Like the buffalo, single women were scarce and sought after even before they reached puberty. The more fortunate males were out sparking some farmer's young daughter. Others would have to pay for a girl's favor or enjoy the evening gambling their hard earned pay at Lucy Stone's poker tables. Clean shaven, hair slicked down with the latest pungent hair tonic bought from a peddler's wagon, they crowded Lucy's house of promise.

Roulette wheels were spinning, poker chips being staked out while a sullen Albert McFadden stood at the bar, a half empty bottle of whiskey in front of him. His late arrival found him minus his favorite female companion, Tess Wheeler. Buxom, scatterbrained Tess, tired of waiting, had taken up with a young cowboy.

At first McFadden took the joshing of his predicament in good spirits but with each drink his patience was beginning to wear thin and he became belligerent. Several times Lucy tried to console him by pointing out the fine attributes of some of her other girls. McFadden didn't appear interested until he saw the young Mexican girl standing at the opposite end of the bar watching him. There was something hauntingly familiar about her pretty oval face as she openly stared at him.

An engaging smile curled the corners of McFadden's lips and he winked at the girl. -He caught a glimpse of the red dress she was wearing as she weaved her way through the crowded room towards him. On approaching his side she hesitated, reached out and touched his arm.

"I would like a drink, Al," she smiled, with large, brown eyes flashing.

He was flattered that she knew his name and smiled, "Sure thing, Honey. Lucy give us a glass will'ya," he yelled out. "What's your name, Honey?"

"Juanita."

"How is it you know my name?"

"It was easy," she laughed. "Tess never stops talking about you and you the only towhead in the room."

"Why haven't I seen you before?"

Juanita shrugged. "Tess, she keeps you pretty busy when you come here, no?"

The humor in her honest answer made him laugh.

A solemn-faced Lucy set the empty glass down with a bang. She was somewhat surprised at seeing Juanita interfering with another girl's steady. Let them fight it out between them, she thought and walked away. They were both welcome to the likes of Albert McFadden. As far as she was concerned, he should have been at home consoling his poor wife, whom she heard tell, had lost her first-born child a few months ago. Her only disappointment was in how she had misjudged

Juanita. She never figured her to be one to take up with another girl's customer. She couldn't shake the feeling that there was going to be trouble.

McFadden filled the two glasses that sat before him on the bar and held one out to the girl. "So Tess talks about me," he grinned. "What does she say?"

Juanita tongued her dry lips and took a sip of whiskey. She leaned closer and said, "You are the best."

A glint of amusement flashed into his blood shot eyes. "The best what?" he asked.

"The best lover she's ever had."

Her frank answer brought a smile to his face. He not only liked what he heard but suddenly the girl interested him.

Playfully Juanita ran her index finger the length of his arm and brought it to rest on his shoulder. She nestled close. "Why didn't Tess wait for you?"

She didn't have to look at his face to know her words cut him like the clean, sharp edge of a machete. She felt the muscles in his arm tighten in rage. She blew in his ear. "If I had a man like you waiting, I'd need no other."

McFadden's arm shot out and tightly gripped her about the waist squeezing the breath out of her. With his free hand he picked up his drink and drained the glass in one swallow. Using the back of his hand he wiped his mouth dry. "Where's your room, Juanita?" his hoarse voice asked.

She held tight to the arm around her waist and steered McFadden through the crowded room and into the empty foyer.

From behind the bar, a baffled Lucy watched as the couple climbed the staircase and disappeared from view.

With trembling hands, Juanita closed the door behind her. She watched as McFadden, who stood in the middle of the room, began fumbling with the buckle on his holster. She had envisioned this moment many times. Some nights she'd awaken in a cold sweat from the nightmare of her plan. She had pampered his ego to get him here and now she had intentions of killing him. Killing him would be easy; there'd be no qualms about it, she thought. It would be like killing a mad dog. Making it appear that it was in self-defense was another matter. The good people of Abilene would think nothing of hanging a Mexican woman who dared to kill one of their upright citizens, unless she could make it appear to be in self-defense.

Well hidden beneath his boyish charm, Juanita knew lurked a mean streak of cruelty, and this was what she was counting on. She trembled. Whether in fear or hate she was uncertain. McFadden slung his holster over the bedpost at the foot of the bed and came staggering toward her. Juanita stood frozen with a pasted smile on her lips as she felt his hand roughly snatch a hand full of her hair. He pulled her hair making her neck taut as his slobbering whiskey smelling mouth came down hard on hers. His free hand began to take inventory of her body. Juanita struggled to free herself but the weight of his body pinned her against the door as his mouth hungrily smothered hers. Out of desperation, she clamped her teeth down hard on the tongue that forcefully defiled her mouth.

"You little bitch," he howled, face distorted with pain. He struck out, cuffing her hard under the chin; the back of her head hit the door.

"You like to play rough, do you?" He lashed out at her again with the back of his other hand. The heavy gold ring he wore was cutting deep into the flesh of her cheek. Juanita whimpered, her eyes flashing with hate.

Breathing heavily, McFadden pounced on her, mistaking the look in her eyes for that of agreeable excitement. He fiercely shook her by the shoulders. "I know your kind. You like to be roughed up a bit before the main event," he told her. "Well, you picked the right man for the job."

Juanita spat in his face. "You call yourself a man! A man doesn't rape defenseless young girls like my sister!"

McFadden wiped at his face. He shook his head as if clearing it. The shiny black hair, the high cheek bones and the pretty oval face suddenly became hauntingly familiar to him.

Unexpectedly, he reached out, his hand invading the bodice of Juanita's dress and with one forceful yank he ripped it open, clear down to her waist. A sneer covered his lips as he ogled her nakedness. "At least you have more to offer than your sister did," he grinned.

Blindly, Juanita's long nails clawed at his face. With one violent push he sent her sailing across the room. Her body hit the wall and bounced to the floor like a rag doll heedlessly tossed by a child. Slightly stunned, she slowly rose to her feet and inched her way along the wall toward the bed.

With the sting of her nails still burning his cheeks, McFadden roared, "You little hell cat, you're going to pay for this." In one fluent move he removed the heavy leather belt from around his waist and lashed out at her.

Juanita bit into her lower lip to keep from screaming as the buckle on the belt cut into the flesh of her chest. She spun around to ward off the next blow, only to feel the buckle cut across her shoulder blades. Repeatedly the belt buckle cut into her body until she couldn't endure the pain any longer. Gasping, she sank to the floor.

Through a blur of silent tears she vaguely saw the head post of the bed. She crawled toward it, reached up and grabbed the bedpost, pulling herself to her feet. Strong hands came from behind her and pushed her down onto the bed. Juanita's heels dug deep into the mattress as she backed away from him. She reached the far side of the bed to find herself cornered. Her eyes never wavered from McFadden's face as he stood at the edge of the bed, towering over it. The boyish grin was gone only to be replaced by a sneering grin like that of a ferocious animal that was about to spring. "When I get done with you," he said from between gritted teeth, "you won't be fit for another man for months to come."

Juanita slid her hand beneath the pillow as McFadden's body came crashing down beside her on the bed, impaling himself on the knife she held in her hand.

He gasped and with bulging eyes looked at the girl on feeling the impact of the knife that had punctured the pit of his stomach. "You little bitch," he gasped. He strained in an effort to grab her by the throat. A groan escaped his lips just before his head hit the pillow. He lay motionless.

Juanita felt the warm sticky wetness of his blood on her hand that was pinned beneath his body. Frantically she pulled at her arm trying to free her blood ridden hand. She became hysterical on seeing her blood covered hand and tried to wipe it clean on the sheets. Trembling and crying, she crawled to the foot of the bed and sat there hunched in the corner, staring at the dead body of Albert McFadden that lay face down on the bed with one eye staring back. The only sound in the room was Juanita's incoherent mumbling in Spanish as she sat frozen in a state of shock. She wanted to run, escape, but the thought of crawling over his dead body was frightening. In death he had blocked her avenue of escape. Cold and trembling, Juanita pulled at the remnants of her tattered dress to cover her nakedness. For what seemed like an eternity, she sat there rocking back and forth. She began to hear voices and people moving about in the room. Her eyes caught the flare of a green blanket being thrown over the dead body on the bed. Then two powerful hands reached out and lifted her up over the footboard of the bed. She whimpered in pain and clung to the warmth and strength of the arms that carried her. She nestled her head in the broad shoulder and began to cry like a child. She didn't have to look up to know it was Blake Saunders.

He carried her over to the chair by the window and sat with her cradled in his lap. With gentle hands he examined the bruises on her face and body.

A nervous and distraught Lucy Stone watched in dismay. "Why the hell didn't she scream her head off? Someone would have heard her. He deserves killing for what he'd done to her. Why the hell did she have to kill him here, of all places? Jesus, they'll tar and feather me and run my girls out of town."

"Pull yourself together, Lucy. Remember no one knows what's happened here, except you and me. Now run downstairs and get some brandy and some bandages."

Blake waited until the door closed behind Lucy. He clearly remembered the piece of paper he had found in Juanita's baggage with the name Albert McFadden written in childish scrawl. "Juanita? Juanita you knew McFadden long before you came here, didn't you?"

She never answered. He was hoping against hope that what he surmised was wrong. When he felt the slight nod of her head against his chest it shattered him. He could only assume the killing to be that of a crime of passion and even in death he felt a twinge of jealousy over McFadden.

Lucy came storming into the room with a glass of brandy and cut pieces of sheeting for bandages. With uncontrollable shaken hands she held the glass of brandy out to Blake. "Did she say anything?"

"No," Blake said, holding the glass to Juanita bruised lips. "Drink some," he urged.

The brandy stung Juanita's cut lips, but eased the dryness in her throat. She took several sips and relinquished the rest by turning her head back into the warmth and security of Blake's shoulder.

"He came to my village a year ago last summer," Juanita murmured.

Blake and Lucy stared at each other.

"He raped my young sister, Rosa, who was only twelve years old—a saint of a child who never recovered from the shock. Two months later, my father died from a broken heart. You asked me if I knew him. No, I never knew him, neither did Rosa, but what right he have to destroy our lives?" she sobbed. "I no sorry I kill him, it was like killing a mad dog."

"Jesus," Lucy gasped.

Blake listened, his arms gently holding tight the small crumbled body in his lap. "Juanita, why did you let him beat you like this? Why didn't you scream? Someone would have heard you."

For the first time she lifted her head and her eyes searched the soft, gentle blue eyes that held hers. "Who'd believe a woman like me? If people see what he could do to another human being, then they believe me."

"He could have killed you," Blake said.

"Why the hell did you have to pick my place?" Lucy said, in despair, more or less to herself. "For sure they'll close me down when Reverend Finch's pious committeemen hear about this. There's no telling what they'll do to you."

Blake thought hard for the moment. "First of all, Lucy, no one knows I'm here and no one knows what's happened here except the three of us."

She nodded her head in agreement.

"I'm going to leave the same way I came in, by the back staircase, only this time I'm taking him with me. His body will be found on the other side of town. It will look like drifters robbed and killed him while he was heading home. Lucy, take all the money out of McFadden's pockets and that ring on his finger."

Lucy cringed. "I don't want to touch him."

"Just make believe your rolling a drunk," Blake said in exasperation. "Now don't try to tell me you never done that before."

"But what about her," Lucy frowned, "if anyone sees her looking like that they're liable to put two and two together and——-"

"After I get rid of McFadden's body, I'm going to rent a rig and come back for Juanita."

"Where are you taking her?"

Blake smiled, "Where she belongs. . . home with me."

"Damn it to hell!" Lucy swore, while pulling the ring off Albert McFadden's cold finger. "I sure as hell feel sorry for his wife, Abigail, after losing a baby and now this. I wouldn't wish it on my worst enemy."

Chapter Seventeen

As the days passed into weeks, and the last snows of winter melted into the ground, the green grass of spring began to appear. During these days the haunting dreams Abigail had, night after night, of a baby crying troubled her waking hours. She finally got the courage to walk up the hill to the cemetery to visit her child's grave. Physically she recovered from childbirth, but mentally the death of her child left her in a state of gloom. That she had never seen or held her baby girl, or had named her, weighed heavy on Abigail's mind. Mentally she referred to the child as my little girl, but she and Albert would have to think of a name to put on the gravestone. Despite the efforts of Jenny and Timothy to cheer her, some mornings, after everyone left the house, she'd go back into her bedroom and would sit for hours lovingly fingering all the clothes that she and Jenny had made for the child.

Another thought that kept recurring was the fact that her only chance of ever having another child had passed her by. Albert had accused her of being cold and indifferent towards him and with the death of her child it had become twice fold. That he would seek the companionship of other women to fill his masculine needs was obvious. Many a night he'd come home from Abilene smelling of cheap perfume and whiskey. Other nights he wouldn't come home until morning. Sadder still was the fact that Abigail couldn't find it in her heart to care about him.

335

It was on one of those mornings she sat on the front porch watching the sun come up and wondering when her husband would be returning from Abilene that she heard the sound of wagon wheels long before sighting the wagon coming over the hill. Accompanying the wagon were two other men on horseback. As they turned into the road leading to the house, Abigail recognized all three men. Sheriff Saunders was driving the wagon and accompanying him on horseback was Reverend Finch along with Mr. Thompson, the proprietor of the hotel. Abigail suddenly realized that the horse that was tied to the back of the wagon was Charger. Immediately she knew something was amiss on not seeing Albert.

With a sinking feeling, Abigail rose from the rocker and went down the porch steps to meet them. "Morning, Mrs. McFadden," Saunders said, tipping his hat.

"Morning Sheriff, Mr. Thompson, Reverend Finch," Abigail weakly smiled. "I see you have my husband's horse."

Blake jumped down from the wagon while the others dismounted. Forming a semicircle they more or less stood blocking her sight of the wagon. It was Blake who took the initiative to speak. "I'm very sorry to have to tell you this, Mrs. McFadden, there's been an accident. Albert must have met up with a band or robbers last night while on his way home. We found his body this morning on the outskirts of town. He was stabbed to death."

Abigail felt her knees go weak and the Sheriff grabbed her by the arm to steady her. "He's. . . he's dead," she gasped, her lips a quiver. "Albert's dead?"

"Yes, ma'am."

"Sorry for your loss, Mrs. McFadden, we came along to help," Reverend Finch explained. "Seeing how there only be Timothy to help you, we thought you could use the help of some men folks."

"Yes, yes, of course," she murmured, silent tears running down her cheeks. "Would you please carry my husband into the parlor so I could get him washed and properly dressed before Timothy or Jenny wake up, I'd be ever so grateful."

Abigail left her three guests in the kitchen drinking coffee and eating some apple tarts that she had made the evening before. With a large basin of water, lavender soap and towels she proceeded to undress and wash down her husband's body that was lying on the sofa. Automatically her deft hands turned to the task while her thoughts lay elsewhere. She managed to wash the bright red lip rouge from his taut lips and the dried caked blood that covered his chest before struggling to put on his best shirt and suit. All the while her thoughts kept reflecting on her husband's youth. He was too young to die, but by the same token he had never grown up to be a man. Perhaps in death his restless spirit would find the peace that seemed to have evaded him in life, she thought. She stared down at the blankness of the blue eyes that looked up at her and thought of all the money he had wasted on drinking, gambling and women; money that was needed to run the farm. Not wanting to waste two copper pennies to slip beneath the eye lids and close them; she resorted to needle and thread. She was combing Albert's hair when the Sheriff walked into the parlor.

Sheriff Saunders could not hide the admiration in his eyes. "You've done a real fine job, Mrs. McFadden but I wish you would have let one of us help you."

Abigail raised a weary hand to her head. Yes, she thought, Albert does look nice, just like on our wedding day. "You can help me, Sheriff," she said. "Would you be so kind as to take Albert's measurements and see to having a pine box sent from town? It will save us the trouble of making the trip."

"Yes, ma'am. I'd be glad to," he said. "And if you be telling us where the grave is to be dug, we'll be doing it before we leave."

For a confused moment she tried to remember the graves on the hill side. "Next to his mother's grave," she said finally, having decided the grave next to their child's would be left for her.

It wasn't until after the funeral that Abigail realized the job that lay in store for her. Running the farm was one thing, but keeping up a courageous spirit was another. For Jenny and Timothy's sake she knew she had to be strong and not let her own anxieties show. There was only one person whom she knew she could count on and that would be Jason, for he loved his half sister and brother as much as she did. Although his name was never allowed to be mentioned in the house, she was certain that Jenny and Timothy would often sneak off to visit with him and his mother.

"Since Albert's gone," Timothy said, in choked voice. "That means I'll have to be the man of the house."

"Oh, Abigail, what's to become of us?" Jenny sniveled.

"Hush, Jenny," she said, setting a pitcher of milk on the table. "We'll manage, somehow."

"I'll be leaving school come September," Timothy announced. "I'll start working the farm."

"You'll do no such thing, Timothy McFadden; you'll be finishing your schooling."

He looked at her and sighed. "You and Jenny can't run this place on your own. After last years drought we'll be needing money for seed, and we haven't the money to pay for hired help, so it's best I leave school and start to do my share around here."

"Has Jason given you any advice?" Abigail asked, only to see the look of guilt that passed between the two of them. "Don't look so guilty, I've known all along that the two of you ride over to see him."

Jenny's eyes grew enormous. "Did Albert know?"

Abigail shook her head. "No, I don't think so and I didn't think it was my place to tell him. As his wife, I had to respect his wishes, but now I think we can be open about it. Has Jason given you any advice on running the farm?"

"Oh, Abigail," Jenny sobbed. "Jason left months ago. He took a job at Fort Riley and he met some girl and got himself married. We ride over to see Gay Feather and he writes to us there."

"Jason's married?" Abigail said, trying to keep her voice on an even note and was thankful she was sitting down.

"From what Gay Feather has told us he went to visit her people and that's where he met the girl; she's Cheyenne," Timothy offered.

"Oh," Abigail said, for want of anything better, while trying to recover her shock. She sat in numbed silence until she noticed them staring at her. Forcing a smile to her lips she said, "Well, now you have another sister-in-law besides me."

"That's not all," Jenny smiled, "his wife is with child. When she has the baby Timothy will be an uncle, and I'll be an aunt. Isn't that great?"

Abigail's mouth went dry and she sat there with a strange feeling inside her chest. Little by little, as if someone had taken a chisel, she could feel her heart beginning to splinter away until nothing remained but a hollow space. She listened with half an ear as the two of them spoke about Jason and for one unexplainable moment wished she had never spoken his name.

That evening with quill in hand, Abigail started going over the accounts. Timothy was right; they couldn't afford to pay for hired help and at the same time set aside money for his education. There had to be some way to do both but at the moment she couldn't even think clearly; the whole of the night, her thoughts strayed to Jason. When she finally crawled into bed, she cried herself to sleep.

It was by chance a solution presented itself the next morning at the breakfast table. Timothy starting on his third piece of toast declared, "Abigail, you make the finest bread west of the Mississippi. Not one woman in town can hold a candle to your bread making."

"And she makes the best soap with lavender and rose fragrance," Jenny added.

"Yes," Timothy agreed, "that's true."

"Stop it, the pair of you," Abigail laughed. "Before you know it, you'll be turning my head."

"Upon my word, Abigail, it's the truth. Myrtle Thompson's bread that she serves at the hotel is bone dry. I bet she'd do anything to have your recipe."

"Even steal it," Jenny giggled.

"With all that Myrtle has to do, it's a wonder she has time to bake bread," Abigail said, in defense of the women. Suddenly quick thoughts began to flash through her mind. "Timothy," she said, apprehensively. "Do you really think my bread is that good. . .I mean in comparison with Myrtle Thompson's?"

"Yes, Abigail, it's far better and tastier than a number of breads I have eaten. Why do you ask?"

Abigail sank to the empty chair at the table, mind bogged in thought. From across the table Jenny stared at her. "What is it, Abigail? You have this funny look on your face."

"I was just thinking. You don't suppose that Mr. Thompson would be interested in buying my bread for his hotel? It would save Myrtle a lot of time not having to bake and . . .and if I make enough money selling him bread, we could afford to hire ourselves a helper to run the farm."

Open-mouthed they stared at her.

In order for her idea to succeed, Abigail knew she'd have to have their wholehearted support. "Jenny and I could bake the bread and you can deliver it on your way to school, Timothy. And we'd be selling the bread and making money to hire a helper."

"Do you honestly think we can manage it?" Timothy said doubtfully.

"Oh, we'll manage it all right," Abigail said with determination. "With hard work and our good name, we'll manage it."

Her enthusiasm suddenly spread to Jenny. "Yes, we could sell our bread and what about your soap, Abigail? I bet half the ladies in town would die just to have a cake of your fragrant soap."

Jenny's words swept over her like a sudden burst of energy that she had been lacking for months. "Why not," she said. "Why not sell soap as well?"

After seeing to the care of the animals, with Timothy driving the wagon, they rode into Abilene. Neatly wrapped in towels were four loaves of Abigail's bread and wrapped in paper lay ten cakes of soap; five lavender and five rose fragrances.

"How much will you be asking for a loaf of bread?" Timothy asked.

She hadn't given it a thought. "I honestly don't know. What would you say a fair price would be?"

Timothy, the mathematician in the family, began giving it serious thought. "You have to take into consideration not only your time, but how much it will cost you to bake the bread and the cost of the ingredients you use."

"What about the cost of the soap?" Jenny chimed.

The next half hour of their journey was spent calculating the cost of the making of one loaf of bread and that of a cake of soap.

A surprised Mr. Thompson looked at the three people walking towards his desk in the hotel lobby. The young widow, in her black widow's weeds, the young boy with a black band around his arm and his sister dressed in dark blue. He felt a pang of pity for them. "Mrs. McFadden," he smiled, and looked at the basket she set down on his desk. "What have we here?"

"Good day, Mr. Thompson, I hope we're not intruding, but I would like you to taste a slice of the bread I baked this morning."

With that, Jenny pulled back the covering on the basket offering him to take a slice. Somewhat baffled he obliged and bit into it. As if holding their breath the three of them watched as his black mustache twitched with movement in time to his chewing. "Mmmm. . .mighty tasty, that much I'll say for it."

"I thought perhaps it would be to your advantage to order your bread from me rather than have your wife bake since she has so many other chores, what with five children . . ."

Myrtle Thompson, who was in earshot of the conversation, came out from behind the door. "What's this," she frowned, "am I to understand, Abigail McFadden, that you have intentions of selling your bread?"

Abigail smiled. "Yes, Myrtle. I thought perhaps you'd be interested in buying weekly for your business and saving yourself the chore of having to bake."

Without ado, Myrtle's hand reached into the basket for a slice of bread and she stood there eating it. Already the thought of less work she found appealing and hating to admit to herself the bread was tastier than hers. "How much are you asking for a loaf?"

Again the three McFadden's held their breath. "I'll be asking ten cents a loaf," Abigail said.

"That's a bit high," Myrtle balked. "We'd be ordering in quantity, at least ten loaves a week."

"Oh," Abigail stammered.

"Sorry," Timothy interjected, "I can't see Abigail doing all that baking for less than ten cents a loaf, what with the cost of firewood."

"If you're not interested in Abigail's bread," Jenny smiled, "maybe you'd be interested in buying some of her lovely fragrant soaps. I'm sure your guests would be pleased bathing with fragrant soaps. I know the ladies would."

Myrtle turned up her nose sniffing the air as Jenny held out a cake of soap to her. "How much is a cake of soap?"

"Five cents," Jenny answered.

"Hum," Myrtle snorted, "that's too expensive for hotel quests. But you can put me down for an order for my family. Two cakes a week we'll be buying. And. . . and make that ten loaves of bread."

It wasn't until they left the hotel that the three of them burst into peals on peals of uncontrollable laughter. They had anticipated selling the bread for eight cents a loaf and a cake of soap for three cents in order to make a profit. With what they thought was good bargaining on their part they had solicited the Thompson's business for ten cents a loaf of bread and five cents for a cake of soap, never taking into consideration that their products were far superior to others available.

With renewed confidence, they started down the main street, going from door to door selling their wares. By late afternoon, on approaching the last house on the outskirts of town, a smiling Sheriff Saunders quickly crossed the street to greet them and nonchalantly stood there blocking the gate to the house. "Mrs. McFadden, Jenny, Timothy, it's good to see you again," he said, politely tipping his hat. "Heard tell you've been canvassing the town, Mrs. McFadden, selling your good bread and fancy soap."

"Yes," Timothy smiled. "Abigail's bread sure is a seller. Jenny where's your manners? Offer the Sheriff a slice."

With a shake of his head, Sheriff Saunders declined the offer.

It was the look of embarrassment on the man's face that set Abigail to thinking something was wrong. "Is it against the law, Sheriff, to canvas the town?" she asked

"No, ma'am," he sighed. "But the residents of this house in particular, I honestly don't think they'd be interested in your wares."

"Oh," Abigail murmured. "Why would that be?"

Blake Saunders found himself at a loss for words. "It's. . . it's not the proper house that a lady, like yourself, would want to be seen entering, ma'am."

On grasping the implication of his words and his good intentions, Abigail smiled while saying "Thank you, Sheriff. Thank you very kindly for your concern. But since I'm in the business of selling my bread and soaps, I'm hardly in the position to be prejudiced. I'm sure the people who reside here do eat bread and wash."

"Yes, ma'am. Yes, ma'am, I'm sure they do."

"Good," Abigail smiled. "I'll take your word of advice and instead of using the front door we'll go to the back door to sell our wares. Good day, Sheriff."

With mouth agape, Sheriff Saunders watched as the three of them went down the side street heading for the back door of the house. He stood there for some time shaking his head from side to side.

Abigail, Timothy and Jenny waited in the kitchen while the woman who answered the back door went running off into another part of the house to call her mistress. "If ever you make a delivery here, Timothy, you're to use the back door and you're not to linger a minute, do you understand?"

"Yes, Abigail," he answered, while anxiously waiting to see what a wayward woman looked like. He often heard stories about the women who lived in the house; stories that boys kept to themselves. He was beginning to have second thoughts of not heeding Sheriff Saunders words and having allowed his sister and Abigail to enter such a house.

To the sound of clicking heels coming down the hallway Abigail's voice dropped to a whisper. "I'll do all the talking," she warned.

Surprise touched Lucy Stone's face on entering the kitchen and finding the three McFadden's standing there. "I understand you wanted to see me, Mrs. McFadden," she said coolly, eyes sweeping them.

"Thank you for your time, Miss Stone," Abigail said, forcing a smile to her lips. "I'm starting a small business, so to speak, and I thought perhaps you'd be interested in having a weekly delivery of my homemade bread or perhaps my fragrant soaps."

A baffled Lucy Stone just stared at them for a second until realizing the tremendous amount of guts it had taken for them to enter her house. She found herself admiring the woman standing there in her widow's weeds.

Although somewhat shocked by the lady's painted face and gaudy dress, Jenny stepped forward offering her a taste of the bread. An obliging Lucy Stone dipped her hand into the basket and began chewing at a small corner of the slice in her hand. Suddenly taken with the taste she asked, "Where did you learn to bake bread like this?"

"It's. . .it's an old family recipe," Abigail said.

"Best I've ever tasted in these parts that's for sure. How much are you asking?"

"Ten cents a loaf."

"A little bit high in price. . .but it's well worth it."

"Then you'll want to place an order?" Abigail frowned.

"Sure thing," Lucy smiled. "You can put me down for three loaves a week. And what's this about fragrant soaps?"

With quick hands Jenny unwrapped two cakes of soaps and held them out to the woman. "One has the fragrance of lavender, the other is of roses," Jenny offered, still appalled by the women's outlandish clothes.

With a cake of soap in each hand, Lucy Stone stood there sniffing away at them. "Haven't smelt anything as good as these in years, all the soaps you buy around here smell like disinfectant. My girls will go crazy over these. How much are you asking?"

"Five cents a cake."

She thoughtfully looked at the cakes in her hand. "Is there any chance you could make them a little larger? Soap just seems to disappear in this house."

"Larger," Abigail frowned. "Why I suppose I could, but of course that would cost extra for twice the size."

"That's fine with me," Lucy smiled, sniffing the soaps again. "You can put me down for four cakes a week, two of lavender and two of rose."

Abigail looked at the woman and in all sincerity said, "Thank you, Miss Stone. Thank you for your order."

"Thank you for dropping in," Lucy smiled. "Will you be making the delivery, Mrs. McFadden?"

"No," Abigail answered, surprised by the question. "Timothy will be making all the deliveries."

Their eyes locked for a moment.

"I see," Lucy said, somewhat disappointed. "You can put your mind at rest, Mrs. McFadden; I don't take to having young boys loitering on my property."

Her words sent the color rising in Timothy's face.

"Thank you," Abigail murmured, and on impulse reached out and offered her hand to Lucy Stone in a gesture of friendship.

On their way home, after calculating what their profit would be, the three McFadden's in jovial spirits began to sing, something they hadn't done in months.

The weeks seemed to fly and with all the work that had to be done, Abigail had very little time to think about herself and in a way she was thankful. She was too tired at night to let her thoughts drift and slowly, although it hurt her deeply, she began to accept the fact that Jason would never be part of her life again. Her last thoughts at night came in the form of prayers asking for the strength to carry on.

On a mild September morning, Abigail's deliverance came. After seeing to Timothy taking off in the wagon to make his deliveries and attend school, she had turned to the task of feeding the chickens and gathering the eggs in the hen house. When she came out of the barn the surprising sound of someone whistling, drew her attention. Raising a hand over her eyes she gazed into the distance and could see someone walking along the road, a rare sight. She watched with interest, as the tall lean figure of a boy turned into the roadway heading for the house. Leary of strangers, Abigail's footsteps quickened and before he could get to the front porch she had met him halfway. She had left Jenny in the kitchen churning butter.

"'Morning, ma'am," he smiled warmly, "my name is Jonathan Ames." He politely removed the blue cap from his head and wrung it in his hands. "Would this be the McFadden farm? I'm looking to speak with a Mrs. Albert McFadden."

"Yes, Mr. Ames, how may I help you? I'm Mrs. McFadden," Abigail said apprehensively on noticing his shabby appearance. The coveralls he was wearing were high above his ankles and his shirt sleeves were frayed and the blue cap was that of a union soldier.

Jonathan Ames stared at the young woman in her widow's clothes. "Sorry, ma'am, I didn't mean to gawk like that, but I was expecting a much older woman. Sheriff Saunders told me you might have some work for me."

On hearing the Sheriff's name, Abigail relaxed a moment. "Oh," she murmured, "did he drive you here?"

"No ma'am, I walked."

"All the way from town?" Abigail said in surprise.

"Yes, ma'am, I started before sunup."

Two schools of thought penetrated Abigail's mind, either he was a liar or he was in desperate need of work to walk that distance. "Do you know anything about farming, Mr. Ames?"

He chuckled. "I was raised on a farm, ma'am, before the war. My Pa died at the battle of Vicksburg; this be his cap I'd be wearing, and my Ma died soon after. That's when we lost our farm. My younger brother and sister are in an orphanage back in Ohio. I came here hoping to find some land I could settle on and then send for my brother and sister but that takes a heap of money."

"Unfortunately it does," Abigail said sympathetically. "To be honest, Mr. Ames, we couldn't afford to pay you much, we're just about holding our own."

"That's fine with me, ma'am. Right now, I'd settle to work for room and board."

"Well, Mr. Ames," Abigail smiled, "since you put it that way, you have a job." Having noticed the way he eyed the eggs in her basket, and the leanness of his body, she added. "You can start right after I cook you some breakfast. Is that agreeable?"

"Bless you, ma'am. That's. . .that's more than fair." Quickly setting the cap back on his head and covering the unruly curly sandy head of hair, he politely reached out for the basket on her arm.

Chapter Eighteen

Time and time again, Abigail would find herself staring at Jonathan Ames while he worked, wondering if he was her father-in-law reincarnated. He had a natural reverence for the land, was a hard worker and had an even-tempered personality. The first week he took over the farm he accomplished more than she had imagined. She never had to give voice as to what had to be done, since Jonathan seemed to have the natural instinct for knowing beforehand. At the back door there was always an ample load of chopped fire wood to keep her stove going on the days she and Jenny baked bread. The hogs and chickens were looked after and the fields plowed in time for planting. More importantly, it gave Timothy some leisure time to study. Within a month of his living with them, Jonathan became part of their family.

It was Jenny's idea to move her things down from the attic and into her father's room so Jonathan could sleep in the house instead of the barn. At the same time Abigail rummaged through Albert's clothes and, with a few alterations, Jonathan acquired a new wardrobe. Although he was a few years older than Jenny and Timothy, the camaraderie between the three of them was quite noticeable, and for this Abigail was grateful. She was also pleased that her business was turning a nice profit and she could afford to pay Jonathan a weekly salary.

As the four of them rode home from church in the buckboard one Sunday morning, Jenny thoughtful said, "It's a beautiful day; why don't we ride over and visit Gay Feather today? She's never met Jonathan, and Timothy and I haven't visited her in some time."

"I would like to meet her," Jonathan smiled, "you've told me so much about her."

Abigail sat frozen, momentarily at a loss for words. She hadn't seen the woman since the night her child died. There was a part of her that wanted to visit Gay Feather, if only to thank her. But at the prospects of having to hear about Jason, his wife and child, she shirked at the idea. "The three of you can go," Abigail said. "I. . .I have to go over the accounts this afternoon."

"Today is the Sabbath, Abigail," Timothy reminded her. "Enough is enough, you work hard all week; the accounts can wait. We won't go without you and that's that. Furthermore, Gay Feather keeps asking about you all the time."

From where she sat in the backseat of the buckboard, Abigail could see the small log cabin in the clearing. It was the sight of the barn beyond the cabin that brought back memories, memories that seemed so long ago. She remembered the day she had fallen from Charger and the night the foal was born. Suddenly her whole body seemed to ache with longing, longing for the man she loved and would never have and she had nobody to blame but herself. Unconsciously her hands had tightened on the rim of the pie plate in her lap, her fingers crushing bits of the flaky crust. God, she thought, when will it end, how long does it take for love to die?

No sooner had they pulled up in front of the cabin when the door opened and a smiling Gay Feather came down the steps to greet them. She was taken aback on seeing the substantial loss of weight of the girl in the black mourning dress. "Abigail," she smiled, circling an arm around the slim waist. "I'm so glad you could come. It's been such a long time."

"Yes," Abigail murmured, "almost a year."

Clearly remembering the sadness of their last meeting, Gay Feather's arm tightened around the girl. "That long," she sighed.

"I'm sorry for the looks of this apple pie," Abigail said. "The crust seems to have broken in several places."

"Well, it certainly smells good," Gay Feather smiled. "Jenny, would you be seeing to making the tea while Abigail and I sit out here on the porch."

The afternoon dwindled away and the surprising thing about it, Abigail realized, there was never made mention of Jason or Albert's name. They sat watching the camaraderie between the younger members of the party.

"He seems like a very nice boy," Gay Feather said, in reference to Jonathan Ames.

"That he is," Abigail smiled. "He's taken on the job of running the farm and he's such a hard worker."

"That's good. Maybe now you can get some rest. Timothy is real concerned about you, Abigail. He's told me how hard you work with all the baking and soap making that you do."

"Timothy and Jenny work just as hard as I do, believe me."

"Yes, but you're shouldering all the worries, I can see that," Gay Feather frowned. "You're certainly doing a fine job of raising them, and I know Hugh would be proud of you."

For a moment an acute silence hung in the air.

"I really miss Father McFadden," Abigail sighed.

Gay Feather bit into her lower lip. "Yes, he's a man to be missed. He'd come over here at least once a week just to see how I was getting on and he'd do most of my shopping for me, knowing what a burdensome task it was for me to go to town."

Puzzled, Abigail looked at the woman. "I would think that going to town would be a nice change for you, seeing other people. I know I look forward to it sometimes."

Gay Feather wanly smiled at the naive statement that was made. "That's because you're a white woman."

"What has ———-" Abigail stopped.

"The name calling doesn't bother me as much as having to stand there and wait until everyone else has been served. It was a very hard thing to explain to a child."

Envisioning the injustice, Abigail could see the humiliation the woman as well as her son had to suffer over the years. "I usually go to town about once a month," Abigail said. "I'd be only too happy to have your company if you'd care to join me."

Gay Feather warmly smiled at the girl. "Thank you, Abigail, that's very kind of you. I just may do that."

"If there's anyone who should be doing the thanking, it should be me," Abigail said in strangled voice. "I never thanked you for your help the night. . . I . . . I lost my little girl."

On seeing the pain in her green eyes, Gay Feather turned her face away. "No need to thank me," she murmured.

The afternoon ended on a happier note with the eating of Abigail's apple pie and Jonathan and Timothy seeing to the splitting of logs for Gay Feather.

Over the months, in Abilene, it became a rather common sight to see Mrs. Albert McFadden driving her buckboard into town with an Indian squaw sitting beside her.

There was something else that Abigail began to observe over the months, the radical changes that were taking place in Jenny. To a degree she was slowly coming out of her shell of shyness. She also noticed how Jenny, at times, appeared moonstruck in Jonathan Ames's company. Rather then create a disharmony in the family; she decided to approach the subject with Jonathan.

With lunch basket in hand, Abigail headed for the south field to help Jonathan with the planting of the winter wheat. They had worked side by side for hours and when the noonday sun came up directly overhead, they decided to have their lunch under the shade of a cottonwood tree.

"It's a nice lunch you made, Miss Abigail," Jonathan smiled while finishing his second portion of baked beans and bread.

"Jonathan," Abigail said, hesitantly. "There's something I've been meaning to talk to you about."

"What might that be?" he said, good-naturedly, while eyeing the fields.

"It's about Jenny," she said, only to see the high color rise to his face. "I know she's smitten with you, Jonathan, and I thought it best to talk to you since you're older and would understand rather than create a discourse in the family."

"You have nothing to worry about, Miss Abigail, I wouldn't hurt a hair on Jenny's head. As much as I love her, I know I have nothing to offer her. Jenny is far above the likes of me," he said, shaking his head from side to side.

"Don't say that about yourself, Jonathan. You have a lot to offer any woman, but what I'm trying to say is, for you to be patient and wait. After all, she's only sixteen. If and when Jenny decides that she wants to marry you, I'll not stand in her way."

"Do you mean that?" he beamed. "Do you honestly mean that, Miss Abigail?"

Abigail laughed at his joy. "Yes, I mean it."

He jumped up, grabbing her by the hand and jerking her to her feet. He loudly whooped and hollered while lifting her clear in the air and swinging her around. "I'll wait . . .if it takes forever, I'll wait, Miss Abigail."

Abigail watched in amazement as he went back to planting the field with twice the energy that he started out with.

Chapter Nineteen

It came as no surprise to Abigail when Jenny turned seventeen the following year; she announced her intentions of marrying Jonathan Ames come spring. For the next few months ever spare moment they had was spent in planning the wedding and making Jenny's trousseau. The sewing of the wedding gown was placed in Abigail's capable hands. She spent painstaking hours sewing on small beaded pearls that she had ordered from New Orleans. If anything she wanted Jenny to have a beautiful wedding, one she would remember the rest of her life. When it came time for the final fitting of the gown it was Abigail who was surprised even more than Jenny.

"Oh, Abigail," Jenny sighed, turning from side to side in front of the looking glass. "It's gorgeous. I've never seen anything like it in my life."

Abigail pulled at the large puffy sleeves and with a critical eye checked her work. Satisfied, she smiled at Jenny in flowing white gown. "You'll make a beautiful bride."

"Dear, dear, Abigail, how can I ever thank you?" On sudden impulse, Jenny ran to her side and planted a kiss on Abigail's cheek. "I only wish that someday you'll find the happiness I'm feeling. Oh, did I tell you I received a letter from Jason? Gay Feather gave it to me yesterday when we stopped by for a minute. Guess what? Jason will be here for my wedding, isn't that wonderful? Being my oldest brother, he deems it a privilege to be asked to give me way. I only wish that he finds happiness after all that he's been through. I would like everyone in this world to feel the joy I'm feeling," she giggled.

Abigail finished rolling the spool of thread in her hand and placed it in the sewing basket. "I don't understand," she said, "what makes you think that Jason isn't happy?"

"How could he be with losing his wife. . ."she stopped and stared at Abigail. "Didn't I tell you? I could have sworn I told you. About a month ago he lost his wife in a fever epidemic."

Abigail swallowed the lump in her throat. "No . . .you never mentioned it."

"I'm sorry. With all this wedding business I've been in such a tizzy, I thought I told you. We'll just have to see to making him and his daughter happy while they're here. Gay Feather is counting the days; she can't wait to see them."

"I can imagine," Abigail said, her thoughts elsewhere. "Three years is a long time."

***

The hour was late as the last two wagons of wedding guests finally departed in an uproar of song and laughter. Abigail stood on the porch and waved good-bye until they were out of sight. She breathed a deep sigh of relief and turned and entered the house. After closing the door she stood there for a moment with her back leaning against it. Nothing stirred in the house and the stillness of it seemed to engulf her.

In the doorway to the parlor, Abigail hesitated. She was pleased by the sight of the room and the fashionable way in which she had decorated it. The small delicate vase containing the flowers that she had cut from the garden earlier that morning, were beginning to wilt from the heat of the day. All around the room traces of guests could be seen, empty tea cups, plates, forks with traces of white cake frosting. On the sideboard sat a saucer that held a half smoked cigar. Ordinarily, Abigail would have been bustling around the room picking up and straightening before retiring for the night, but she felt completely drained. Instead, she walked over to the fireplace mantel and with one hand leaned against it looking down into the blackened hearth. She complimented herself on how smoothly and tastefully she had managed Jenny's wedding, sparing no expense. For months to come it would be the main topic of conversation at church and town meetings. But more than this, she complimented herself on how beneath the facade of her forced smiles she managed to cover the overpowering feeling of loneliness inside her. She would miss Jenny and Jonathan something terrible although they'd only be gone a short spell.

Her thoughts reflected on the day's events and the first incident that came to mind was the most stirring of the day; the sight of Jason entering the church with Jenny on his arm. After three years, Abigail thought, she had succeeded in erasing him from her mind and heart, but she was mistaken.

Next to Jenny's small frame he appeared taller and more stately then she remembered. Even with age he was still handsome. When he lifted Jenny's bridal veil and placed an affectionate kiss on the young girl's forehead, Abigail imaged herself the recipient of the kiss, and could almost feel the warmth of his lips on her own forehead. Smiling he left Jenny's side and came walking over to the pew and unexpectedly stood beside her. He smiled, "The family pew, I take it."

Too choked to answer Abigail nodded her head and vaguely remembered the rest of the wedding ceremony. She went through the motions of smiling and shaken hands with their guests while inconspicuously searching the crowd for another glimpse of Jason as they left the church.

Back at the house she was more at ease thinking he wasn't coming to the reception; again she was wrong. It was while she was busy setting out trays of food on the make shift tables that she and Timothy had put together that she caught sight of him in the yard. He was standing there with a glass of punch in his hand talking to Sheriff Saunders and his wife Juanita, when suddenly he turned and looked her way. Under his straight forward gaze Abigail could feel the heat of color rise to her cheeks and was thankful when Jonathan sudden grabbed her by the arm and steered her toward the dance platform. "Come on, Abigail," he urged. "It's high time I had a dance with my new sister-in-law."

To the tune of a fiddle and a banjo, Jonathan waltzed her around the platform that he had built out of wooden planking that someday would be used to build him and Jenny a house.

With half an ear, Abigail listened to Jonathan's youthful jubilant praises of his new bride and his undying devotion. Abigail found herself wishing that his happiness was contagious and somehow would spread to her.

To the creaking sound of footsteps coming down the staircase that led to the attic, Abigail pasted a smile on her lips on the anticipation of seeing Timothy. Instead her smile gave way to that of surprise as Jason entered the parlor. "Where's Timothy?" she asked.

Jason smiled, shaking his head from side to side. "I put him to bed. Seems he bit off more than he could chew."

"Is he all right?"

"Nothing a good night's sleep won't cure. He hasn't learned how to hold his liquor yet."

"Thank you, Jason. Thank you for taking care of him," she said and detected a flicker of anger in his eyes.

"You say that as if you were addressing a servant, Abigail. Aren't you forgetting something? Timothy is my half-brother."

"I'm sorry. I'm sorry if you misinterpreted——"

"Forget it," he shrugged and continued studying the room. "You've done a real fine job with the house and a real fine job of raising Jenny and Timothy. They idolize you. I've never heard so many praises sung about one woman in my life time."

"I assure you," she lightly laughed, "the feeling is mutual where Jenny and Timothy are concerned."

"Not to hear them tell it. You've brought the farm back to making a profit. You have a bread business going and you have all the ladies buying your soap and smelling like roses," he smiled.

Hearing his praises made her uncomfortable and hoping to change the subject she asked, "Would you care for a brandy?"

"That would be nice," he answered.

Annoyed at herself, Abigail walked over to the sideboard, conscious of him watching her. She picked up the crystal decanter and with shaking hands start filling a small glass.

"I'd like to thank you for taking my mother to town with you. That's very thoughtful of you. She wrote and told me what it meant to her."

"No need to thank me, I enjoy her company. It is a rather lonely drive." She turned to find him standing where she had been with one hand leaning on the fireplace mantle.

"Aren't you joining me?" he asked, eyeing the glass in her hand as she came across the room.

"No," she smiled. "I'm afraid, like Timothy, I haven't acquired a taste for strong liquor."

He reached out for the glass and instead his long lean fingers curled around her wrist steadying her shaking hand. "You're thinner," he murmured, his eyes studying her face. "And more beautiful then I remembered." Their eyes locked. "Are you happy, Abigail?"

The unexpectedness of the question, the earnest note in his voice and the powerful touch of his hand on her wrist shattered her. "Happy?" She repeated the word as if it were foreign to her vocabulary when suddenly the glass slipped from her fingers. As if symbolic to what she was feeling the glass shattered into pieces on the stone hearth.

"Now look what I've done," she gasped, wrenching her arm free and falling to her knees. With quick fingers she began to pick up the slivers of glass and tossed them into the fireplace.

Puzzled, Jason watched in silence as she drew a handkerchief from her pocket and began mopping up droplets of wine from the carpet. There was something so desolate about seeing her before him on her knees picking up the bits of glass. "Does the carpet mean that much to you?" he finally asked.

She stopped and sat back on her haunches. "No damn it, it doesn't" she cried. Uncontrollable tears welled-up in her eyes as she looked down at her bleeding finger tips. "Why?" she asked in anguish. "Why did you have to touch me?"

Strong hands gripped her beneath each elbow drawing her to her feet. She swayed against the lean hardness of his body as his arms encircled her waist drawing her close. He bent his head and she stood on the tip of her toes to reach the lips that passionately sort hers. The next thing Abigail remembered was being in her bedroom and Jason helping with the laces of her corset as though it was an every day occurrence between them.

Abigail awoke with a start on feeling the warmth of an arm that lay across her waist and the fact that someone was sharing her bed. After three years of widowhood, she grew accustom to sleeping alone. She smiled to herself and looked over at Jason with his face half buried in the pillow next to hers. The faint scar that cut across his cheek brought back memories. If only she knew then how much she loved him. Lightly, she ran her index finger down the length of the scar.

"Every time I look in a mirror it's a reminder of you." His voice came muffled against the pillow as he opened his eyes and look over at her.

She drew back her hand not knowing whether to laugh or cry. "Can you ever forgive me for that day?"

"I have. . . a long time ago. In fact," he grinned, "it makes for interesting conversation when I meet people. They're always inquisitive as to how I got the scar in the first place. So I tell them about the night I was rolling in the hay with this redhead——"

"You can't be serious," she said, in shocked voice. "You don't actually tell people about that night."

She could hear the deep rumble of laughter caught in his chest.

"No," he laughed. "It wouldn't be the gentleman thing to do."

"Honestly, Jason," she said in exasperation. "I never know when you're serious or teasing me."

"Me tease you," he laughed. "If my memory serves me well you did a pretty good job of it the whole of the night, I hardly slept a wink."

The truth of his words brought the color rising to her cheeks. "I was trying to make up for the three years of missing you," she honestly admitted and quickly added, "But I wasn't teasing you. I think the correct words here would be; I seduced you. Yes, I seduced you. Teasing is without affording one satisfaction. Correct me if I'm wrong but my seduction of you was not without gratification on your part. Am I right," she smiled triumphantly.

"Let's see about that," he said, making a grab for her and kissing her soundly.

For the longest time in peaceful solitude they lay with their arms around each other. It was Jason's voice that suddenly broke the stillness in the room. "I wonder what time it is?" he said.

Abigail shrugged and looked at the daylight that came seeping through the curtained windows. "It's early yet," she sighed. "Judging from the light of day it must be going on six o'clock."

Jason sucked in his breath. "I better get a move on."

His words surprised her. "What about having some breakfast before you leave?"

"No, I'm afraid not." He was already sitting upright on the edge of the bed slipping into his pants.

Somewhat stunned by his anxiousness to leave, Abigail bit back a million questions that triggered through her mind. Three years away certainly left his land in dire need of work, but she couldn't see how one more hour spent with her would make that much of a difference. She rose on her side of the bed and quickly slipped into her dressing gown. For want of something to say she asked, "Just how many acres do you own?"

Jason's hands froze on the belt buckle. He turned around and looked at her for a few seconds before answering. "Not much," he said, "compared to Safe Haven. Sixty acres to be exact."

"Are you sure you won't stay for some breakfast?" she asked again, while rounding the foot of the bed to his side.

"Sounds good," he smiled, "but I honestly can't stay."

"Yes," Abigail said, trying to cover the hurt she was feeling. "Maybe it's best you leave before Timothy wakes up. You wouldn't want him to know you've been sleeping in his dead brother's bed."

His hand shot out roughly grabbing her by the arm. He spun her around to face him before she could reach the door. "That's not it, Abigail. It's my daughter, Mary. Ever since the day she was born, I've been at her bedside the minute she wakes up in the morning. My face is the first face she sets eyes on. It's bad enough my having to leave her some nights in the care of strangers, but I want her to know that no matter who puts her to bed at night, her father will be there each day to greet her. It's bad enough she hasn't a mother."

For a fleeting second Abigail wished the ground would have swallowed her up for the way she was acting. "I can truly understand," she said. "Mary is very lucky to have you for a father." She reached up and straightened the collar of his jacket. "I would have thought you'd have given your daughter an Indian name."

"I would have," he honestly admitted, "but she's going to have to face enough prejudice in this white man's world without her name adding to it. Mary is as Christian as you can get, don't you think?"

"That it is," Abigail smiled. "It's a nice name. I imagine your mother must be pleased having a grandchild."

"My mother," he laughed, "is going to spoil her rotten."

In silence they walked to the back door of the house and in the doorway Jason hesitated. He bent his head and his lips lightly brushed hers. "Take care, Abigail," he murmured.

"I will," she answered and watched as he headed for the barn to get his horse. She stood there for the longest time looking out and seeing nothing. God you're a pitiful person Abigail, she told herself; envious of a three-year-old child and a death woman who had his love for the last three years. Suddenly, with an air of certainty, Abigail turned to the stove and poked at the red embers while adding more kindling. What she needed was a cup of tea. He'll be back, she told herself while recalling the memorable night they had spent together.

After a week went by, without Jason's not having paid a call, Abigail was beside herself with anguish. Nearing the end of the second week her anguish turned to anger. For no apparent reason she had words with Timothy that morning for which she had to apologize.

Her behavior was getting out of hand and that's when she decided to do something about it. From the cupboard she took down a jar of her wild berry jelly and tossed it into a basket along with a loaf of her bread. Children like jelly and bread, she told herself, and Gay Feather always welcomed her company. What better excuse for paying a visit. In fast gate she head for the barn to hitch up the buckboard.

Disturbing thoughts triggered through Abigail's mind as she caught sight of the log cabin in the distance. Was it possible that Jason was still in love with his wife? After all she was dead only a couple of months. Never once did he say he loved me. Could it be she meant nothing more to him than a port in a storm? On reaching the road to the cabin, Abigail slowed the pace of the horses. She could see a small girl sitting on the steps of the porch. The child cast a glance in her direction and appeared preoccupied with something in her hands. Abigail tied the wagon to the hitching post and with basket in hand approached the child. At the moment, the child was trying to figure out which moccasin when on the proper foot.

"May I help you," Abigail smiled, reaching out with her free hand.

"No, no, I can do," she said, waving her off with her left hand.

"I'm afraid she has a mind of her own," Gay Feather said, opening the screen door for her guest.

"She's beautiful," Abigail said, noticing the wavy chestnut brown hair and hazel eyes set behind dark black lashes. Her tan creamy skin coloring was striking again her gleaming white teeth and the whiteness in her eyes.

"She's also a handful," Gay Feather laughed.

"See I do!" The child said excitedly while thrusting her feet out in full view with each moccasin on the correct foot.

Inside the cabin they chatted over a cup of tea while the child played in a corner of the room with her rag doll and a small woven pink blanket. It was on the tip of Abigail's tongue to ask about Jason's whereabouts but she refrained from doing so.

"Oh my," Gay Feather smiled, on opening the basket. "You couldn't have brought a more perfect gift; wild berry jelly is Mary's favorite."

"Mine too," Abigail smiled. She watched as Gay Feather sliced the bread and spread the jelly on top.

"Mary, come over here, dear, and see what Abigail's brought you."

Dropping her doll on the floor Mary rose to her feet and came running over to the table. She climbed up on the empty chair next to her grandmother and smiling, picked up the slice of bread and jelly that was set before her. About to bite into it her grandmother's stopped her.

"No, no, Mary. How many times must I tell you to use your right hand?"

Abigail watched as the child awkwardly switched the slice of bread to her right hand and suddenly as if buried deep within the recesses of her mind shocking memories came floating to mind. She shuttered. She remembered how as a small child in the orphanage her left arm had been taped to her body rendering it useless thereby forcing her to use her right hand. Also came to mind how other children had shunned her claiming it was the work of the devil if one ate left-handed or wrote left-handed. On impulse Abigail reached across the table and took the slice of bread out of the child's hand and switched it to her left hand. "What difference does it make what hand she uses as long as she is comfortable," Abigail said.

A shocked Gay Feather stared at her guest. "You don't understand. Mary is going to have a lot of obstacles to overcome in life, more than other children. I was only trying to spare her by teaching her to use her right hand which is more acceptable in society."

"That's all the more reason why she should enjoy her childhood. There's plenty of time for her to learn about the cruelties that life has to offer."

Mary's eyes darted between the two women, not knowing who to obey.

Abigail leaned over and patted the child's arm. "It's all right, Mary, eat your bread and jelly."

A few seconds later Mary lost all interest in the bread and jelly. It dropped to the table as she scrambled out of the chair. She went running across the room and went sailing out the door.

"I swear," Gay Feather laughed, "she's got the ears of a fox. She always knows when her father is coming home."

Together they walked over to the screen door and watched as Mary went running down the road. In the distance Abigail could see the familiar figure on horse back. Her heart skipped at beat at the sight of him. She watched with interest as Mary stood at a standstill with her arms raised in the air. On spotting the child Jason sent the horse into a fast gallop and leaning halfway out of his saddle charged toward his daughter. In one scoop he picked her up about the waist bringing her to rest in his lap. Their joyous laughter echoed across the open fields as they rode up to the cabin. Jason dismounted and after tying the reins to the hitching post, with both hands reached up for his daughter. She hugged him about the neck and kissed him several times. "I swear," he laughed, hugging her to him, "if I didn't know better those were wild berry kisses."

Mary giggled with delight. "That lady brought the jelly," she said and pointed.

The smile on Jason's face faded on seeing Abigail standing behind the screen door. His eyes quickly darted to his mother.

"I was just telling Abigail that she couldn't have brought a more perfect gift, that Mary's favorite jelly is wild berry."

"That it is. Thank you, Abigail," he said stiffly.

"You're welcome," Abigail answered automatically while stepping onto the porch. She was suddenly conscious of the strained atmosphere between them, like that of a stranger, a strange who wasn't welcome. She was glad to have a legitimate excuse to leave. "I have to get back," she said, "we're expecting Jenny and Jonathan home tonight."

She avoided looking at Jason and turning deliberately to the child leaned over and patted the child on the head. "It was nice meeting you, Mary," she smiled.

Shyly the child took her finger out of her mouth and said, "Good-bye."

Abigail pulled herself up to her full height and on legs that felt as wobbly as wild berry jelly, headed for her wagon. Silent tears streamed down her cheeks, tears of anger knowing she had made a complete fool of herself by coming. Jason didn't love or need her; he had his daughter and his mother. She never felt so used in her life since Albert's death.

The arrival of the newlyweds that evening helped to lift Abigail's spirits. She didn't have time to think about herself or Jason. The evening meal was a hum of conversation listening to Jenny and Jonathan talking about there honeymoon in Topeka.

"Oh, Abigail," Jenny sighed, when they were alone in the kitchen. "I'm so fortunate for having Jonathan as a husband. He's by far the most considerate man I know."

"If you ask me," Abigail teased. "Jonathan got the best of the bargain. He got himself a pretty wife who can bake bread, work in the fields, and look as fresh as a daisy come evening."

"Yes, that's true," Jenny giggled. "I'm so happy that you and Timothy like him as well as Gay Feather and Jason. Speaking about Jason, have you seen him and his daughter? Have they stopped by?"

"I was there this afternoon," Abigail said and quickly added, hoping to change the subject, "they're doing fine."

"Isn't Snowflake adorable," Jenny smiled.

"Snowflake?" Abigail frowned.

"Jason's daughter, Mary. He calls her Snowflake; that's her Indian name. He said the first time he set eyes on her, she melted his heart."

"Yes," Abigail agreed, "I can see where she'd melt anyone's heart. She's a beautiful child."

During the night sleep was evasive and a restless Abigail lay in bed with strange thoughts churning over in her mind. Was left-handedness hereditary? Could it be passed down from one generation to the next? Was it a coincidence that wild berry jelly was their favorite? Why the Indian Snowflake? Had it any connection with the name, White Snow? Suddenly the women in the Indian village came to mind who kept tugging at her curly hair. Not one of them had curly hair; it was straight and black. Abigail shook her head as if trying to clear it of the farfetched thoughts that plagued her sleep but found herself wide awake and sitting up on the edge of the bed trying to remember the night her child was born. Jason claimed to have stayed to bury her child, but why did Gay Feather leave without him? If Mary was her child, what possible reason could they have for taking her? What did they hope to gain?

Suddenly, in the dimness of the room, the child's face loomed before Abigail. "Merciful God," she gasped. "It wasn't Albert's child I gave birth to; it was Jason's. Snowflake is our daughter."

377

Chapter Twenty

Abigail tied Charger to the hitching post and on seeing that the large doors of the barn stood ajar, she headed directly towards it. The only light inside came from the open doors and her shadow cast a giant figure as she stepped over the threshold. As her eyes became accustomed to the dimness she saw Jason. His back was to her and he was busy pitching hay over the railing of the last stall. She could envision the strong lean muscles beneath the shirt he wore, straining in motion with his toil. At the sight of him all the anger within her seemed to dissipate.

As her eyes slowly drifted around the barn warm, vivid memories came floating back. She raised a hand and fondly touched the gate of the stall next to her. It seemed so long ago, and yet, each moment of that night was clearly etched in her mind. A faint smile crossed her lips on remembering that the filly that Timothy named Grasshopper was born, and it was the night her daughter was conceived. Slow realization set in, and deep within Abigail's heart she was aware of having loved Jason all these years. No matter what was to happen, she would still go on loving him.

Her hands became buried in the folds of the blue calico dress as she lifted her shirt. She looked up to see Jason leaning on the pitchfork; he was intent on watching her. She felt the heat of a blush rise to her cheeks wondering if her thoughts were visible to him. Raising her head high, she closed the distance between them and held the steady dark brown eyes that held hers. She searched for a speck of warmth, a speck of love, even a speck of surprise as to her being there; they were devoid of emotion. Within a few feet of him she stopped.

"What do I owe this honor to?" he asked.

She was surprised by the empty tone of his voice more so than the uncivil manner in which he had addressed her. And for the first time in her life, words failed her. Where to begin, she thought, when everything she wanted to say suddenly became strangled in her throat at the sight of him. "I know Mary is my daughter." Her voice was soft and calm that for the moment she was uncertain as to whether she had actually spoken. Then she saw Jason's hand that gripped the handle of the pitchfork turn white. He stared at her in silence as if seeing clear through her body and beyond. He thrust the pitchfork deep into the hay and turned away from her. Like a man defeated, he stood staring down into the stall. Suddenly, his hands came down hard on the top of the railing with such force it startled the life out of her.

"And you came here to tell me you want her and you need her. Is that it?" he asked, voice dripping with sarcasm.

To keep from reaching out and touching the sleeve of his shirt, she rung her hands together. She was wishing he'd turn around to face her. Her wish was granted.

Every muscle in his face was distorted in anger and his eyes blazed into hers. "Tell me," he roared, "for the love of God, Abigail, tell me what you want. At least give me an inkling so I know how to fight you!"

Fight. Oh God, she thought despairingly. There wasn't any more fight left in her; couldn't he see that? She had fought blizzards, dust storms, hail storms, brush fires and droughts until she thought she would die of exhaustion. God, she was so tired of fighting. Yet that's what he was expecting. He was expecting her to fight over their child when she had come in the name of love and peace, deeply hoping they could become a family. Fear brushed at the corners of her mind, the fear that he didn't love her.

"I don't want to fight, Jason," she said, holding onto what little pride she had left. "I just want Mary to know that I'm her mother and that I love her. Is that too much to ask?"

The anger went out of his face only to be replaced by a look of skepticism. "No," he said coolly, "that isn't too much to ask. And I promise you, that when she's old enough to understand, I will tell her about you. God knows, I'll even try to convince her of your loving her, although I know you to be incapable of loving anyone."

The cruelty of his words sent her hands flying to her breast to ease the pain of her constricting heart. He had made it quite clear that she would never see her daughter again and there was no room in his life for her. But to say she was incapable of loving was more than she could bear. "How. . .how can you say such things to me? Do you hate me that much?"

"Hate you," he snorted, running a hand through his hair in exasperation. "I wish to God, I could hate you, Abigail. Hating would make it easy compared to the torment of wanting and loving you. God knows, I've tried to hate you. I've even tried to understand that insatiable greed of yours for material wealth; like marrying Albert for his name and the hundred and sixty acres that went with it. I made no bones about disliking Albert, but when he married you, I found myself pitying the man. What a blow it must have been to his ego to find his wedding bed containing a land deal instead of a loving wife. He might still be alive today if you had kept up your half of the bargain. If he had a loving wife at home, he wouldn't have gone running off to Abilene to have one of Lucy Stone's girls fill his needs. Does that shock you, my dear lady?" he asked, on seeing her face drain of color. "Well, where the hell do you suppose he was the night Mary was born, in church?" He stopped; a faraway look came into his brown eyes, like one remembering. "I thought of that night so often," he said, as if speaking to himself. "It still scares me just to think about it. What do you suppose would have happened had Albert seen the child you bore him? Do you think he would have let her live and raised her as his own? And what of you, Abigail? Would he have forgiven you for bearing him another man's child and his half-brother's at that? No, it wouldn't have ended there, knowing Albert's deep seated hatred for Indians; he'd seek revenge. Don't misunderstand, I wasn't afraid of him and I wasn't afraid of dying if it meant saving Mary's life. I was more afraid of living. Of living with the torment of knowing I killed my half-brother over you. . .I'd never be able to face Jenny or Timothy. That's what made me decide to tell you that your child had died. All my thoughts were for her safety. And. . .that morning, in your bedroom, I wanted to hold you and comfort you, and share the joy of our daughter's birth I never wanted anyone to be hurt, least of all you. I figured in time you and Albert would have children of your own that would help to ease the loss you were feeling. My main concern was for the safety of our child. And with time, hopefully, I would forget you."

"Oh, Jason," she sobbed, reaching out to touch his arm. He shrank from her touch.

"I went to Fort Riley and I lied about having a wife who had died in childbirth. I hired a wet-nurse to take care of Mary during the day. I thought most of my troubles were over. . . but I was mistaken. Each day she was a constant reminder of you. You might not think it, because of her coloring, but in a lot of ways she is like you. She has the same habit of throwing her head back when she laughs and the same pout of her lower lip when she's sleeping. And though she is extremely shy with strangers at first, she could be just as stubborn in wanting her own way. And all the love I harbored for you, I gave to her. The child is a godsend, just like my mother, giving freely of their love without want or reward. Something you wouldn't understand, Abigail."

Suddenly she was frightened, but not of the thought of losing him. Now more than ever, she was certain of his love. There was more to what he was saying; something deep inside him that was yet to be revealed. An inner peace seemed to steal over him as he spoke, a man self-contained, and this is what she feared would destroy their love.

"I used to sit for hours reading Jenny and Timothy's letters, over and over, anxious for a word about you. I remember receiving a letter from Timothy once, that included five pages about Grasshopper," he laughed. "I can laugh now, but at the time I felt like strangling him with my bare hands for not mentioning a word about you. And then, a letter would come from Jenny spilling over about the two of you and what you were doing. They love you, Abigail. Their letters were filled with loving you. But then," he sighed, "they don't know you like I do. When Jenny wrote and told me about Albert's death, I felt no remorse. All I could think about was coming home and seeing you. But I never found the courage to face you, with nothing to offer but myself. You rejected me once without benefit of explanation, and you could easily do it again. Only this time I had more to lose besides my pride; I had Mary, our child. The thought that you might accept me solely for the sake of the child was shattering. I even had doubts as to whether you could love her and admit to being the mother of a half-breed."

"Oh, God, Jason, that's by far the cruelest thing you've ever said to me," she gasped. "How could I deny my own flesh and blood, my daughter? How could you even think that I . . ."

"I've been in that position most of my life, Abigail. My own father denied me. Why wouldn't I think that? Although one of the things I have often admired about you is your fair sense of justice. Like delivering your bread to Lucy Stone's place, despite what people might say or think."

"You knew about that," she said, and her hopes began to soar on seeing a speck of warmth in the brown eyes. All too quickly it faded.

"Blake wrote and told me," he said. "I stayed on at Fort Riley for another year and then I took Mary to live with my mother's people for the summer. When we returned to Fort Riley, I found Jenny's letter waiting for me, asking me to come to her wedding. I was so confident that after three years I could look at you without wanting you." He raised a hand in the air and it helplessly fell to his side. "That night, in your bedroom, I was foolish enough to think that you changed. I was out of my mind with loving you and so scared it was all a dream I couldn't close my eyes. I just lay there watching you asleep in my arms, thinking it was a dream and come morning you'd be gone."

"It wasn't a dream, Jason. It never was a dream. That night was real. What happened between us was real."

"Was it?" he sneered. "I would like to think that it was, but for a lady, my dear, you could have shown a little more decorum. You could have at least waited a day or two before asking me about the acreage I owned."

The shock of his words sent the blood draining from her face. She could well understand his misinterpreting her question. "Believe me, Jason. You have to believe me," she begged, making a desperate grab for his arm. This time she succeeded and held fast to steady herself. "My question stemmed from curiosity—nothing more. I'm not interested in your land. I don't care what you have; I just want us to be together. Believe me, Jason. God, you have to believe I love you."

With a sad smile edging his lips he stared down at her. "Whether I believe you or not, Abigail, it really doesn't matter anymore. I've sold my land to Blake and the day after tomorrow we're leaving here for good."

The finality of his words momentarily stunned her. A cold shiver of chills ran through her body at the thought of his leaving. After all his years of working the land he wouldn't sell it. Surely this was his way of testing her. It was a cruel test but she would forgive him. She searched his face for the faint show of a teasing smile that she had come to know so well. There wasn't any. Then she felt the warmth of his hand over the cold numbness of fingers. He removed her hold on his shirt sleeve. Totally confused she stared up at him. "Where? Where are you going?"

"Where I belong," he said, "with my people."

Nothing made sense. With his people? What was he talking about? Jenny, Timothy and me, she thought, aren't we his people? As slow realization set in her heart pounded wildly in her chest; she was shattered. "Why? Why on earth. . ." She made a grab for the gate of the stall to steady her.

"I don't expect you to fully understand," he said solemnly. "I hardly understood it myself. All my life I've been searching for a place to fit in comfortably. I've tried the white man's world, so to speak, and found it filled with nothing but greed. Yet I've seen these same greedy men go out and die for the freedom of other men, under the pretext that all men are born free and created equal. For a while I believed them, until I saw the hypocrisy of their turning on my people who have lived freely on land that rightfully belonged to them for generations, breaking treaty after treaty and stripping them of their freedom and dignity and forcing them to live on reservations. Their so-called idea of freedom consisted of conforming to their way of thinking and their beliefs. God knows, I'm not a heroic man, Abigail, but there comes a time in one's life when you have to make a stand and be counted for what you believe in. Day after tomorrow we're leaving to join my mother's people to help in any way that we can."

The mistreatment of Indians on reservations was common knowledge; she knew what lay in store for them. "And. . .and this is what you will subject Mary to, life on a reservation? How, in the name of God, can you do this to her?"

The muscles in his jaw line tightened in anger. "I suppose you think your world would be better suited for her. You can bring her up as a refined lady; a lady that no white man would marry. Is that what you want for her? People will shun her because she is different. I've seen what my mother has suffered all these years and it's not going to happen to Mary. She'll be raised with people who will love and fully accept her and be proud of her heritage."

"Please, Jason," Abigail begged, "don't do this, not now. Let me at least get to know her. I lost her three years ago; please, for the love of God, don't let me lose her again. I don't think I could stand it."

He drew in a sharp breath on hearing the pain in her voice. "Why prolong it, Abigail?" he softly murmured. "Getting to know her would only make your suffering that much harder. My decision is final; we'll be leaving the day after tomorrow at sun up. If you think about it, you'll know it's for the best. Now if you don't mind, I have work to do."

The finality in his words had brought tears to her eyes and out of desolation she turned to leave. "Oh, God," she bitterly wept. "What have I done to deserve such punishment?"

The Journey

Chapter Twenty One

The haunting words, day after tomorrow, ran rampant through Abigail's mind. The whole of the night she hadn't slept knowing she had no options. If she wanted to be with her daughter, she had to leave everything else behind; it was as simple as that. The thought of leaving Jenny, Timothy and Jonathan was heart-rending. Rather than face them with the truth, she sat down and wrote them a letter explaining how Mary was her child and her reason for leaving. In closing, she asked for their forgiveness. Come morning she'd place the letter on the kitchen table before leaving. She was beginning to think that it was the fate of women named Abigail to write such distressing letters. With all she had to accomplish in one day, she thought the letter would make things easier without having to come face to face with their downtrodden spirits as well as her own. In fact, she decided to make the evening meal a festive occasion, one that they'd all remember and could look back on with fond memories.

There was so much she had to contend with that morning that she thought her head would explode. First, she saw to getting Timothy off for school and packing his lunch and his deliveries. A half hour later, with sheepish grins on their faces, the newlyweds sat down to breakfast. "Will you be working the south field to day?" she asked.

"Yes," Jonathan smiled, over the cup of coffee in his hand. "I'd like to finish planting it, once and for all."

Abigail nodded her head in understanding. "Jenny, why don't you pack a nice picnic basket for you and Jonathan? It's such a nice day to be outdoors and I'm sure Jonathan would appreciate having some company. It will save him the time and trouble of coming back to the house for lunch."

A surprised Jenny asked, "What about my chores?"

"They can wait until tomorrow. I'll see to whatever has to be done around here."

"Are you sure, Abigail?" Jenny smiled.

"Positive. Now make Jonathan a good lunch."

Alone in the house Abigail began the planning of the evening meal and at the same time the planning of what clothes she would take with her. She kept running back and forth from the kitchen to her bedroom trying to accomplish the two feats. While rummaging through a dresser drawer, well-hidden beneath her underclothes and wrapped in paper, she found the pair of moccasins that Great Bear had given her; over the years she had forgotten about them. She stood there holding them to her while remembering the day they were given to her and his words, "May your moccasins make tracks in many snows yet to come, my daughter." She laid them on the small pile of clothes that she would be taking with her. It was while she was in the kitchen rolling out pastry dough for tarts that would be filled with her homemade preserves; she saw the three jars of wild berry jelly on the shelf. She removed two jars from the shelf and ran into the bedroom setting them down next to the pile of clothes on the bed. Lastly, out of habit, she made certain to toss sewing needles and a couple of spools of thread into her purse.

By sunset Abigail had the table set with the best linen, flowers from her garden and candles. At each place setting she had placed a gift. The aroma of delectable food permeated the house and when Jenny, Jonathan and Timothy entered, the surprised looks on their faces stirred her heart.

"Heavens," Jenny said, on seeing the table. "You must have been working all day. What is the occasion, Abigail?"

"Your homecoming," she said, while placing the platter that held a roast chicken and potatoes down on the table. "I thought it would be nice to celebrate."

"By the looks of this spread," Timothy laughed, eyeing the table. "You and Jonathan should leave the house more often, Jenny."

"Never," Jonathan laughed, "we'd miss all this good cooking."

"Sit down and open your presents," Abigail smiled.

"Presents?" Timothy frowned, seating himself. "I think the heat of working over a hot stove must have gotten to you, Abigail. Christmas isn't for a couple of months yet."

Jenny fingered the small package at her place setting. "I think mine is a book," she said, and began tearing the wrapping off. "It is a book," she smiled and began leafing through it. On discovering it was written in Abigail's hand surprise touched her face. "Oh, Abigail," she said in delight. "You've written down all your recipes for me."

"Now that you're a married woman, I thought you should have a cookbook of your own. I've been working on it over a month now," Abigail smiled.

"I can't thank you enough for that," Jonathan grinned. "Jenny's cooking sure needs direction."

They all laughed and watched as Jonathan opened the envelope with his name on it. "A twenty dollar gold piece," he said in astonishment. "You're giving me twenty dollars? I've never seen a twenty dollar gold piece before."

Abigail smiled. "I know how hard it's been for you trying to save enough money so you can send for your sister and brother. I think it's about time that they came here to live. There's ample room in the house and I'm sure Jenny and Timothy wouldn't object."

"Bless you, Abigail," he said in choked voice, brushing at tears that clouded his eyes with the back of his hand.

"I don't know," Timothy said, "I'm a little leery about opening my envelope."

"You should be," Abigail smiled at him. "It's going to mean a lot of hard work on your part. I was going to give it to you for your sixteenth birthday, but decided today is a good a day as any."

"You sure got my curiosity piqued," he said, toying with the envelope in his hands.

"Open it," Jenny insisted.

All eyes were on Timothy as he opened the envelope and took out a letter. He glanced down at the page to see that it was a formal letter from the University of Kansas, in Lawrence. "Holy cow! Holy cow!" he yelled in jubilation.

"What is it?" Jenny asked.

"It. . .it states here that I've been accepted to the University of Kansas and that my tuition is paid in full for two years. Good God, Abigail, how on earth did you ever manage this?"

"Your father started saving for you and over the years I just added to it. It was his wish, as well as mine, that you should attend a University. I chose the University of Kansas because it's close to home and you wouldn't have far to travel on holidays. I'm afraid the rest was all your own doing by keeping up such good grades."

"I. . . I don't know what to say, Abigail."

"Thank you will do nicely. But if you want to be a lawyer, Timothy McFadden, you better not lack for words."

The evening couldn't have been more festive nor merry had she taken days to plan it. Giving Jenny the cookbook containing her bread recipes would allow her to carry on the business. The money she gave to Jonathan would help him to bring his sister and brother to Kansas and in doing so, Jenny would not lack for company. As for Timothy, a whole new world would be opening up to him and in time, no doubt, he'd forgive her.

From her bedroom window Abigail could see the promise of a new day breaking on the horizon as she quietly moved about the room rolling up the two jars of preserves and her clothes in a blanket. From the closet she took down two leather belts that belonged to Albert and used them to tie each end of the blanket roll securely. She picked up her purse and threaded the belt of her dress through the drawstring handles so she wouldn't have to carry it. Lastly was the letter she had written. Softly she crossed the floor, opened the door and headed for the kitchen. Tears clouded her eyes as she laid the letter down on the kitchen table. She was halfway out the back door when a thought struck her that sent her scurrying back into the parlor.

On reaching the fireplace mantel, with her free hand she reached up and took down the rifle that was hanging there and a box of ammunition that lay on the mantel. She drew in a deep breath balancing the rifle beneath her armpit as she headed for the back door. By chance, next to the back door hanging on a nail she spotted the small leather drawstring purse that once contained the money that Maggie had given her. Over the years Abigail had put the purse to good use. It contained flower seeds that she gathered each year for her garden. Who knows, she wishfully thought, maybe someday I'll have another flower garden. She reached up and slipped the small pouch from the nail.

In the barn with deft hands she saddled up Charger, tied the blanket roll to the back of the saddle, and securely slipped the rifle into place before mounting. As she rode out she never looked back, well knowing her heart would break at the very sight of leaving what had been her home for the last five years. Another thought the came to mind was the fact that she was leaving, more or less, with the same amount of belongings she had arrived with five years ago, with the exception of the two jars of preserves, two cakes of lavender soap and the rifle.

Within a mile of the log cabin, well aware that the sound of horse's hooves carried in the stillness, Abigail dismounted, removed the rifle and blanket roll before giving Charger a hard slap on his hind quarters that sent him heading back in the direction he had come from.

With blanket roll under one arm and rifle in the other, she trudged through the ticket of grass until reaching the stone wall. She set everything down and sat there with her back leaning against the wall and waited. While she waited, she loaded the rifle with ammunition.

As the sunlight brightened on the horizon, Abigail heard the sound of the wagon wheels on the other side of the stone wall. She rose to her knees and peered over the wall. She saw Jason fast at work, hitching a team of horses to the wagon. His horse, Thunderbolt, was already saddled. She watched as he began loading the wagon with supplies that were lined up on the front porch. Suddenly Abigail grew anxious for a glimpse of her daughter. To the sound of the screen door banging, Abigail looked up and saw Gay Feather coming down the porch steps with her daughter in tow. She watched as Gay Feather picked up the child and sat her down on the front seat of the wagon before walking around the back of the wagon to the other side. From this she gathered Gay Feather would be driving the wagon.

"I guess that does it." She heard Jason say while putting the last load on the wagon and heading for his horse.

With quick hands Abigail picked up the blanket and the rifle while lifting her skirt and petticoats. In one fluent movement she scaled the wall. As she ran across the lawn heading for the back of the wagon, she caught a glimpse of Jason's back as he mounted his horse. On reaching the back of the wagon she tossed the blanket roll over the side and made a dash for the front end of the wagon. A shocked Gay Feather looked at her as she climbed into the seat next to her daughter. Breathless and uncertain, she sat there with rifle in hand.

"Abigail what...."

"Start the wagon," she ordered, her eyes darting from Gay Feather to that of Jason's back. He was halfway down the road, leading the way.

"Abigail, do you know what you're doing?" Gay Feather asked, snapping the reins.

"God only knows," she honestly admitted. "But I'll never leave my daughter."

For the first time she looked at her daughter. The child's eyes were enormous in her face as she looked at her. Frightened, she sat cringed next to her grandmother, holding tight to her rag doll.

Abigail reached out and gently patted the child's knee. "It's all right, darling," she softly murmured. "There's nothing to be frightened about. I brought you a present." She reached into her purse and took out the small purse containing the flower seeds and rose petals. "See," she said, "you can hang it around your doll's neck. Doesn't it smell pretty?"

Shyly the child took the small purse from her hand and sniffed at it. "Flowers," she smiled.

"That's right," Abigail smiled back. "Now let's see if you can put it around your doll's neck."

"Abigail," Gay Feather said in warning.

She looked up to see Jason blocking the road. He sat perched on his horse staring at them. "Whatever happens, hold tight to the reins," Abigail warned. Within a few feet of her son, Gay Feather pulled at the reins stopping the wagon.

"Where the hell do you think you're going?" Jason asked, faced masked in anger.

"On a journey with my daughter, whether you like it or not," Abigail said boldly.

"We'll see about that," he said, while dismounting from his horse.

Abigail picked up the rifle and cocked it. She stood up in the wagon with gun pointing at him. "You once told me that no man in his right mind would come within twenty feet of a woman holding a gun in her hand. I'm warning you, Jason, get back on your horse. If you don't, I'll shoot and our daughter will be fatherless."

With eyes boring into hers, he took a step forward and the crackling sound of the rifle made the horses jump. A shocked Jason looked down at the puff of dust that rose from the ground where the bullet was buried but a few inches from his right foot.

"That," Abigail announced, "was a warning shot. Next time I won't miss."

For the longest time he stood frozen looking at her and the bullet hole in the ground. Finally, as if resigning himself to his fate he swore under his breath, turned and mounted his horse and rode on.

After setting the rifle down, Abigail looked at her daughter. God, she thought, all I'm doing is scaring my child.

Suddenly, a soft chuckle of laughter escaped Gay Feather's lips as she set the horses in motion.

"What are you laughing about?" Abigail asked, in bewilderment.

"You. . . my son. I've never seen Jason scared before. He honestly thought that you were going to shoot him."

"I would have," Abigail said with strong conviction.

Gay Feather shook her head from side to side. "No. . . not when you love a man as much as you love him."

Abigail was speechless.

For the longest time neither one spoke until Abigail's curiosity got the better of her. "Why is he doing this?" she asked. "Why did he sell his land? What does he hope to gain by all this?"

A deep sigh escaped Gay Feather's lips. "Sometimes I think there's no one to blame but myself. It's been hard on him having to live in two worlds; it's been eating away at him for years. He's seen the great injustice my people have suffered under the white man and the breaking of treaties. He believes that he can be of use to my people when it comes to writing up new treaties since he knows the way of the white man's world. It's his dream that all men should be able to live free and roam free, especially Indians, since this land rightfully belonged to them."

Abigail peered into the distance at the lonely rider leading the way and swallowed hard the lump in her throat. With a small spark of hope in her heart, she thought, perhaps he can make a difference.

At all times throughout the day Abigail made certain that the rifle, as well as her child, were within reach since they were her only weapons of assurance. There was no doubt in her mind that given the first opportunity, Jason would leave her behind. It wasn't until they had camped for the night that he decided to approach her. He came over to where she lay on the blanket with the rifle close at hand. Within a few feet of her he stopped and got down on his haunches facing her.

"Abigail," he said, in exasperation, "you are by far the most pigheaded woman I've ever met. You know, as well as I do, that there is no sense in what you are doing. Come morning, I'll unhitch one of the horses from the wagon so you can leave. This isn't your fight. . . you don't belong here."

She raised herself up on her elbows and in the dimness her eyes searched his. "Tell me where I belong, Jason. Tell me, so I'll know. Should I go back to the

401

farm with Jenny and Timothy or should I be with my family? Yes, my family. Mary is my daughter, whether you like it or not; you can't separate us. She's part of me and always will be. It will be easier on all of us if you will accept that fact because I'm not leaving. Like it says in the Bible: Do not ask me to abandon or forsake you! For wherever you go I will go, wherever you lodge I will lodge, your people shall be my people, and your God my God. Wherever you die I will die, and there be buried."

For a second he was too choked to speak. "Even if it means following me into the jaws of Hell," he said in despair, "because that's what it will amount to, Abigail, pure Hell." When she didn't answer he dejectedly turned and headed for his blanket roll on the other side of the campfire. He was at his wits' end trying to figure a way to make her leave, well knowing the hardships that would lay in store for her.

In the days that followed, although Jason rarely spoke to her, Abigail got to know her daughter better, and for this she was thankful. Little by little the child's shyness gave way to trusting friendship and love. At times she would seek out Abigail's company. It was on a warm evening that they had stopped to set up camp for the night near a small river bed that Abigail decided to take advantage of the time to wash out some of their clothes. She was busy thrashing the clothes against the smooth stones of the river bed when her daughter came down to join her.

Squatting down beside Abigail, Mary announced, "I can do." She picked up an article of clothing and began imitating Abigail. Before long Abigail burst out in peals of laughter at her daughter's fruitless attempts which only managed to soak the child clear through to the skin.

After spreading the clothes over some nearby brush to dry, Abigail turned to the task of undressing her wet child. On sudden impulse, she undressed, picked up the bar of lavender soap and hand in hand, stark naked they went wading into the water to bathe.

On a grassy knoll for the longest time Jason sat watching them. Now and again he'd smile to himself on hearing their joyful laughter. The happy picture of the two of them together not only touched his heart but would be etched in his memory forever. Suddenly, it became very clear to him, come what may, God help him, they belonged together.

Later that evening as Abigail lay sleeping, she sat up with a start sensing someone was watching her. In the moonlight, standing but a few feet away from her was Jason. At the sight of him her hand automatically reached down for the rifle lying beside her.

"You won't need the rifle," he murmured. "If you're foolhardy enough to want to come with us. . . so be it. I won't stop you."

Puzzled she looked up at him. "What made you change your mind?"

"I haven't," he honestly admitted. "I still think you should go back. I have enough to contend with without having to worry about you."

"Oh, I see," she said. "But it's all right for me to go back to the farm and sit there day after day and worry as to where you might be or my child. Love has a double-edged blade, Jason, and the more you love someone, the more you worry over them."

As if struck powerless against her words, he stood there before sinking to his knees beside her. With a gleam of admiration in his eyes he looked at her. "Damn my luck," he smiled, "for falling in love with a stubborn woman who knows all the answers."

Shamelessly, she reached out, pulling him down beside her on the blanket by his shirt sleeves until her arms could circle his neck. "And damn my luck," she whispered against his lips, "for falling in love with a half-breed."

In the days that followed, Abigail was beside herself with joy; they were a family now and nothing in the world could ever change that. Come what may, they would face it together.

Chapter Twenty Two

Bracing against the harsh cold winds that blew in over the open plains, on the crest of a hill Abigail and Gay Feather stood beside the wagon looking at the small caravan of Cheyenne Indians who were marching overland while they waited for Jason to return. In number Abigail estimated there were about one hundred and fifty people; one third of whom appeared to be children. She had often heard of them referred to as the Beautiful People, but by the impoverished look of them it was hard to believe. Their clothes looked tattered and laden travois's carried their meager supplies as well as the sick, wounded and the infirm.

Within the next few days, after having joined the caravan, Abigail soon learned what courageous people she was living with. Far into the night as they lay huddled beside a campfire Jason would tell her of their misfortunes as told to him by Chief Dull Knife. On good faith, over nine hundred strong, they had traveled over three months to reach Fort Reno to take a look at the reservation. They soon learned that the water was foul as well as the meager rations allotted them. When they finally got permission to hunt, there wasn't any game to speak of and found the land to be barren. They had to resort to eating coyotes and before long they began to eat their dogs in order to survive. With the summer came mosquitoes, measles and a malaria epidemic; without quinine or medical care a number of them died. That's when they decided to leave Fort

Reno and head back to their own lands, but permission to leave was denied them. At the first light of day they packed their meager belongings and with teepees left standing stole away. They had fought skirmish after skirmish with the soldiers as they headed north.

"What is our destination?" Abigail asked out of curiosity.

Jason couldn't help but smile to himself. He had seen how in the last few days without complaint she had truly become one of them. She had given up her seat on the wagon so that an old woman could have it, and willingly shared their supplies with the less fortunate. "In the north," he said, "there is an Indian reservation run by Chief Red Cloud and we're hoping he will take us in and give us refuge over the winter."

"Where are the others headed who escaped from Fort Reno?"

"They're headed further north to the Tongue River; that's where our people come from. You'd love it there. It is beautiful country with trees and forest and streams to fish in. Only the summers are rather short and the winters can be severe."

"We'll manage," Abigail smiled, snuggling closer to the warmth of his body. "Your mother and I will weave more blankets."

Jason reached up and removed the kerchief that was tied around her head and lovingly ran his hand through the softness of her hair. He had noticed how in the last three days she had taken to covering her head with a dark kerchief which gave his cause to wonder.

"Are you cold? Is that why you wear this?" he asked, setting the kerchief aside.

"No. . .," she said hesitantly. "Some of the other women are afraid of me. They say the color of my hair is the work of a bad spirit or the devil. I thought it best to conceal my hair until they really get to know me."

"Oh, Abigail," he said in anguish, "you have to forgive them; they don't know any better."

"You don't think my hair the work of the devil, do you?" she smiled.

He frowned as if giving her words some serious thought. "Yes, it could be," he grinned. "I was bewitched by you the first time I saw you."

The noonday sun felt good upon Abigail's body as she trudged alongside the wagon. The sun's rays helped to take the chill out of her bones caused by the cold night air and sleeping on the cold ground. Now and again, Abigail would study the horizon hoping to catch a glimpse of Jason. He had left camp early that morning with a group of men to go hunting.

"Abigail, will you take up the reins?" Gay Feather called to her. "I'd like to stretch my legs a bit."

Abigail welcomed the turn. Not only at the thought of sitting down for a spell, but being able to spend time with her daughter. While she waited for Gay Feather to stop the wagon and climb down, Abigail made a fast check on the other passengers in the back of the wagon who, one by one, began to replace their dwindling food supply, three in all. A young boy with a bullet wound in his shoulder, an old woman with a lame leg, and an old man who hadn't the vaguest notion as to what was going on around him. The whole of the day he sat in the wagon chanting to himself.

With reins in hand Abigail started the wagon. It was moments like these that she would become lost in another world with her daughter. She taught Snowflake songs to sing and told her stories, but most of all she spoke about her dreams. Someday, they were going to have a house of their own and a garden so that Snowflake could plant the seeds in the small pouch that was tied around her doll's neck. Little by little, the child began to accept the fact that Abigail was her mother as she washed, fed and dressed her each day. But in the evening, when it came time for the child to go to sleep, she sought the loving arms of her grandmother.

The sun was beginning to set and with it came cold air drifting in over the plains. A little apprehensive about not having seen Jason the whole of the day, Abigail began to worry. In another hour they'd be breaking up the caravan and making camp for the night. It was then that Abigail noticed the small band of men who came riding in. She thought it remarkable that at such a distance she could spot Jason on his horse. She stopped in her tracks falling behind the wagon and just stood there smiling to herself as they approached. She watched as the other men dispersed in all directions to greet their families as Jason came riding towards her.

"Any luck?" she asked, as Jason reined his horse beside her.

"Not as much as we had anticipated," he said disappointedly, "but we did get a deer and some rabbits."

"Well, that's good," she said, forcing a cheerful note to her voice. "Maybe you'll have better luck tomorrow."

"Yes," he said, "maybe we will at that."

Leaning all the way over in his saddle he stretched his hand out to her. "Come on," he urged, "grab hold of my arm and get behind me."

With what seemed like effortless ease, before Abigail realized what was happening, she was being swung in the air and seated on the back of the horse. "If you want to ride with me, lady, you have to take that damn kerchief off your head."

Laughing, Abigail bid his command before circling her arms around his waist as he set the horse into a fast gallop. Within seconds they had caught up with their wagon, but to Abigail's surprise, Jason spurred the horse on. The wind played havoc with her long red hair as they rode the length of the column, circled round and came back down again. Once more, Jason spurred the horse on circling the column, only this time at a remarkable racing pace. Suddenly, to Abigail's surprise, the whole column came alive in an uproar of hoops and hollers as they sped past. Finally, on reaching their wagon, Jason reined the horse and the uproarious hoops and hollers slowly dwindled.

"What. . .what was that all about?" Abigail breathlessly laughed, as he helped her down from the horse.

For a second his hands came to rest on her small waist as he stood there looking down at her. "Nothing," he grinned jauntily, and planted a kiss on her forehead.

"I just thought you could do with a ride after walking all day. Now what must a man do to get some supper around here?"

It wasn't until the next afternoon when Abigail, sitting next to Gay Feather, with her napping daughter in her arms, found out the truth about Jason's actions.

"You and Jason were the talk of the campfires last night," Gay Feather smiled. "They Who Ride like the Wind, that's what they're calling the two of you."

"They Who Ride like the Wind," Abigail laughed, "we sure did. I don't know what got into him."

"Didn't he tell you?" Gay Feather frowned.

"Tell me what?"

Gay Feather hesitated, having second thoughts. "It's really not my place to tell you, but he was upset that some wagging tongues should think your red hair to be the work of the devil. It was his way of showing everyone that you are his woman, and no matter what they say, he has chosen you and together you will ride to the ends of the earth."

Shimmering tears of joy glistened in Abigail's eyes. She was deeply touched that he had defied all on her behalf. They Who Ride like the Wind. The words hummed in her head the whole of the day.

Chapter Twenty Three

Within the next few days one hardship after the other seemed to follow. An axle on the wagon broke and they had to leave it behind. The food supply that they had carried with them had dwindled down to nothing. Each day's hunting party returned empty-handed. Even the weather had turned against them as they trudged and struggled over the open plains through a blinding blizzard of snow.

With each passing day Abigail could see the strength of the older woman who walked besides her beginning to diminish along with her own. At the evening meal she had seen Gay Feather scooping out the bits and pieces that floated in her soup and feed them to her hungry granddaughter. The sight of it had brought tears to Abigail's eyes, but she refused to let it discourage her and continued to pray for deliverance out of the very jaws of Hell that Jason had warned her about.

Late afternoon deliverance came in the form of a cavalry troop of soldiers who, without their knowledge in the blinding blizzard, had surrounded their camp.

A strange atmosphere of doom seem to hover over the women as they sat huddled together trying to keep their children warm while their men went off to parley with the soldiers.

"What's wrong with them?" Abigail asked. "I would think they'd be happy. There's a good chance that the soldiers will give us food."

"One can not eat with the stench of death in the air," Gay Feather replied. "They are afraid the soldiers will come back and kill us."

"Nonsense," Abigail said. "Tell them that the starving and killing of innocent women and children is not an article of war."

Gay Feather sadly shook her head from side to side. "I can not tell them that. They will not believe me. You have much to learn, my daughter. They have seen treaty after treaty broken, and without provocation soldiers riding into their camps at night to slaughter them. They have good reason to fear the white man and his treaties."

"Things are different now," Abigail said with strong conviction. "You can be sure that they won't harm us."

A deep sigh escaped Gay Feather lips. "You are my only hope, Abigail. They won't harm you, because you are a white woman. You and Snowflake may be saved. And in time to come, she will speak of my people and we will be remembered."

Tired, cold, and weak from hunger, Abigail shrugged off Gay Feather's pessimistic attitude and crawled beneath her blanket, hoping that sleep would help to alleviate all her miseries. For a timeless time, she could dream. She could dream about food, the way things use to be. The beautiful gown she wore at Fort Riley and Jason dancing with her and a large tub of hot water to bath in. Sleep was becoming her only refuge.

An hour later, Abigail awakened to the strange bustling sounds of people moving about in the camp.

But a few feet away from her Jason sat cross-legged on the ground, busy cleaning his revolver. She crawled over to where he sat on the edge of the blanket. "What happened?" she asked. "How did you make out with the soldiers?"

"It seems the government went back on its word again," he said in disgust. "There isn't any reservation here. They moved Red Cloud and his people further north. Dull Knife agreed to our being escorted to Fort Robinson in the morning rather than see us suffering in this blasted cold."

"Is that bad?" Abigail asked in all innocence.

For a moment he blankly stared at her. "I don't know. I honestly don't know. It all depends on what their next move will be. By any chance, can you think of a place to hide this?" he asked, holding the revolver out to her. "In the morning they will want us to give up our weapons and. . .and our horses."

"Oh, no," she said, throwing a comforting arm around his shoulder well knowing what Thunderbolt meant to him. "I'm sure it's only temporary."

"I hope so. I hate for one of those greenhorns they call cavalrymen to lay hands on him and mistreat him."

Deep in thought, Abigail looked down at the revolver in her hand. "What do you think of my hiding this inside Snowflake's rag doll? I can slit it open and sew it inside the doll."

"That's a great idea," he said in astonishment, "they'll never think to look for it there. But Snowflake is bound to wonder why her doll suddenly put on weight when the rest of us are losing it."

Throughout the night the camp was a buzz of activity as they worked at taking guns apart to be concealed beneath the clothing of the women. Small items such as tying springs, pins and cartridges were camouflaged in between the beads of their moccasins.

With fingers numb and stiff from the cold, Abigail's progress was slow as she worked at sewing the rag doll together after carefully concealing the revolver in the doll's stuffing. Several times over she had to blow on her fingers, trying to warm them. She was putting the finishing touches on her work when she looked up to see Jason watching her. She caught the warm speck of admiration in his eyes and somehow knew that his thoughts were running parallel to hers. "The last time you saw me with a needle in my hand you were scared to death," she laughed.

"Can you blame me," he smiled. "I still have the scar on my arm to prove it."

Abigail sighed in deep despair, "Oh, Jason, that seems so long ago."

He reached out and took the doll from her hands and carefully examined it before pulling Abigail down on the blanket beside him. He tossed another blanket over them to keep out the snow flurries. It had pained him to watch what effort it had taken on her part to sew up the doll with fingers crippled by the cold. As his arms circled round her he said, "You've done a real good job on the doll—almost as good as the one you did on my arm."

Even in sleep their thoughts ran parallel, wondering what tomorrow would bring.

Starving, cold and weak they had marched for two days through the driving snow before reaching Fort Robinson where they were given a log barracks for housing. Although overcrowded and cramped, they were grateful for the food, medicine, blankets and shelter provided by the soldiers.

Being kept cooped up in the barracks with so many people and nothing to occupy her mind, Abigail found the days long and empty. She could also see the effect it was having on Jason; with each day he grew more restless. She was glad when, along with a few warriors, he was given permission to go hunting. She herself asked permission from the guard on duty to walk the grounds in front of the barracks with her daughter. Although the weather was brutally cold, the solitude of just a ten minute walk each day, alone with her daughter, helped to lift her spirits. It was on such an afternoon after their walk that she got up the courage to ask one of the young soldiers on guard duty for writing paper, ink and pen.

"I'll see what I can do ma'am, I can't promise you."

"I understand," she said, smiling up into his youthful face. "I just want to write to my sister and brother in Kansas and tell them that my family and I are safe."

Three days later, when the young soldier came back on duty, with an apology he handed Abigail two sheets of paper, two envelope and a writing stick. "I'm sorry ma'am, I couldn't get you ink and pen; all we have are writing sticks."

"It will do nicely," Abigail said, taking stick and paper from his hand. "Thank you very much."

Suddenly, he appeared ill at ease. "I was wondering ma'am, if it's not too much trouble," he said, "could you write a short note for me on the second piece of paper to my family. I'm afraid I don't know how to read or write and I know they'd be happy to hear from me. I'd be very much obliged to you ma'am."

That evening Abigail sat down to the task of writing a short letter to a Mr. and Mrs. John Bodmer of Ohio telling them that their son, Samuel, was stationed at Fort Robinson and was in good health and fine spirits. It was the second letter to Jenny, Timothy and Jonathan that was time consuming. She didn't want to disclose the true nature of their circumstances so as not to worry them. Nor could she acquaint them with any future plans on their part since they were being kept prisoner at the fort. A considerable part of the letter pertained to her daughter Snowflake's escapades and how truly happy she was to be with her family. And in closing she stated that they need not worry, for the soldiers were taking excellent care of them.

Exactly one week to the day after Abigail had written the letter, a new commander took over the fort. Captain Henry W. Wessells, by all accounts, was a stern man. At any given time he took it upon himself to come barging into their barracks and openly spied on them. If that wasn't enough, Chief Red Cloud was brought down from Dakota to counsel with them, but nothing was resolved. Although the Chief had welcomed them to join his people, the fort's commander refused to grant them permission to leave.

"Where do we stand now?" Abigail asked, watching Jason playing with their daughter on the floor.

"Now. . . now we sit and wait until the Great White Father in Washington decides what to do with us," he said sardonically. "We told them we will not go south again and that we want to live in peace. We want to stay here in the north where we belong. They've had their share of suffering living in the south."

"It's so little to ask," Abigail said hopefully. "I'm sure they'll let us stay here. And when spring comes we can move on."

Jason saw the flicker of hope that shone in her green eyes and quickly squelched his anger, not wanting to destroy it. Too often now he had come in contact with the bureaucracy of government agents which gave him cause to believe that the only goal of the white man was the annihilation of the Indian race.

"Okay, apple of my eye," he said, rising to his feet and taking his daughter by the hand. "That's enough playing for one night. It's time for you to go to sleep. Kiss your mother good night."

With open arms Abigail received her daughter's kiss. "Sweet dreams, Snowflake," she said, and watched as the child crawled up on the cot next to her grandmother who lay sleeping. "Do you think there will come a time when she will seek the comfort of my arms?" Abigail asked dispiritedly.

Jason seated himself next to her on the cot they shared drawing her close. "Give her time, Abigail. Having a mother is a new experience for her."

"I know. . .I know. But I love her so much."

"She knows that," he said, and softly laughed.

"What are you laughing about?"

"We have a very perceptive daughter. You don't suppose that Snowflake realizes if she sleeps in your arms that I'd be left out in the cold."

"Yes," Abigail smiled, "maybe she does at that."

It was the first day of the New Year and Abigail optimistically thought that with it would come peace on earth and good will towards men, but she was mistaken.

The news from the War Department, a couple of days later, was discouraging to say the least; they were ordered to return to the reservation in the south.

With arms folded across her chest and fingertips tucked beneath her armpits trying to warm them, Abigail stood at the barracks window looking out. The raging snow storm that fell blanketed drifts from previous days. "How can they possibly expect us to travel in this weather?"

"Can't you see," Jason said angrily, "that white men have no rhyme or reason for what they do. Some bureaucrat in Washington sitting behind a desk, warm and comfortable, has issued orders far from knowing the situation at hand and expects us to follow his orders. That's how it's always been."

Hearing the bitter note in his voice, Abigail turned from the window to look at him, almost afraid to ask the next question. "What have you and the other men resolved at your meeting with Chief Dull Knife?"

He turned from the questioning look in her eyes and stared out the window. He drew in a sharp breath and said, "We will not go back. . . if they want us to die. . . we will die here. That's our stand."

Stunned by his words, Abigail was speechless for the minute. "And. . .and," she stammered, "what was Captain Wessells' answer to that?"

"He has given us five days in which to change our minds," he said flatly.

Five days, five days, Abigail thought with a ray of hope; a lot can happen in five days. Suddenly she felt Jason's hands on her. She was being pulled close to his chest as his arms tightened around her. "We have to be strong, Abigail," he murmured. "It will be five days without food or wood for the stove."

"Oh, my God," she gasped. "How will we survive without food or wood? They don't mean it. They're just saying that to frighten us. It can't be true . . . they're Christians."

Chapter Twenty Four

The very next day deliveries of food and wood for the stove had ceased. Their hands as well as their faces became frostbitten. All they had to sustain them was a watery soup made from the scraps and bones of their previous meals. Abigail tried hard to console her daughter, but found it difficult to convey to a child of three that there was nothing to eat. Each time her beseeching hazel eyes looked up at her, Abigail's heart broke into pieces. She could keep her warm and comfortable by wrapping her in a blanket, but there was no way of soothing the pains in her child's empty bloated stomach. For want of food, her daughter began sucking on her thumb until it was raw and bleeding. At night the pitiful wailing sounds of the children's suffering echoed off the walls of the barracks, tearing at the very hearts of their parents. Throughout it all, a weak and exhausted Abigail tried to keep her sanity. At times she'd sit with her hands cupped over her ears trying to shut out the pitiful cries. Other times strange thoughts would trigger through her mind. Was the taking of a life of lesser value to a man than that of a woman? Men hadn't the slightest inkling of the pains of childbearing. The discomfort of a cumbersome body and the tiresome months of waiting, only another woman would know of such things. Only another woman would resolve a problem before seeing her child suffer or sent to a senseless death, such as war. Why wasn't the voice of women heard? Perhaps tomorrow the commander would relent and give them food and wood; he had made his point. It would be the Christian thing to do.

By the third night a strange stillness seemed to invade the barracks. Listless and weak, fewer children had the strength to cry. The low moaning groans of adults as well as children could be heard as hunger gnawed at them. Sleep was their only recourse to hold onto what little physical strength remained. For in sleep their bodies relaxed and their minds became partly lost in an unconsciousness that momentarily helped to ease their suffering.

Abigail was awakened from a state of stupefaction. She dragged herself up on the edge of the cot, not knowing what time it was. It took her a few seconds to realize it was still night; the brightness of moonlight glistening on the snow outside the barracks window had confused her. She shook her head to clear it. What she thought to be the sound of Snowflake crying had awakened her. From the other end of the barracks came the cries of a wailing child. Strange, she thought, how the mind plays tricks on one. Out of all the children she was certain it was her daughter crying. To put her mind at ease she rose to her feet swaying dizzily while inching her way over to the other cot where Snowflake slept with her grandmother.

Crouching over, Abigail looked down at her daughter clutched in Gay Feather's arms, her face half hidden beneath the blanket. It was the shimmering tears in her child's eyes that drew her attention. "What's wrong, sweetheart," she whispered, and on reaching out accidentally touched Gay Feather's arm. Appalled by the shocking coldness of the arm, Abigail pulled her hand back and glanced up at her face. The brown eyes that once sparked with warmth were wide open blankly staring up at the ceiling; Gay Feather lay dead. "Oh, no! Oh, no!" Abigail sobbed, tears spilling from her eyes. She made several fruitless attempts to free her daughter from the stiff icy arms that were locked around her. Frantically, Abigail tried pulling her daughter free, but failed.

It was a hellish nightmare to awaken Jason with news of his mother's death. But having to bear witness and listen to the crunching sound as Jason and another man were forced to break one of Gay Feather's arms, in order to free Snowflake, was even worse.

Abigail tried hard to muffle the sounds of her sobbing as she sat there rocking her child in her arms. She would miss Gay Feather dearly; she had become her mentor, teaching her the ways of the Cheyenne people, but more than this she loved the woman. "Her serape . . .and moccasins," Abigail sobbed, "make sure you take them before anyone else does."

A bewildered Jason stared down at her.

"Oh, God," Abigail moaned, "I can't believe I said that, how selfish of me. Forgive me. Please, forgive me. What's happening to me, Jason?"

"Nothing's happening to you," he said in choked voice. "It's the position we have been put in, trying to survive, that makes each man selfishly think about their own needs. You're only human, Abigail. I know she'd like you to have her things."

Gay Feather wasn't the only one to be buried that day. Another woman lost her life to the bitter cold and a boy of ten named Running Legs.

For two more days their relentless struggle to survive continued and a party of three men went to meet with the fort commander only to be put in irons for refusing to go south again. In the barracks they could hear the shouts of Left Hand that came to them in warning before the soldiers dragged him away. By late afternoon another ultimatum was set forth by the fort commander as he talked to them through a barracks window. "Let the women and children out," he ordered, "so they will no longer suffer."

"We'll all die here together sooner than be sent back." They answered.

Within a short time the soldiers came and put chains and iron bars over the barracks door.

Suddenly a surprising force of energy seemed to burst forth and run rampant through the barracks. If they were going to die, they would face death on their terms, fighting. The cold stove was lifted and beneath the floor planking they retrieved five gun barrels that they had hidden. They tore free the pins and springs that had been camouflaged in their moccasins and reassembled their rifles. The young men began to paint their faces while the women piled up little bundles beneath each window thereby making jumping out easier.

In silence Abigail watched as Jason tore open the back of the rag doll to retrieve his revolver and loaded the chamber with the three remaining bullets he had in his possession. Three bullets against a cavalry of men, she thought dispiritedly, and turned to the task of tossing their few possessions into a blanket; every article of clothing they owned was already on their backs. The two other blankets they owned she rolled up and tied together before handing them to Jason.

"I want you to listen carefully to what I have to say," he said, taking the blankets from her hand. "We haven't much time. I've been giving this serious thought and decided that you and Snowflake should stay here in the barracks where you'll be out of harm's way. There's a good chance when this is over they'll send you and Snowflake back to Kansas. When we break out of here, I'm going to try to steal a horse and work my way to Canada. There is no hope for my people in this country, outside of being forced to live on a reservation. In Canada, I'll be a free man. God willing, when I get there I'll send for you."

"No, Jason, don't ask this of me," she begged. "I have to take my chances just like the rest of the women. You wouldn't ask this of me if I were Cheyenne. I won't leave you. Don't ask me to leave you."

"Please, Abigail, I'm begging you," he said in desperation. "My mind will be at rest knowing you and Snowflake are safe."

"You promised," she cried, "you promised that we would ride to the ends of the earth together."

"Oh, Abigail," he said, anguished by her words. "I love you more than life. Nothing can separate us if you remember that wherever you and Snowflake are, my heart will follow."

She was shocked to see the shimmering tears in his eyes as he bent his head to kiss his sleeping daughter's cheek. It was the first she had seen a man cry. Then she felt the strength of his hands clasp her face as he kissed her good-bye. Before she could say anything, he was across the room with the other men standing in front of one of the windows.

With heart wrenching pain, Abigail screamed after him only to have her screams drowned out by the sudden burst of gunfire which was quickly followed by a loud deafening noise as every window sash was pushed out and men, women and children clamored to leave the barracks.

Jason was no more than a fleeting glance, revolver in one hand and blankets tucked beneath his arm. His tall lean body framed the window before he jumped through it and disappeared from sight.

Hands crippled by the cold, Abigail tightly wrapped the blanket around her daughter and lifted her to her shoulder. With her free hand she snatched at the blanket containing their meager possessions and through a maze of cots half ran to the nearest window. She was being pushed along with the crowd and managed to climb the heaped up stakes beneath the window. A blast of cold night air swept over her as she jumped to the ground, the drifts of snow cushioning her fall. All around her there was chaos and confusion, mothers yelling for their children and people running in all directions. For a second she stood paralyzed. On the ground lay the dead bodies of the soldiers who had been standing guard. Vivid red blood stained the white snow. "Your son, Samuel is in good health and fine spirits."—the words she had written came back to haunt her on seeing his lifeless body lying in the snow.

Over and over again, the word Canada began to run through the corridors of her mind. She knew it to be in the far north but was at a loss as to which direction was north when suddenly she remembered what Jason had taught her about the North Star. As she trudged through the snow, trying to put distance between herself and the barracks, her eyes studied the sky in search of the North Star. Her heart sank; the stars were hidden behind heavy clouds that held the promise of more snow. It was then that she remembered where the horses were kept and headed in that direction. Behind her she could hear the sound of gunfire, men shouting, women and children screaming.

Abigail suddenly realized that in the open clearing she and her child would be targets for the soldiers. She headed for the woodland area, the first tree but a few feet away from them. Exhausted and weak of limb she took cover behind the tree and set the blanket down, clutching her child to her chest. Her ears kept listening for the horses. The cold night air bit at her face and hands and her arms began to tremble under the weight of her daughter. It seemed like an eternity, but she knew it to be but a few minutes since she had left the barracks.

Over the uproar of cries and screams the sound of a horse's hooves plopping through the snow drew Abigail's attention. As the familiar silhouette of rider and horse appeared in the distance, she snatched up the blanket and went running forward screaming Jason's name on the top of her lungs. At first she thought her efforts were in vain when suddenly she heard the horse neigh and buck while unmercifully being reined. Abigail stopped in her tracks as if frozen and watched as horse and rider turned in her direction.

"Damn fool woman! You are by far the most obstinate, pig-headed——" Jason gave up and reached down for the precious blanketed bundle that she held up to him. With his free hand he grabbed hold of her arm. Within seconds Abigail was seated behind him, her one arm circled his waist while she held fast the blanket containing the meager possessions in her other hand. Jason spurred the horse into a fast gallop heading for the woodland area.

Abigail rested her weary head against Jason's strong hard back and a faint smile edged her lips as the words, They Who Ride like the Wind, came floating to mind. Behind them could be heard the shrill sound of a bugle rallying the soldiers in the Fort; soon they would follow.

Chapter Twenty Five

They had ridden most of the night, stopping only to give the horse a much needed rest before continuing on. A new dawn was breaking on the horizon and with it came the hope that somehow they had managed to elude the soldiers by taking to the mountainous area instead of the open plains. The other enemies now facing them were those of hunger and the bitter cold. It wasn't until their second day of traveling that Jason chanced to build a fire. He worked at cutting down two lower limbs from beneath a large pine tree and built a wall of snow on the outer edge to break the harsh winds. He gathered stones and set them in a circle before starting a fire with the dried branches of wood that had been gathered. Their search for something to eat was futile. Weak, exhausted of limb, they sat huddled beneath the pine tree thawing their hands and feet in the warmth of the fire.

"Why don't you get some sleep, I'll look after her," Jason said, reaching out to take the bundle from her rocking arms.

"She. . . she hasn't said a word all day. All she does is sleep," Abigail said in dismay.

"She'll come round. The minute we get some food into her she'll be a regular magpie and you won't get a word in edgewise," he said, hoping to sound convincing.

Abigail weakly smiled, "She does talk a lot for her age, doesn't she?"

"Just like her mother," he smiled.

On reaching over to take the child from her, the serape that Abigail had draped over her head slipped to her shoulders. With quick hands she pulled it up but it was too late, she saw the shocked look on Jason's face.

"What in God's name happened to your hair?"

"I cut it," she murmured.

"Cut it? If you ask me you butchered it. Whatever possessed you to do such a thing?"

Abigail could well imagine what she looked like with bobbed hair. She drew in a sharp breath and avoided looking at him. "I cut it to stuff inside Snowflake's moccasins, her feet felt like ice last night," she murmured.

Momentarily at a loss for words, he looked at her quietly, unable to hide the warmth of love that shone in his eyes. Few women he knew would have thought to make such a sacrifice; she never ceased to amaze him.

"It will grow again," Abigail said.

She felt the touch of his hand on her head pulling the serape down to her shoulders. Lightly his hand caressingly fingered the short curls on her head as he stared at her. "You are by far the most beautiful woman that I have had the good fortune to fall in love with, but it's your inner beauty that far outshines your physical, Abigail. Snowflake is blessed to have you for a mother."

Bright sunlight came streaming through the pine tree overhead and awakened Abigail from a sound sleep. She just lay there somewhat confused trying to recall how she got there. Despite her dazed state, she began to focus her thoughts and little by little she began to remember placing Snowflake between them, making certain she wouldn't be exposed to the elements while they slept. She became conscious of the blanketed bundle lying beside her and struggled to her elbows, every muscle in her body stiff and aching with pain. A nausea that was compounded by hunger swept over her. She leaned over and looked at her child lying beside her and gently pulled at the blanket that partly covered her face. The emaciated, gaunt look of her child in the bright morning light tore at Abigail's heartstrings. Her eyes were closed and she could hear the sound of her greedily sucking on her thumb. Abigail reached out and gently removed the thumb from her daughter's mouth. "Snowflake, its mother," she murmured, "wake up, dear."

The child turned in her sleep as if seeking comfort and automatically raised the raw bleeding thumb to her mouth again. In anguish Abigail glanced around while wondering what to do. Red smoldering embers were all that remained of their campfire. On her hands and knees she crawled over to where their few possessions lay scattered beside the tree trunk. Jason had taken the blanket they were wrapped in to cover the horse. That much she remembered, but where was he? She sorted through their belongings, tossing tin plates and other articles aside while searching for the tin cup she had packed. It was the sight of the tin plates that angered her. Of what use were they, she bitterly thought, when we have nothing to put on them. Finally she found the cup and with fingers crippled by the cold dug into the snow. The loss of dexterity in her fingers only angered her more. She scooped up small amounts of snow trying to fill the cup. She crawled over to the campfire, set the cup down in the smoldering ember and warmed her hands while waiting for the snow to melt.

For the longest time Abigail sat with her back leaning against the trunk of the tree with her child in her lap coaxing her to drink the warm water. "Come on, sweetheart, just another sip," she said repeatedly. It was the vacant look in the hazel eyes that tore at her heart. She doesn't even know who I am, Abigail thought in despair.

At the sound of horses' hooves, a dazed Abigail awoke after having fallen asleep again. Puzzled she looked down at her daughter cradled in her arms. It was then that she remembered melting the snow and giving it to her daughter to drink. She looked up to see Jason leaning over making his way under the branches to where she was sitting.

"How is she?" he asked.

"She . . she took some water."

"Well that's good," he said, and opening his jacket began placing things down on the ground in front of him.

Abigail blinked with uncertainty as if seeing a mirage as he placed two eggs on the ground, a dead chicken and an ear of corn still in its husk. "Where. . .where did you get the chicken?"

"I didn't want to tell you yesterday, but I noticed a small settlement in the valley. I rode back early this morning and found it. So I borrowed two eggs and the chicken. I found the ear of corn in the field on my way back."

"You borrowed the eggs and chicken?" she laughed.

Jason smiled. "It wasn't much of a hen house, three hens in all, and I was kind enough not to take their rooster."

Abigail watched, her mouth salivating, as Jason broke open the eggs and tossed them into the tin cup along with a handful of snow and set the cup down in the embers to cook. She was trying to remember the last time she had eaten an egg but her memory failed her.

"If you hand me the chicken," she said, "I'll start plucking it."

"It can wait," he said. "After you and Snowflake eat the eggs we have to move on. When we make camp tonight we can cook the chicken."

Fear brushed the corners of Abigail's mind. "Have the soldiers picked up our trail, is that it?" she said.

"No, I haven't seen any sight of them. But the farmer I stole the chicken from may get it into his head to track us down and I'm afraid we'll have to leave the horse behind and travel the rest of the way on foot. There's no way we can ride him over this mountain; we'd only have to drag him."

Making good use of the horse's blanket, Jason cut part of it into long strips and bound Abigail's feet and legs. Thin leather strips cut from the reins were used as laces to hold the bindings in place. Another blanket

433

with two ends knotted together was slung over his one shoulder and around his waist to pocket his daughter on his back. Throughout their journey north, trudging through the snow, the one thought that helped Abigail to bear up was that of cooking the chicken. It would be their first substantial meal in eight days and God knows how long they could make the chicken last.

Four days late, when the last of the broth made form the chicken bones was gone, Abigail could not find it in her heart to question Jason as to what they were eating. Some of the weeds he gathered looked vaguely familiar to her. The unmistakable boiled leaves of frozen dandelions and chickweed that she had pulled out of her flower garden and tossed aside considering them unsightly were now helping to sustain her. One morning she watched as Jason struggled in vain to roll over a large dead branch that had fallen from a tree. He got down on his hands and knees with tin cup in hand and picked at the grubs that squirmed beneath the log. At the very thought of having to eat them, Abigail thought she would vomit. Surprisingly the hunger pangs that gnawed at her stomach took precedence over the unsightly meal on her plate that evening.

With each passing day Abigail became conscious of the thinness of her body. Her skirts and petticoats hung on her frame and began to trail on the ground becoming caked with snow and weighing her down. At one point she took to cutting a good three inches off her hemline. She could also see the radical changes taking place in Jason. Having to forage for food left him tired, worried and worn. Bracing the bitter cold, he had sat outside a burrow the entire night until he succeeded in catching a rabbit. She didn't know what she hated more, the bitter cold or the hunger. But it was her daughter that worried her the most. The listlessness of her child was heartrending, but it was the spasms of convulsions that now and again shook her body that frightened Abigail.

By early afternoon they descended the mountainside, heading for the valley below when the light flurries that had fallen during the morning turned into a blinding blizzard. They were forced to take shelter in a small cavern on the side of the mountain. The cold dank dampness slowly dissipated as Jason started a fire with the bundle of sticks and branches that they had gathered along the way.

In the dim grayness of the night Abigail fought the sleep that taunted her eyes. Now she knew what pain and suffering was, but it was her conscience that troubled her more. Was it possible that her child was suffering in retribution for her sins? She had been living a lie for so many years that she couldn't fathom where the truth left off and the lies began. Worst of all, she had deceived the man she loved, the father of her child, into thinking she was a lady born of gentility.

"Jason," she murmured.

Smiling, he crawled over to where she sat carrying the tin cup in his hand. "Try this," he urged, "it's the closest I can get to making you a proper cup of tea. Careful you don't burn yourself; it's hot."

She glanced down into the cup at the clear orange colored liquid before taking a sip and found it to be sweet and refreshing. "It's delicious, what is it?"

"I was lucky to find a few frozen wild persimmons clinging to a branch."

Abigail sipped at the liquid in the cup thinking it an irony that Jason deemed it necessary to apologize for not making a proper cup of tea for her. She swallowed another mouthful and could feel the warmth of it spreading through her body giving her the strength to speak on. "Jason, there's something I have to tell you," she said.

The solemn note in her voice drew his full attention. He curled up beside her pulling her close. "Yes, what is it?" he asked.

"I'm. . . I'm not who you think I am; my real name is Beth Carney," she sighed. Suddenly, like that of a heavy weight being lifted off her chest, she began to speak in a profusion of words. She spoke at length about her childhood, Maggie Cosgrove, Mr. Carver, the death of Abigail Whitcomb abroad ship, her reason for marrying Albert, her love of the McFadden family and the true happiness she finally found being with him and their daughter.

Jason listened intently, a couple of times deliberately brushing his cheek against her forehead thinking she was delirious from a fever. As he listened a lot of things began to make sense to him and fall into place.

An acute silence seemed to hang in the air as each became wrapped up in their own thoughts. Jason finally found his voice, "Why. . . why did you think it was necessary to tell me the truth after all these years?"

"I deceived you; I deceived you for so long," she murmured. "And I didn't want you to go on believing that I was something that I'm not. . . a proper lady."

Jason smiled to himself, the seriousness of the moment stopped him from laughing out loud. His arms tightened around her. "A proper lady," he said, "is that what this is all about, my dear? Having deceived me into thinking you're a proper lady. It's not what one is born into that makes them proper or improper, Beth," he smiled. "It's the true nature of a person that counts. Their kindness, generosity and warmth and the woman I fell in love with has all these attributes, be her name Abigail, Beth or White Snow, it doesn't matter. A person of many names, I would think is much loved."

Her head fell to his shoulder and lulling her into a deep peaceful sleep came his words, many names much loved.

Twice that morning Abigail noticed the spasms that shook her child's body. She had crushed the remainder of the wild persimmons into a cup coaxing her daughter to drink the warm tea. A distraught Abigail held fast the child in her arms in an attempt to stop the uncontrollable spasms that shook her small body.

Their progress was slow as they trudged through the deep snows of the previous day's blizzard heading across a small meadowland hoping to reach the other side. By mid-afternoon their attempts seemed futile as harsh winds came blowing in over the open land. They took refuge beneath the overhang of a small cliff to rest, but one thing Abigail was certain of, she couldn't go on; defeat was imminent.

The soles of her moccasins were worn thin and her legs, from her knees down to her feet, were numb and blue from the cold making each step unbearably painful. Added to this was blinding headaches caused by the brightness of the sun's rays on the glistening white snow. She had passed the point of feeling hunger; even if there was something to eat, she doubt she could swallow it. All her strength gave out and she was too tired to go on, too tired to care. She closed her eyes and lay back on the blanket that Jason had spread and curled up into a ball. Vaguely she heard him moving around her, talking to their daughter.

When Abigail opened her eyes it was night and in the moonlight that came streaming through the trees, she saw Jason sitting cross-legged but a few feet away from her. He was softly chanting while rocking their child in his arms. Clearly visible in the lines of his face was the agony of his suffering. He loved his daughter dearly.

"Is she. . . is she. . ." Abigail couldn't say the word but the alarm in her voice was evident.

"No," Jason said in choked voice. "It's. . . it's just a matter of time."

Abigail tried to rise to her knees but couldn't feel her legs; they were dead weight. Instead, using her elbows she dragged herself, inching her way over to where Jason sat rocking their child. She reached out and gently pulled at the blanket that partially covered her daughter's face and peered down at her.

438

This wasn't the child she remembered with full rosy cheeks and the faint pink color of a rosebud on her lips, and beautiful hazel eyes that sparkled with life. Abigail shuddered at the sight of the child with the hollow cheek bones, blue lips and eyes that appeared to be rolling back in her head with each spasm that shook her body as she labored to breathe.

With tears streaming down her cheeks Abigail reached out. "Give her to me, Jason," she sobbed. "Give her to me."

With a slight measure of reluctance he placed Snowflake in her lap and watched as she held the child close to her bosom while tears spilled from her eyes.

"God forgive me. God forgive," she bitterly wept, placing her hand over the child's mouth and nose. "I won't let her suffer anymore. God forgive. God forgive me. I won't let her suffer anymore."

The full impact of what her intentions were suddenly struck Jason. For a few seconds he sat stunned until realizing her actions stemmed from the tormenting anguish of seeing her child suffering. "God forgive us," he corrected, placing his hand over hers. "God forgive us."

In the palm of her hand Abigail felt the last warm whisper of her child's breath and took strength from the hand that covered hers. "She's at peace Jason; she's at peace," she sobbed, brushing the tears from her eyes. "Her suffering is over."

A blood-curdling scream of agony escaped Jason's lips and for the longest time they laid in silence with their child closely nestled between them. Abigail took the small pouch from around her daughter's neck and sprinkled the seeds and petals it contained over her body. "She always liked flowers," Abigail sobbed.

"Just like her mother," Jason said solemnly.

"What were you singing to her?" Abigail asked.

He drew in a ragged breath. "An old Cheyenne song my mother would sing to me when I was a child, about the sky, birds, trees and the beauty of nature."

"Jason, I want you to promise me something. When morning comes I want you to leave here and continue on to Canada, I know you could make it. I'd only be a burden to you. I want to stay here. . . I want to stay with Snowflake. It's only a matter of time."

He avoided looking at her as he spoke. "Is that what you truly want?"

"Yes, my love. That's what I truly want."

"So be it," he said.

Unmindful of the snow that came blowing in over them, they lay huddled together beneath the blanket and in soft whispers reminisced of happier times. "You know, Jason you were the first man I ever danced with. Remember that night at Fort Riley?"

"How could I forget?" he smiled. "Every man in the room was envious of me."

She reached up and touched his cheek. "The words, the words of the song you sang to me. Do you remember them?"

Jason cleared his throat and softly sang, "Drink to me only with thine eyes and I will pledge with mine. Or leave a kiss within the cup and I'll not ask for wine."

"Such pretty, pretty words," she sighed, shaking her head from side to side. "Such pretty…pretty…words.
. ."

He felt her head fall to his shoulder and glanced down at her face masked in the relaxed state of sleep. "Good-bye my love," he whispered while leaning over and tenderly placing a kiss on her lips.

Chapter Twenty Six

After ten years of searching, Timothy McFadden knew better than to let his hopes rise when reading the letter that came in over his desk at the Bureau of Indian Affairs in Washington. Over the years he had tracked down every lead that had come his way without success, although it was his burning desire to find out what happened to his half-brother Jason, Abigail and their daughter, Snowflake. In his wallet he still carried the letter that they had received from Abigail. It was written in pencil and postmarked Fort Robinson; it was yellow with age and the writing blurred in spots.

Five years ago, Timothy had taken the job with the Bureau of Indian Affairs solely to right the injustices Indians were suffering on reservations. Progress was slow and at times downright discouraging but he traveled from reservation to reservation meeting the people and seeing more of the country than he ever anticipated. He always traveled with one thought in mind: someday he'd meet up with the rest of his family.

Timothy's last lead, three years ago, had brought him to South Dakota and the Pine Ridge agency where he chanced to meet up with a young Cheyenne boy in his teens. The boy remembered as a child being kept prisoner at Fort Robinson and how they escaped only to have the soldiers catch up with them several days later. The soldiers had them pinned down in a deep buffalo wallow and kept shooting at them until there were only nine survivors left out of thirty-two people, mostly women and children.

"Do you," Timothy said, as he looked at the young boy sitting cross-legged across from him on the ground, "think it was possible my brother and his wife and child could have been killed there that night?"

He shook his head from side to side. "No. They were not with us."

"How can you be so sure? You were only a child at the time," Timothy frowned.

"I remember; I remember everything about that night," he said with a note of obstinacy in his voice. "One doesn't forget the night his mother and father were killed."

"I'm sorry," Timothy said, "I didn't mean to bring back such sad memories, but I've been looking for my half-brother a very long time."

A heavy silence seemed to hang in the air.

"I remember the woman," he finally said, raising his hand and touching his head. "She was the first woman I ever saw with that strange color hair. And I remember how they said her hair was the work of the devil. That I remember."

Timothy smiled to himself, knowing how superstitious some Indians were. "Yes, I could see where some of them would think that. She did have beautiful red hair."

"Oh, there is one more thing I remember," he frowned, in thought. "It happened before we got to Fort Robinson, before the soldiers came. Your brother, who you call Jason, rode this beautiful stallion with

444

his woman sitting on the back of the horse." With two fingers pointing in the air he said, "Twice, your brother raced around us circling the caravan. They made a pretty picture together, her long hair flowing in the wind. Some people even cheered. After that, when people talked, they called them, They Who Ride like the Wind. That I remember."

The train was pulling into the station and Timothy rose from his seat and grabbed at his luggage overhead. It had been a long, tiresome journey. He was anxious to leave the train and stretch his long legs. He was also anxious to meet with the woman who had written the letter. A well-written letter by all accounts, conveying the facts about a couple and a child who had been found dead many years ago and no one knew the truth of their origin. She wasn't certain whether it was a true story or just a fable since she was quite young at the time when she had first heard the story. She had thought it ironic that it should spring to mind when reading the article in the newspaper about Timothy having been promoted to a job in Washington. It made mention of his missing half-brother, wife and child. Although it had been a number of years, she was certain that she could trace the source of the story and would willingly accompany him if he thought it worth looking into.

With luggage in hand, Timothy stepped onto the station platform, his eyes scanning the crowd. How will I know you? He remembered asking in his last letter. I'll be dressed in green; it's my best color, was the written reply.

A good head taller than most of the passengers around him, Timothy craned his neck looking for the woman dressed in green as he moved through the dispersing crowd. He was taken aback on seeing the pretty young woman sitting on a bench dressed in an emerald green skirt with matching jacket. The sash on her straw hat matched her outfit. She was far younger than he had anticipated and quite pleasing on the eyes. He studied her while slowly closing the distance between them. The long tiresome journey suddenly seemed worthwhile.

"Miss Albright?" he said hesitantly.

Her hazel eyes quickly swept him and went back to searching he crowd. "Yes," she replied, "what can I do for you?"

"I'm Timothy McFadden."

Her head snapped round and a high flush of color rose to her cheeks. "I. . .I was expecting a much older man for a lawyer."

"Sorry to disappoint you," Timothy grinned.

"No . . no, it's not that. . . " Molly Albright stopped, thoroughly embarrassed.

"It's very kind of you to go through all the trouble of meeting with me," Timothy said.

"It's no trouble," she said, recovering her embarrassment. "Do you want to check in at the boarding house first or would you rather we start out?"

"I have to admit I am rather anxious to get to the bottom of this and find out whether the story is a fable or the truth."

Nodding her head in agreement, Molly Albright rose to her feet. "I thought as much," she said. "I hired a rig. It's a good hour's ride from here."

Smiling, Timothy looked up at the fair blue sky. "Well, we certainly have a nice day for a ride in the country."

After a half hour of driving out of town they were on a first name basis. Timothy was surprise to learn that the girl was a journalist on the local paper. "I never met a woman reporter before," he smiled.

"I'm the first one to work on the paper," she said proudly. "When I first started all they gave me to write was the obituary column but now, after a year of working I was promoted to writing human interest stories. Oh, my, I guess I should have mentioned it earlier; that's why I'm making this trip with you. I thought there may be a good story in it. Is that all right with you?"

Timothy's hands tightened on the reins. "I'd have to read the copy first before it goes into print. I'm afraid I'm a stickler for wanting the true facts to be known."

"Certainly," she said. "You have my word on it."

The strained atmosphere between them for that fraction of a moment dissolved.

"Do you speak French?" Molly asked.

"No," Timothy chuckled. "I have a hard enough time trying to learn Arapaho, Sioux and all the other Indian languages without studying a romance language."

"Yes, yes of course," Molly murmured. "The reason I asked, there's a good chance that Mr. Du Bois, like most trappers in this area, doesn't speak a word of English."

"Tar nation!" Timothy swore. "I'll never understand him."

Molly smiled on hearing him swear. "My French is a bit rusty, but I'll try to interpret as best as I can."

Louis Du Bois stood on the porch of his home, a small log cabin. He stood there smiling to himself on seeing the young couple riding up in the rig. Long before he caught sight of the rig he heard it coming. Living alone in the wilderness for so many years had attuned him to any unusual sound. He watched as the young man helped the girl down from the rig and together they came walking toward him. He thought them to be a fine looking couple.

"Bon jour, Monsieur Du Bois," Molly smiled.

The aging lines in Louis Du Bois' face softened into a smile on hearing his native tongue, but more so on hearing the soft feminine voice; it had been years since he had heard a woman speaking his language.

Timothy stood there feeling a bit awkward as he listened to Molly talking to the man in his native tongue. She was far from rusty in speaking French. Perhaps modesty forbade her from telling the truth, he surmised, on hearing the words rolling smoothly off her tongue. Suddenly, the man thrust his hand forward in his direction. Timothy grabbed the gnarled callus hand and shook it.

"He's invited us into his cabin for a cup of coffee," Molly said.

"That's fine with me," Timothy smiled. "I sure could use a cup."

"I hope you like it strong," Molly said in warning, as they climbed the steps and followed Louis Du Bois into his cabin.

The cabin consisted of one primitive furnished room. A cot occupied the far corner and a table and chairs stood smack in the middle of the room. Hanging from the ceiling beams a number of animal skins appeared to be drying. They watched as Louis Du Bois hobbled around the room on a crutch, the foot of his left leg was missing. He was a short strapping man. His unruly curly gray hair matched that of his beard, but it was his eyes that sparked with life, warm soft brown eyes.

With a welcome gesture, Louis Du Bois motioned his guests to the chairs at the table, and hobbled about the room bringing three tin cups to the table and the coffee pot that he took from the stove. With an after thought, he placed a bowl of sugar in front of Molly before seating himself.

Molly thanked her host before taking a small sip of coffee and out of the corner of her eye she saw Timothy take a mouthful. He cringed, gulped and squirmed in his chair in an effort to recover from the bitter taste of the thick, dark muddy coffee. Molly bit into her lower lip to keep from laughing. I warned you, silly, she thought to herself.

Molly toyed with the tin cup in her hand as she began to question Mr. Du Bois as to whether the story that they heard was a rumor or true when suddenly he appeared very indignant. The lines in his face hardened and he raised his voice in answer.

Timothy kept staring at the man completely at a loss as to what he was saying. He kept studying the man's body language and at the moment knew the man was somewhat irate. Molly finally turned to him and said, "He. . . he said that for years no one would believe him; just because he lives all alone in the wilderness, people look on him as being strange. Whenever he took his furs to the trading post he'd mention the fact that he had found the dead bodies of a man, woman and child, but nobody seemed to care."

"Ask him, how long ago did this happen?" Timothy said, bringing his arms to rest on the table as he waited.

Louis Du Bois went on to speak for a lengthy time, his voice dropping to a solemn note while Molly, now and again, would pose a question to him. Quite unexpectedly, Timothy saw the silent tears steaming down Molly's cheeks as Louis Du Bois sat back in his chair as if concluding his story.

"What's wrong?" Timothy asked with concern. "What did he say to make you cry?"

With a quick hand, Molly brushed at the tears and turned to face him. "He. . . he can't remember the year exactly," she said in choked voice, "could have been ten or twelve years ago. All he can remember, it was one of the worst winters, snowstorm after snowstorm, and he was forced to hole up in this cabin. One night he heard the sound of gunfire, two shots, and thought someone was stealing from his traps. The next morning it was bitter cold and he ventured out to check on his traps and. . . and that's when he found them. A tall man with dark hair, a petite woman with red hair and lying between them was a girl child. Their bodies were partly covered in snow beneath a small ledge of rock where they had taken refuge."

"His description fits them well. Abigail did have red hair and Jason was dark-haired and tall," Timothy murmured, swallowing hard the lump in his throat. "I hate to think that their lives should come to such a tragic end because of a snowstorm."

"No . . .not exactly," Molly said, and consolingly reached out to touch his arm. "Mr. Du Bois said, by the appearance of the thinness of their bodies, they had to have been starving to death. There was a bullet wound in the woman's head as well as the man's and the gun was still in his hand. As for the child, she appeared to have died from natural causes." Molly drew in a sharp breath, tears clouding her eyes. "Apparently the man shot the woman first, before taking his own life. He. . .he tied a long strip of rawhide and bound all three of their wrists together as. . . as if signifying that death could not separate them."

For the longest time, Timothy sat with his head buried in his hands as he visualized the tragic death of Jason, Abigail and their daughter. All these years, in his heart of hearts, he knew they were dead and he wanted closure, but now having to face the truth was hard.

"Attente! Attente!" Louis Du Bois said, as he excitedly rose from his chair and went hobbling across the room.

Timothy and Molly stared after him.

"I think he wants to show us something," Molly said.

They watched as Louis DuBois, with one hand holding fast his crutch, began rummaging through the shelf noisily tossing objects aside with his free hand. He came back to the table and placed a revolver down in front of Timothy along with a small leather pouch.

With shaking hands Timothy reached out and gingerly picked up the familiar pouch. He sat mesmerized, fingering the softness of it in his hands while remembering. "This belonged to Abigail," he said in strangled voice. "Each year she would cut the dead heads off the flowers in her garden and store the seeds in this pouch for next year's garden. She loved flowers."

"Oh. . . " Molly murmured, "I'm so sorry. Then it truly was your brother and his wife and child who died here."

"Yes," he nodded, "it appears that way."

From the sorrowful looks on their young faces, Louis Du Bois surmised that they knew who the couple and child were.

Molly suddenly became conscious of the man standing over them at the table patiently waiting for an explanation. She pulled herself together and quickly went on to explain Timothy's relationship and the significance of the small pouch he held clutched in his hands.

The man nodded his graying head in understanding, but when the girl spoke of the pouch containing the flower seeds he could not contain himself. He excitedly began speaking to the girl.

"What's he saying?" Timothy asked.

"I'm not sure," Molly frowned. "Something about the fact that the pouch was empty when he found it and we should go and visit their grave. Because of the deep snows he couldn't bury them properly but mounded the area with rocks and it's in walking distance of the cabin."

"I'd like to go," Timothy said, and added with an after thought, "if you wouldn't mind."

"No, of course not," Molly answered. "I'll show you the way. It will save me the time of telling you the directions given to me by Mr. Du Bois."

"One more thing," Timothy said solemnly, "will you ask him if I could keep the pouch?"

Instinctively, Louis Du Bois had already reached out and clasped his hands over Timothy's.

From the porch of his cabin, the old man smiled after the young couple and watched as they followed the path through the woodland area and disappeared from sight over the crest of the hill.

Molly searched her mind for something to talk about, but it was far from an ideal moment to make light conversation. She was conscious of the somberness of the man who walked beside her and could only imagine what he was feeling. On approaching a fork in the path she hesitated. "Here's where we take the path to the right. He assured me we will know the spot when we see it."

"Judging from this path," Timothy said, "Mr. Du Bois must come here often."

"Funny you should say that, that's the impression I got when he spoke to me."

They had climbed the crest of a hill and stood at a standstill looking at the small meadow land below. Clearly visible was the mound of rocks that marked the grave site on the side of the hill. From the foot of the grave and as far as the eye could see was a breathtaking blaze of magnificent colors. Rippled by the soft summer breeze waves of wildflowers swayed, their fragrance permeating the air.

An awestruck Molly reached out and grabbed his arm. "I've. . .I've never seen anything like it in my life. It's like a beautiful painting. You don't suppose that the seeds in the pouch. . ."

Timothy weakly smiled down at her, covering her small hand that rested on his arm. "I'd like to think that," he said. "I'd like to think that Abigail's seeds were carried in the wind. She and Jason would love it here, of that I'm certain."

~~***~~

About the Author

For years, Delores B. Nelsen (AKA) Sissy Nelsen has been entertaining friends and family members with her unique stories. Her books are smart, clever and full of twists and turns, with surprising conclusions. Mystery is usually her forte but over the years she has compiled a novel titled, 'Moccasins in the Snow' that incorporates the true and tragic facts of the Cheyenne people.

An ardent gardener, she was born and raised in New Jersey. She claims gardening and writing go hand in hand. While working a plot of land it gives her time to plot another story. She doesn't lay claim to being a writer per se, but a born storyteller.

She is the author of, 'Sweet Essence of Murder' and 'Cloned.'

Printed in the United States
24449LVS00001B/1-18

9 781420 807417